21ST CENTURY CHINESE LITERATURE

21ST CENTURY CHINESE LITERATURE

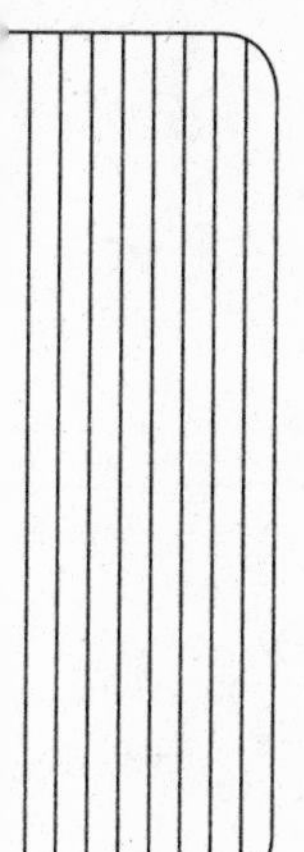

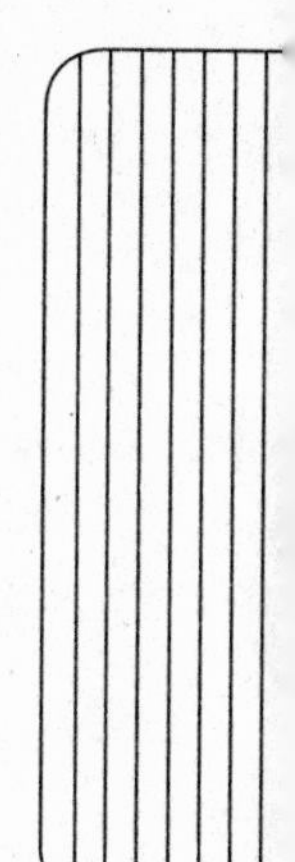

HOW FAR IS FOREVER

AND MORE STORIES BY WOMEN WRITERS

FOREIGN LANGUAGES PRESS

First Edition 2008

ISBN 978-7-119-05436-0

Published by Foreign Languages Press
24 Baiwanzhuang Road, Beijing 100037, China
http: //www. flp. com. cn

Distributed by China International Book Trading Corporation
35 Chegongzhuang Xilu, Beijing 100044, China
P.O. Box 399, Beijing, China

Printed in the People's Republic of China

Contents

21st Century Chinese Literature — Points of Departure

By Wang Meng

The *21st Century Chinese Literature* series aims to introduce contemporary Chinese literature in English, French and other languages to readers all over the world.

Chinese literature's recent path, along the country's trajectory, may not resemble a smooth highway, yet it is still the main channel toward understanding China and the daily lives and inner-world of the Chinese people.

China has been experiencing soaring development, and its links with the rest of the world have been growing closer. Even if you might not know anyone from China, "made in China" still can now be found in most aspects of your life, or as expressed in a Chinese idiom, "Look up, and see it everywhere." News about China appears regularly in newspapers, on TV and the Internet, trying to tell you what is happening in this remote yet near country called China, and what China is thinking and planning. In this way, peoples of the world have developed their general views of China.

Many of those views are often insightful. Chinese writers, like myself, have also been keeping an eye on the world. We often discuss the US, Japan, Russia, South Africa, Italy and other countries, as well as the interesting or ingenious views about China held by peoples of such countries. But we feel much regret to find

---

Wang Meng is an illustrious writer and China's former Minister of Culture.

sometimes that others' views about China are full of illusions and misunderstandings, more often than not, preconceived, arbitrary and overgeneralized. Thus, my fellow citizens and I have become powerfully aware of how little the world really knows about China, and thus we feel that the world is so near, yet still so remote.

Literature can draw us closer to communicate views and imagination about the world and life, and share each other's joys and sorrows beyond language barriers, different cultures and backgrounds or long distances. It can make you feel that people living afar are like your next-door neighbors, as you perceive and share the secret interiors of their lives and dreams. To illustrate this point, I shall borrow a poetic line from the current Indian ambassador to China, Mrs. Nirupama Rao:

"...making sense of each other,
even as realization glimmers
that, we are little morsels
tossed by the history of these parts."

It elucidates the point of departure of this series. Readers from all over the world, who are used to learning about China through foreign newspapers, TV and the Internet, may now open up these books to see China through the heartfelt thoughts and writings of Chinese people themselves. The many authors of these new short stories, living in this rapidly developing and changing, yet ancient nation, have strived to describe all that is happening in and around themselves, to give genuine dynamic expression to the intricate recent experiences of the Chinese people. Through the power of their words you will be able to catch glimpses of the real, complex and living China, as well as other possibilities for all humanity, including yourself.

The Foreign Languages Press has long devoted itself to enhancing mutual understanding between China and the rest of the world. China followers in every country probably still remember *Panda Books*, mainly published in the late 20th century. Those books collected a wide range of contemporary Chinese literary works. The *Panda Books* series helped many Chinese writers become known to the world. *21st Century Chinese Literature* can be regarded as the continuation of *Panda Books*, though its selection and editing methods vary greatly from the old series. All the three volumes of new short stories were edited by Chinese scholars, with in-depth understanding and research in contemporary Chinese literature, whose judgment and views are highly respected among Chinese writers and readers. They accomplished this editing work independently, conducive to this new series better reflecting the highly diversified spiritual quests and artistic creativity of contemporary Chinese literature.

Thus, the other vital impact of this series is to provide international sinologists and Chinese literary researchers with the view from inside, from within the Chinese literary circles widely recognized among Chinese writers and readers. These points of view are likely to differ from the general views held by other countries toward contemporary Chinese literature. It is this very difference that engenders the great potential for new knowledge and discovery.

Modern Chinese writers have been deeply influenced by literature from all over the world. We have been deeply convinced by Goethe's concept of "World Literature." We are committed to the invaluable dream of a "Tower of Babel" promoting mutual understanding among all the peoples of the world. I believe the *21st Century Chinese Literature* series will provide our own enduring great bricks in this skyward "Tower."

Introduction

The "Soul" in Her Body

He Xiangyang

He Xiangyang. A graduate of Zhengzhou University with an MA in Chinese Literature, she is a renowned literary critic in China, a research fellow at the Henan Academy of Social Sciences (HASS), and the director of the HASS Literature Institute. Her major works include *Stories on the Pilgrimage* (1996) and *Retrospectives through a Mirror* (2004). As editor-in-chief, she conducted the compilation of *21st Century Chinese Literature – Short Stories* (2002), *Intellectual Women's Literature* (2004), and other books. She was the winner of the 2nd Lu Xun Literary Award – Prize in Criticism of Literary Theories, one of over 20 professional awards she has garnered through the years.

The "Soul" in Her Body

In the Western classical belief system, woman was "created," through Eve originating from one of Adam's ribs; while in Chinese mythology, a woman "created" men, since Nüwa made men with earth. When it comes to literature then, do women of different cultural origins have completely different writing mindsets? What kind of transformation and progression do narratives experience as a result of long historical evolution and the changing roles of women?

Certainly, these eleven contemporary stories with eleven Chinese female protagonists from a certain period cannot answer all the questions concerning women. Moreover, most of the time women's literature does not answer questions, so much as raise them. Different from "his" stories, "her" stories pay more attention to questions carried by the "ego" or where to place the sense of self in various social questions. This is naturally closely connected with the cultural evolution of the female personality and role definitions over several thousand years. This question is universal for women around the world, whether in the West or the East, at present or a hundred years ago.

There is a famous feminist saying about patriarchal writing, "He is the Subject, the Absolute – she is the Other."

It summarizes how patriarchal culture had remodeled women, whether idealizing them as angels or demonizing them as whores, embodying a deep-rooted misunderstanding of women. How can women writers recreate these female images in such an environment, where men have dominated the right to speak and the general literary approaches? In other words, although women may be dissatisfied with their state of being objects of creation, being named and restricted, how can they, as creators, name-givers and rule-setters, build a new "self" among all the past overlapping images? Even when "she" has the right to name as the One, can "she" completely shake off the shackles of language conventions and cultural definitions? With what materials will the One create a real "self"?

By the 1880s, "feminism" had come into in the English vocabulary, considered as the demand for equal political and legal rights for women. Forty years prior to that, philosophy and sociology scholars had put forward the significance of and conditions for the emancipation of women. At first, such terms as "women's rights" and "women's issues" were inevitably imprinted with sociological marks, gradually growing into historical practice. At the very beginning, "Women Studies" were placed in a certain context. Although spontaneous, incidental and local events and experiences cannot all be covered or recorded, the world today is now in an era where diverse identities and fragmentary experiences make up individual life. Literature, shifting between individual experience and historical narrative, also hints that Women Studies will certainly move away from certain feminist absolutes and tend toward the more specific experiences of all the different aspects, and thus within this framework would be able to truly accomplish its humanistic objectives and potential.

To understand women writers' consciousness of the self to express, change and develop itself from a special position over a certain span of time, and where it is headed, is, I believe, the approach of this book. I prefer works that effectively express women's personal experiences within a social framework, rather than those overly influenced by feminist concepts. I deeply value the dramatic process through which literature deals with life's complexities; rather than hoping for some all-knowing person to tell me the conclusion even before the prologue.

This was the basic criterion for selecting the stories for this book.

Women writers should not be studied as a distinct group. They write about women, but they only describe fragmented aspects of individual women. For this reason, short stories published around the turn of the 21st century were selected, given the profound fascination toward the question, after the 20th century when a series of grand events constituted people's daily life, of what were the waves stirring Chinese women's hearts at the very end of the 20th and beginning of the 21st century? As a woman, I am also a drop of water in the waves, clear yet vulnerable, experiencing the turmoil of both the body, the heart and the soul, while sharing similar fates with other women within this social framework. I, too, want to know the answers to these complex questions.

Bai Daxing in "How Far Is Forever," written by Tie Ning, represents one of the ubiquitous, fun-loving girls from the hutongs of Beijing, who seemed "at a times a bit brainless." "Daxing was still pure and conscientious even after she grew up, and I thought she was the last of her kind in this world." "Daxing always let other people go first," or as Mrs. Zhao in Yard Nine would say: "A very kind child she is." From the very beginning, Daxing was locked up by a culture that determined that she could not have any personal demands. As long as others were around, Daxing would always first sacrifice herself. An unknown force, her family background, and her education joined together to make Bai Daxing a person "bearing a cross," from her childhood. Kindness, helping others, tradition, integrity and all such things are reflexive in Daxing. For her, kindness is an instinct, not a performance or pretension. But, as a pure and true pan-moralist, a transparent person knowing nothing about hatred, in this world what would be her fate?

The ten-year-old Bai Daxing let all the other girls play "Xi'er" with the desirable Dachun in *The White-haired Girl*, while she herself retreated again and again. But her inner desires differed greatly from her outward manifestations. As a young girl, Daxing regulated and restricted herself conscientiously or reflexively regardless of her inner desires, and realized her raison d'etre that dominated her life by sacrificing herself. She suffered a great deal between these two choices – choosing for herself or abiding by the group. Compared with her, the rebellious character of "Xidan Xiaoliu" appeared much simpler. At nineteen, she was an immature yet charming girl. Her big eyes were forever half-closed; her hair always in a loose bun, with several strands hanging out; her toenails painted bright yellow with balsamine petals. As beautiful as Cleopatra, with only a glance, she immediately attracted Chun.

Eventually Bai Daxing finds a number of boyfriends, yet her marriage plans never quite work out. With a later boyfriend, Bai Daxing becomes self-defeating enough to yell, "Go! You'll never find anyone as good as me!" In fact, in terms of psychology, Bai Daixing remains in the stage of pure childhood compared with her changing social surroundings.

Always honest and sincere toward people, Bai Daxing is the type of woman who stays unchanged even after her surroundings have changed, and becomes isolated and cut off from help. There is a detail that is repeated in the story – the "birthday party." Daxing, for every new boyfriend, would hold a birthday party, yet do the three men ever remember to buy her even a rose? She is a woman trying every means to bring happiness to her partner, but none could adapt to such good treatment, or really cared about her and "her frustration, her fatigue, her hopeless expectations, her longings, and her childhood wishes." Bai Daxing sticks to this incurable childish mentality while trusting the person she loves is also childish. The two mentalities are both fatal in adult love affairs. When someone tells her, "you're kind, …you're pure, …you're a good person," Bai Daxing could only wail, "I'm a good person, yet I never wanted to be like this!" To which the other replies, "Did you just say you wanted to be someone else? But that's impossible! You can never be someone else!" Thus, Daxing's kindness is used once again. Because she is a good person, she seems incapable of escaping the kindness rooted in her heart since a very young age, nor can she escape her exposed benevolence and incurable childlike innocence.

In "Maiden Days in the Boudoir," written by Wang Anyi, "she" grew up in a lane of Shanghai, who "swam around in time, always following the trends," and is "so compliant, free from any struggles, thus without any scratches left by time." The author also thus described "her" mother; from this female blood relationship and lineage, "she" is sophisticated, at ease and impervious to fame and fortune, just like her mother, a young woman of a past decade, ladylike, carrying old-fashioned marks of the previous generation. "She" is not given a specific name because the author wanted to generalize about women who had experienced their own independent life, or "little women" going through history. An individual name could not represent all these women. However, beneath "her" self-sufficient and smooth appearance, there is still something awkward, carefully protected through all the small, inner affairs of the heart, so is her heart truly at peace? Although "she" had her mother's attic to live in, something seems buried in her heart beneath this serenity, without leaving traces, but perhaps later with unexpected exposure it may be awakened from its long sleep. This woman, who closed herself in the boudoir, has remained numb and satisfied with her insular heart, perhaps because at least a closed heart is safe, bringing neither happiness nor harm. The question is, has this woman really made her own choices, or is it that she had no option but to accept a "captive" fate?

Su Suhuai in "A Rose in Full Bloom Overnight," written by Chi Li, is a top academic, thus a very different type of heroine from the above characters growing up in traditional city lanes, yet also in her own way overly insular. From her youth considered most capable, Suhuai "always maintained her wisdom and frostiness" as a female intellectual. Her routine life turns her public behavior into a sort of performance. She is divorced but still has some romantic feelings, though she remains rather aloof and depressed. Walking home by herself late at night, although an accomplished professor, she would feel lonely and sad "as a paltry woman," suddenly finding herself on her own. An unexpected taxi then takes her into a fairytale of sorts. The driver tells her, "I can take you to the end of the world." Suhuai becomes totally transformed, "her eyes… beautiful with the excitement, bright as the sun rising over the sea," as she experiences new thrills, as before a breakthrough, before dashing through the wall of reason and rules. At the very moment of dashing through,

Suhuai realizes she is doing something extremely inappropriate for her status and age, something she would never do at normal times. She blurts out, "No—!" but at the same time expressing an incomparable excitement in her voice. The story is a witness to a turmoil suppressed deep in her heart, an irresistible rebellion driven by life instinct, fully describing the two sides of a woman's personality. Can Suhuai, an intellectual with higher educational background and considered a mainstay and model of the university, escape from powerful cultural influences? Momentary rebellion, against long-term cultural repression and manmade rules, exposes something much stronger melting inside her blood, coursing through her body, controlling her brain, becoming an inner imperative. How will this high-profile professor become reconciled again to her cover, to her former ordered life? Which is the genuine Su Suhuai, and will her suppressed true self and desires wither overnight like a rose in full bloom? This story leaves us with the question, for intellectually brilliant and "successful" women, what is the fine balance between "breakthrough" and "breakdown," between social deception and the honest torn heart?

In Wei Wei's story "Big Lao Zheng's Woman," the name of this woman is erased and omitted. Her existence is only identifiable through her relationship with Big Lao Zheng. The term in Chinese for someone's "woman" has a double meaning, normally referring to "wife" and sometimes also implying "mistress." Big Lao Zheng, a tenant from Putian in Fujian Province doing business in the city, is diligent, thrifty, easygoing and compliant – "all the right ingredients for an eldest brother." Big Lao Zheng's woman is "tall, skinny and rigid as a pole"; "if I had not seen her face, I would have thought she was a man." However, she is "shy, reserved, out of place." Although others living in the courtyard immediately discern that she is not Big Lao Zheng's wife, they accept her for giving a hand to the four Zheng brothers, and for the couple's apparent quiet love; "she unconsciously played the roles of wife, mother, housekeeper, hostess…, but she was really no more than an accidental acquaintance of Big Lao Zheng." Although fifty percent good woman and fifty percent "bad," such women "provided solace to the male wanderers with their inborn feminine qualities: attentive, tidy, and diligent." The story emphasizes the willing participation of both parties and the compassionate nature of these women beyond social stigma. The concept of Big Lao Zheng's woman oversteps the gender-based ethics found in traditional literature. The author, as a woman herself, takes a lenient view of the easygoing life of Big Lao Zheng's woman.

In Xu Kun's story "Kitchen," this traditional confinement for women is the place in the house that Zhizi comes from, walks out of, and then voluntarily returns to. She was a homemaker who had turned into a so-called super woman. As a rising business star and successful woman, she begins to again long for her home kitchen, where she "hopes she could kill time with a mild and hollow heart." Such a reversion from socialized gender and modern roles to nature-based gender and traditional roles seems to pose a challenge against feminism. The reason for her return to the kitchen is her love for a male artist, Songze. He notices her skilled, graceful cooking movements and her expressions of love and affection through her "kitchen language," toward him, the man in the living room. When Zhizi, feeling love and helplessness, anticipates further action from him, however, how will Songze respond to her in his "living room" etiquette and language? This subtle story looks at issues of how power can be manifested not only by direct acts of oppression, but more often than not by distance and polite civility.

In the end, will Zhizi still return to the hollowed-out kitchen – the so-called safe harbor for women?

In Pan Xiangli's "Forever Autumn," Madame Autumn's "Kitchen," in seemingly total contrast to the above private kitchen, is an entertaining place gathering all sorts of people. Although Autumn tactfully handles all the worldly affairs in her successful restaurant, she keeps a low profile, appearing extremely taciturn, rather aloof and even proud. But beneath this smooth surface, she is so much more than that, since her extraordinary composure comes through the experience of so many dramatic changes of life and fate. What is the use of lasting beauty if love cannot survive? This story, in a sense, allows the readers to appreciate yet regret the hidden pain of a heart resisting against the waves of chaotic times, illuminating a lonely beautiful flower blooming through the dark night. "This begonia seems to have been painted with a layer of burnished finish, so the torrents of time and the dusty fallout of gossip have not been able to leave any mark. She seems completely oblivious to the vicissitudes of the ways of this world, and the rise and fall of the fates of the people around her." If Autumn's aloofness and secrecy are the result of the repeated wounds in her heart, then perhaps even the course of love that later comes her way is somehow fatefully forged by her unique personality?

In Sun Huifen's "Sowing," Dafeng is a fifty-four-year-old woman living in the countryside, whose husband had been enticed away by the twenty-six-year-old daughter of Shoulan. Both of the two women suddenly come upon each other while opening up sandy wasteland, in a long-deferred confrontation. "She had done nothing bad, she was worthy of her husband, her children…. The only one that she felt unworthy of was herself…." "Who could guarantee that one had no evil intentions all one's life?… The most difficult thing for a good woman to do is to muster the power to rid evil ideas once they did appear." "I am a decent woman!… I had never purposely lured men." "Yes, my husband ran away with another woman, but I was stainless, decent and aboveboard." The individual thoughts of the two women focus on one question, leading to unavoidable conflict.

In Fang Fang's "Ending Where I Started," the protagonist in a transformative moment stands before the mirror, "she had a white neck and high breasts, and her waist and buttocks formed perfect curves which made her resemble a dark green vase. Her face was expressionless like quiet, dead virgin soil; her eyes were confused, as hollow and white as a fog-dominated morning." It became a game of splitting one into two. She "began to make up an alter ego, elaborately. …with thick foundation, her face turned plaster-white…. Her lips were dyed so red she felt they were bleeding. At last she sprayed perfume all over her body and allowed her unbound hair to cover half her face." Staring at the woman in the mirror, Huang Suzi is startled, yet she recognizes something clearly now. "It's so easy to get rid of a person," she realizes, transformed into Darling Yu.

Down the passage which we did not take
Towards the door we never opened….

The author Fang Fang uses an excerpt from T. S. Eliot's Four Quartets to start her story. "*What might have been and what has been/Point to one end, which is always present*," reads like a prophecy, to be confirmed by the life of a young woman. Huang Suzi was not such a bright girl, always shy, quiet and solitary, feeling separate even from her own family. Her taciturnity from long suppression, in the university brings her the nickname "Corpse Beauty," which will come to haunt her. As Suzi had nowhere to vent her resentment and anger, she has developed the habit of silent swearing. Under her silent surface, her curses have piled up in her mind, ready to be triggered off at any moment like a volcano. After suffering a distorted love affair, she also finally tastes the happiness of venting all she had suppressed. "She was Huang Suzi by day but Darling Yu by night. Huang Suzi was the graceful and silent, pretty office lady on the surface, but inside she was a dirty woman who constantly cursed others with filthy words; at night she would become Darling Yu…, cheap and obscene on the surface but desperate inside."

In looking at the question of, what did this contrasting "Darling Yu" come out of, her own answer is, "I do it as a test, whether a person can have another lifestyle, and whether one can develop several alter egos." "What a complex creature a human is – three-dimensional and made of different material, yet only paying attention to one dimension in life and becoming its slave because of vanity of contentiousness, afraid of being three-dimensional and making every surface shine…, making their lives attached to their bodies languish…." This is, of course, her own rationalization. She defends herself, rebels, chooses her own lifestyle, loses her acquired power, love and virginity, but the ultimate question is, what will her extreme "test" cost her?

Through complex problems, powerful temptations, indescribable thoughts and irrational behavior, the author conveys the message that there is no perfect or whole person in any case and everyone is split in terms of body, soul, personality or spirit. Huang Suzi is merely one of us, only a quiet, depressed girl who took a rather extreme way of dealing with her split body and restless soul.

After reading all these short stories, perhaps the overall question is, what is the relationship between all the heroines and us?

First, who are we? Then, who are they, these many-voiced women? These older and younger sisters....

Perhaps the characters all represent "her" multiple identities played out in the role of "woman," and all "our" unresolved alter egos. The eleven writers, whose stories are brought together in this volume, courageously discuss and portray various aspects of the mentality of women. They based their stories upon the "real" experiences of individual women, rather than old stereotypes or more recent generalizations that have grown out of gender power struggles. "She" is created one after the other, each different from the others, and set into these diverse tales of humility and everydayness, passion or apathy, disappointment or betrayal, sense and sensitivity, sexuality and desire; in ongoing struggles, for goodness, or against self-destructiveness or self-sacrifice. Despite even at times their helplessness or despair, the women portrayed are always vivid, alive, caring and genuine. Discontented with their fate, despite confinement of self, they still bravely try to open their hearts, to show to the world their life journeys and human growth.

These short stories express to the world the degree of commitment and pain of women still caught in ongoing "battles" to emancipate their spirit from captivity and to break through besiegement. The power of these women's stories is comparable with that of humanity engaged in any struggle for independence and freedom.

How Far Is Forever?

Tie Ning

Tie Ning. Born in 1957 in Beijing, of Hebei origin, Tie Ning was once the chair of the Hebei Writers' Association and vice-chair of the Chinese Writers' Association, and in 2006 she was elected the chair of the Chinese Writers' Association.

Tie Ning began to publish her writings from 1975. Her representative works are four novels, including *Rose Gate*, *Bathing Beauties* and *Benhua Village*, and 15 novellas and short stories, including *Xiangxue*, *The Twelfth Night*, *A Red Shirt without Buttons*, *In the Opposite Building*, and *How Far Is Forever*. She has also written prose and informal essays totaling 4 million Chinese characters, and published over 50 anthologies of fiction and prose, including the five-volume *Tie Ning Collection* in 1996 and the nine-volume *Tie Ning Series* by People's Literature Publishing House in 2007. Tie Ning has won the Lu Xun Literary Prize, along with five other national-level literary prizes, and over 30 prizes for her fiction and prose given by major Chinese literary periodicals. The film *Xiangxue*, adapted from her novella, won a prize at the 41st Berlin Film Festival, as well as Chinese Jinji and Baihua film awards.

Some of her works have been translated into English, Russian, German, French, Japanese, Korean, Spanish, Danish, Norwegian and Vietnamese, among other languages.

How Far Is Forever

You once lived in the hutongs of Beijing, did you not? You were once a Beijing child, were you not? Then you should remember the ubiquitous, fun girls in the old alleys who could be at times brainless, right?

I once lived in a hutong of Beijing, and I was at heart a child of Beijing's hutongs. I always remembered the ubiquitous fun girls from the hutongs who were at times a bit brainless. I always thought, without them, the hutong would not be even half as special. Without these girls, Beijing wouldn't even be Beijing. Maybe I have offended you by these words. Yes, you may think that Beijing today is quite different from what it used to be. So many outsiders now reside in Beijing. The cerebral and somewhat uppish Beijing dialect is no longer popular in the hutongs anymore. The girls used to hang out in these old lanes, with their distinctive dialect, clean hair, modest clothes, amiable disposition, and gullible instinct. It has been twenty years, and whenever I come to Beijing and see girls anywhere, I naturally assume that they are children from the hutongs. If Beijing was a leaf, then the hutongs would be the veins of the leaf. If you observe this leaf under the sun, you will see it is so clear, so beautiful, because of the girls who move inside the veins of the leaf. They are the essence of a city. Hutongs feed these girls onto the streets of Beijing, brightening up the city and giving it a sense of warmth. They are the reason I shall remain a fan of Beijing forever, and this will not change even in a hundred years.

I left Beijing and grew up in B City. Every year I have some chances to return to Beijing. I have visited many writers who write children's books, in my search for interesting manuscripts for my publishing house. I also visit many of my relatives, the one I see the most being my cousin Bai Daxing. Daxing often comes to me for advice, though in the end never follows any of it. She seems helpless in many ways, but we always see each other. I see it as my responsibility as her older cousin.

Right now, on this June afternoon, I am sitting in a taxi watching the sprinkling of rain outside the window. Daxing and I agreed to meet at the Shidu Department Store on Wangfujing. It is not far from Kailun Hotel. Daxing started working at the four-star Kailun Hotel right after graduating from university. She started out as a union representative and then got promoted to be a manager in the marketing department. I told her she was lucky to be a manager, a leader, upon first entering the marketing department. She sighed and said, "Everyone in our marketing department has donned the title 'manager,' but only the supervisor is the leader." I understood, but on the business card it looks prestigious, "Bai Baixing, Marketing Department Manager, Kailun Hotel."

The taxi got caught in traffic after arriving at Dengshikou West Street. I get down at the intersection, because it is not far from the Shidu. The rain is getting heavier, and I discover I am standing in front of one of those traditional hutongs. There are two limestone steps close-by, and an old gray tile roof above. There is a door under the roof, but it is now sealed with blue bricks, as if someone had turned his or her back on you. I step up the stairs and stand under the roof, shielding myself from the rain. Escaping the rain is not important. I just want to be here, with these stairs under my feet, because on such stairs I truly feel like I am in Beijing. The broken steps beneath my feet, the door behind me, and the ageless roof over me confirms that, yes, I am in Beijing, and I'm standing on authentic Beijing soil. Yedu Plaza, Sunworld Dynasty, New Dong'an Mall, Lao Fu Ye, Leimeng.... None of these new shopping centers distinguishes Beijing from anywhere else. They have no idea how simple doorsteps can summon up my clear memories of the frigidity of Beijing.

Twenty years ago, during those hot summer afternoons, my cousin Daxing and I would usually run errands for our grandmother and go buy iced soft drinks with the vacuum cooler. Our lane was called the "Prince Consort Hutong," and at the north entrance to the hutong was a grocery selling pastries, canned foods, condiments, meats and fish. Outside the grocery door, they sold fresh vegetables on yellow bamboo shelves that the store clerks had set up. They were not afraid of the vegetables being stolen at night time. Their logic assumed that no one would be in a hurry to eat vegetables. If anyone wanted any, they can just wait till the store opened at dawn to buy some. On the south entrance of the hutong was the small store we got our soft drinks from. We usually called the grocery "North Side" and the other store "South Side."

"South Side" was actually a small tavern. There were a few steps leading up to the door, and I always thought the things you could buy must be very precious if you had to climb so high for them. "South Side" never sold condiments, but only liquor and the traditional snacks that went with liquor. In the summertime, it also sold ice-cream, popsicles, and soda. There are only two small round tables in the whole store, covered in fairly stiff, crisp tablecloths. Around the tables always sat old men drinking and eating snacks. The reason I fell in love with the traditional pig-spleen snack was because of "South Side." Do you know when the spleen tastes best? It is from the store clerk placing it on the chopping board and slicing it. The sharp knives cutting this delicacy help diffuse the aroma of food throughout the store. I would always inhale at the counter, because I thought it was the best smell in the world. I would stand smitten by the aroma until the clerk asked me what I wanted to buy. "Give us soda!" was the typical opening line of a Beijing child to buy something during that era. No one said, "I'd like to buy...." Everyone just said, "Give me...." "Chilled or not?" "Chilled," and we would hand over our cooler. I had returned from my spleen-aroma trip. I wanted plum soda badly at that moment. There was a white refrigerator beside the meat counter, and when the clerk opened the fridge, we ran over excitedly. Cold blew out from the fridge, and cooled our faces in small punches. There were huge chunks of ice in the fridge, and plum soda bottles sprawled all over the ice. The clerk filled our cooler with chilled plum soda, and Daxing and I opened the cooler as soon as we descended those old limestone stairs. I always got the first sip, although I was older. Daxing always let other people go first, regardless of whether they were older or younger than she. I took the first sip of plum soda, but I have no memory of how the soda got past my tongue and my esophagus to settle into my stomach. All I would feel was my skull freezing, as if one thousand steel needles were pricking my temples. The lower part of my eye sockets was hot and immensely painful from the cold. *That* was cold. That is what is called *chilled*. When there were no fridges, people knew "cool," and when fridges came, "cool" went out. But fridges can never create the profound and needling frozenness that the icebox would deliver. Daxing took a huge sip next, and shivered. Goosebumps surfaced onto her plump arms. She was out of breath, and told me she had peed a little bit in her pants. I laughed and took the cooler away from Daxing and took another large gulp. A thousand steel needles pierced my temples again, and my eyes hurt, but I was more alert. I shot a glance Daxing's way, and we ran through the quiet hutong, only waking up the orange cat on the roof — that was Niu Niu, the feline of No. 9 Yard, who was always looking out for our family's male cat, Little Xiong. We ran on the ground and Niu Niu ran alongside us on the roof. Niu Niu, have you ever tried iced soda? You'll never be able to try it in your whole life! We ran all the way home in a flash. That was what *cold* feels like.

Daxing never complained about the fact that I drank more soda than she did on the way home. Why didn't I know how to share? One time, when we were getting ready to watch the movie *Prince Sihanouk Visits China*, we had boiled some water to wash our hair. The water was steaming, and I went first, using egg-yolk shampoo. It was a type of shampoo that was colored and textured like egg yolk, costing eight cents a packet, but it smelled like lemon. I hogged the basin, rinsing many times. By the time it was Daxing's turn, the movie was about to start. Grandma came many times to tell her to hurry up, and I told her to hurry up also, although I had been the one causing the delay. She went to the movie with us without thoroughly rinsing her hair. I walked behind her and saw some shampoo still on a strand of her hair. She had no idea and shook her head in the wind to make it dry faster. I knew in my heart that Daxing's shampoo residue was my fault. Twenty years later, I still think that the fleck of shampoo is still on her head. I thought about telling her about the incident, but she has a way of not understanding how others have wronged her. She would extinguish any thought of apology. Daxing will always be Daxing.

Now I simply stand in the hutong off Dengshi West, waiting under an abandoned roof thinking about soda and egg-yolk shampoo until the rain recedes. I proceed towards the Shidu Department Store.

I am waiting for Daxing in the café on the second floor of the Shidu. I like the café, especially the seats by the window because they make you feel as if you're floating on thin air, giving a false illusion of superiority. You can see everything from there, the glass walls, the modern buildings and the shoppers of the Shidu beneath you. My cousin Daxing will eventually appear in the sea of shoppers.

There is still some time to go until our appointment, with enough time to just sit tight. I could even go look at the women's clothing and household items on the second and fourth floors, respectively. I have a special liking for towels of different shapes and sizes. Whenever I am in the presence of such items, I have an impulse to shop. I order a cup of Spanish coffee, the big mug feeling more substantial than cappuccino. I drink my coffee while watching the people. Daxing once told me that she liked to watch the sides of things: buildings, cars, shoes, even alarm clocks. Of course this applies to people as well, men or women. I laugh at this habit of Daxing's, but that is what makes her special. How does she differ from everyone else? She is overly enthusiastic. She gets infatuated with boys, but always gets dumped. Ever since she was little, she has been easygoing. Mrs. Zhao in No. 9 Yard always said, "What a kind child she is."

1

Back in the 1970s, when Daxing was seven or eight years old, she was labeled "kind" by the hutong elders. During that period, "kind" was a mysterious and suspicious word. An antediluvian word that reeked of old roofs and wooden boxes, a word not to be openly spread, a word that did not arouse much excitement. It was not a word that struck us like other words. Once when I was visiting Granny Zhao I read the diary of her granddaughter — a quiet teenager. Her diary was on the teapoy, as if inviting people to read it. In her diary were those words, "I come from a politically incorrect family, but I cannot extinguish my passion for the revolution." Yes, the words "extinguish my passion for the revolution" struck me, and I didn't even know what it meant back then. I thought they were words that belonged to the learned, and thought of ways how I could use them in my own diary. I cherished these words, although I did not understand them. I cherished them and protected them so much, I dared not ask adults for a definition. I wanted to bury the phrase in my heart, and define it myself with the help of time. If Daxing was "kind," so let her be.

Daxing was indeed kind. When she was only in first grade, she carried (or more accurately, supported) home Granny Zhao, who had fainted in the public restroom. In second grade, Daxing volunteered to empty Grandma's chamber-pot every day. Our grandmother couldn't use the squat toilets in the public restrooms, so she had to take care of her personal business inside her room. Our parents were not there during those years; it was only Grandma, Daxing, and me. When Daxing was in third grade in elementary school, many cities in China were showing a North Korean film called *Flower Girl.* This movie made everyone who watched it cry. I cried as well, when Daxing and I watched the movie together, but I did not cry as hard as Daxing. The grownup sitting in front of me cried really hard. With every sob, he arched his back and slammed it on his chair. He made a ton of noise but no one bothered to complain about it, because everyone was too busy crying themselves. The grownup sitting to my left stared at the screen and let his tears flow down his cheeks along with the mucus from his nose. To my right was Daxing. She seemed to be choking on her tears because she was hiccupping really loud, and she was hiccupping incessantly. It was there and then that I discovered that my cousin had a habit of hiccupping. Her hiccupping made her sound like an old man loitering around with nothing to do. Especially when she ate radishes in the winter, she would burp loud and stinky. I was unhappy about associating Daxing with an old man. She was neither old nor idle. However, after *Flower Girl* was widely shown, her schoolmates began calling her "Landlord Bai," because her last name was Bai and Landlord Bai also happened to be the evil landlord from the movie. Some boys would yell, "Beware of Landlord Bai," as Daxing walked through the hutong.

This nickname made Daxing feel self-abased. She almost had an emotional breakdown over being teased. There were always "gray" grownups walking through the hutong. They were members of the so-called "four types of enemies" under surveillance. They swept the streets and scrubbed the public restrooms. After watching *Flower Girl*, Daxing would always hold her head high whenever she encountered them to show that she was different from them, that she was not an evil landlord. She always asked me, "Except for sharing the same family name with that evil landlord, we have nothing else in common, right?" Daxing had nothing in common with the evil landlord, but neither was she ever compared with the best characters. *Flower Girl* aroused many fantasies in the young girls of that era, making them think that they were as beautiful and righteous as the protagonist Huani. After I saw the Albanian film *Never Surrender*, I fantasized that I looked like the courageous soldier

Mila. The only evidence and assurance I had was a blue plaid shirt, which Mila also wore. I wished everyone in school would comment on how much I looked like Mila. I wore that blue plaid shirt every day during that period of time, indulging myself in my fantasies. I still remember a quote from the movie, when the Nazi officer questioned Mila and gave her a glass of water, Mila rejected and said, "Thanks, but I can see through the humanitarian face of fascism." I thought it was a brilliant quote; so proud, and so effective. I started practicing a frigid smile in front of the mirror, and asked Daxing to play my counterpart. I told her to fetch me a glass of water, and when she brought it to me, I would say, "Thanks, but I can see through the humanitarian face of fascists."

Daxing laughed and commented on how good my impersonation was. She loved my performance, rather than getting mad just because she had to play the fascist, although she was still labeled "Landlord Bai" at that time. She had an innate ability to follow me, and even when I made her play the fascist, she didn't even get mad at me. "Fascist" was not greatly different from "Landlord Bai," both equally bad, but Daxing never got upset with me. I thought maybe she had been labeled "Landlord Bai" for so long that, even she thought she was an evil landlord. Landlords should listen to the people, and I was the "people." I was prettier, and brighter. Grandma always chastised Daxing for not peeling the garlic properly and making a mess, and for her lack of ability to swat flies, and also for losing money and ration coupons. Back in those days, buying oil required ration coupons. Without ration coupons, we had to pay twice the money to buy peanut oil. Once when Daxing had been sent to buy oil from "North Side," she lost the money and the ration coupons even before entering the shop. Grandma scolded her for the whole day, about concentrating and not losing her head.

In my opinion, concentration and mindfulness are two different things. Why did Daxing lose the money and the coupons? It was because Mrs. Zhao had a visitor — Uncle Zhao. Daxing had her full concentration on Uncle Zhao, therefore she started losing her head. Uncle Zhao was Mrs. Zhao's nephew, and he was a dancer from a troupe in another province. He played Dachun in their troupe's production of *The White-haired Girl.* He had a small tumor on his neck and was receiving surgery in Beijing, so he was staying at Mrs. Zhao's place. "Dachun" was the most handsome man this hutong had ever seen. He was in his twenties, curly hair, big eyes, pouting lips, and a good physique. He wore an army uniform without badges, clothing that could only be worn by actors of important art troupes. He did not button up his collar, revealing his crisp white shirt, evoking an inviting feeling. Women fell for him, but the people who spent the most time with him were girls like us, who could not yet be called women. Where were the women during those times? Women were not like us, crowding around Mrs. Zhao's yard all the time. Dachun was more than patient with us, and he taught us how to dance, and rehearsed his plays with us. He would put a square table in the middle of the yard, and two shorter chairs beside it, so we had a stage just like the cave scene from the play we were rehearsing. The climax of the scene was when Dachun held the hand of Xi'er and climbed up the "stage" to see the light at the end of the tunnel. The scene ends in a beautiful pose with both characters immensely overjoyed. It was a grand scene to behold, and it was our dream. Many girls in the hutong wanted to play Xi'er in this scene, not because of the light at the end of the tunnel, but because we would get the chance to hold hands with Dachun. We waited anxiously for our turn, and jealously applauded each other. Dachun was fair, and invited each one of us to be Xi'er, except for Daxing. She refused to work with Dachun, although she frequented his yard more than anyone.

Since she always wanted to go to Mrs. Zhao's yard as quickly as possible after dinner, Daxing came close to quarreling with Grandma a few times. Every day after dinner, Grandma would do her "business," and Daxing had to empty Grandma's chamber-pot before she could go out. At the same time, the stage had already been set up in Mrs. Zhao's yard for the play. It was a gruesome time for Daxing; Grandma took ever so long to attend to her "business," smoking and sometimes reading *Quotations of Chairman Mao*. It made Grandma appear as a mean person, because she didn't understand what Daxing was thinking of. I was happy that I wasn't the one who had to empty Grandma's chamber-pot, but I felt sorry for my cousin. Every time I told Daxing that I would go first, Daxing would beg Grandma to go faster. She pleaded across the curtain for Grandma to go faster but her pleading evoked a reverse psychology. Daxing was supposed to be the "kind" one. Grandma yelled through the curtain, "What's wrong with you today, child? How can you talk to your elders like that? Why did I raise such an ungrateful child as you? You can't even let me do my 'business' in peace...."

Daxing waited for Grandma outside, and as if punishing Daxing, Grandma prolonged her "business." By that time, I was already in Mrs. Zhao's yard. I felt guilty because I had not waited for Daxing, though I wished that she would come faster. Daxing always came and sat in an unnoticeable corner, although she desperately wanted Dachun to notice her. Only I knew of this yearning. One day Daxing told me that Uncle Zhao would leave after his surgery because his residence was not registered for Beijing. When I said yes, Daxing stared straight at me without really seeing me.

I gently tugged at her hand, which was ice cold, reminding me of the plum soda, as if her hands had come straight from the icebox. She was only ten then, but her hands were so cold, not something ten-year-olds supposedly had. That was an unstoppable passion, an indescribable yearning. I looked at Daxing and wished that Dachun would give her some attention. I yelled, "Uncle Zhao, Daxing hasn't been Xi'er yet, let her be Xi'er this time." Uncle Zhao, or Dachun, walked towards Daxing in a friendly manner. He extended his hand towards her, inviting her. Daxing rejected the proffered hand, stuttering, "No… I can't… I don't know how…." Daxing was always so agreeable, what had happened to her? I knew she wanted it, so why did she reject something she wanted so badly? I thought she was being shy, so the other girls and I chanted words of encouragement. We were cheering Daxing on, who was really scared, to be still not as good as we were. Dachun's hand remained extended, and Daxing appeared perturbed. She began yelling words of rejection, and moved back. She was sweating and helpless. She leaned backward, as if denying the world. Dachun extended both of his hands and his arms, trying to lift her up from her stool. We all saw Uncle Zhao's actions, and were surprised. Surely Daxing was not stupid enough to reject a gesture like that. Of course, she did not protest loudly, because with a loud thump, she collapsed on the ground and fainted.

Many years later, Daxing told me that when she had fainted ten years ago, it marked her first love. She said she hated herself at the time, but just could not summon up the courage to deal with herself. To this day, Daxing, in her thirties, still thinks that Uncle Zhao was the best-looking Chinese man she has ever seen. I, on the other hand, all grown up, no longer agreed with Daxing. I did not like men who had creases on their eyelids, though I did not reject Daxing's opinion. I can only sigh at Daxing's passionate yet naive "first love." That Uncle Zhao, who we never saw again, would never have imagined that ten-year-old Daxing from Prince Consort Hutong could really have fainted because he was, according to her, the handsomest man.

A man of Uncle Zhao's age would never think about the thoughts of a ten-year-old girl. In his eyes, we were just children, and he hugged us like little kids. He never knew when he extended his arms towards us, it would arouse such palpitations. He recklessly hurt so many little girls, after what happened between him and Xiaoliu of No. 3 Yard of Xidan, known as Xidan Xiaoliu. After that, the little girls who played Xi'er with him came to realize that he was never paying any real attention to them. He liked the notorious Xiaoliu. How come a ten-year-old girl could faint because of a grown man; while Xiaoliu, who never even looked at Dachun, could make him so lovesick?

2

Xidan Xiaoliu was about nineteen years old at that time, or perhaps seventeen. Her family had only moved to Prince Consort Hutong several years before. They took over the five rooms at the north end of No. 3 Yard. The northern rooms had belonged to Mr. and Mrs. Jian, but they had been banished to the outhouse because they had been proprietors of a pharmacy, while Xiaoliu's father was a carpenter.

Xidan Xiaoliu's parents were short and skinny, but they were good at bringing up children. They had four sons and four daughters. Their sons were big and strong, and their daughters were beautiful. They were tough people. When they moved in, they had no beds so they slept on boards. They ate tough food also, consisting of vegetable porridge and cornmeal buns. Yet their food and home produced Xiaoliu, a girl who, though not the prettiest of her sisters, yet still had a certain charm about her that attracted men. Her flawless tanned skin glistened, emitting freshness; her big eyes were always half closed, as if she couldn't see anything in front of her, but also as if she were concealing passionate eyes with her lush lashes. She belittled the "good girls" who had their hair tied up. Her hair was always in a loose bun, with several strands hanging loose. It made her look fearless, yet laid-back, as if her head had just left the pillow after spending the night with a man. Actually, she had probably just finished scrubbing the pots, or eaten a cornmeal bun with some preserved cabbage. Every day after dinner, she would scrub the pots and eat the bun, and then just stand against the door for awhile or go across the street to the public toilet. When she crossed the hutong to get to the washroom, she would display her luscious physique. Back then, it was an era of baggy pants, but for some unknown reason Xiaoliu's pants were tight and perfectly hugged her curves. Her steps were relaxed but her body was straight, and it was the combination of relaxed and straight that brought out the sultriness in her. She usually wore sandals, with her toenails painted a bright yellow with balsamine petals. At that time, no one in the hutong, not even anyone else in Beijing, dared to engage in such vanity as painting of nails, except for Xiaoliu. She did not look at anyone when she walked, because she knew that not many people in the hutong paid attention to her, so she never talked to anyone either. She lacked female friends, but she could care less because she more than made up for it with male friends.

She had joined a gang called the "Xidan Brigade," hence her nickname Xidan Xiaoliu. Her name came from the fact that she was in the Xidan gang and she was the sixth child in the family (*liu* meaning "six"). The Xidan gang was made up of ten or so young adults who neither went to school nor work. They all came from good families, so they were invincible. They mugged people for their army hats and stole bicycle bells. They then sold the stolen goods to shops, and bought cigarettes and liquor with the money. During that era, army hats and bicycle bells were the epitome of desire for young people. If you had a cotton army hat with soft nap, it would be like owning a wool jacket nowadays, and to have a bell on your bike was like having the newest cell-phone in your pocket now. Xiaoliu never took part in the stealing, as the only girl in the gang. Her enjoyment was sleeping with all the boys in the gang. She needed no special reasons, she was purely seeking attention. She liked it when men fought over her.

She could not hide her wild ways from her parents. Her carpenter father tied her up once and made her kneel on the washing board in the courtyard. Everyone thought Xiaoliu was a disgrace to her other siblings, but in fact they had a strong bond. Every time Xiaoliu was punished, her siblings would ask for forgiveness on her behalf from their father. Her punishments usually lasted a long time, from afternoon until midnight; and each time she was stripped down to her undergarments. Her siblings' pleas were futile, and they could only watch her kneeling there hungry and cold. Once, when the Xidan gang found out about Xiaoliu's punishment, they snuck into the hutong in the middle of the night and freed her, carrying her out in a red-and-white blanket. Then, they rode their *Phoenix* bicycles out of the hutong, ringing their bells and carrying Xiaoliu away as fast as they could.

That night, both Daxing and I heard the piercing bike bells going off in the hutong, and Grandma heard them as well. She half-consciously said it must be Xiaoliu's family. The day after, our hutong was filled with gossip of how Xiaoliu had been "kidnapped." This rumor evoked much excitement from Daxing and me. We were curious, excited, and somewhat nervous. We ran about the hutong, especially hovering around No. 3 Yard, trying to catch some details about the incident. We then heard that it was one of Xiaoliu's older brothers who had told the Xidan gang about her punishment, that Xiaoliu had never told the gang herself. Who had actually seen Xiaoliu being carried away in the blanket? Who could've actually seen clearly the colors of the blanket in the dark? We didn't care about the facts. All we cared about was that there was a group of men who had worked together to save a woman they all loved, and the way they did it was so earth shattering. Xidan Xiaoliu became even more mysterious and intriguing. Several days later, Xiaoliu returned home as if nothing had happened, and resumed her daily routine. Crochet needle in one hand and a ball of white yarn in her pocket, she took to knitting a cheap-looking tusk collar. Maybe it was then that Dachun spotted Xiaoliu, and Xiaoliu probably gazed at Dachun with her large dark eyes.

It was like they were fated for each other and nothing could stop it. Mrs. Zhao told Grandma that the shrewd Dachun had finished his surgery long ago, and his employer had written several letters asking him to return. Of course, he ignored all the letters and, despite Mrs. Zhao's rebuffs, asked Xiaoliu to marry him and leave Beijing with him. Xiaoliu chuckled without saying a word but continued to date him secretly. Some time later, the Xidan gang caught them in Mrs. Zhao's yard, and they carried the naked Xiaoliu out of the hutong and gave Dachun a good beating. Then, they forced Dachun to leave Beijing by threatening his life.

Some rumors in the hutong claimed that Xiaoliu had seduced Dachun deliberately only to humiliate him; when she gave them the signal, the gang then appeared. That she loved to see men humiliated in front of her. If the rumor was true, then Xiaoliu was a truly cruel person. Beautiful yet cruel, since it seemed that Dachun would definitely have been deeply hurt.

Mrs. Zhao cried about it to Grandma, saying that it was such bad karma that our hutong had a whore like Xiaoliu. Grandma wept with Mrs. Zhao and told us never to go play in No. 3 Yard again and that we were never to speak to Xiaoliu's family. She was afraid that we might turn out like Xiaoliu.

I left Beijing at about that time, and returned to my parents in B City. My parents had just ended a period of labor at a "May 7th Cadre School" in the mountains, and the first thing they did was to send for me and make me continue my schooling in B City. My parents cherished our reunion, but my own heart was to remain forever in Prince Consort Hutong. I know the adults from the hutong would never miss an irrelevant child like me, yet I always thought about the grownups from the hutong: Dachun, Xiaoliu, Mrs. Zhao, and even Mrs. Zhao's cat. Sometimes I wished I could be Mrs. Zhao's cat, then I would be with Dachun day and night, and watch his and Xiaoliu's story unfold. I heard that when the Xidan gang had gone to attack Dachun, Mrs. Zhao's cat meowed nonstop on the roof. Was she yelling for help or yelling with the joy of watching the incident? Why did I want to be the cat and see their stories? At that age, I had no idea what men and women did together. I wasn't jealous — it was simply some kind of vague feelings of melancholy. I did not "love" Dachun like Daxing did, yet I did not hate the "whore" who everyone talked about. I liked the couple, especially Xiaoliu. I could not believe that she had humiliated Dachun on purpose. Even if she did humiliate Dachun purposefully, what of it? I was rooting for her in my thoughts, and I felt guilty. This woman with painted toenails unleashed the liberated woman within me, arousing my desire to be just like her. More than ten years later, when I watched Elizabeth Taylor as Cleopatra, being carried out in a Persian rug for Caesar, I thought of Xiaoliu, the beauty of our hutong. A woman as beautiful as Cleopatra, a woman cursed by many.

For a very long time afterwards, I had not told Daxing what I thought of Xidan Xiaoliu because I thought it was taboo. It was Xiaoliu who had "stolen" Dachun from Daxing; Daxing, who had fainted for Dachun. At the beginning of the eighties, the five northern rooms in No. 3 Yard went back to Mr. Jian's family and Xiaoliu's family moved away. She had already disappeared from our hutong, so why mention her to Daxing? Until one day about two years ago, when Daxing and I were in a bar in Sanlitun called "The Oak Barrel," and we saw Xiaoliu there. She was not a customer, rather she was the pub's owner.

It was a small bar imitating foreign trends, with the smell of various foreign spices permeating the air. Business seemed to be good at the bar, with lots of customers, the majority of them foreigners. There were stuffed bear heads and bows hanging on the walls and a South Americanish songstress singing "Kiss Me, Jimmy" with a Spanish guitar. It was then I saw Xiaoliu. Even though we had not seen each other for more than twenty years, I recognized her immediately in the dim light. I never believed those stories that said if you have not seen a certain person for a number of years you will never recognize them. This was not possible, at least it was impossible for me. I recognized Xidan Xiaoliu. She must have been forty years old then, but she had not aged at all. She was wearing a low-cut black dress, and sunflower earrings. She was curvaceous but not corpulent, still beautiful and confident of her beauty. She was walking towards us, in the same way she used to walk in our hutong. She looked more pleasant, and she looked happy, yet somewhat common, I told Daxing. "Hi, Xiaoliu." She also recognized us and walked up to us and asked if we used to be her neighbors. She smiled and asked the waiter to bring us two glasses of complimentary cocktails, called "Midnight Bash." Her smile was nostalgic, not resentful and not weathered. Daxing and I smiled at Xiaoliu as well. We had friendly smiles, somewhat astounded at the fact that she could still recognize us, two kids from the hutong. We were not sure how to address her, so we politely yet not truthfully complimented her on her business. She was happy to hear our feedback, and called over to the busy broad-shouldered young man, and introduced him to us. He was Xiaoliu's husband.

Daxing and I had a good time at the "Oak Barrel." Xiaoliu and her young husband mesmerized us. We sighed at this mysterious woman, this impregnable mystery. It was that night that Daxing told me she had never hated Xiaoliu. She asked me to guess who she had admired the most, and I couldn't guess. Daxing said she admired Xidan Xiaoliu the most, that she had admired Xiaoliu ever since her childhood. Daxing had wanted to be like Xiaoliu, proud, beautiful and attractive to men, able to date whomever she wanted to. Daxing often stood in front of the mirror, trying to tie a loose ponytail like Xiaoliu had. She also imitated Xiaoliu's pose of standing against the door frame, looking demure, then leaving the doorway and walking around the room. She used to look at herself in the mirror, excited yet sneaky, confident yet hopeless. She had really wanted to bolt out the door out onto the street, but of course she never ran out onto the street. No one had ever seen Daxing's imitation of Xidan Xiaoliu, not even me.

That night I looked at the tall Daxing beside me. I looked at her sideways, and I thought, I really did not know her.

3

My cousin Daxing remained pure and conscientious even after she grew up, and I sometimes thought she was the last of her kind in this world. At high school and university she had always been a good student, and in her junior year in university she was on the student council. She loved to help people and involved herself in social activities, sometimes even falling behind on her coursework because of this. I thought perhaps she didn't really like studying. She majored in psychology, and sometimes she would sneak away from class to go nap in her dorm. All of this did not deter her from graduating. She graduated and went to the Kailun Hotel's marketing department, and has stayed there ever since. Daxing's main job was renting out the rooms, since there were not enough individual customers and tour groups, so the hotel had to do proactive marketing. Her target was the foreign corporations or branches of foreign corporations in Beijing, and she had to visit the offices of these companies and promote the hotel's rooms at a discount. Kailun's employees called this practice "building sweeping," which sounds more like warfare, being a serious business. I had no idea what strategy Daxing used in her public relations, because she didn't have any advantageous looks. She was average-looking, with blunt short hair. She liked wearing masculine blouses without adornments. Even though she was not short, her legs were, and her oversized bottom sagged when she walked. However, her sales were the best in her department, and I often wondered why. Maybe it was because of her "kindness," which she had carried over from her childhood. Maybe it was her truly warm and friendly nature.

I had enough personal experience of Daxing's true kindliness. When she was in her sophomore year in university, she came to B City to attend military-style university boot camp. After boot camp had ended, I called her and asked her to hang out in the city for a few days and stay with me. I had just got married back then, and I was happy. I wanted Daxing to see my new home and meet Wang Yong, my husband, whom I had unrelentingly told her all about. Daxing gladly accepted and talked to Yong nicely on the phone. We welcomed Daxing to our home and cooked lots of food. We reminisced over our days in the hutong and of how we used to buy plum soda. I even bought pig spleen, our favorite childhood food. My parents — Daxing's aunt and uncle — also came to dinner. Everyone said Daxing had got a tan from boot camp and looked really fit. The topic having been brought up, Daxing then told us about her boot camp experiences. No doubt she had enjoyed it. She told us about her daily routine, from waking up to going to bed, how the knapsacks were prepared, how camouflage was worn, and even what they sold in the boot camp concession. She also talked about how her platoon leader was kind yet strict but how everyone fully respected him. The captain was from Shandong Province and had an accent when he talked, yet he was not at all rural. He was very talented and played the violin and even knew how to play *Butterfly Lovers*. Oh, and also their company instructor....

Throughout the whole meal, Daxing remained engrossed in her boot-camp nostalgia. She did not see the food in front of her nor the pig spleen I had bought her. She did not see her aunt and uncle, nor Yong. She did not see our new comfortable home. Nothing, except for boot camp, the platoon leader, the instructor. It was as if it made no difference where she was or who she was with at that moment, as long as she was still in boot camp. That night, when Daxing went to shower, I gave her a towel, but the towel made her cry. I asked her what happened, she did not answer. Later, she walked out teary-eyed and said she could not bear to see the color green. Everything green reminded her of the military, of the army. Before she could finish her sentence, she buried her face in the green towel and cried, as if it was the uniform of her platoon leader.

Daxing's never-ending thoughts about army men annoyed me, and made her appear disagreeable. I did not want to hear about her boot-camp stories, and I was worried that Yong might not like my cousin. After breakfast the next day I suggested we go out and see a bit of B City. Daxing agreed but asked me if there was a post office nearby. She said she had written letters last night to her platoon leader, and she wanted to send them because she had promised she would send them as soon as she returned. I told her she hadn't returned to Beijing yet. She said, if sent locally, they would be received faster. Such was Daxing's logic. Luckily, soon after that, some major events overtook Prince Consort Hutong, or else who knows how long Daxing would have obsessed over the army.

First of all, our grandmother passed away. Before her death, Grandma had been paralyzed for three years. Grandma was living with my aunt and uncle, who were Daxing's parents, but because they had not returned to Beijing until the eighties, Grandma had spent most of her time with Daxing. In my memory, Grandma used to chastise Daxing the most. Especially after she became paralyzed, she took immense pleasure in tormenting Daxing. Her words never changed in twenty years, it was always about "stupidity" or "lack of concentration." However, when Grandma chastised Daxing like that, it was always when Daxing was helping Grandma with her excretions. Daxing's brother Daming never even lent a hand, but Grandma favored him more. All the money that our uncles sent to

Grandma, Grandma gave to Daming. Whenever Daming moaned in front of Grandma's bed, Grandma would reach under the pillow for money. Once I told Daxing that the problem with Grandma was that she played favorites, treating Daming like a prince. Furthermore, if Daming was a prince, that would make Daxing a princess. Daxing immediately told me that she wanted Grandma to favor Daming because of all the ailments that Daming had suffered. Poor Daming! Daxing's eyes were teary again. She said, when Daming was born, he had whopping cough; when he was two, he choked on a pea; when he was three, he had intestinal surgery; when he was five, he fell into a well; when he was seven, he caught polio, and when he was ten, he was shoved by his classmates and bumped his head on the stairs; when he was eleven… when he was thirteen… why did all misfortunes happen to Daming? Why didn't I get any bad luck? Whenever I thought of this, my heart ached…. Oh… the pain!

Daxing's speech was as if she was guilty for being healthy, full of guilt that she had not been as unfortunate as her brother. I could not say anything further. Anything further would seem like I was trying to wreck their sibling relationship, although I disliked Daming passionately.

Grandma died, and Daxing fainted many times from crying so hard. I tried to guess the reason for her tears. Grandma had never been kind to her, but in Daxing's heart, Grandma was the best. Once she told me that Grandma was a knowledgeable woman. In the late seventies, when cosmetic counters in stores first carried nail polish, Daxing had bought a bottle. Grandma told Daxing to buy polish remover as well, or else the polish would not wash off. Daxing then realized that polish and polish remover were equally important. She went to the store for polish remover, only to meet a sales associate who had never heard of polish remover. Daxing said Grandma knew things even the sales associates did not, and that made Grandma knowledgeable. I thought knowledge about nails did not qualify one as knowledgeable, but I did not rain on Daxing's parade. I just thought that Daxing admired people too easily.

After Grandma's death, my aunt's workplace — a prestigious high school — gave their family a two-bedroom apartment, as a part of the teachers' housing program. After deliberation by the whole family, my aunt and uncle moved into the new home with Daming, and the old house in the hutong was left to Daxing. Ever after, Daxing would be the owner; she could get married and have children there. In the expensive area of Beijing's west business district, Daxing's hutong home was much admired. At that time, she was a senior in university and, once her friends discovered that she had her own place, they often partied there, and sometimes her friends from other cities would stay there. Daxing's classmate Guo Hong's mother came to Beijing for medical treatment, and stayed in Daxing's hutong home for almost a month. After that, Hong became Daxing's boyfriend. Hong was from Dalian, and Daxing said he looked like Chen Daoming, a famous Chinese film star. Hong did not talk much, but he was bright; I had a gut feeling he did not really loved Daxing. Yet how was I to convince Daxing, since she was so engrossed in her relationship. If you think about her obsession with the army, you can probably picture Daxing in love.

4

During that period of time, Daxing often asked me if I were to marry a man, would I choose someone who loved me as much as I loved him, or choose someone who loved me more or choose someone whom I loved more? She said, "Of course, you would choose equal love, since you and Wang Yong love each other equally." I asked her what she would choose. She said, "I would probably choose to be the one who loves more...." She did not finish expressing her thought, but from then on I knew that from the beginning she had set a low standard for herself. She was altruistic, giving, and thus it was a heartbreakingly low standard. It was like she already had a premonition that no man on earth would ever love her as much as she loved them. The problem was that I pursued an even crueler question: could any man ever really love Daxing? Guo Hong dated Daxing because he wanted to stay in Beijing after graduation, and I had already seen through that. I told Daxing that Guo Hong had no home in Beijing, and Daxing said he would if they got married.

Maybe Guo Hong wanted to marry Daxing, since they were living together. Daxing thought taking care of Guo Hong was the single happiest thing in her life. She bought him cigarettes, washed his socks, and cooked for him. She even threw a birthday party for him in her hutong residence, to show everyone that their love was serious and bound for marriage. When Guo Hong's family came to Beijing, she paid for everything. She even started asking her family for money just to satisfy Guo Hong. Once, because she wanted to buy a puppy for Guo Hong's young nephew, she secretly sold an old electric fan in the house. Why did she do go to such lengths? Just before graduation, Guo Hong started seeing a Japanese exchange student and stopped coming over to Prince Consort Hutong. One of Guo Hong's friends once said Guo Hong was set on being dependent on women; he wanted to go to Japan with the Japanese girl. If he could go to Japan, he would have no reason to try to stay in Beijing. If he didn't stay, he did not have to marry Daxing.

To this day, I can remember the day Daxing came crying to me about that matter. Her eyes were red and her hair was messy. She sat cross-legged on the bed, biting her lips (I then realized Daxing could bite her own lips), and said how she wanted to take revenge on Guo Hong, so he would be unable to stay in Beijing, forcing him to return to his hometown. Then, she plotted many possible ways of revenge, but they all seemed to me like childish schemes. When Daxing got very emotional, she started hiccupping really loudly, sounding sad yet noisy, as if weathered by the events. However, when I encouraged her to actually take revenge, she went quiet and dumped herself onto the bed and fell asleep. Staring at the "cotton mountain" in front of me, I thought that being under covers is a great way to shield oneself. It can give you warmth, pacify your loathing, relieve your pain, and cover your sadness. Daxing slept under the covers for a whole day, and when she woke up she never talked about revenge again. When I asked about it, she said she wished she could be more like Xidan Xiaoliu, because Guo Hong would have never treated Xiaoliu like that. But it was as if Guo Hong was supposed to treat Daxing like this.

Daxing received her work assignment upon graduation along with her heartbreak over Guo Hong. She went to the Kailun Hotel and started a new chapter in her life. She was enthusiastic about her job and treated people nicely. She gained two kilos when she went through restaurant training (which every employee had to go through), but nothing else changed about her. She was still like a student, not affected by the phoniness and chilliness of large hotels. Sometimes when she was alienated by her colleagues, she just laughed it off or did not even notice it. She was quite popular. Even the lady who worked in the locker room liked her, and said, "Never mind all the pretty girls here, Daxing is the best. She always greets me politely when she sees me, and it makes me warm inside. Even my daughter-in-law doesn't greet me like that nowadays. Daxing, why did you tie a scarf below your collar? I thought scarves are worn on the neck!" The lady in the locker room thought of Daxing as family, talking to her incessantly whenever they met.

Some time later, Daxing started another relationship. This time, the man was called Guan Pengyu, an employee in the Guest Room Department at the Kailun Hotel. He was one year younger than Daxing and as tall as her. They met at the hotel Christmas party rehearsal. Guan Pengyu was to sing the *Song of Yangtze River*, and Daxing was to sing the folksong *Returning Home*. Daxing had known this song ever since she was in college, and she was not nervous onstage. Maybe it had something to do with her being the public coordinator for the student council. She only had minor problems during the rehearsal, that is, when she sung the line "left hand a chicken, right hand a duck, and with a baby in tow," she was supposed to extend her left hand first, and then her right hand, but she always did the opposite. It was a minor problem, but it seemed awkward. Guan Pengyu, who sat in the audience, signaled her to extend her left hand first. Daxing saw Pengyu's reminder and heard him as well. His gesture warmed her inside, as if she had support, so she extended her left hand with Pengyu's cue. After that, whenever she rehearsed, even before she got to that line, she would glance at Pengyu, somewhat signaling him, yet flirtatious. She reminded Guan Pengyu of his cue, as if saying "I'm going to make a mistake, don't forget to remind me!" When it came to the point for her to gesture, she already knew to extend her left hand first, but she pretended to hesitate. Pengyu was anxious and extended his left hand immediately. Daxing loved it when Pengyu was anxious, because that anxiety was especially for her, and no one else. Daxing's flirting was at its zenith, but it was also the only thing she knew. She had nothing further up her sleeve.

Guan Pengyu was different from Guo Hong, he was a family guy. He paid attention to fashion, he knew how to knit and play the piano, and to make a bed. The first time he went to Prince Consort Hutong with Daxing, he demonstrated his professional bed-making routine. He never seemed to hate his job, and as part of his professionalism, whenever he saw a bed he wanted to tidy it. He told Daxing to bring him a set of bedding and stood at the foot of the bed and with a few waving motions, made the bed in a flash. He patted the pillow and sat her on the bed, showing off to her his accomplishment. Guan Pengyu and Daxing were on the bed together, but they did not realize what could happen on a bed. People who make beds are far from beds, just like people who build houses are far from houses. Daxing only saw pure work-evoked bliss on Pengyu's face. No desire, no sex.

They still moved in together. The hotel was liquidating some furniture, selling the pieces at a huge discount to employees — a three-set sofa was only 120 yuan. Daxing bought many things: sofa, carpet, microwave, lights, wine cabinet, and a desk. Guan Pengyu helped her refurbish her home. Daxing remembered that Pengyu liked playing the piano, so she made a difficult decision to spend 500 yuan on a second-hand piano (and piano stool) for Pengyu. Daxing did not need to ask for money from her parents again, although she was far from rich. She threw a birthday party for Pengyu in their newly furnished home. This time she did not invite many people, like she had on Guo Hong's birthday; it was only her and Pengyu.

She ordered a "black forest cake" from the hotel's restaurant and bought a bottle of moderately priced *Great Wall* wine. That night, they ate cake and drank; Pengyu even played some piano. While

Pengyu played, Daxing stood at his side and looked at him. She was really close to him, his ear almost brushing against her shirt. His ear was red, like a rabbit's. Daxing told me later that she really wanted to bite the ear. Guan Pengyu kept on playing, but lost track of what he was trying to play. The hot air around him blocked his thoughts, and he was torn between staring at the piano keys or turning to the mass of hot air. When he turned around, his head was in Daxing's arms. It was a defenseless pose for Daxing, maybe she wanted to hold on to the head in her arms, but her knees sank and collapsed onto the floor. Her kneeling position made her look saggy yet bulky compared to Pengyu, who was sitting on the bench. However, she was still shorter than him. She tilted her head up to him, in a very compromising pose. He leaned down toward her and kissed her, and touched her body. She clasped his neck around her arms, and hoped it would continue, that he was supposed to pick her up or pin her down. He was scared, he did not have the energy to pick her up nor the weight to pin her down. Maybe he was already regretting turning his head. Maybe he had nothing better to do than to turn his head. He soon realized that Daxing was quite big, and too big to be manipulated. Maybe he felt inferior because of his height or his diploma? Daxing had a bachelor's degree, and he had gone to a vocational college. Perhaps it was not any of that. Guan Pengyu was never sure he loved Daxing. He crawled out from Daxing's arms. He sat at the table, and so did Daxing. They both looked tired.

Daxing suddenly said, "If we're going to live together, I should change the gas cylinders."

Pengyu said, "If we're going to live together, I should change the light-bulbs."

Daxing said, "If we live together, I would never let you do anything."

Pengyu said, "You're too kind. I saw it a long time ago."

He was telling the truth, and he knew that not every man could experience her kindness. Just because he saw the kindness in her early enough, he kissed her again. Then, they peacefully said goodbye.

They still did not talk about marriage, but they understood each other. When her colleagues asked, Daxing just laughed it off. If it wasn't for one of our other cousins coming to Beijing, I think Daxing would have married Guan Pengyu. However, Xiaofen arrived on the scene.

Xiaofen was the daughter of our uncle who lived in Taiyuan. She had failed to get into university three years in a row, so she came to Beijing. She wanted to be a fashion designer, and chose a textile school that did not offer a diploma or boarding. She spent a fortune getting into that school, and demanded to live at Prince Consort Hutong with Daxing.

She was adamant.

5

Xiaofen had never been to Beijing before but she was not shy when it came to dealing with people. She shamelessly thought of Daxing's home as her own. She opened Daxing's closet and squished all of Daxing's clothes to one corner to make room for her own "fashions." She then examined Daxing's dresser and pushed aside Daxing's photographs to make room for gigantic photographs of herself. Xiaofen hung one of the largest photos of herself in front of the entrance, so whoever entered the room would see her face first. At last, Xiaofen thought about the bed, since there was only one bed in the room. She told Daxing that she had bad sleeping posture and demanded that Daxing give up the bed to her, and set up a bunk for herself. Daxing did not have a bunk, so she had to buy one. The last question was food, and Xiaofen had plans for that, too. She laid down the rules that they eat breakfast separately and whoever comes home first cooks dinner — and Xiaofen always came back later than Daxing. As for lunch, Xiaofen would eat with Daxing at the cafeteria in Kailun Hotel, because lunch was free for employees. Daxing was reluctant to agree on the lunch deal because she did not want to stir up talk. Xiaofen tried to convince Daxing by telling her to get a double order, or just share Daxing's own meal, because Xiaofen said Daxing clearly needed to lose weight in order to be Xiaofen's fashion muse. Daxing thought she wasn't fat, though she did not exactly have a flawless physique; and then she thought of Guan Pengyu, who was clearly smaller, so she caved in. Xiaofen thus started eating lunch at the Kailun Hotel, and although she called it "sharing," Xiaofen always ate more than half, leaving Daxing to chew on crackers in the afternoon.

The Kailun Hotel broadened Xiaofen's horizons. She introduced herself to all of Daxing's colleagues, and asked for their phone numbers. Soon after, she was closer to them than Daxing ever was. Xiaofen went for free facials and haircuts at the hotel salon behind Daxing's back, called for room service to wash her clothes; and this other guy from Daxing's department who had his own car drove Xiaofen to school every morning, because he claimed it was "on his way." This way, Xiaofen saved on bus fare. Xiaofen shamelessly enjoyed all these privileges, and of course she knew how to thank the men who provided them to her. Her way of "thanking" the men was gently touching their thighs and adding a "you're so funny!" These men were bedazzled by her touch and the vague "you're so funny," but they dared not do anything with her. Randomly touching men's thighs was a sign of ill-breeding, but when applied to Xiaofen, it was not as simple as a lack of breeding. She was only five feet tall, with her short bobbed hair, and her small hands gave a sense of her being between a girl and a woman. She was pampered yet bitchy, shrewd yet unworldly. And she carried a hidden agenda: to whip into Prince Consort Hutong, mess up Daxing's life, and finally steal Pengyu away.

One afternoon, after a meeting with her clients at Ford, Daxing did not return to the hotel but instead went straight home. She had been successful in the business venture; the bald man from the US had agreed to sign the contract to lease guest rooms at Kailun for a year. It also meant that Daxing would receive a 0.2% commission from the deal. Since Daxing did not need to return to work that day, she wanted to go home and celebrate. When she opened the door, she saw Xiaofen and Pengyu on her bed.

I can't use "messing around" to describe Xiaofen and Pengyu. If it was simply messing around, maybe things would have turned out otherwise. Xiaofen did not just want to mess around with Pengyu, and Pengyu also thought he should better marry Xiaofen. Now, Daxing's fiancé had become Xiaofen's, in less than two months.

After much thought, Daxing decided she didn't hate Guan Pengyu like she hated Guo Hong. What made her sad was the fact that she had never slept with Pengyu in their year-long relationship, yet Pengyu slept with Xiaofen after only meeting her a few times. And in her bed, it was Daxing's bed!

Xiaofen moved out of Prince Consort Hutong without a word of apology, only leaving Daxing a buttonless blouse, which would cover her sagging butt. Guan Pengyu was the apologetic one. One day he asked Xiaofen for the key to Daxing's house and, when Daxing was at work, he moved her old bed out of the room and bought a new bed for Daxing along with new linen. He made Daxing's bed meticulously, more carefully than he would ever make Xiaofen's bed. He did not leave a single crease on the linen, nor one speck of dust. Then, he opened the bed, like he did every day in the hotel, and fluffed the pillow, tucked the blanket in neatly and put a yellow carnation on top of it. It looked as if he wanted Daxing to forget what had happened on that bed, and also as if to wish Daxing good luck in her new life.

When Daxing came home from work and saw the bed, she knew it was Pengyu's special way of apologizing to her. Daxing sat on her bunk, staring at the new bed, because she really missed the old bed Pengyu had moved out, the bed that had hurt her so deeply. If she could lie on the old bed again in the middle of the night, she would still be able to feel Pengyu's lingering smell, even though not with her. The other part, the part occupied by Xiaofen, could be omitted. When Daxing was on the old bed, she had ached, both physically and emotionally, but it had helped capture that pain — however painful, it had been with Pengyu. There was nothing about the new bed except meaningless wood.

Pengyu's new bed brought a certain frigidity to Daxing's home. It was like a man who was determined to leave the woman who loved him but before he left did every house chore imaginable. It was the cruelest compliment, and a woman could wither in this tribute or find a revelation in it.

My cousin Daxing was more kind of withering, and still no where near any revelation, so she just refused to sleep on the new bed. The first person to sleep on the new bed was me, when I was in Beijing for a youth literature conference. I lay on Daxing's new bed, and she lay on the bunk and told me about Xiaofen and

Pengyu. She said, after Xiaofen and Pengyu got married, Xiaofen quit fashion school and moved in with Pengyu's parents. He lived on the first floor of an old apartment and Xiaofen opened up her own "prêt-a-porter boutique." Daxing did not go to their wedding, because she was adamant about hating them forever. Daming, in support of Daxing, swore never to talk to them again, but for some strange reason still gave them a wedding present — a dishwasher. Daxing said the customer service department told her that Pengyu had sent her some wedding candy. She asked me to guess what she did with the candy, and I said it was surely not eaten. She pointed to the ceiling and said she threw them all up on the roof.

I close my eyes and think about the moldy roof. The roof is still there, but the two cats are not there anymore, or else the wedding candy would have aroused immense interest. Daxing started blaming herself for not being alert enough about the whole situation. I didn't think it had anything to do with attentiveness. Daxing asked, "Then, why did it happen?"

I could not answer Daxing's question, so I took her to the cinema. We watched a Hollywood film that was not yet at the public theaters, called *A Perfect World*. I had got the tickets at the conference. We both cried watching the movie. We tried to hold back our tears but wept silently, unlike when we had watched *Flower Girl* back when we were young. Daxing hiccupped occasionally but smothered the noise, so only the people near her could hear it. The criminal and the kid who was held hostage in the movie made an impression on Daxing, and she retold the story to her colleagues more than four times. After I returned to B City, I got a phone call in which Daxing said she loved children more than ever after seeing the movie. She was envious of my profession and asked me if I could get her a job in a children's book publishing house. I told her to stop being crazy, because work wasn't easy in the publishing business. Daxing did not pursue her idea, not because of me, but because she was in love again.

6

Daxing met Xia Xin on Prince Consort Hutong when Xia Xin crashed into Daxing on a bicycle. It was nothing serious, with Daxing only getting a tiny bruise. But Xia Xin apologized repeatedly and took out a band-aid from his jacket pocket and insisted on placing it on Daxing's leg himself. Then Xia Xin told Daxing that he had gone to No. 3 Yard to look at a place for rent; Xia Xin had been interested in the houses belonging to Mr. Jian and hoped Mr. Jian could reduce the rent, but the latter refused, so Xia Xin gave up.

Xia Xin thought of himself as a gifted person born at the wrong time, the good positions in society being filled already. He had graduated from a community college, and over the years had established about eight or nine unsuccessful companies, including a photo lab and a pharmacy. None of the ventures lasted long nor were they ever lucrative. He had a bad relationship with his parents, so he wanted to move out. He asked Daxing to look out for affordable housing for him because he dreaded seeing his parents. Daxing gave Xia Xin some listings and even accompanied him to look at two places. After the excursion, Xia Xin wanted to treat Daxing with dinner, but Daxing insisted on paying, telling Xia Xin he could pay after he became rich.

Daxing took Xia Xin to her home on Prince Consort Hutong, and from then on Xia Xin often ate there. While he was eating, he would tell Daxing about his plans to start a business and make a fortune, or to partner up with his schoolmates to open up a chemical factory on the outskirts of Beijing. He sometimes made changes to his plan, but Daxing believed in him nevertheless. Since Xia Xin lacked the funds to open the factory, Daxing offered to withdraw ten thousand yuan from her account to help Xia Xin. In the end, Xia Xin did not take her money because he no longer wanted to open up a factory.

I did not approve of Daxing and Xia Xin's relationship. I didn't think it was appropriate for a man to shamelessly eat, drink and talk in the home of a woman. I told Daxing that Xia Xin was not worth her while, but Daxing said I just didn't know Xia Xin well enough. She said, despite the fact that Xia Xin was poor right now, what she liked was his potential. Oh? He had potential? And Daxing liked it? I asked Daxing to list some of Xia Xin's abilities, and after some thought Daxing said Xia Xin was adept at catching flies with his bare hands. I asked her what kind of relationship they were in, and she said they didn't have a relationship. Xia Xin was very gentle, and one day they even chatted until midnight and Xia Xin stayed over. Daxing slept on the big bed in the bedroom and Xia Xin slept on the bunk outside. Nothing happened.

The purity of their relationship was as pure as ice, but also as boring. Were they just friends? Or did they have a familial relationship? Her whole life Daxing could never analyze something like this. She only wanted the affection of the man she loved, and no doubt she loved Xia Xin. However, she could never figure out what Xia Xin thought. After the lessons learnt from Guo Hong and Guan Pengyu, and after my numerous warnings, Daxing had learned to be modest in terms of relationships. Or maybe she was just pretending to be reticent. She told herself to slow down and lower her expectations, and she told herself to be subtle, and she even wanted to present herself the way Xiaofen and Xidan Xiaoliu did… maybe a little of both. Unfortunately, theories and practice were two different matters. Whenever she tried to slow down, she only moved faster than ever. Likewise, when she tried to be more toned down and subtle, she would only be more fidgety than ever. When she tried to put on makeup, she looked a thousand times worse than before. And when she smiled "coyly" into the mirror, her coyness was so extraordinary that it even scared Daxing herself.

Time flew, and after Daxing and Xia Xin must have known each other for more than six months, just like for Guo Hong and Guan Pengyu, Daxing threw a birthday party for Xia Xin in Prince Consort Hutong. Daxing seemed so forgiving, yet so very persistent. No one ever knew why she always did the same things for the men in her life. Just as before, Daxing offered to throw Xia Xin a birthday party and of course Xia Xin agreed and said, "You are too sweet," which he had never said before. "You are too sweet" made Daxing anticipate the turn of events that night, and she became busier than ever before, trying to plan Xia Xin's birthday party. Maybe it was the "You're too sweet" that made Daxing jittery. It was a Saturday, and she spent almost the entire day trying to pick out what she was going to wear that night. After many combinations, she still could not decide. She ransacked her trunks and boxes, and found her new clothes unnatural and her old clothes too insipid. If she wore simple clothes, it would make her look old. If she dressed up too much with bright colors, it would make her look cheap. She became so frustrated she decided to go and shop for new clothes. The Lufthansa Center and the Scitech Center were too far away, so she went to Xidan instead and picked out a pullover with black and red dots. She thought the pullover was the perfect combination of loud and quiet in a perfect blend of black and red. When she came home with it and looked at herself in the mirror, she thought she looked like a stagecoach. Xia Xin was going to arrive any minute but the dinner table was still empty. She took off her pullover to attend to the cake in the fridge and to take out the vegetables she had cooked the night before. However, she knocked over the bowl containing the vegetable dish and it landed on her new slippers. What was wrong with her? It was as if she had gone crazy.

When Daxing finished preparing dinner, she realized that she was running around the room in only her bra. As she looked at her own breasts, she became embarrassed about the way they looked. They could not be described as either big or small, they were just two bundles of flesh and also sagging. It looked as if there were some curves, but upon closer examination they had none. This fact made her reluctant to look at herself at all. She returned to her messy pile of clothing and pulled out a baggy shirt.

That night Xia Xin ate a lot of cake and Daxing drank a lot of alcohol. The atmosphere was fine but a slightly drunk Daxing destroyed any ideas of being subtle and coy. She was not content with just a "good atmosphere" any longer. Her frustration, her fatigue, her hopeless expectations, her yearnings, her childhood wishes, all of these things turned into firecrackers, and they exploded with fiery sparks. She demanded that Xia Xin talk, her strategy straightforward and simple, as if forcing him. It was as if her reward for the birthday party was to be Xia Xin's commitment, and she would not even allow him time to think. She never thought that this way, he had nothing to lose while she had nowhere to get to.

"Say something," Daxing said to Xia Xin, "You should say something." Xia Xin said he had a premonition that Daxing would become the person who he was the most grateful to. Daxing questioned further. Xia Xin thanked her sincerely, but it sounded very awkward. Daxing asked if he had anything else to say other than

"Thank you." Xia Xin was silent for a moment, and then said he did not want to say too much on his birthday, although he knew perfectly well what Daxing wanted to hear. Maybe he wanted to say something about their relationship, but perhaps tomorrow or the day after.... Then he thought he probably would not get through the day if he did not say it, so he would say it. He threw away his reluctance and the words just spilled out. He said he could never maintain a relationship with Daxing because one incident had made a strong impression on him: one day when he was eating there, she had taken a phone call while the pot was boiling, and when the pot started burning, she was still talking on the phone. Finally, the pot caught fire and the whole kitchen almost burnt down. Xia Xin could not understand why Daxing did not tell the person on the phone that she had something on the stove, because it was not an important phone call to begin with. Or she could have turned off the gas and then talked on the phone, but she didn't. She just kept on talking and the pot kept boiling at the same time. Xia Xin said this type of lifestyle made him uncomfortable.... Daxing interrupted him and asked him what it had to do with "lifestyle." Xia Xin said maybe it was a one-time thing, but he could not stomach it. Then he said, Daxing had offered to lend him ten thousand yuan for his business venture soon after they met. What if he were a con man? Xia Xin could not believe how easily Daxing trusted strangers.

Once Xia Xin started talking, it was hard for him to stop. Everything he listed was the truth, so he was cruel but correct. Here he was, a man without a decent job, not even capable of maintaining himself, sitting in Daxing's home shamelessly enjoying her cake. He was cruel to Daxing, talking about her faults and shortcomings. Poor Daxing, kept yelling, "I'm willing to change! I'm willing to change!"

In the end, they never talked about marriage. Xia Xin left Daxing after the birthday party. Daxing cried, and shouted at his back, "Go! I was going to tell you that Prince Consort Hutong will be relocated soon, and these two old rooms will be exchanged for a three-bedroom apartment! Three bedrooms!" Xia Xin did not turn back, as no smart man would have turned back at this point. Daxing became even more frustrated, so she yelled, "Go! You'll never find anyone as good as me! Do you hear me? You'll never find anyone as good as me!" After hearing this, Xia Xin turned back and said to Daxing, "I'm afraid so. I'll probably never find anyone." This was true, but he left. The solicitous way Daxing tried to obstruct Xia Xin only made him go faster. He did not owe her anything. He was not a customer who said he would buy but didn't, and he wasn't a customer who took the merchandise without paying. He had never even touched her hand.

For long time after, Daxing did not clean the table nor did she tidy the beds. The leftover cake from the dinner with Xia Xin went moldy on the table, and beside it stood two oily wine glasses. All the clothes she dug out for Xia Xin's birthday lay scattered on her bed, and when she came home from work she slept amidst the heaps of clothing. One day, Daming came to Prince Consort Hutong to visit Daxing, and the moment he entered, he could only shout, "Sister! What's wrong with you!"

7

Daming was surprised at Daxing's state of mind, but he did not worry. He knew his sister well, and he knew his sister could not possibly have anything on her mind. Daxing's state of mind only hindered Daming's original plan for the day, which was to try to talk to her about the demolition of Prince Consort Hutong.

Daming had got married before Daxing. His wife Mimi taught music in a preschool, and Daxing had introduced them. Daming didn't move out after he was married, because neither he nor Mimi got housing from their workplace, so they lived with Daming's parents, whom Mimi worked hard to establish a good relationship with. Although this type of living arrangement did make Mimi uncomfortable, it could not be helped. Mimi thought that after she gave birth, Daming's parents would take care of the baby and the cooking, so Mimi and Daming would not have to do anything around the house. After much thought, Mimi thought it was after all a pretty good arrangement, but it was still no self-consolation. If not for the demolition plans for Prince Consort Hutong, Mimi and Daming would have lived at home for years to come, since Mimi had already worked out how to establish a positive relationship with the in-laws. However, at that time, news of the demolition of the hutong was confirmed. Daxing had already done the paperwork to ensure that she would get a three-room apartment with gas and heating near the Fourth Ring Road. The whole Prince Consort Hutong was in a state of havoc. Sighs and frustration mixed with excitement and eagerness filled all the courtyards. Many people did not want to move, not wanting to leave the golden Beijing locality they had all lived in for so long. Granny Zhao, in No. 9 Yard, whose teeth had all fallen out, said she had been a Beijinger for her entire life, and now when she was old they were moving her out of Beijing. Daxing told her the Fourth Ring Road was still Beijing, and Granny Zhao retorted, "Then even Shunyi (the airport) is Beijing!"

Mr. Jian in No. 3 Yard told everyone he saw that the development company had made a deal with him to give him a four-bedroom apartment, and he could even choose the floor. He also said he was going to ask them about his lilac and cherry-apple trees, and whether they could move the trees into his new apartment as well. Mr. Jian shook his head full of white hair, as he let the "capitalist" in him shine through.

Daxing had deep feelings for Prince Consort Hutong, though she was neither like Granny Zhao nor Mr. Jian. She did not want to hinder the demolition process at all. A new life, and a new home with modern amenities appealed to Daxing more than the location of the hutong did. At that time, she even thought of Xia Xin, thought of him trying to find an affordable place to live, haggling with landlords. Daxing said, to herself only, many times, "Marry me, I have a home! I'll have even better houses in the future!"

The demolition of Prince Consort Hutong triggered great interest in Daming and Mimi. To be exact, the first one to react was Mimi. One night, Mimi tossed and turned and could not fall asleep, so she woke Daming up and said to him that, if they knew the hutong was going to be demolished, they could have switched living quarters with Daxing at the time of their wedding and make Daxing live at home with their parents, so then the new three-bedroom apartment would be theirs. Daming said it was too late to say anything, and besides, the way they were living was just fine. Mimi said it was not up to him to judge whether their living conditions were good or not, because he was his parents' son while she was an outsider. She said, of course he thought it was a good life, because he did not have to make the effort to establish a relationship with in-laws and maintain a good relationship. Mimi said she had always dreamed of having their own place, to decorate and live in. Daming asked what Mimi intended to do, and Mimi said they should approach Daxing first before they speak to their parents about it, because if Daxing agreed, their parents would have no reason to refuse to have Daxing move in again. Daming said that he could not possibly treat his sister like that, because she was in her thirties and still husbandless, and it was not possible for them to take away her own space. Mimi said, of course, even his sister needed private space and she was single, but does a married couple not need more private space? Mimi further convinced Daming by saying that Daxing could live at home and keep their parents company. Daming finally caved in and talked to Mimi about approaching Daxing together, but Mimi refused and said it would be easier if Daming went alone. Daming asked Mimi to reconsider, but Mimi said it should be done as soon as possible; she almost dragged Daming to Daxing's place then and there, in the middle of the night. Several days later, under pressure from Mimi, Daming finally went to see Daxing.

Daming sat at the edge of Daxing's messy bed, her pullover with black and red dots under his buttocks. He knew something bad had happened to his sister, and he poured her a glass of water. Daxing drank the water, and told Daming about Xia Xin. She talked and cried, her tears falling like beads, and Daming felt really bad. He thought of how well his sister had treated him, he thought about that one time he had thrown a banana peel in the courtyard and Grandma had slipped over it. He had told Grandma that Daxing had done it, and Daxing had to write out an apology, in addition to being chastised the whole day. Daxing silently admitted to this false blame, but never told on Daming nor held a grudge against his false accusation. Daming thought about all these things and did not know how to bring up the housing issue to Daxing. Finally, it was Daxing who asked him what he wanted from her.

Daming had no choice but to tell Daxing about their housing idea. Daxing was extremely unhappy, and said it had to be Mimi's idea because it totally sounded like an idea of Mimi. Mimi was someone who would think of such things, and Daxing said she was sorry she had introduced Mimi to Daming and welcomed Mimi into the family. She demanded to know why Daming had sided with Mimi to gang up on her — did they not see the condition she was in? Or had they just decided to pretend and forget the past? She called Daming evil and ungrateful, and she became so angry that she asked Daming if he had been under the illusion that she would never get mad. She said, "If you thought I never get angry, you are absolutely wrong because I have a very bad temper!" She demanded Daming go home and fetch Mimi and demand that Mimi tell her the plan herself, because Daxing had said that Mimi would not dare tell her of it to her face.

Daxing's voice grew louder and louder as she talked, until she was yelling as she had never yelled before. She had become a completely different person speaking those harsh words. She did not even notice when Daming had slipped away silently, and after realizing he had left, she calmed down. Daming's departure scared Daxing, and for awhile Daxing imagined he had not only vanished from the hutong, but he had vanished from the earth. He had never really done anything wrong! When he was born he caught whooping cough, and when he was two he almost choked on a pea, when he was seven he went through intestinal surgery, when he was five he fell into a well, when he was ten he chipped his tooth on the stairs … oh, poor Daming! Why did he encounter all these misfortunes! Daxing thought she was lucky never to have had such misfortune befall her, therefore in the end, she decided to give the new apartment to her brother. The more she thought about it, the more remorseful she became, for she felt as if she had been pushing him and adding to his pressures. She had to go and find him now, to tell him that she was willing to trade homes with them and move in with her parents again.

Daxing found Daming at his office and announced her decision. When she thought of what she had said about Mimi, she felt guilty and called Mimi at her office to tell her again that she was willing to switch homes with them. She spoke to them nicely, even when it really should have been Mimi and Daming pleading with Daxing. Now, Daxing was the one asking to switch with them. It was as if, perchance they hesitated in their answer, Daxing would have felt bad.

So she gave up her own house, and the day Prince Consort Hutong was demolished would become the day she move in with her parents again. The notion was supposed to be painful and regretful, yet she felt a sense of warmth from it all. Every time she walked through the hutong she was able to think of many things from the past, from when she was young and those ordeals with her "boyfriends." She wanted to calm herself through the hutong, before it was demolished, without seeing anything. It was only herself and the old rooms. She did not answer anyone's knocking. When she came home from work every day, she did not turn on the lights. She did everything in the dark, creating the false impression that no one was at home. One day, just as she was planning to do the same thing as usual when she got home, there was a man carrying a child standing waiting for her. It was Guo Hong.

Guo Hong had managed to break Daxing's vow to avoid everyone, only because she just happened upon him, and could not pretend then there was no one at home. She invited him in and got him a drink.

Over all these years, Daxing had never seen Guo Hong but had learned of his situation. He had not gone to Japan because the

Japanese girl had suddenly changed her mind and refused to marry him. He did not go back to Dalian either, but had stayed in Beijing. Afterward, he had found a wife and a job in Beijing, becoming an editor for a beauty magazine. Several years after their marriage, his wife gave birth to a girl. His wife was an interpreter for a translation company and, after giving birth, she had taken the chance to go to England with a corporate team. She never came back, and their child was left to Guo Hong. The whole marriage seemed surreal to Guo Hong. If it was not for his daughter, maybe he could have pretended the marriage was just a dream and everything could start over again, since he still was not very old. But his daughter was in his arms and not even two years old yet. She already recognized her father, and she needed to eat and to sleep. She was alive and not a dream.

Guo Hong sat on Daxing's couch drinking his drink, while his daughter lay half asleep beside him. He said to Daxing, "You see my situation." Daxing said, "Indeed I do. I see what you're going through." Hong said he knew Daxing was still single, and Daxing said, "So what?" Guo Hong demanded she marry him. He told her she could not refuse, and he said he knew she would not refuse. Then, he knelt before Daxing. It resembled a proposal, yet was more like a threat.

It was a sight to behold, a man kneeling in front of you. Daxing, who had wanted to get married for so long, felt like a proud princess. For one moment, she really felt pride, victory and comfort, along with even a little sense of nausea. Although Guo Hong's prostration involved not only marriage, Daxing still suddenly felt full of herself. No man had treated her like this before, and it was probably going to be the only time in her life. She could not be level-headed. She bent down to look at Guo Hong, who was kneeling in front of her, she smelled his hair, and it was the same smell he had had when they were in university. The scent made everything near yet far, so she could not answer him, and only asked, "Why?"

Guo Hong, who was kneeling on the ground, said to Daxing, "Because you are kind, because you are pure. Because you are a good person. You are better than anyone I've ever met or anyone I will meet."

Daxing nodded bitterly. Maybe it was what she wanted to hear. But she wanted to hear a man tell her how beautiful she was, how unforgettable she was, just like men had said to Xidan Xiaoliu, Xiaofen, and many girls around Daxing. Just as my own husband Wang Yong did, when he held me tight and nibbled on my neck as he told me so. But the man kneeling in front of her did not say those things to Daxing, and instead he was saying what everyone said to Daxing, about who she was in their hearts. Just because this sense of injustice stabbed at her, she suddenly exclaimed in a wail, "Just because of that? Isn't there anything else you can say about me?"

The kneeling man replied, "I have said everything in my heart. You are a truly good person. I have realized this after many years…." Daxing interrupted him and said, "But you don't understand…! I may be a good person, but I never wanted to be like this!"

The kneeling man still knelt, and was confused. Daxing continued, "Why do you still not understand? I never wanted to be such a good person!"

The kneeling man said, "Are you joking? Did you just say you wanted to be someone else? But that's impossible! You could never be anyone else!"

"How far is never?!" Daxing screamed.

So I am sitting on the second floor of the Shidu Department Store when Daxing finally arrives. I order an iced cola for her, and tell her I knew she still wants to talk to me about Guo Hong. I tell her not to hesitate anymore, because she cannot possibly marry him. Daxing nods at my advice, but only says she is not as stupid as before. She assures me that she is no longer as naïve as before. She says, "He can't just ditch me for another woman and come back to me years later with someone else's child." Daxing assures me that, even though Guo Hong had knelt down before her, she would not take him back.

I am surprised at Daxing's "epiphany," but I am still afraid that she will cave in and change her mind. I try to convince her further by saying, "Everyone matures, and things are never that simple to begin with. You've already given your house to Daming, and even if you wanted to marry Guo Hong, your parents wouldn't allow him and his child to live at home with you." Daxing says, "Not only are they not welcome in our family, Guo Hong has been staying at his sister in-law's place and now she wants to kick them out. I'm not going to take them in."

"The point is, he is just not worth it," I say. Daxing says she'll never talk to someone like him again, and I tell her she still has a long way to go. Daxing vows to become a new person and drinks all of her soda in one gulp, then asks me to go and purchase new cosmetics with her. She says she wanted to switch brands; she has always used *Opera*, but now she wants to use *Dior* or *Clinique*, though they are too expensive. Or perhaps she won't shell out the money, but just resort to baby lotion instead, since many Hollywood stars swore by it.

Daxing and I tour every floor of the Shidu, and in the women's department she tries on clothes that she would never wear: flamboyant, transparent, or too-tight ones. I want to stop her, but she is both stubborn and frustrated. Not only does she not listen to me, she starts arguing with me. I tell her I do not like any of the blouses she likes, and she asks me why I always never like what she likes. I tell her they do not suit her. Daxing demands to know why she cannot even decide what she wants to wear. I tell her those clothes would never suit her. Daxing asks me, "What is never? What is forever? Tell me, what is forever! How far in the end is forever?"

I shut up right there and then, because I have a premonition, though my premonition is not as simple as I think. The next day I get a call from Daxing, who tells me she is calling from her office because there is no one in her office at that time. She asks me to guess what she had found in a crevice of her couch. She says she found a wrinkled handkerchief in the crevice of her couch — left by Guo Hong when he brought his daughter over the other day. Daxing says the dirty little handkerchief made her feel bad, because the handkerchief had reeked of rotten milk, so she washed it. As she was washing it, she had felt pity for the little girl because she didn't even have a clean handkerchief to use. Daxing then comments on what a bad time Guo Hong and his daughter are going through… and says she cannot treat Guo Hong this way. Daxing keeps on saying, "Poor Guo Hong…" several times, and then she tells me, after much thought, she still is not able to reject Guo Hong's proposal. I remind her that she had rejected him already, and Daxing says she would feel forever guilty if she really did reject him. I ask her, "How far is forever?"

Daxing is silent for a moment on the other end of the phone, then she says she does not know how far forever is, but she doesn't think she will ever be the someone she has wished for her whole life to be. She says, that is really hard, even harder than marrying Guo Hong.

So Daxing is going to marry Guo Hong. I do not want to argue with her over the phone, or try to convince her otherwise. I just tell her, I should have known long ago this was coming.

That night, my husband Wang Yong and I walk down Chang'an Jie, or the "Boulevard of Eternal Peace." He has driven all the way down from B City to pick me up. I have never felt happier to see him, and feel an abundance of love and passion for my husband. I want to put my head on his shoulder and tell him I will be good to him forever. We park our car in the parking lot of the Nationalities Hotel, and walk to Prince Consort Hutong, which is just across the street. We walk through the hutong without disturbing Daxing. I ask Wang Yong, without any purpose, if he will be good to me forever. He takes my hand and says he will love me forever. I ask him, how far is forever, and he asks if I am alright. I tell Wang Yong that Prince Consort Hutong is under demolition, and Daxing is going to marry Guo Hong, and she has handed her new apartment over to Daming. I also want to tell Wang Yong how hopeless Daxing is, with a shampoo clump in her hair, and washing the handkerchief of a little girl she barely knows.

Just because she is hopeless, I will hate her forever. How far is forever?

Just because she is hopeless, I will love her forever. How far is forever?

Just because of this love and hate, even if all the hutongs in Beijing are destroyed, I would still be a loyal devotee forever.

So, how far is forever then….

(Translated by Lian Wangshu)

Maiden Days in the Boudoir

Wang Anyi. Born in Nanjing, Jiangsu Province, in 1954, and the following year Wang Anyi and her mother moved to Shanghai. Since 2001 she has held the post of chairperson of the Shanghai Writers' Association, and from 2004 has been a professor of the Chinese Department of Fudan University. She was elected vice-chair of the Chinese Writers' Association in 2006.

Starting from 1977, Wang Anyi has published writings totaling over 5 million Chinese characters. She became famous for *The Rain Whispers*, published in 1980. Since that time, she has won many awards and honorary titles, including the 3rd Lu Xun Literary Prize for "Confidences in a Hair Salon" in 2005; 2nd prize in the national 2nd Children's Writing Awards for *Who'll Be the Young Pioneers Secondary Team Leader?*, 1981 China Short Story Prize for "This Train's Terminus," 1981-82 China Novella Prize for *Lapse of Time*, 1985-86 China Novella Prize for *Xiaobao Village*, Top 10 Books of *Asia Week* for *Heroes Everywhere* in 2006, and the 2007 Outstanding Writers Award of the 6th Chinese-language Literature Media Prize for *Enlightening Age*. In particular, her novel *Song of Everlasting Sorrow* was listed among the Top 10 Books of 1996 by Taiwan's *China Times*, and won the 4th Shanghai Literature and Art Prize, the 5th Mao Dun Literary Prize and Malaysian *Sin Chew Daily*'s 1st Huazong Prize for Chinese-language literature across the world.

Many of her works, including *Xiaobao Village*, *Love on a Barren Hill* and *Song of Everlasting Sorrow*, have been translated into English, German and French and other languages, and published in places such as the UK, Germany, France, the Netherlands and Russia. Wang Anyi has been a visiting scholar or guest professor at numerous universities, including Harvard, Columbia, Yale, Cambridge, Hamburg, Waseda, and Lingnan (Hong Kong).

Maiden Days in the Boudoir

Time seemed to have glided over her, leaving no traces. You could hardly guess her age, for she still looked nubile: a delicate body and a porcelain-like face with fine features. What made the vital difference was the expression on her face: that imperceptibility between anger and joy in a maiden. Her lips curved up a little at both ends, as did her eyes — one of the causes for such an expression. With hardly any wrinkles not even when she smiled, her skin was also smooth, with only slight tracks at the outside corners extending the line of her eyes along their upward curve, actually making her more charming. Anyway, since her figure did not show her age at all, not as old, or even mature, there was only a certain sense of growth. Still, you could feel some uncertainty, or even incredulity, that she was really so young. From somewhere, age had seeped through, and moreover, expanded once it seeped through. Under the fine and smooth, yet delicate, surface, there was something frozen, turning harder. How to say? Though nothing had changed, still the held-in substance was increasing and accumulating. Who was to know? Probably, to some extent, it would eventually change the figure. Therefore, when people said she looked young, it actually implied, she could not be young.

However, you still could not guess her age, it was hard to determine. After all, and quite obviously, she had passed the blossoming age, well past it in fact. Why? Because of that purity, without any traces of lust. Inside the purity, there was also something jelling up and turning harder. Time without experience had condensed to show a denser quality. Therefore, this was a different purity compared to that of a young girl; for a young girl's purity would show something wild, with some unfounded experiences and would be, thus, somewhat lumpy. This same purity over time, however, becomes frozen, and to some extent, almost fossilized. Such frozen facial features could reveal age even more than a rugged face, which would normally contain some flowing elements: a life force, which swallowed and changed the composition and shape of the muscles, lines and skin. Probably, or for certain, it would become somewhat unsightly, however, it provided a certain vibrancy. That type of personality would contain some quality of youth for ever, and youth, because of its nature of movement and its very uncertainty, would often appear on the outside as distorted, skewed and rough.

So, you could not really say that she had not experienced time, it was just that, time seemed to have slipped over her. She had grown, but not grown up. You would see a little girl in her when you watched her squeeze and tuck in a segment of snack, such as mandarin fruit or dried banana, into her pinched mouth, wry-necked and with a raised little finger. Moreover, when she smiled at you, with the corners of her lips and eyes turning upward, she looked her utmost like a teenager. Her hair was quite dark without a single white strand, reaching to her waist gently and tied up together loosely at the end with a handkerchief, which would then make her look a bit older than that girl now, or one from an older time, dressed up in the style of about twenty years ago, like a daughter from a middle-class family, whom you could have seen either indoors or outdoors, in the lanes or a doorway facing the street, looking half languid, or half purposefully dressed up. Therefore she still looked a young woman, but as a girl of more than twenty years ago. She would spray some perfume into her handkerchief, folding fan, or behind the ears before she was about to go out. If she were to have used eau de cologne instead, then she would have been that young woman of thirty or forty years ago. Now using something more up-to-date, say an international fragrance, then the times retreat a little closer. When attending some important events, she would dress herself up in a black velvet midi, with a pair of stilettos to raise her petite body, to look slimmer. A wine-red silk shawl and a beaded handbag would turn her into a lady of an older time, which coincided with the fashion then, thus zipping up the distance torn apart by the years. It was in this way that she swam around in time, always following the trends, without that type of unwilling, fighting personality. If she had fought, then that would have left traces. Therefore, it really looked as if she had actually slipped through time.

She was just so compliant, free from any struggles, thus without any scratches left by time. But she was also not the kind of sleeping beauty in the middle of forest, who had slept all the way through time. She did go through life, from primary school to middle school, graduated during the "cultural revolution," waited for job allocation, then worked at a kindergarten as an accountant. By adding up these periods of time, you would be able to gather her age in a rough way. However, who would believe it? Age was not something to joke about, one year different from another, and this was involving almost decades of time. People would not ask her to her face, but check with each other behind her back: "How old is she?" If she happened to overhear it, she would turn her head back with a sweet smile to say: "An old woman now!" Though her smile looked so irreconcilable with an old woman, however unnatural, there was something there to make you believe. To be honest, when combining these two elements together, there was something a bit, just a bit, horrifying. It would always be strange, for at this stage, it was no longer about whether still young or good-looking, but about something else, yet what else? Nobody knew.

Nobody knew about her life, not because of how complicated her life had been, but rather on the contrary, it was far too simple, to be known by people. She had always lived with only one person, her mother. Who was her father? Either passed away or left, yet if taken off, where to? Nobody knew, nor did they ask. At that time, which was the beginning of the fifties, many families had been split in half. It probably had something to do with the times, which at a transformative stage, seemed to have been cut short, without head or tail. Behind the tens of thousands of gleaming windowpanes, how many families were short of a mother or a father? Children grew up day by day unaware of all that drama, and how many of them would go through the fuss to track the traces? With a mother and a daughter, the combination is rather good, simple, stable and peaceful, with the young well looked after and the old having someone to rely on. No arguments like those between husbands and wives, neither are there fights like that between brothers; the relationship between a mother and a daughter being somewhat like that of sisterhood, especially easy to be companionable with each other. In the streets and lanes of the city, however, there are crowds of people, who do not know each other, all having their own concealed feelings. Therefore, under the surface of crowdedness, there is privacy. Friends tend to reside within one family, such as sisters, or in-laws, and of course, mothers and daughters.

Her mother now, at first sight, actually looked more like her sister. Like her, petite-bodied, also the kind with pretty eyes and brows, and fair skin. Her dress was also quite attractive. Moreover, she looked young as well. However, at least she had gone beyond a certain border, the hard core condensing through time having transformed the outside figure from deep inside. Her figure showed a tendency to contract, not thin, not wrinkled, yet she still looked smooth and neat, just not with the same kind of gloss as before, a dimming due to change of texture. Moreover, the mother at least had experienced something more than the daughter, not to mention others; simply being that marriage and childbirth and marital changes to some extent, had at least changed the emptiness of time, leaving its marks. Therefore, her expression was also more sophisticated than that of the daughter, and more relaxed and at ease, having ultimately coped through the times. Just this little bit of difference also made her slightly more vivid than her daughter. Therefore she looked even better than her daughter. However, mother and daughter were the same, genetically speaking, of that type of personality impervious to fame and fortune, so their markings by time looked much smoother than others. Individually speaking, she was already an old woman, that type of "petite old woman," a pretty and lively petite old woman. When together with her daughter, they looked just like sisters.

They even dressed up in about the same style. When she was little, her mother used to dress her up as a lady, with her long hair done up with a bow, in the shape of a drooping bun. She would be dressed in a camel-fur-lined cotton jacket made of brocade fabric with coiled buttons, made out of her mother's cloth remnants. Underneath was a pair of her mother's worn woolen pants, modified upside-down and inside-out, with slightly tight pant-legs, and a pair of black cowhide shoes lined with synthetic gray mouse fur. When hanging out together, they looked just like two ladies of different ages. When she had grown up a bit, at around thirteen or fourteen, she was the same height as her mother and acquired some new ideas. So the mother and daughter would go to the silk store together, then after much calculation, buy some material to bring home to sew for the two of them. When there were readymade clothes, they would buy something slightly different, however still belonging to the same style. During this period she had looked rather old-fashioned, since she would dress up similarly to her mother, with overtones of a mature woman. Even during her adolescence, she looked old-womanish. Those were the days of the "cultural revolution," when the trend was the rough yet somewhat dramatic style of workers and peasants. Actually it rather coincides with the fads today, which are also quite unconventional. Wide pant legs, with a broad belt to wrap around the waist, with girls favoring dressing up in men's clothes, and fully buttoned up from the throat down. At that time, this mother and daughter had looked just as if they had been left over from the last century. Locked in their attic, they would loosen the pant legs to six inches, which was the standard then, and dismantle the lace and embroidery on the blouses, to get rid of the characteristics of corrupt older times. However, secretly they still figured out certain ways. During that time, there was a silent spreading of all types of knitting arts, such as the Albanian pattern. On getting back home and closing the door of the attic, the pair would take off their outfits, revealing their bright-colored and uniquely styled sweaters. It blurred their age. You could say they were glamorous, two beauties, but fallen behind, not with the times.

Especially her, it should have been her time; however, instead of following the trends, she had retreated. At this time, she had graduated from high school and should have gone into the hills or down to a village; however, this pair would not even give this a thought. The school and the neighborhood, after considering their pathetic situation of having only one mother and one daughter in the family, thought it would not be fair or reasonable to tear them apart, so had not really pushed them hard to do so. Eventually she was classified to be on the waiting list to be allocated work. Anyway, the mother had a job as a cashier in a local foodstuffs company. One person's salary to be spent on two had never seemed a burden. During the days waiting for her work assignment, the pair fell in love with crocheting. At that time, everybody was relegated one coupon for yarn every quarter, with each permitted to buy four clusters. They used their other coupons for fish, meat, eggs, or even grain, to exchange with others for more yarn coupons. Luckily both of them had little appetite and did not have overly strong desires to satisfy their taste buds. Having thus bought balls of yarn, they would crochet them into tea towels, tablecloths, couch covers or gloves. Crochet patterns also multiplied silently. She crocheted a jacket all with black yarn, with loose sleeves, an apple neckline, and without buttons. During spring or autumn, it could be worn to cover a blouse. Under the fishnet of the crochet, the color and pattern of the blouse would show through, which at the time, could well be called flamboyant. The unease and disorder of adolescence thus had passed by quietly in peace within a disrupted world, leaving a whole houseful of crocheted decorations. At a glance, there was a certain eyeful of exuberance. However, because of the color white, everything ended up as pure again. Later on, she was allocated work at a neighborhood kindergarten, coincidentally as an accountant, the same as her mother. It was by then already the final stage of the "cultural revolution," in the mid-seventies, and the trends on the street were regressing, starting to reveal again the realities of life. As for her, she had turned into a real adult. Her dress, therefore, no longer appeared to be too old for her, but just right. Her style was conservative with a bit of fancy — for example, between winter and spring, she would don a grayish beige checked woolen jacket, with a red and green silk scarf around the neck, a pair of Western-style navy woolen pants, and a pair of short T-string black cowhide shoes. Her hair would be plaited into two braids, gripped together with a plexiglass barrette. At that time, the trends were still quite exacting, though not as tense as before. This style took on a slight tone of townspeople, which was anyway becoming the new fashion.

She and her mother, in those early years, pretty much lightened up the scene on this street of Shanghai. Her mother would normally appear the same as she did, with the only difference being her hair style. Her mother would plait the hair into one braid, as both mother and daughter kept their hair long, and coil it around the forehead, then secure it with a pin. By the end of the seventies, when things were more open, her mother would coil up a bun and cover it under a black hairnet. As for her, she then began to loosen her braids, and tie her hair into a ponytail. At that time, her age was beginning to catch up with her dress style, with a tendency indeed to overstep. However, the clothing style that the mother and daughter favored was capable of lasting over time. Like the leading ladies in the Beijing Opera, from their youth to adulthood, so long as their personality did not change, they could always dress up in the same way. She then looked even younger than before. With the great changes in the trends, they also added one more type of dressing up, which was makeup. In the beginning, they made up each other's face. Once familiar, they started to put the cosmetics on themselves. They would each face a mirror — that kind of old-styled dresser with three panels of mirrors. They would each face one panel, to even out the powder, draw in the eyebrows, then the eyeliner, slightly raising the eye-line at the ends. Since their mouths were small, therefore the corner of the lips also needed raising. Finally, some loose powder to stabilize the makeup. At that time, skirts were also becoming fashionable. They both loved wearing skirts, long skirts reaching the feet. In winter, it would be woolen skirts, to go with short boots, which could cover the legs of the long underwear worn inside. This style lasted until long velvet stockings started to become popular. Skirts were much easier to match than trousers. They could go with wool sweaters of all colors, long or short jackets, giving a more decent tone. On the outside, there would always be a long overcoat, with collars up. After all their dressing up, they would go downstairs, go outside, and go dancing.

They would most frequently go to the ballroom dances in the neighborhood, or those held by bankrupt factories for middle-aged and older people. The ticket prices would normally be inexpensive, and the atmosphere would be quite proper. Also, they would go to the dances held by their own organizations for socializing purposes, also very decent, without troublesome people or issues. They took no partners, and danced only by themselves. They cooperated really harmoniously, able to handle all types of steps. Of course, sometimes someone would also invite them to dance a round. It had always been a hiding place for some real gentlemen, these dances for the middle- to old-aged. They would walk in front of the mother or the daughter, bowing forward slightly, with a seeming bent to their knees, which actually was not there, and then they would hold on to one of the hands reaching out, and quietly glide into the dance hall. Most of the dance floors were built of cement, but smoothened and flat enough just by the grinding from the bottoms of shoes. Luckily the mother and daughter pair were both light and easy to dance with. Led by the gentlemen, they danced quite elegantly. After one piece of music, they would return as a pair and dance face to face with each other again. Even if they danced to the last song, it would not be too late, normally half past ten or eleven. The two of them would then put on their coats and walk out, along a street or lane, twist and turn, left and right, before finally reaching home.

They lived in an attic of an old lane. This was a double attic, compared with the normal ones, between different floors with north-facing small rooms, about twice the size of two side-by-side north windows and a back window looking down on a courtyard. She had been living there since she was born, and had never left. The washroom was shared with the people on the second floor, and the kitchen was right outside the door, with a single gas stove, commonly called a "turtlehead," at the corner of the stairway, for cooking and boiling water. The mother and daughter's home could reasonably be called simple and plain, but, because of their whole roomful of rosewood Western furniture, it still looked quite fine. Moreover, with all the crocheting they had done at that time, piles and piles of silk and yarn, it did display something special, a kind of delicately silky girlhood of a boudoir. The pair had been through life long enough to become a bit squeamish, therefore the twelve- or thirteen-square-meter small room was always wiped spotless. Inside the mottled walls, where the doors and windows had nearly rotted to bits, who could imagine, that there was this small world in this niche?

For their fans to be used in summer, they would line the edges with fine hemp, and wrap the handles in spirals of thin bamboo strips, and finally attach some silk thread. They would put the fans away on the hook behind the door of the wardrobe, after thus tidying them up. Such hooks would have normally been used for holding men's caps or ties. The hot-water bags to be used in winter would be put away in the last drawer of the chest, with covers made of leftover fabrics. Together with these, there would be a can of buttons removed from old clothes, a bundle of knitting needles, and a metal box once holding chocolates. Inside the box, there were all sorts of odds and ends: empty perfume bottles, useless but they would begrudge throwing them out; also three or four old postcards, very scarce, in some remote relative's hand, making you feel like he had once written it in a surge of blood, and then never remembered to send more again. During every year's spring cleaning, they would consider whether to throw these things out and then resort to postponing it until the next year. They would change only the lining paper to new sheets, and put everything back again, one thing at a time. The paper to line the drawers used to be old newspapers, since it was said that the ink could keep boring insects away. However, gradually they could no longer think of the reason, and therefore started using stiffer and smoother calendar paper instead, and thus an old habit was altered. They would change the lining in the drawers one by one; finally reaching the top of the chest. On top of the chest, there were two abacuses, which represented their basic means of livelihood, as well as also their toys. After dinner, before there used to be television, they would take one each, compete over a "double-nine adding skill," which was "one two three four five six seven eight nine," plus nine times of "one two three four five six seven eight nine," to see who would be the first to finish the calculation and who was accurate. Two people using six fingers on numerous abacus beads, not to mention looking at or even just listening to it, was a quite enjoyable phenomenon. Later on, abacuses were upgraded to calculators, and therefore no longer used; however, the game went on for some time before it gradually ceased. No more playing with the abacus, then, they started watching TV! The abacuses were relocated to the top of the chest. So, there were still changes, however, meek and smooth, just no world-shaking revolution.

But their home was not as quiet and lonely as it might have sounded. There used to be several regular visitors! There was one old friend of the mother, some kind of relation, whom her mother called Brother Yun, and for her he was thus "Uncle Yun." He lived in Pudong. Pudong at that time was a place where people had their own distinct accent. When he came, he would always bring some sweet sugarcane, tough or tender water chestnuts, homemade cakes, and once in a while, the quite precious gift of a yellow-beaked, yellow-footed hen. On the mother's side, she would fill up his empty bags to be as full as when he came, with thinly sliced glutinous rice cakes, egg pancakes, or a kilo of white cake. When they sat down, they would normally chat; nothing much but something like, how the house of a family had caught fire during a burial ceremony; or how someone had disguised himself as a ghost at the Dongjia Ferry Road to rob people of money, and how some lady from a certain family had been scared to death. It all sounded similar enough to the neighborhood gossip, spread through the streets and lanes, but, when mentioned by them so seriously, the gossip turned out like a kind of truth. After that many years of being spread, the scary and ghostly atmosphere in the stories had already faded away, therefore transformed to real normality.

This Uncle Yun, when she was waiting for a job, introduced

someone to her for marriage. He was a technician, five years her senior, from Pudong, where his family had a house, with three rooms upstairs and three downstairs. Normally speaking, this would have been considered quite good prospects. But she could not see any future in it then. Just knowing he lived in Pudong was something unacceptable to her. She had always lived in Shanghai's western district from birth, if only in a shabby north-facing small room in a lane of this flourishing area, cold in winter and hot in summer, even leaking during typhoon season, but she was used to it. She was someone even unfamiliar with places only a couple of bus-stops away. In high school, she had gone to villages to work as a labor helper in the autumns, to places like Fengxian, Songjiang and northern Xinjing. Every time she went, her mother would prepare her a pack of panties along with a pack of pins, the number of panties and pins calculated according to the days she needed to be there. If fourteen days, then there would be fourteen packs of each. Mother would ask her to change her panties every day, but pin them all up with the four sides rolled up to protect the crotch in the middle, and then bring them home to wash. The rivers in the countryside would contain, who only knows how many types, thousands or tens of thousands, of germs and filth. Because of this failed matchmaking, her mother even got into some difficulty with this Uncle Yun, wondering what made him consider her daughter as someone old and unwanted. What they did not know was how many job-waiting girls were hoping for marriage into just such a family! Therefore that Pudong guy soon found someone to marry, who was even two years younger than her, from a big family, who also did not wish to go to the village and was determined to stay in Shanghai. When Uncle Yun talked about it, mother and daughter simply smiled, not at all feeling the regretful commiseration that he had expected.

Other regular visitors included two or three of her primary or high-school classmates. All average girls, close to her in personality, relatively unambitious and blasé. When they were together, they also had their fun: gossiping about other girls and rumors in the lanes, or going to the nearby cinema to watching movies — tragedies being the best to shed some tears together over. When walking out of the cinema, it would be getting dark, and streetlights would have been turned on, therefore adding a feeling of a change of world, though still with the same characters. They would not come back to reality until after having walked a block. Parting from them, she would go inside the lane, reach the back door, and see the light in the north window of the attic, through whose crochet curtains, you could see an eyeful of shadows. The drama on the screen was then suddenly sucked far away. The girls would always have some secrets to share between them. In the days of waiting for a job, they were all eighteen or nineteen years old, and who would not think about marriage? However, who could speak out about themselves? They could only talk about the others. For example, a girl from some school, who had gotten involved with a certain teacher, and had even gotten pregnant by him, and used a white band to tie around the tummy. When playing basketball on the playground, and asked by a classmate how she'd gotten so fat, she had flown into a rage and told off the classmate for talking nonsense. Or something else like, two sisters in the lane falling in love with their cousin at the same time, and how the three of them would always go everywhere together. Feeling it too hard to make a decision, the cousin ultimately married one of his classmates instead. These sounded really touched up, with a flavor of those Jane Austen novels, mixed in with some of the worldliness of street rumors. Underneath their secret gossip, there was a feeling of the forbidden, therefore scary but exciting. Yet, those stories seemed somehow even further away to her than the tragedies on the screen. The roles and events in movies were at least linked to her sense of aesthetic appreciation, but those rumors seemed not at all related to her. In her life, such things were definitely not going to happen. All those extremely terrible, plague-like disasters. Her own life was safe however. These frequent visitors also left one by one. One went to Anhui to settle down in a village; one was assigned to work in a factory, busy juggling a three-shift life, with no more free time to enjoy a maiden's life in a boudoir. Another one, same as her awaiting a job allocation, with a third-degree heart problem, hung out together with her for a while; and it was this girlfriend who introduced crocheting into her family. They would put their heads together to crochet all the designs and styles, which certainly brought about a close friendship, because of the similar simple and plain life and experience. Because of their closed-in life, they would be somewhat poor intellectually, without much to talk about. Therefore their association was merely chatting and knitting. By then, there were even no more films available. Soon afterwards, the girl got herself a boyfriend, and gradually stopped coming.

After she started working, there were one or two colleagues who got along well with her. However, at this age, relationships had become hard to get too close in. As mentioned earlier, she was not that type of enthusiastic person, therefore her association with such friends also stayed at an ordinary level. Yet one of them hoped to introduce her husband's brother to her, and she really did go to see him once. In the park on a Sunday, there were chattering kids everywhere. The two of them walked along the cement path, a couple of rounds, with a distance of one person between them. She did not know whether the other one looked at her, but she did not look at him. However, she did see he was wearing a pair of black three-part cowhide shoes with shoelaces, inside which were a pair of thin nylon socks, smoothly covering his ankles without any skips in the weave. That somebody talked about something, his job probably, how he was in charge of instruments at a metallurgy factory. Whatever he talked about was beyond her understanding, though she did not feel bored at all. With someone by her side, somewhat noisy, still, it was not so bad. In fact, at this time she did start to think of getting married. However, once back home and after discussing thoroughly with her mother, they considered it somewhat inconvenient to become in-laws with a colleague, so it would not be good to have such a marriage, and in this way she turned it down. There were a couple more introductions like that later on, since there was always someone who was overly warmhearted. By that time, she had passed the most ideal age for getting married. It was like missing a bus, and thus she had missed one whole load of potential compatible partners. Those people introduced to her were either not good enough here or with regrets there, not satisfying her at all. Though she had the intention to get married, she was not eager to do so, or even not so purposefully conscious about it. If she were really to get married, she would still have had some fears at least about it. Another few years later, even that little bit of something unconscious from the bottom of her heart also diminished.

Life, rather like lukewarm water, glided over her. All those whirlpools or undercurrents that could have caused an impact in life just passed by, moving straight forward on their own. She was still like that younger little girl, who had slept with her mother in the same bed. The bed was a double bed, about five feet wide. The two of them happened to be both petite, thus not taking up too much space. A couple of decades later, even the palm-woven mattress had not unraveled at all. Only once or twice, her mother had called in a handyman, some country folk repairing palm mattresses, to slightly tighten it by adding in a few palm fiber threads. The bed cover was for a long time the old bubble-weave cotton in red, blue and yellow stripes, and later changed to a white poplin base with red strawberries stitched all over. Time seemed never to advance, but rather to go backward, back to those naïve childhood times. Because of regular waxing, the rosewood furniture still looked new and gleaming. And nowadays, mahogany furniture had become popular again, in a Victorian style, with heavy and complex carving and ornamentation. Therefore it matched the changing trends. Those covering crochets and embroideries, since their time was more recent, of course had not become misshapen but were still useful. There were also new add-ons, like the refrigerator. On its handle, there was a sage green cloth cover decorated with red strawberry flowers, introducing another ten percent of the taste of a boudoir. The television was a comparatively frequently changed item: from twelve-inch black and white, to a fourteen-inch color one, and most recently a twenty-five-inch flat screen. The channel would always be locked on Hong Kong or Taiwan soap operas. After dinner and washing up, and finishing whatever they had to do, it would then be about the time when the drama would continue from where they had left it in the last episode. They sighed, they shed tears, but still only indifferently, like watching a fire from the other side of the river. Their life was so much abstinence, that they consumed extremely little, therefore, there were nearly no expenses.

Every morning when she got up, her mother would cook breakfast, also very light: rice porridge, with preserved bean-curd, homemade bamboo shoot and beans. She would wash her face and brush her hair, the sunlight still not reaching inside. Their attic was on the other side of the sun, and the dresser was placed in between the two north windows under the wall. Unable to catch the light, the mirror was also in the dark. That was also quite fine, for in the mirror, she looked really young, as if she were still in her late teens: a moist and smooth complexion, pitch-black hair, and eyes glimmering in the deep darkness. After their ablutions, the rice gruel would be thirty percent cooler by then, held in a gilt-edged fine porcelain bowl, which had also been used for many years. It would be quite difficult to see bowls like that anymore these days! Even if there were, they would be replicated ones, the imitation none too good, either using rough porcelain with the bowl line not fully round, or they were extremely expensive, luxurious show-offs for big banquets, together with gold and jade glasses and cups. Nothing came as delicate as these ones for daily use. After breakfast, she would go downstairs, to go to work. Lucky for their old lane, many times, new planned blocks had missed it within an inch right next to them. All around, there now were erected high buildings, the road also having been widened, leaving only their patch of lane. The population had changed quite a lot in this lane as well, especially those her age — they had either married and left the lane, or changed or bought new apartments — until more than half had left. Some of the older people were still there, those who had already been old now were just older, and not changed much in their appearance. When seeing her, they would still call her "*meimei*" (little sister). The children were not as many as before either, when there used to be flocks of small ones rushing out of one family door. Now there were only two or three, and normally you could not see a soul, other than in the morning and evening, though from the windows of the courtyard, you might hear children howling or adults growling. Occasionally there would be one or two cries of a baby, which would be so scarce as to make it feel precious. Some time on, the crying would also disappear and be replaced by babbling.

The bus she took to work changed routes several times. She used to get on the bus from the road not far away from the lane, later on the bus stop shifted to a small street on the back; and then it stopped running completely, and she had to take another bus which involved transferring in the middle somewhere. Still later, she could use the underground subway. When she walked down into the wide and bright tunnels of the subway waiting for the train to come in at its typhoon speed, standing beside the platform would make her feel the advance of the time, and a feeling of pride would ooze from the bottom of her heart. But not for long, since soon she also started to take it for granted, the fact that she could not remember what the street used to look like before the subways had been built. Those crowded small shops, residences, little schools, noisy and dirty entrances of the lanes, had all disappeared in the face of the now straight and wide roads, like none of it had ever existed. The former local specialty shops or dairy shops, and their products, such as preserved peach halves, salted orange-peel pellets and flattened olives, were all now displayed together in the grand shelves of large or small supermarkets. Therefore, the earlier fun of trivial picking and choosing, and calculating, was devoured by wholesale-like consumerism. At first she would not know where even to put her hands, but soon she got used to it. To take home bags and bags of goods from the grocery shelves made her feel wealthy and fulfilled. Although she was not that type of self-motivated person, she also was not the kind who would stick to the past, loathing to part with it. She just lived in the moment, no past, no future; only the present moment was real. This was her way of submitting, imbedded with a certain positive significance.

The organization that she worked for, a kindergarten, changed its premises a couple of times, and went through one or two mergers. Because of the one-child policy, the number of children kept getting fewer and fewer, until, about three years ago, the kindergarten she was working for was turned into a home for the elderly. However, she remained its accountant. This job had become popular in the last decade or so, and even many young women who had had high education would still go to evening school for continuing education in this subject, in order to be able to obtain a certificate for such a job. However, most of them fancied sino-foreign joint ventures or exclusively foreign-owned companies, not like her, an accountant in a small neighborhood kindergarten, a position nobody would fight with her for. She was always cautious when doing the accounts, never making any mistakes, and the appearance of the books was also kept clean and tidy. Her career life was very peaceful, as she never came across even the smallest risks. If there really were any, probably only two occasions could count. Once, an accountant, from a neighborhood kindergarten in the same area, the hearsay being she had been allocated there from the famous Lixin Accounting School, had embezzled 170,000 yuan from the children's lunch fees, in order to please her boyfriend, and was ultimately sentenced to death. This shocked the whole kindergarten education system. Though she knew clearly she would never commit such a crime, she felt inescapably frightened. Who was to know that one day she might keep the accounts wrong without realizing it? Still, she was not the sickly nervous type and this stress swept over swiftly. Another scare was from reading in the newspaper, that according to statistics, one tenth of those affected with venereal diseases were accounting personnel, because they came into lots of contact with paper notes and bills, which, especially banknotes, were the most extensive carriers of numerous bacteria. This greatly horrified her. However, the report also said that so long as you kept washing your hands, any infection would be thwarted. From then on, whenever she touched bills and notes, she would wash her hands, as well as before or after the toilet, before or after meals, always washing her hands. She thus safely survived another crisis.

It went on like this until the point of retirement. This was a serious warning of an age dividing line, warning people that time had come to a certain limit, and life would soon follow to enter another stage. But for her it was not so serious. Mother's retirement life had already given her a great model. Mother had retired the second year after she had started working, which had made the pair both feel relaxed. They would no longer have to fight for the dresser to brush their hair and do their makeup, or finish breakfast without having time to do the dishes, therefore leaving them upside down in the pot, with no time to consider the grime. When coming home from work, they would have to start cooking straight away without a rest. The whole day thus used to pass by in tension and disorder from morning to evening. After the mother had retired, she would get up one hour earlier than the daughter, do her hair, prepare breakfast, and even do the grocery shopping for lunch and dinner as well. After she left, her mother would tidy up the room, and also have some free time to kill in the park enjoying the sunshine. After lunch, the mother would doze off for a siesta, to make up for the one-hour loss of sleep in the morning. When she came home, she would find hot steaming dishes awaiting her on the table. In the park, the mother got to know some other retired women, one of whom was fond of singing Shaoxing Opera. That park was also quite amusing, with a corner especially set out for opera fans. In the morning, those in roles for ladies or gentlemen, plus the musicians, would gather there to perform. Another two were into Mulan-style swordplay, and taught her with great enthusiasm. Therefore, the mother was also quite busy in the park, playing with Mulan swords, and listening to Shaoxing Opera. Later on, a retired teacher had a crush on her, who even sent her a big bunch of roses on the Mother's Day. That day, she had walked home through the lane, with her face showing a mixture of embarrassment and sweetness, really looking somewhat like a maiden. Because of this, she stopped going to the park. Not long afterwards, half of the park was also annexed by a real estate developer, who dismantled its fences and turned it into a promenade park in the middle of a street. As for her mother, she had found another resort, that was, the church. At the persuasion of a neighbor, the mother was converted to Christianity. Every Sunday morning, she would go to church. In the meantime, because of the hymns, she fell in love with singing. For sure, the mother had something in her more open than the daughter, not because she was more experienced, but because of her childish sense of fun. As for her, though closed-in, because of the lead of her mother, she was able to step out into new lives, which did not worry her at all.

Before retirement (at age fifty-five), the company arranged for her to take part in the district union's tour to Hunan's Zhangjiajie zone. It was a big issue for both the mother and daughter. Neither of them had ever vacationed outside city, unbelievable as that might seem. Farmers from the countryside would be normally considered ones who would never leave their fields, though as a matter of fact, people in the city were the same, and even more possibly so, since they were not even as curious about the outside world as farmers would be. They thought any life beyond the big city would be unbearable. However, the times were changing and new and fresh things were sprouting, for example, package tours. Though they were not such passionate people, still they were also not without interests either. When the opportunity presented itself, they also liked to go around taking a look and having some fun, why not? It was not like migrating somewhere to make a living. TV, newspapers and tourist advertisements had brought closer those faraway places, which no longer felt so remote and frightening. All these things were secretly changing people's view of the world.

Quite a few days in advance, the mother and daughter had started their exciting and nerve-wracking packing. Hygiene was their priority consideration. Mother had bought alcohol cotton balls, disposable wet napkins, paper serviettes, and toilet tissues which were folded into small piles and packed in small-size plastic bags. To avoid cross contamination, they also prepared antiseptic for disinfection purposes. The second consideration was food. This mainly consisted of instant noodles and biscuits, in case she came across food that she could not eat; these were supposed to fill her up. There were many things that she did not eat: mutton, beef, chili, garlic, cilantro, radish, pepper, and egg yolk. If she happened to eat something unclean, that would not be a problem, since she would carry a large amount of berberine with her. As for clothing, it would mainly be for the purpose of keeping warm. Though it was early autumn, long underwear, woolen jumpers and dustcoats had to all be taken along. Thinking of the inevitable walking and mountain trekking, they purposefully went to buy a pair of sneakers, which really marked a breakthrough in their dress style, bringing in an atmosphere of sport, and something modern into their silky maiden style. Finally they had to consider the travel companions; though both easygoing, they took things seriously when it came to mixing with people. Especially when traveling in a group, people would need to look after each other even more so, and thus would need better communication to understand each other better. Therefore, they went to the supermarket and bought a whole load of snacks: marinated orange peel, Taiwan-style plums, hawthorn slices, *Wang Wang* rice crackers, nut chocolates.... Then packed them into small packs, and squeezed them into every corner and slot of the already filled-up travel bags, and surprisingly they managed to fit it all in. Thus, her luggage became huge and heavy.

That day, when catching the train, there were the mother and daughter, with Uncle Yun also called upon, who was by that time an old man, with a big bald patch in the middle of his head, but still capable of managing heavy weights, with one big bag in each hand. The mother and daughter were each carrying something itsy-bitsy as they followed Uncle Yun. When getting onto the train, her luggage alone occupied a whole section of the luggage rack. Their travel-mates were from different organizations, therefore not known to each other at all, but all considering the long journey they would go through together, plus the exciting feeling of travel, everyone came up to help, with no regrettable complaints at all. The mother then relaxed, and hurried her to share the snacks with everybody. Therefore, the just-loaded luggage was pulled down again in search of the snacks, with everything soon scattered all over the place. When, finally when they did find something, it was already time for the conductor to chase the visitors off. As they distributed the snacks and said goodbye, the train started moving in the chaos, which somewhat lightened the feeling of departure between the mother and daughter, and no embarrassing scenario ensued.

The hygiene on the way was better than expected. They were lucky to be on a new train, with the carpet, bedding and curtains all new. Even the uniforms of the conductors were in a new style. Sitting in the bright car with clean windows and tables, they soon felt familiar. Traveling outside without being tangled with daily troubles, their hearts felt light. Speaking and listening became extraordinarily exciting activities, with frequent bursts of laughter. The tour group had about a dozen people. Six were women, so they filled one compartment of the sleeping car exactly. On reaching their destination, if there were three-bed rooms, they would be divided into half, while if there were two-bed rooms, they would be divided into three pairs, which they formed automatically. The one who paired up with her was a staff member from the trade union who had actually organized the tour, Xiao Hong, who was not yet thirty, but already had a toddler at home. She seemed to have won Xiao Hong's favor. Xiao Hong took the initiative to stay in the same room with her. If it were a three-bed room, the other partner would then be Xiuping, a model worker at the district level, and the director of a neighborhood committee, only forty years old but looking much older than her. In a big group, with two closer companions to go everywhere together, she felt relaxation and calm deep down in her heart. The first meal on the train was like a potluck party. Everyone put down whatever they had brought, turning it into a banquet: ham sausages, tea eggs, half an electric-oven-roasted chicken, cakes, hamburgers, instant noodles, all kinds of fruit and drinks. The second meal, they were divided. The men went to the dining car together, while the women finished what was left over. Xiao Hong did not eat anything, and just climbed into her bed and slept. People said she was missing her son. The lights in the car came on, while outside the window there was the darkness, making people feel even cozier inside.

She had seldom experienced staying out overnight. This was for her almost like a changed world. She sat on the bed, watching the dark open country outside; occasionally a cluster of lights would pass by. When they reached a station, the lights would become denser, even looking splendid. When the train stopped, there would be people squeezing in the door, bringing in a tense and rushed feeling. Vendor trolleys were being pushed along under the windows, which, in contrast, looked more relaxed and at ease. She was assigned to take the floor berth, due to her age, since she was the only one among the group who was about to retire, though she looked about the same age as Xiao Hong. She did not sleep well that night. Every station the train reached, she would wake up and look outside through the window. In the middle of the night, the stations were fully bright. So many people were moving around, getting on or off the train. What a lively night! Just in between moments of waking and sleeping, she felt herself getting further and further away from Shanghai, embarking on her tour.

She was more adaptable to the environment than she had thought. The climate in the Hunan area was quite damp, so clothes would not dry even two days after washing, and they would soon be on their way again wearing damp clothes, feeling the stickiness and dampness on the body. Sometimes she thought she would fall ill, but she did not. It was Xiao Hong who felt unwell because of the change in the local climate: She got a rash, and her stomach also became disorderly. In the end, she had to look after Xiao Hong instead. The meals there used a lot of chili pepper. In the hotpot would float some scarlet peppers, which you would not taste at the beginning, but would get spicier as time went on. Learning from experience, they would scoop the chili peppers out first thing when a hotpot was brought to the table, a bit like some firefighting. However, they were not able to scoop all the peppers out. There would always be the ones missed, and they had to let it be. Later on she found that she was able to eat hot and spicy food as well, and even found it quite delectable with rice. Once she had a kind of meat, but did not know what it was at the beginning. Afterwards she was told, by the lady boss, that it was turtle meat. It gave her an unusual feeling, however the meat had already been eaten and what else could she do about it? The next time, on coming across turtle meat again, since it was not the first time, she just ate it.

She also found she was quite good at hiking, for she was nimble and light in weight. When trekking in the mountains, she found it even easier than the men did. She did not even need that pair of sneakers. She would have felt awkward if she had worn them, since they were not her usual style. Those moderate-heeled, boat-shaped brown shoes, she felt nothing inconvenient in using them. On the Mengdong River, they even went on bamboo rafts. A few women holding hands and cuddling together, following the raft's ups and downs in the turbulence of the current, and they laughed until their bodies turned to jelly. The mountains and rivers were like from a painting, and they themselves felt as if no longer belonging to themselves, but to the painting.

The things she favored the most were the souvenirs at each scenic spot. The stuff was about the same, but she had always had a penchant to check them out from one stand to another, selecting, and bargaining. Those roughly made and vulgarly designed small knickknacks looked extremely interesting to her. She was not that experienced after all, with about the same knowledge as a village girl. Soon the little things she bought were able to fill up the space opened up by the finished snacks. When checking out and buying the stuff, there would be chitchat when the stall owner was a lady, with questions like, where she had come from, what she did, how many children she had, or her age. At first, she would answer with the truth, not married yet. However, gradually she was starting to grow concerned, and therefore changed to a vague and tricky answer, "Left behind in Shanghai!" When coming across someone serious, or nosy, who would dig even further, asking whether she had one or two children, boy or girl, how old, she could only grin, and turn to leave. Later on, she became more tactful, and learned how to brag and tease with these women. Sometimes she would say a boy, and sometimes a girl, sometimes one child, sometimes two. When asked for their age, she would sometimes say at kindergarten, and sometimes in university. When hearing that, people would not believe her and would delve further, and she would have to repeat her answer. After a couple of times, she started to fall in love with such chitchat, and sometimes would bring up the topic herself. For example, when seeing a child, she would ask the mother how old the child was, where they planned to send the child to study. People would then ask her the same questions. Once, after a long chat, a woman pointed at the men in her group, asking which one was her man. She was not married, after all, and could not really fend this off by joking. Shy, embarrassed and defeated, she then fled.

Going down the Mengdong River was a village called Wangcun. It used to be a quiet village, but was now famous because of once being chosen as the site for a film shoot. In the village, there were restaurants and scenic spots named after the film characters, places, scenes or plots. On top of that, there were performances to display the folk customs: singing, antisphonic singing, dancing, dragon-boat racing, praying for rain and deity worshipping ceremonies, etc. Wangcun was right by the Mengdong River, with a dark mountain's silhouette in the distance, the water crystal clean and the trees emerald green. It may have been a prosperous important town in the old days because of its closeness to the waterway. The residential buildings in town mostly had dark roof tiles and blue bricks, and the walls were tall and thick. The Chu area had a kind of charming and gentle style, something quite seductive about it. There was a woman standing by the door to be part of the clamor, holding a baby girl in her arms, who was at most a little more than one year old. The baby girl was wearing a kylin-design hat, red lipped, dark eyed, and she suddenly glanced at them with an expression in her eyes. That expression certainly belonged to an adult woman, with the corners of the eyes raised high, and a smile emerging on the cheeks. The baby girl's flirtatious look was surprisingly uncanny, and she could not help feeling shocked.

In the black-bricked streets, or under strutted pavilions, there were ongoing performances about folk customs from love to marriage. Some young boys and girls, seemingly not-so-professional actors, without special training in singing and acting, showed inharmonious coordination and a lack of fluency. Their expressions even were restrained and therefore not as lively as the normal mountain villagers walking on the streets. However, their performance contained something unusually sweet to enjoy. The girls were all quite pretty and fresh, with bright eyes, and hiding underneath their awkwardness were their early-to-mature flirtatious expressions. They would have all been little foxes when the age of that baby girl. The boys were small, thin, not as exceptional as the girls, yet looking very witty. Just an eyeful of a glance at a girl looked as if thousands of words were being sent. What they were singing was not understandable, the tone flat, the drum and music also not correctly adjusted, but with rhythmic beats and stops, it sounded quite fluent. The boys and girls first sang while sitting down or walking, then as the singing got going, they started to throw silk balls at each other, and afterwards paired up together and started holding hands. Then came an ugly old woman, supposedly played by a boy, as matchmaker, and they would drink, and sing, turning the scene into an obvious banquet for a marriage proposal. But the singing did not seem to get them anywhere, and the atmosphere became tense. Finally a sedan-chair showed up from somewhere, and was carried down from the pavilion, going straight towards the tourists. A girl announced in standard Chinese, that the boys were about to grab a bride!

The sedan-chair was moving through the heavily gathered crowd, and the performance was at its climax. The crowd suddenly started jostling about, and hustled to give way. The sedan-chair was wrapped in silk and colorful cloth, bright red, carried on the shoulders of four boys, and led by four girls in the front. It wobbled its way through the crowd, followed by trumpets and flutes, blowing out complete happiness. There were suddenly auspicious clouds gathering, floating on top of the dark mountain ranges. A couple of rafts also came along, some more guests gathering. The girls' faces now beamed with smiles, looking more at ease than earlier on when singing and dancing. Obviously this was also their favorite part of the show, with a bit of a mischief, also with some secret yearnings towards their own futures. They checked left and right, to see who would be suitable to play the role of the bride. Their sights pierced through the crowd halfway down the street. All the women began to scream and laugh, dodging away from these girls for fear of being pulled onto the sedan-chair. But in actual fact? They all kind of hoped for it. The girls merely smiled without stopping their steps, and went straight toward her. The four girls exchanged this look in their eyes, and quickly altogether stopped, also stopping the four boys, leaving the sedan-chair on the ground, waiting. Four pairs of hands reached out to grab her, producing a red robe like magic, and before she could scream, she was already hooded and wrapped, tucked into the sedan-chair and carried away. This time, the four guys and four girls marched across the street, and the trumpet rang out even more powerfully. Everyone was clapping their hands and screaming, especially her group, whose palms went red from clapping so hard. They were greatly surprised, for she was not the youngest, nor the prettiest, but how could these people tell that she was the maiden who was still waiting in the boudoir?

The young men and women marched along the black-cobblestone street, carried the sedan-chair one more round, and stopped only when they were back to where they had picked her up, and then released her. Her face was bright red, though it was unclear whether it was because of the reflection of the red silk coat, or because of the laughter. Xiao Hong and Xiuping snatched her back, peeled the costume off and threw it back to the young men. She laughed with all her body until it was like jelly, without being able to say anything, her heart pounding heavily. The music and the drums slowly moved far off, and when it ceased the crowd also dispersed. The happy excitement was gone but she was still smiling. Her companions were also smiling, embracing her all around. At this moment, she became their star.

She did not know how to handle the whole scene other than to laugh, which echoed on the already lonesome black stones. This village, without the noise of the tourists and related activities, was quite peaceful. They could hear their own steps, crisply clicking on the cobblestone street. She laughed for a while, and then suddenly felt exhausted. She abruptly drew in her smile, and her eyes welled up with tears.

(Translated by Wang Zhiguang)

A Rose in Full Bloom Overnight

Chi Li. Born in Hubei Province and now living in its capital Wuhan, Chi Li is the chair of Wuhan's Provincial Federation of Literary and Art Circles, a deputy to the 11th National People's Congress and an executive member of the Chinese Writers' Association.

Her representative works are the seven-volume *Collected Works of Chi Li*; the novels *Comings and Goings*, *Good Morning Miss*, *Water and Fire's Lingering Love*, and *Therefore*; the novellas *The Pain of Living*, *Foxtail Grass*, and *Shout When You Feel Joy;* and her prose collections *Old Wuhan*, *Endless Love for You*, and *Becoming a Drop of Water*.

For over 20 years, Chi Li has been inspiring and enlightening innumerable readers through her unique understanding and penetrating perspective of social reality, and her reflections on and genuine concern for the lives of people of all backgrounds. Her works have been translated into many languages. With her maturing wisdom, rich experience, polished language and witty expression, she has gained a wide loyal readership in China and abroad. She is the winner of over 50 national literary awards, including the China Novella Prize, the Lu Xun Literary Prize, and *Fiction Monthly*'s Baihua Prize. Several of her works have been adapted into films and TV series, among which the film *Life Show* garnered three international film festival awards.

A Rose in Full Bloom Overnight

The approaching figure was that of Su Suhuai. Suhuai emerged bit by bit out of the dark night. In that dimness, she appeared as a blurry woman, her tall slanting figure beneath her heavy, stiff denim dress blurring out all her shape. Upon a closer look she seemed to have a bit of a limp. Suhuai was no doubt an eminent personage, but she could stand close scrutiny no better than any ordinary person.

Suhuai came out of the night from the college where she worked. This was the broadest college boulevard, lined with shady trees and hedges of scarlet sage, stretching across stylishly. She had spoken in public of her love for that boulevard, so that her students who adored her kept writing essays about it. Elated, the president had asserted repeatedly that for Suhuai there only remained the path to the podium for a Nobel Prize in Chemistry. For years, Suhuai behaved exactly as a role model, as a potential nominee for the prize.

Su Suhuai was approaching, with her wise, cool color and her lined face. In fact, that color and those lines were composed of pigmentation, acne and wrinkles caused by kidney deficiency, meridian blockage and pathogenic fire according to traditional Chinese medicine, but nobody would be taking her at face value. The inner character of a woman was much more important than her appearance, as many experienced people thought. So did Suhuai naturally believed. A young woman who had reached such monumental heights in this masculine world, could she have been so successful without experiencing some difficulties? Yet only Suhuai herself knew how difficult it had been. So day and night, she maintained her wisdom and frostiness.

Suhuai was coming nearer, her footsteps clearly heard now. Regrettably again, her footsteps were also rather commonplace, a bit coarse, a bit sluggish, with her heels dragging on the ground. Women with such footsteps could not have elastic, long straight legs. Suhuai knew well about her legs, so she stuck to her long skirts even in winter. She carried a square bag full of books, while holding a stack of lecture notes in her arms. The heavy bag was pitching her one shoulder so high that the round accumulated fat of her thirty-five-year-old underbelly had burst open the buttoned slit at the front of her skirt. Her white woolen sweater beneath was also shamelessly squeezing out. How important an overhanging belly could be for a woman, Suhuai also knew. What was there that she did not know? But the better known she became, the more she needed to be extra careful, so she had recently found herself in this double squeeze. A few female students brushed past her and noticed the gap. They nudged each other, lowering their eyes shyly and giggling after her. Suhuai had her own assessment of the situation: aware that the girls recognized her, she supposed them to be awkward out of awe for her. She walked on confidently, with her face, of course, displaying that permanent wisdom and cool.

It was five minutes past ten in the night, so the road became more and more deserted. The early winter gusts stirred the gathering leaves by the roadside, which rolled briskly past her skirts, secretly singing with almost personal passion. Suhuai shot a glance at the leaves, and something deep inside her thudded. She suddenly realized that she was walking alone! How could she be all alone? Where had all those around her gone? Suhuai halted, hugging her lecture notes and looking about herself. She was reassured by her solitude. She then felt amazed. In swift succession emotions surged through her bosom and other ideas came to mind. She passed unkind judgment on the daily hustle around her. She wondered about the people who usually bustled around her. Was it only because of her excellent work? Or was it to prove their own excellence? Suhuai stirred the crisp leaves with the tips of her toes, feeling sad as a paltry woman: why was there no suitor to woo her after the divorce, since she was in fact so extraordinary? Why was there nobody to walk her home after these occasional late meetings into the night? Out of spite, she thought, "That's fine! It is comfortable to be alone, with a rare sense of secluded quietude!"

The usually elegant well-behaved Suhuai now fell into a sullen state of mind. She sadly said to herself, "Am I an old hag?" She shook her head and smiled to herself, "No!"

As Suhuai disappeared into the roadside shadows, she took out her shawl to keep warm. This was a traditional Scottish shawl, which she had bought on an impulse while abroad. It took three winters before she had dared take it out from the square bag and use it. In this college, it was impossible for her to use anything less than dignified to adorn herself. But tonight, with nobody around, Suhuai could with desperation finally wear it!

Suhuai put on her bright, expansive Scottish shawl, with its tassels dangling leisurely at her waist. She found her figure all the more graceful under the streetlight. Between this sudden realization and a look around, she had missed the crossroad leading to her own apartment. Suhuai did not seem to recognize her apartment building, or to realize where she was headed from the college. She had a sense of indefiniteness; as if she could slip away unawares. She could be taken by surprise any time.

Suhuai turned onto the street, where a breath of freedom caressed her face. There were a few pedestrians, who went their way separately, as if sure that someone was waiting for them in the distance. There was a couple of cuddling lovers before the closed department store, quietly forgetting themselves like statues. A few tricycle-carts were cruising ingratiatingly on the sidewalks. Cars whizzed by, not giving a damn. Suhuai walked on for a bit quite comfortably. After an interlude of this carefree state of mind, she began to chew on the purpose of this journey. Maybe she should take a cab across the Yangtze to Hankou, to have a look at the empty rooms locked up after the divorce? Or go back home to visit her parents? Suhuai hesitated in the street, draped in her Scottish shawl, and looked back at the campus reluctantly, time and again. The streetlights made her shadow waver, rather resembling a miserable student vacillating on her life's journey.

A red cab, after passing by her, returned audaciously on the sidewalk, pulling up abruptly in the deep night in defiance of traffic regulations. Suhuai should have been taken aback, but somehow she did not feel frightened. She just put her feet together, pulled her shawl tight and showed interest at the driver's head sticking out the window. It was a male driver. She first noticed his high-quality black leather jacket. He had thick hair, a heavy build, a rather unconventional appearance. Suhuai felt merrily ashamed of her unexpected worldly wise perspective.

The driver looked in her eyes, and said with good judgment, "Hi."

Suhuai bashfully blurted out, "Hi."

The driver came out energetically and pulled open the door for her. He said in a humble yet tyrannical tone, "Get in, please."

Suhuai was immediately stunned by his self-assurance. She thought, "This is a gentleman!"

Suhuai involuntarily pulled up her skirt, her desire to be waited on and dominated rising to the surface, while rationality miserably struggling at the brink of emotional turmoil. She hesitated, "I'm still far off. I want to cross the river."

The driver smiled confidently, "I can take you to the end of the world."

He spoke a bit ironically, only to stir the tranquil lake of her mind. She had to admit she had been looking forward to hearing those very words for a long time. But why did they have to come out of a total stranger — a taxi driver — today?

Anyway, Suhuai was doomed tonight. She looked down and stepped into the cab while pulling her skirt. The last tassel of her shawl caught in the door, to be scooped out with his fingers and then allowed to slide slowly to her thigh. Quietly watching this detail, Suhuai was again stunned. She felt a gush of warm liquid oozing where she was stricken and her eyes became moist.

Now Suhuai was flying. The driver was beside her. They were flying together shoulder to shoulder. Her shawl covered her brow and cheeks, so that showing through the Scottish tartan was only a bit of thin face with moist and hazy eyes. She sat upright and reserved, with sweating palms at her bosom. Suhuai had totally changed, tonight endowed with a lamb-like emotional appeal.

They began chatting.

The driver started, "Are you a graduate student by day?"

The mistakes that drivers made were often even funnier. In general, they liked to ask her, "What is it that you do?" She had lost her sense of humor over such humorless questions.

Suhuai retorted to the driver, "Why could you not take me for a professor?"

The driver said, "I'd like to so flatter you, but you are just so young. Honestly, how old are you?"

Suhuai asked in return like a girl-student, "How old do you think I am?"

The driver looked her up and down, quickly reaching a conclusion, "I think you're twenty-five at most."

Tonight, Suhuai was unable to reject his crooked compliment. She said craftily, "If I were asked to guess your age, I would say you are fifty-two."

The driver was amused, "What a clever girl!"

Suhuai said, "You're being rude."

The driver said, "From the bottom of my heart, I mean that it's a modern society. The traditional belief that women are virtuous without knowledge is now outdated."

Suhuai said, "You're also familiar with such traditions? You shouldn't have taken this career then."

The driver said, "It is said that college girls are all plain, so why stay there?"

Suhuai said, "Then I might not be a college girl after all."

The driver laughed heartily, "Damn it, then I'm definitely not a taxi driver."

This driver was a macho type. His manner of speaking and behavior was daring and resolute, yet with wit hidden in his attractive rashness. Only thus would he be a real man! Suhuai again sighed to herself. Such a man was different from all the men around her, who almost invariably restrained and resigned themselves at the sight of her. Only this driver was an exception, from first sight silently aggressive and unreserved before her. Tonight Suhuai fell into such a state, of a woman hoping for another's opening and attack on her. So when he turned around to look at her, she met his eyes in a new bold attitude. Just at this very moment, something unforeseen happened.

After passing the Yangtze River Bridge to approach the Jianghan First Bridge, the driver suddenly let out a vexed cry. It occurred to him just then that today he was not allowed to drive across that bridge. Due to the congested traffic, cars were allowed to pass that bridge on specified days according to the odd or even number on their license plates. Today was an odd-number day, but his plate was an even number, so he could only drive her to this side of the bridge, instead of all the way to Hankou. Suhuai could not control her terrible displeasure and dejection when she heard this. She looked at the driver for a moment, until seeing nothing she turned her face to look out the window. Then, she slapped a hundred-yuan bill on the dashboard, and as she was trying to open the door, the driver grabbed her arm. He said, "Miss, take it easy. I was only thinking of you, otherwise I would have dashed through. It is so late, with so little traffic; it would be inconsiderate of them not to allow me past."

Suhuai said something she dared not believe possible herself, "Then dash through!"

A light more intense than diamonds glinted from the driver's eyes. He said, "Then I will dash through with you!"

Suhuai said, "Go."

The driver said, "If we are caught and you don't want your teachers to know, you could pretend to be my wife."

Suhuai confidently protected her pride. "I would be greatly honored."

The driver would not let Suhuai prevail, saying, "It is me who would be honored."

This was something she wanted to hear. She often likes to think men are stronger than women, though she was always considered more powerful than men. The driver was now her born bosom buddy.

Now they were dashing through. The driver had buckled her up, and again she was holding her shawl tightly, looking adventurous. Her eyes were beautiful with the excitement, bright as the sun rising over the sea. The driver energetically switched on his stereo and chose Michael Jackson the star, with his wild cry. Suhuai's heart beat vehemently like a drum.

As the cab started to pick up speed, she realized she was doing something extremely inappropriate for her status and age, something she was forbidden to do. She blurted out, "No—!" but at the same time expressed an incomparable excitement in her voice. In the midst of the pulsating rock music, Suhuai opened her eyes and saw the whole world suddenly going horizontal before them and swiftly retreating. Bright apartment windows, flickering neon lights, sturdy lampposts, huge steel supports, followed by the stunned faces of policemen. What a world-shaking moment!

It seemed that a whole century had elapsed, before the taxi stopped on a small street in Hankou. He switched off the stereo, and the silence felt unprecedented. Suhuai heard her own delicate sigh coming from a faraway place, and somehow her hand was shaking the driver's hand. They shook their hands tightly, hot and moist. They excitedly affirmed to each other the incredible result: "We did it!"

Seeing her shawl sliding down, Suhuai was ready to catch it

when the driver stopped her. He embraced her completely with his intense and enchanting eyes. She could easily sense his deep approval. Suhuai, usually worried about her own plainness, became so ignited that her person became bright and transparent and her hair secretly danced, graceful as seaweed.

The driver picked up a bottle of water and forcefully opened it. He put it in the hand of Suhuai, who drank. He took back the bottle and, raising it as a salute, put the bottle mouth where her lips had touched to his own lips. While drinking, the driver still fixed his eyes on her. His bold and explicit overture finally frightened her. She needed to escape, turning down the car window and sticking out her head. The cold night slapped her hard in the face.

But the driver gently said behind her, "Put your head back. I'll drive on."

Suhuai submissively pulled in her head, but she had become uneasy at her own enthusiasm. He reminded her, "Where should I drive you? You never mentioned your exact destination."

Suhuai had to obediently give out an address, but it was not the real address. The moment before she told him the fake address, she squeezed her thighs very hard, saying to herself, "He is only a driver!"

Now the driver took her to her false address. It was empty there, at the side of the road there was only a department store. He opened the door for her, putting his hand over to help her out. Suhuai felt so weak in her legs that she could hardly walk. She stood before the huge rolling gate, leaning on a pillar of the corridor. She felt close to tears. She said weakly, "You may go."

The driver took the fare Suhuai had placed on the seat. Approaching her, he slipped it into her square bag. Suhuai was too weak to resist. The driver said earnestly, "What I want to tell you is, I am usually not like this; I was not this type of person before I met you. I am usually a very discreet man. So I have to thank you for that."

Suhuai began to tremble in spite of herself.

Greatly moved, she said, "Me too." Suhuai also intended to confess her lie, but she was trembling too hard.

The driver put his warm palm on her shoulder to sooth her, before holding her against his chest. Suhuai slowly but surely melted, so that with warm tears dripping, she found her hands slowly penetrating his jacket and embracing his strong waist. They kissed a long, deep kiss. Suhuai had never in her whole life experienced such a kiss.

After the long kiss, they were panting with their necks still touching. The driver asked tenderly after her name. Suhuai wanted to tell the truth, but she uttered the name, "Li Lanlan." She gasped as she lied a second time, but she was not brave enough to correct herself. Fortunately, the driver was so romantically intoxicated that, off-guard, he praised her false name, "That is just the name I expected." Then he rewarded her with his own sincerity, and told her his name and phone number. He was called Qin Wenwei. Suhuai felt so sorry, that she resorted to ingratiatingly praising his name, "Your name is truly apt."

It was deep in the night when Suhuai parted with the driver. At the last moment, while the driver was opening the car door, she ran over to offer him some truthful assurance to make up for her slip-up. She said, "I will call you."

The driver waved to her, and the night fell on her gradually, as the red taxi disappeared quickly.

The next morning, the bright sun cruelly woke her up in her and her ex's nuptial bed. She sprang up, in a cold sweat. She kept running her fingers over her brow nervously. She thought, "This is so ridiculous! The man is only a taxi driver! They had only met casually!" Suhuai was a bit frightened. She made hasty work of her makeup and sneaked out. After getting in a taxi, she just pretended to sleep. The driver dropped her right at the lab door of the Chemistry Building, and she quickly hid herself inside the lab.

Suhuai gradually settled down again. In her life, there were no signs of any cab driver searching for her or harassing her, but when it was confirmed that there was indeed no sign of that driver, she became vexed again. After passing a few normal days of appearing respectable and esteemed, she dialed the number of the driver, on the pretext of being a lady faithful to her word. But the actual turn of events ended up cruel: the number she had been given was a false one, and the name the driver gave also appeared to be false; there simply was no driver with such a name in the city. Suhuai had never put so much energy and willpower into searching secretly for someone, and for a casual acquaintance at that. Suhuai was nearly driven mad by this guy. What was even more awkward was that, her mistreatment could never be confided to others. Thus, such a young and capable professor suddenly collapsed for the first time in her life. She found the air was as if filled with fiberglass, and so refused to breathe. How could a person refuse to breathe? Suhuai could indeed.

Her amazing willpower nearly killed her. To force her to breathe, people sent her to a mental hospital. All those who knew her or knew of her were shocked. Everybody could not but ask why. Then some people would play god and explain this was simply fate. On Suhuai's part, she became utterly disinclined to have anything to do with all these vulgar people.

(Translated by Wang Zhiguang)

Big Lao Zheng's Woman

Wei Wei

Wei Wei. Born in 1970, She holds the professional title of "First-ranked Litterateur," and is now working at the Guangdong Provincial Writers' Association.

Wei Wei began writing in 1994 and her fiction and informal essays to date total over one million Chinese characters. She was conferred the 3rd Lu Xun Literary Prize for "Big Lao Zheng's Woman," the 2nd Chinese Fiction Society Prize in 2006 for "The Great Masque," as well as the 10th Zhuang Zhongwen Literary Prize, the 2nd Youth Literature Prize, and awards from the periodicals *People's Literature*, *Selected Stories* and *Chinese Writers*, in addition to many other honors. Her works have been included in various annual anthologies and selected for the Chinese Top Fiction List in 1998, 2001, 2003, 2004 and 2006. Some of her works have been translated into several languages, including English, French and Japanese, Korean and Polish.

Big Lao Zheng's Woman

1

Looking back, it must have been well over ten years ago now. At that time, Big Lao Zheng, a tenant at our house, was only in his forties at most. Back then, our family had more rooms than we needed, all situated along the curbside of the street. So my mother emptied several rooms to lease out to merchants, who had come from outside our town to set up businesses. I cannot remember exactly since when, but it seemed our small sleepy town gradually took on the appearance of a busy, or even a bustling, place.

Before, our town used to be quiet. There were hardly any people from outside of town. Existing businesses were few, and they had been established for generations. Anyway, those businesses usually had been no more than a small stand in front of the owner's house, selling candy, dried food, tea leaves, etc. The townsfolk generally lived ordinary and relaxed lives for the most part, whether office workers, factory workers, or schoolteachers. They went to work in the morning and finished in the afternoon. On weekends, they might go to the park, or go out as a family to watch a movie.

The town was small. A river, a number of small bridges, a front street, a back street, east gate, west gate... we lived within these confines all our lives, from the first days of our childhood to the last days of our life.

Every household had some dirty laundry that made the rounds, nothing too outlandish, just the usual gossip: whose daughter-in-law quarreled with her mother-in-law, who was divorcing or remarrying, who was a philanderer, whose son had a run-in with the law... the sort of things that, if it was your own, you swallowed it, but if it was someone else, then you spread it. A quiet cough and a suggestive smirk... then, that was the end of it. You went back to your own business.

The town was ancient. Nobody could really tell how old it actually was. It was just said that the town was already here when Xiang Yu had battled Liu Bang before the founding of the Han Dynasty. And here it still is today, with people seeming to live now pretty much the same way as they did in Liu Bang and Xiang Yu's time, thousands of years ago.

There was a time when the small town seemed to move very slowly. Year after year, those streets and alleys stayed the same, but if you looked back, you saw that people had aged — or perhaps the streets and alleys had become old but the people stayed the same, still alive. If you accidentally walked by a house, you would see a small woman squatting by the door, shucking soybeans at an amazing speed from a basket resting on her lap, with a sea of green pods scattered about her. At a tranquil moment, perhaps tired of the intense labor or briefly detained by an injured fingernail, she would lift her head, shake her hand, put the finger in between her lips, and blow air on it. That action, the act of blowing air, turned a "being" into a live person. And such a live person she was — her whole small body was filled with it: the way she was shucking the soybeans, her head lifted, the shaking of her hand… just like old times.

Another example: when you walked by the entrance of an alley, you would see a group of old folks sitting under an old locust tree in the dusk. They seem to be aimlessly chatting — probably talking about the ancient town. One of the old men, probably in his eighties, would stop abruptly in the middle of a speech, lift his head, scratch the nape of his neck with one hand, and say, "Hey, you stingy worm…."

Countless years have passed, but our town has remained standing on its own: simple and unadulterated, with its alleys, its old folks, its slang, its perfume from the flowers of the locust trees at dusk… ancient customs and values that have defied time.

Yet at other times, our town could be quite lively. The pulse of times elsewhere could be felt here, as if brought to us by the passing wind. It would evolve at its own pace, gradually fading until it became part of us. The most palpable pulse, or change of the times, first manifested itself in the women in our town. Most of the women from our town were a quite fashionable bunch. I do not remember which year it was, but I remember reading in the newspapers that women in Guangzhou had started wearing makeup on their faces, lipstick, eye shadow and all. It was even said the employees of some shops open to foreign customers had to put on makeup, or they would be punished. Of course, that was Guangzhou, not just any place. But before anybody realized it though, makeup became a trend in our town as well.

Speaking of women in our town, we did not have to look too far back to see how trendy they could be: beginning with the "Lenin" suit, to the yellow military uniform, to dresses, and then to mini-skirts.... How wide a time span was that? Did we ever miss any of the vogues?

Still, our town was far from being very developed. But it was also never closed to the outside world. At one time, all people talked about would be reform, economy, and *xiahai* (diving into the sea of business), because this was the new vocabulary.

And then, came the *waidiren*, from outside our town.

No one knows how these people found our town. They came to start businesses. Some of them made it, while others went bankrupt, and in the end they all left. And then, a new wave of outsiders would follow suit.

The first who came were two sisters from Wenzhou. They were very attractive: fair skinned and elegant. When they spoke, their voices were so soft and melodic that it sounded as though they were singing. Their apparel was different from the locals as well. In fact, it was not so much the clothing itself, since their same clothing would look quite different on our bodies. Perhaps it was because they carried a certain air of foreigners, of modernity, of someone who had seen the world. Simply put, they brought a breath of modern times to our small town, a breath that reminded us of words such as, "open," "coastal cities," "Guangzhou," and so on.

It was almost as though the sisters knew what they symbolized for us, since they named their hair salon, *Guangzhou Hair Salon*. The salon was located on the town's back street. It was a very old street. It had been there forever, with a Xinhua bookstore, an old post office, a police station, a cultural hall, a hospital, and a grain store... and then, there came the hair salon.

This was the first-ever hair salon in our town. At first, it did not draw much attention, because it was very small and inconspicuous. Besides, we had never heard of such a thing as a "hair salon."

We went to a *lifadian*, or barbershop, to get a haircut. Ordinarily, only men went to the barber every once in a while. They would go there to get a haircut, a face scrub, or have someone massage their shoulders and backs. Occasionally some ladies showed up, too. Almost without exception, they would just come for a little shampoo, a haircut, then look at themselves in the mirror, and that was it. Back then, there was no such thing as a perm. If by any chance someone on the street had naturally curly hair, the beautiful wavy hair above her shoulders would be the envy of the whole town: "How foreign! ...a living modern doll."

The Guangzhou Hair Salon brought reform to our small town. It was like a mirror, said some, that reflected the times and changes of our town. Through hair, we came to grasp that our lives could be like the hundreds of sorts of flowers competing for resplendence and beauty. From here we learned a multitude of facts about our hair that we had never heard of before: we could style our hair according to the shape of our face and head; we could shampoo and condition our hair; we could have our hair straightened and separated; we could even have a perm so that our hair could become curly.

By the time I heard about the Guangzhou Hair Salon, it had already been around for two or three years. One day after school, a classmate and I went over to take a peek. It was a small room, no bigger than ten square meters. Yet, it seemed as if all the fashionable women of our town were there. They took numbers and waited in line: some sitting, others standing, some looking at hairstyle magazines, others chatting with each other, exchanging ideas... quite a dizzying scene for someone my age. I felt intimidated. So I only hung around at the door for a little bit before I took off.

I heard that the reason the Guangzhou Hair Salon business was booming was because it did not just do business with women: there was business from men as well, and it was understood that the men's business was not a haircut. It was something else. As to what this "something else" was, this was a mystery to most folks. For those few who knew, they would first give a smug smile, and then explain to you: the salon did business with women during the daytime, and it did business with men at nighttime. Upon hearing that, the listener would put an expression on his or her face, as if saying, "Sure, I knew that," while in fact they might still have been in a complete state of confusion about the "business." It was no wonder. At that time this type of "business" was still unheard of and completely foreign to everybody's experience. Since it was such a new and curious business, people loved to clandestinely chitchat about it.

Big Lao Zheng came to our town pretty late. He was from Putian, in Fujian Province; his business was selling utensils made of bamboo. At that time, our town had already gathered quite a number of *waidiren*, folks from different locales. In addition, there were already a good number of locals who had started their own businesses as well: small hardware shops, electronics shops, and clothing shops.

By then the Guangzhou Hair Salon was no more. But more hair salons had popped up, like Wenzhou Hair Salon, Shenzhen Hair Salon.... Most of these joints were owned by *waidiren*, not locals, and they were all doing well. The two Wenzhou sisters had left a long time ago. They only stayed here for three or four years, made tons of money, and called it quits. No one circulated rumors about them anymore, as if they were ancient history. Whether or not those rumors were true, one thing was certain: people had learned something new, their horizons broadened, and they came to accept the reality. Nothing was too odd anymore.

Big Lao Zheng rented a room from us facing the street. Pretty soon, his three younger brothers came along also, so he rented two more rooms in our courtyard. The addition of a whole new family to share our courtyard made us a little uncomfortable at the beginning, but before long we got used to it. We even started to take a liking to them. All four brothers were honest and clever, but with different personalities. When they got together, they were a really fun bunch. The thing was, they did not have the air of businessmen, but did we even understand what "the air of a businessman" was? Of course not.

Let's look at Big Lao Zheng first. He was honest and serious, and also seemed mild-mannered and softhearted — all the right ingredients for an eldest brother. He did not talk much and was at his best when he worked: polite but not standing on ceremony, he knew what was just right. In those days, there was a grapevine in our courtyard that was growing beautifully. In the summer, juicy bunches of grapes would hang above our heads from the ceiling trellis. My mother would ask Big Lao Zheng and his brothers to pick and eat them; or she would pick them herself, wash them up, put them on a tray, and ask my brother to take them over to the Zhengs. Big Lao Zheng would habitually decline at first and then accept the grapes. A few days later, he would buy a variety of fruit and bring them to our table, all the while saying that it was no big deal to him: he had had to go to the country for some business, saw these fruit fresh from orchards along the roadside, looking so good and being cheap, only a nickel and dime, so he bought them. The broad smile on his face gave the impression that he had really enjoyed himself buying these fruits since they were such a bargain.

He was also very diligent. Every morning he would get up when there was still barely any daylight. The minute he came out of his room, he started sweeping the courtyard, watering our garden, weeding… as if it was his own home. My grandma loved to praise him as: "considerate, competent, careful and nimble. Whichever woman he was going to marry was going to be the luckiest woman on earth."

In fact, Big Lao Zheng was already a married man. His wife lived in their hometown, Putian. She married Zheng when she was only sixteen, and had borne him a boy and a girl. We often asked Big Lao Zheng about his wife and his kids. Most of the time, he only smiled, with no comment, good or bad. And that was alright.

We would say, "Big Lao Zheng, why don't you bring your wife and children out here to stay with us for a while?" He just said, "Sure," and smiled as always.

For a long period of time, we all believed Big Lao Zheng, and hoped that one day he would surprise us by bringing his woman and two children to the courtyard. My brother and I especially held high hopes, because summer was always slow and boring, and a playmate or two in the courtyard would be great fun. And to think, not just any playmates, but children who came from a different place… one that was far away and coastal. They would have beautifully tanned skin, and smell of the sea. Where they lived, there were even high mountains, wide-open plains, and forests upon forests of bamboo.

Big Lao Zheng told us all of this, though he rarely mentioned his hometown. Only when asked would he say a thing or two, and even then he would usually use plain words, nothing extraordinary. But somehow, in my mind's eye, I always saw a picture of a small coastal town that was nothing like our town. I saw narrow streets paved with blue stones, blue moonlight, and women in blue floral country apparel, bamboo hats on their heads and bamboo baskets on their backs…. Like our small town, theirs would have seen moments of purity and honesty, their inhabitants enjoying peaceful lives, their hearts filled with kindness and tranquility.

I do not know why I envisioned this picture in my mind about Putian. It was probably because of Big Lao Zheng. Since we lived together day after day, sentiments, trust, along with many unrealistic fantasies of Big Lao Zheng, had formed in our heads. We all liked him. And his three younger brothers were also as likable and charming as he was. Take as an example, his next younger brother, Second Lao Zheng as we called him — such a character: lively and lighthearted, loving to talk and laugh, and a fine singer too. He was particularly good at singing folksongs from their hometown:

Girl, oh girl,
You have the waist of a bucket, a bucket.

The odd lyrics, along with the funny tone with which he sang, never failed to make us laugh. One time, Big Lao Zheng half-jokingly asked my mother if she could match this brother up with some nice girl in town. "You're not going back, right?" asked my mother. Big Lao Zheng smiled, and said that they did not have to go back, he was the only one who had to go back, for he was a married man and had a wife and kids at home.

It had been a few years since Big Lao Zheng had left his hometown. It was said that it was a tradition in Putian for men to leave to make money. A few times a year, they would go back home to visit — whether or not they had made any money did not matter. So one time my mother asked, "Don't you miss your wife and kids?"

Big Lao Zheng scratched his head and sheepishly grinned, "Sometimes."

"Only sometimes?" asked my mother.

"Did I say something wrong? Am I supposed to think about them all the time?" Big Lao Zheng said with a smile.

"So what are you waiting for? Go home," my mother chided.

"I can't."

"Why?"

"Well, I am used to everything now. Besides," he said looking toward his brothers, "If I went, they'd be left with all the work. I can't possibly do that."

Big Lao Zheng loved to chat with my mother. Among the brothers, he was the oldest and by quite a few years, while the other three were substantially younger: one was twenty-six, another was twenty, and the youngest was only fifteen. One day, my mother asked, "Did they all quit school?"

"Yeah. They were no good at it."

"No," said my mother, looking at the Third Zheng, "The third brother looks like he could be smart. He looks intelligent to me, but he doesn't talk or go out much."

Big Lao Zheng said, "He just likes to stay home and play his flute."

In fact, the Third Zheng was very good with his flute. Every moonlit night, he would turn off all the lights, sit in front of a window by himself, and start to play his flute. Those were the rare quiet and pleasant moments, suddenly our town no longer noisy. Instead, it was unusually quiet, as if it had receded to a faraway place.

For a while, it would feel like we were really living in old times again, especially during the long summer nights. We would finish our dinner early, then my brother and I would take out small stools and set them up in the courtyard: ready to *chengliang* (enjoy the cool night air in summer). We would sit together in groups of two or three under the dim starry sky, cattail leaf fans in our hands, and listen to our parents talking about amusing happenings at their workplace, or enjoy Big Lao Zheng's stories about Putian, a place that seemed as far away as the end of the world.

If there was a good television series on, we would take our TV set out into the courtyard so that the two families could watch the program together. But some nights, we would be so immersed in our conversation that we would even skip the TV show.

We would talk about unimportant things and share a watermelon that no one cared who brought. When we got sleepy, we just went inside the house to go to bed. Sometimes my brother and I did not want to go inside the house, so we would just stay in the courtyard and lie on the makeshift bamboo bed enjoying the perfectly undisturbed atmosphere of the summer night: watching the bright stars in the sky, or the shadows of the sycamore tree leaves on the wall under the moonlight. We would listen to the crickets and cicadas chirping, and eventually, amongst the grownups' chatting and the Zheng brothers' soothing flute lullabies, we would fall fast asleep.

Sometimes in the middle of my sleep, it seemed I would hear my father and Big Lao Zheng talk about current policies, things such as economic reform, separation of government and enterprise, township enterprises in Jiangsu, individually owned businesses in Zhejiang.... "Oh...," my father would sigh, "How the times have changed!"

Under the square sky of the courtyard and behind its doors and walls, our two families formed a perfect miniature cosmos. Whatever we were talking about, our world was pure, simple and time-tested.... Later in my life I felt like we had been living in a distant, unreal yet beautiful dream.

2

One day, Big Lao Zheng brought home a woman.

She was not pretty by any means, just a plain woman with a long pointed face on a big bony frame. She was tall, skinny and rigid as a pole; if I had not seen her face, I would have thought she was a man. She wore a black suit and white sneakers, not the typical look of a woman from our town, but neither did she look like someone from the countryside. Countrywomen around here wore typical peasant clothing, not Western-style dress. Their clothes were plain and simple. Even when they dressed up, with their small flowered cotton clothes and cotton shoes, they still looked very proper and natural.

She could not be Big Lao Zheng's wife, for no husband brought his wife into someone's house in this manner: he brought her into our courtyard without introducing her to anyone. Instead, with a smile on his face, he walked her straight into his room. Only moments later, he came back out and stood by the door, again silently smiling at us.

All we could do was smile back.

My mother pulled Second Lao Zheng aside and asked,

"Is she your brother's housekeeper?"

Second Lao Zheng turned his head to look, and then said, "I don't think so. Have you ever seen a housemaid in this type of outfit and carrying two leather suitcases?"

"Looks like she is going to settle here. I know! Your brother's just found you a new sister-in-law," said my mother. Second Lao Zheng stuck his tongue out, and ran off laughing.

Before anybody noticed, dusk had fallen. It was not completely dark yet, and from the half-open door, we could see a dim outline of her bony form. She was sitting on the chair near the bed, her head slightly lowered. Her flat face could only be seen in the flickering light of a nearby lamp, and she appeared to be looking at her feet. Perhaps she was bored, because she briefly raised her head to shoot a quick glance at the courtyard, unexpectedly ensnaring the eyes of one of us, and then lowering her head once more. After that, she seemed to be at a loss. Unsure of where to place her hands, she fiddled with the corner of her blouse, then returned to play with her hands again.

She had the air of a new bride: shy, reserved, out of place, a newcomer in a strange environment who had not quite adjusted herself yet. Even the man in the room did not seem to be an entirely familiar figure to her. Rather, he had the appearance of someone whom she had met a few times in the past, leaving a vague but good impression on her. Knowing he was an honest man and that he would take care of her, she had agreed to follow him along to this house.

That night, her presence gave us the impression of a wedding: solemn, righteous, a bit timid, like the first union of a young couple who had gone through many layers of matchmakings and formalities… and whose day of union had finally arrived. Truth be told, the atmosphere was a little cold for such a day. People around here were simply observing; it was only Big Lao Zheng who seemed excited. He busied himself around the house — sweeping the floor, wiping down the tables… and when all was done, he hesitated a bit before sitting on the bed just a fist's distance from her. He was wringing his hands, a constant smile, maybe he had said something to her, for she was lifting her head to look at him, and then, smiling.

He got up and poured a cup of water for her.

He got up again to bring a stool over so she could set her cup on it.

And now what? Ah, how about peeling an apple? And that was exactly what he started doing. He peeled the apple very slowly, as though he was engaged in some kind of fine craft. Sometimes, he would look at her. More often though, he looked at us: me, my brother, and Fourth Zheng, his youngest brother. The three of us, though no longer so small, could still be considered children — we stood in the middle of the courtyard, talking, playing and laughing… and at times, we would sneak a peek at them through the two Chinese ilex trees and the many pots and planters, as if by accident. Big Lao Zheng saw what we were trying to do, and gave us a long and annoyed stare, before using one of his legs to shut the door.

That night, this woman stayed in Big Lao Zheng's room, but not before some changes had been made to the previous sleeping arrangements. Originally, Big Lao Zheng and Fourth Zheng used to share one room. That night, Fourth Zheng was called into the room first, then moments later we saw him come back out with a blanket under his arm, and then walking into another room unwillingly, pouting. We all laughed.

The atmosphere of that day was very peculiar, we laughed a lot. In effect, there was nothing special about this small event for us to laugh about, for even though our town was a bit on the conservative side, its people were actually quite liberal and open-minded about relationships. Perhaps people believed that when a married man lived away from his wife for too long, it was only normal that he would become restless and go chasing another woman or two. People accepted that kind of behavior as a certain inevitable and universally truth. My father had a friend, whom we knew as Uncle Li, who was generally quite a narrow-minded man. He came to our house often, becoming quite familiar with Big Lao Zheng. Once he jokingly had said, "Big Lao Zheng, why not find yourself a girlfriend?"

Big Lao Zheng had grinned, tried to say something, but no

words came out of his mouth. Uncle Li then continued, "You see, you're a good-looking guy, look at your nice white teeth and how easily you blush…."

My mother had intervened with a smile, "Come on, don't tease Big Lao Zheng. He is a good guy, not that type." But that evening, my mother had to admit — "That tricky Big Lao Zheng, he fooled me." She sat on her sofa, relaxing and waiting for Big Lao Zheng to come over and explain to her about the woman, for she was the matriarch of this household, and had to be informed of any woman that came to her house uninvited.

The woman was actually a local, even though she was from the countryside nearby, and had moved to our town many years ago. First she had worked as a temporary laborer at a flour mill. Then for whatever reason, she had quit and begun to sell sunflower seeds around the People's Theater. My mother said, "We go to the theater often, how come we never saw you?"

"Oh, I go back home frequently," replied the woman.

Later that night, Big Lao Zheng brought his woman over to our house and properly introduced her to my mother. They sat in our living room, the woman not saying much, with her head lowered and her fingers tracing along the lines of the sofa over and over again, so intent was she at doing that during those short minutes that it seemed surely all of her attention had gone into her fingers and the lines of the sofa cloth. The whole time, Big Lao Zheng just smoked away. Occasionally he would say something of no consequence, and then revert back to his silence. This was no way to carry on a conversation. He lifted his head and looked at the moth under the lamp, and smiled. "Why are you smiling?" asked my mother.

"But I didn't."

At that, his woman cracked a smile, too.

It was under these types of circumstances that the woman came into our life and became a member in our courtyard. Matters of this nature were best left unspoken — we saw nothing bad, we heard nothing bad. My mother maintained her spirit as a liberal woman, but sometimes she would feel distressed and complain to my father. "Well, what am I to make out of all this! A wife at home and a mistress at our house! Look at them, living together like a real couple" — and then with a sigh and a smile, would continue, "If other people heard of this, there'd be no end to the gossip. My house — a hiding place for mistresses!"

In fact, my mother was overly concerned. It was already the fall of 1987. Big changes had taken place in our small town. Old professions such as covert prostitution were slowly making a comeback. Security bureaus often distributed documents about eradicating pornography. Our local newspaper where my father worked featured a series of articles on the topic also. Of course, we had never seen an underground prostitute, nor did we have any idea what they looked like anyway, what clothes they wore, and how they talked, walked or behaved. Naturally we were all hugely curious. First, my mother said, "I don't care what you all say, but Big Lao Zheng's woman doesn't look like one." My grandma nodded: "You're right. She doesn't look it. She looks like a good woman. Besides, she's not pretty. You'd starve to death in that business if you don't have a cute little face and pretty body, or aren't good at flirting!" My father said with a smile, "What are you women talking about?"

All in all, in those years, suspicions consumed us. We were curious and suspicious of everything. The peaceful times of our past had truly changed. There was an anxiety inside everyone's heart, so much that one could not sleep soundly at night. Awakening in the morning, the old streets and buildings still remained, and yet you felt that something had changed overnight, or was changing right in our midst, yet invisible to our eyes.

At any rate, the woman installed herself in our courtyard. At the beginning, we were not quite friendly toward her. My mother did not care at all for her ambivalent co-habitation with Big Lao Zheng, but neither could she just chase her out. For one, Big Lao Zheng was considered a good friend, for another, this woman was to be pitied, for she did not have a home to return to. There was her eight-year-old son, but he was in her ex-husband's custody after their divorce.

Besides, she was so dedicated to Big Lao Zheng — diligent and tireless. For all the four brothers, she washed, starched and darned their clothes, and prepared their meals every day. The menu changed daily too: meat one day, fish another. When Big Lao Zheng was in a good mood, the brothers would even drink a glass or two. That family of five sat around the dinner table under the florescent lamp; the newly cleaned floor reflecting a cold light.

Sometimes, their mealtimes did seem a little cold and lifeless, because nobody talked. Every once in a long while, Big Lao Zheng would say a thing or two, but the woman just sat there, smiling quietly. Other times, the opposite was true, when the drinks the brothers had imbibed would turn a lifeless mealtime into a lively one. Second Lao Zheng would use his chopsticks as an instrument and begin to sing, or rather, begin to mumble, completely out of tune. The woman could not suppress a small smile. Between closed lips she once muttered, "Too much alcohol."

The Third Zheng then said to her, "Never mind him. He'll soon behave."

Both of them were a bit startled. But before anyone realized it, they started talking with each other. The Zheng brothers were all good men, but they had all seemed to be indifferent to her, not indifferent as in cold, rather it being the shyness in their nature that got the better of them; and of course, the embarrassing situation they were in did not help either. For example, the woman's last name was Zhang. Well, how should they address her? They could not address her as "Sister," or "Sister-in-law." So, they simply resorted to an "eh," followed by a smile.

The woman was clever. She could see we had our reservations about her, so she did not come out of their room often. During the day, she did the laundry, cooked the meals, as well as cleaned and tidied the house. When it was all done, she would sit on their sofa, watching TV, while cracking some melon seeds. If she saw us, she would smile, bow ever so slightly, but almost never talked. From the day she moved in, the room changed. They added a new sofa, new tea table, new TV…, and she even got herself a cat. On the autumn afternoons, the cat would fall asleep by the door. The afternoon sun between three to four o'clock shone on the sleeping cat, giving the house a comforting touch that felt as warm as the cat's fur under the sun.

One time, I saw her knitting a crimson glove, cute and delicate. "Who's this for?" I asked, "For your son?"

"No, my son's hands are much smaller," she said with a smile, "This is for Fourth Brother."

She set down the knitting work in her hand, went to find the glove she had already finished, and tried to measure it against my hand, "This should be right, not too small, don't you think?"

Among the four brothers, she favored the Fourth, the youngest. The lad was very friendly and easygoing, and did not quite understand what was going on. Once, he called her, "Sister." That had surprised her. Second and Third Zheng had also looked at each other in shock, and then laughed. When there was no one else around, the Fourth Zheng would tell her things about Putian, about his sister-in-law, his two nephews, and about how most of the folk in their town had moved into small two-story houses.

"What about your family?" she asked.

"We don't have one of those yet, but we will soon," answered the Fourth Zheng.

"Is your sister-in-law pretty?" she asked again. That was difficult for the Fourth Zheng to answer. He lowered his head, his hand scratching the back of his neck, and then said hesitantly, "She's chubby." She giggled.

That was about all she asked. After a while, she sent the Fourth Zheng back to his room to check on Second and Third brothers. The Fourth Zheng stuck his face in the window to look inside the room, and then turned around and said, "Why don't you clean the room later? They're sleeping."

"I didn't say I was going to clean the room," she said with a smile, "I needed to wash my bedding, I thought I could wash yours at the same time."

Though she was from the country, she loved to be clean and tidy. Since she got along well with the Zheng brothers, she gave them a hand whenever she could. She would say, "You know, it's not easy for these guys. They come from thousands of *li* away. They don't have any relatives or women to help them out." She would then smile at what she had just said. She was not an easily excitable woman, and she did not like to talk. Nevertheless, even when she was just sitting down, her presence seemed to fill the entire room, as if she was holding it up while she grew bigger and the room became smaller.

It was quite curious. The four loosely connected men we used to know, before she had moved in, disappeared. Instead, the four slowly became one, capitulating to the miraculous spell of this woman. One time, my mother heaved a sigh of relief and said, "You see, women do make a difference. When there is a woman in a house, the house becomes a home."

In this home, the woman unconsciously played the roles of wife, mother, housekeeper, hostess..., but she was really no more than an accidental acquaintance of Big Lao Zheng.

One could say she and Big Lao Zheng loved each other. It was not anything passionate. They just lived together, ate and slept in the same house, nothing extraordinary. Whenever Big Lao Zheng had a moment from his business, he would stop by the house for no particular reason, just to be with her and chat for a while. She would sit on the bed, he on the sofa across from the bed, the door wide open. The wide open door incidentally formalized their relationship, that of husband and wife.

Gradually, we saw her as Big Lao Zheng's wife, forgetting about the existence of his real wife in Putian. We were very careful about what we said, fearing that we might accidentally hurt her feelings. There was only one incident: a letter came from his wife in Putian. That made my grandma happy, so she said to Big Lao Zheng with a broad grin, "What did she say? Does she want you to go home?" My mother cleared her throat loudly. Grandma immediately realized what she had done, and flushed in embarrassment. But the woman pretended that she did not hear anything, and continued quietly peeling apples for us under the lamp, a small smile on her face.

Though I could not quite put my finger on how it happened, still six months later, we had all accepted the woman, and come to enjoy her presence. It must have been time that changed us. We did not dare think twice about her, as if it would have been a blasphemy. My mother one time jokingly called them the "wild love birds." She had even said that the woman was so good to Big Lao Zheng only for his money. But later, she never uttered those words again, because the fact of the matter was, in those ordinary-as-running-water days, it was easy to see that the couple was truly in love.

They loved each other quietly, nothing like love at first sight or ceremonial vow exchanges — they had already been there, done that. For them, it was more like a walk after dinner if the weather permitted. On that type of occasion, my mother would tease them, "Look at you two — acting like two young love birds." They would both smile, while the woman would put a scarf around Big Lao Zheng's neck and flip up his coat collar. Sometimes they would take the Fourth Zheng along if he was out playing with his Chinese yo-yo. He would follow them along, still playing with the yo-yo all the while.

In the evenings when they stayed home, our two families habitually got together just to chat — about the weather, about our food, or about current political affairs. Second Lao Zheng, standing against the door, would toss out a joke that made us all throw our heads back and laugh. At that very moment, the bright and clear sound of a flute would come across from the next room, exploratory and intermittent. The woman said, "It's Third Brother." We all held our breath to listen. This must be a new piece for Third Brother. He was not good at it yet, but it was easy to discern the melancholic tone in the music, rising quietly like fog in the cold night sky.

My family's courtyard saw its happy olden days again. In fact, it was even better than the olden days. On a bright moonlit night, we would curl up in our warm home, or just sit quietly and unrushed, knowing that next door there was a woman sitting on the sofa, knitting a sweater, a napping cat balled up under her feet. During those cold and lonesome winter nights, her presence brought us something everlasting. It was steadfast and wholesome, like the warm breath we exhaled out from our mouths in the frigid winter air. Even though its warmth might dissipate in a moment, within that moment, it still existed.

Wherever she sat, she carried a small wooden stove with her, and the aroma of burnt wood permeating the entire house awakened every sense of our sleepiness, preparing us for a good night's rest.

For some time now, my mother had become really worried about them, saying, "Look at these two, they love each other so much, but what's going to come of this?" But, an outcome seemed to be the last thing that concerned them. It appeared they lived each and every day as if it was their entire life. They were unhurried, calm and collected. Winter afternoons were usually naptime for us, but not for this couple. They would sit in the sheltered gateway, he whittling a piece of bamboo, she sitting on a small stool behind him, playing with the cat, a ball of yarn cupped in her hand. When the cat jumped on her lap, she would leap up, and run, giggling while swinging around to tease the cat some more.

That was the moment when the little girl in her came out — lively and naughty, the very image of a lovely girl. She was indeed very young still, maybe not older than twenty-seven or twenty-eight. Her eyes radiated playfulness whenever she looked at you in a certain way — who knows, in front of Big Lao Zheng and out of the sight of everyone else, perhaps she could also be quite a woman.

Whenever her playful side came out, Big Lao Zheng would smile broadly and gaze at her with an odd look: it was the look of man at a woman, but also, the look of an elder at a youngster. "Can't you stay still for a moment?" he would inquire playfully.

She would come back to sit behind him again, poking his back with her fingers. He would turn around and say with a smile, "What are you doing?"

"Nothing," she would say.

They would gaze at each other now and then, smiling wordlessly, and then go back to their work. If they looked at each other too much, she would say, "Aren't you being silly?"

He would say with a big smile, "Yes."

This time, it was he who was the little one, and she the elder.

3

When spring came the next year, a man showed up at our courtyard. He must have been in his forties, and he was the spitting image of a man from the countryside: navy blue pants, down to cotton cloth shoes. Perhaps because it was early spring, the weather was still on the cool side. He wore an old-fashioned padded cotton jacket; the sleeves too short, giving him the look of being uncomfortably cold and nervous.

We had seen such men before — some wore even more casual clothes. Nothing fancy, yet none had looked as sloppy and laidback as he did.... In fact, he looked downright dumb, slow and lazy, as if ready to submit to anybody at any time. In those years, there were farmers from the nearby villages, clever and bold enough to come to town to do business. But they would talk about money, the economy, commissions and so on, as though they had already been there and done that. But not this man. Everything about this man indicated he belonged to the land, and he would be happy to be bonded to it and fiddle with crops within its confines all of his life.... This may have been the first time he had ever come to town.

He appeared to be looking for someone, timidly. He first looked from outside of our courtyard gate, hesitating whether he should step inside or not, then looking back and forth between our street address plaque and a crumpled up piece of paper in his hand. It was a Sunday afternoon. There was hardly anyone at home. After lunch, Big Lao Zheng usually took the woman downtown; some went out on errands, others went to a bathhouse in town to take a shower, or were visiting friends and relatives.... There was only Mother and I sitting leisurely under the sun, while the Fourth Zheng and my brother were playing marbles on the ground.

It was at that time that we spotted him: smiling contritely, fearful and humble, as though afraid of making someone unhappy. "Who are you looking for?" asked my mother. He lowered his head, bowing ever so slightly, planting his hands in his jacket sleeves, before saying, "I am looking for my woman."

"What's her name?" asked my mother again, waving for him to come inside. He stepped inside, his face filled with gratitude, and then very softly spoke his woman's name. My mother turned her head to exchange a look with me, and then nodded.

He was looking for Big Lao Zheng's woman. Was he the woman's ex-husband?

It had never occurred to us that we would ever see the woman's ex-husband, so we took a good hard look at him: he had a strong build, a broad reddish face, and features more delicate than Big Lao Zheng, except his skin was very rough, with overwhelming traces of weathering: dirt, extreme exposure to the sun, the hardships of working in the fields.... For some reason, this man appeared to have suffered more hardship than anybody we knew. Or could it just be our imagination?

He stood in the middle of our courtyard — lonely, small, and lost. Under the spring sunlight, we were warm, content, and sleepy after a good lunch. But at the sight of this man, all of our senses seemed to be suddenly awakened.

"How about you just wait for a moment?" said my mother.

He smiled. My mother gestured for me to bring a stool out for him. When I came back out with the stool, he was already crouched against the wall, pulling out a pipe from his jacket pocket and tapping it on the cement ground.

Needless to say, we were curious about him. Say, for instance, why had he come to find the woman? Did he want to get back together with her? Did they still keep in touch with each other? Why had they divorced? We hardly knew the woman, she seemed to be a good person, but then so was he…. So why is it, that two good people could not stay together and live a peaceful life?

At first, he was very uptight, without many words to say. But it only took him the space of one bag of tobacco before he loosened up and started to chat with my mother like they were old acquaintances. The fact was he was quite a talkative guy. When he talked, there was a deep and lively tone to his voice. It surprised us somewhat, and also rendered this man more lovable in our eyes. He spoke of the harvest in the fields, his one sow and five piglets, the tree behind the house… altogether, he made several hundred yuan a year after taxes and village dues. However, this income was far from enough, he sighed. After fertilizer, pesticides, the kid's school tuitions and fees, and his widowed mother's medical expenses… not only was there nothing left, but he was in debt, too.

"That's not good," said my mother.

He did not say a word. Instead, he thrust his hand under his armpit, scratched, drew it back, sniffed curiously, and then went on talking about his village: how there was a couple of *wanyuanhu* (households with an annual income of more than 10,000 yuan) in the village, but what made them so rich? "Nothing more than a few extra yuan in their hands so they could contract a couple of orchards or a fishery," he sniffed disdainfully. "These guys abandoned their land," he murmured under his breath, "they'll be punished by the gods." He said those words with a peculiarly calm and melancholic tone.

My mother teased him, "I think you need to open up your mind. Working the soil is not the only way to make a living."

He looked at my mother carefully, and muttered, "But that is still the best way."

"Tell me how," my mother said with a smile. "You'll never make tens of thousands of yuan if you just keep turning up the soil."

He blushed and his rebuttal was immediate, "But working the soil is what farmers do. Ever since the earth existed, have you ever heard of a farmer not having his own land? You tell me! It's only these last few years…" — but what about those years, he couldn't quite articulate — "Well, I don't care if I don't have tens of thousands of yuan. I have my rice, my clothes and my own house with a tiled roof. But…" he paused, resting his elbows on his knees with a smile of acknowledgement on his face, "Almost all the money for the house came from my woman. She got work as some kind of a *ganbu* in town and started earning three to four hundred yuan a month, about the same as I earn in half a year."

We were shocked. *Ganbu* (an official)? What *ganbu*… my mother wondered. "I even don't make three or four hundred yuan a month, who does unless you are in some kind of business? Besides, aren't you divorced?"

"Divorced?" He slowly got up from his squatting position, hands on his knees, eyes wide open, "Divorced? Where did you hear that?"

Seeing the confused look on his face, we began to realize something was wrong. We had been hoodwinked. He was not the woman's ex-husband. He was in fact her husband. My mother signaled me with her mouth to take the Fourth Zheng and my brother out of the courtyard, and then continued apologetically, "I don't know what I'm talking about. Since we hardly see you, and Ms. Zhang lives by herself, we just assumed you were both divorced."

As if wronged by what he had just heard, the man said, "But she wouldn't let me come. And besides, there was so much to do around the house. If it wasn't for our son's school tuition... you see, we didn't pay our tuition last month. The teacher had given us an ultimatum, if we still can't pay, the boy can't go to school anymore. Luckily, the other day when Ershunzi was in town, he ran into her right here at your door. Otherwise, I wouldn't have known where to find her."

He went on babbling about how his life these years had been, how he had to be father and mother at the same time, how their home did not feel like a home anymore, how, if only he had a little bit more money he would not have let her leave the house. How could she work as a *ganbu*? He couldn't hold back a laugh, "I didn't know she had such capability. She could never even lift anything, but I heard she became a temporary supervisor at a textile mill."

My mother and I looked at each other silently. So, the flour factory, the textile mill and selling sunflower seeds at the People's Theater were all fake stories. My mother did not dare say anything;

instead, she just beat around the bush a little longer with the man. What more was there to say? The mystery around Big Lao Zheng's woman had finally unraveled, its veil torn, taking a turn in a direction we least wished to see.

The man, on the other hand, could not stop talking. That afternoon, he gave us an earful about his woman. And what a tone in his voice! Loving, sorrowful and longing. Did he think of her often? Did he not wake up often in the middle of night when all was quiet, looking at the full moon outside his small grid window, and think quietly of things during those rare moments of the day? After daylight broke, he would go down to labor in the fields; in the evening, he cooked and cleaned, year after year, he also took care of his aging mother and his young son.... It had been killing him! Where was his woman? Was she sleeping at this time? The thought of how she slept made him laugh. Oh, he missed her terribly. Yet she took care of the family. Every time she came back, she would bring good tobacco for him, toys for their boy, and some medicine for her mother-in-law. But, he was despondent. He did not know why but he just wanted to cry. Then he thought, when he had a bit more money he would bring her home, let her do what she ought to do, and let their home be filled with smells of cooking again.

Oh, how he missed the smell of cooking. At that moment, he was sitting under the bright noon sun, and slowly squinting his eyes.

He paused for a moment, perhaps tired of all this talk, not wishing to speak. During that noon hour, our courtyard, flooded with bright, white gold sunlight, seemed more spacious than ever before. There was not the slightest sound to be heard. I felt a sweat was about to break out.... Never in my life had I experienced a moment as lonely and desolate as that instant; I felt as if we were sinking bit by bit. I was sitting under the sun for so long that, when I suddenly raised my head, the sunlight turned black.

In the end, the man was not able to wait and left without seeing his woman. However, he was content because he knew that in a few days, his woman would send her salary to him, which he would pass on to the school for their son's tuition. He dragged out half a bag of rice from the doorway and asked my mother to give it to his woman, saying, "This is good rice. If I sold it on the market, I could bring home some good cash. But, let her have it. We at home can manage."

It was not until evening that the woman came home, following Big Lao Zheng, big and small shopping bags in their hands. My mother walked up and asked, "What did you all buy?"

"Some clothing for her," said Big Lao Zheng with a smile. The woman, standing by the bed, took out everything they had bought: leather shoes, shirts, skirts… and a piece of cloth which she tried around her shoulders, and asked my mother if it looked good on her.

"I thought this too flashy, but he said this one was best." Big Lao Zheng smiled and said, "Of all the cloth we looked at, I only liked this one. It's got the right color and floral pattern. You'll look lovely in it."

To be honest, the woman's behavior was not any different from before, but somehow now that we were aware of the situation we started to notice some differences. Say, for instance, she had these long and narrow eyes, when Big Lao Zheng talked, her eyes lifted up ever so slightly, slowly, carelessly… it's hard to describe or mimic…. That simple lifting of eyes, my mother nudged her elbow against me, and whispered, "That shows it."

The fact was, long ago, my mother had heard people mention

that there were two kinds of prostitutes in our town, and it all started after the Guangzhou Hair Salon. One time, someone pointed her to a woman walking on the street, the kind of woman in "*that business*." That was not just any woman, she was like a fairy, said my mother later. Not only was she young, but her outfit was also something that no one in our town had ever seen before. My mother asked, "She isn't local, is she?" That person sneered, "Of course not. No local would do that kind of business in their own town. They wouldn't dare! Even trees are covered by bark. They've got to save some face, if not for their own sake, they've got to do that for their relatives and friends. What if they ran into their own brothers or uncles?"

The other "kind" was in fact local women, like Big Lao Zheng's woman — fifty percent good woman and fifty percent prostitute. My mother had never believed in the existence of such women — you were either a good woman or a prostitute, there simply no such a thing as a half-prostitute, half-good woman. Unbeknownst to her, there were indeed such women in our small town. Most of them were from the countryside, married, with families. They wanted to get away but stay close to their hometown.

These women mostly found their clientele in *waidiren*, or men from outside of town, who were good and kind by nature. Some of the women came from poverty-stricken families, unable to endure life's hardships, but neither were they willing to improve their situation through hard labor; others were just seeking riches and pleasure in life; then there were others who did not get along with family members… they all had their reasons. They would usually hook up with out-of-town businessmen who were married but did not bring their families along. These men typically had some money in their hands, were honest and serious, not stingy, and looked alright too.

Being together day after day, emotions grew, and they eventually fell in love with each other.

The women provided solace to the male wanderers with their inborn feminine qualities: attentive, tidy, and diligent. They washed clothes for these men, cooked their meals, listened when the men wanted to talk, consoled, teased, and strategized when they were in distress and needed help. When the men missed their women, they provided their own bodies to them. When they missed their homes, they built makeshift warm homes for them.... They provided a turnkey solution for these men, while everything they did was within a woman's nature and capacity. Even though they got payment for what they did, it was a mutually beneficial pact in which both parties willingly participated.

If their temperaments clashed, they would go their separate ways without any regrets; if they did get along well, and the man had to go home in the end, then there would be trouble: painful tears, prolonged hugs, keepsake exchanges, reunion promises.... But once separated, life would slowly return to normal. One had to go on living, regardless. After a while, emotions subsided, these women would find another man, and go on to live with him.

Most of these women stumbled into this business through matchmakers. It was said that the practice was not much different from ordinary matchmaking: the man and woman would look at each other a couple of times, and if both were satisfied, the woman would simply follow the man home. There was something in these women's nature that made them different from ordinary women: they were more compassionate, and they easily felt tender and protective toward a man; they might hold onto long memories of the past, but they never became blinded by their love affairs; they were survivors, they could love different men.... This could very well be part of their nature, rather than the result of what they had to do in this "business."

Like us, they despised prostitutes. Big Lao Zheng's woman once said, "*That Business* was so dirty and low! Besides, being unsanitary." She had giggled while she said this. That was a long time ago, before her "ex-husband" showed up at our house. Naturally, they are different from prostitutes. But are they different from ordinary women? That would be very hard to say. In my opinion, the only difference is they make it clear up front, that the purpose of their love or "marriage" is to change or improve their living conditions, while ordinary women keep that purpose to themselves. Therefore, to me these women are more forthcoming and honest; as to whether or not they are respectable, well, that is another story.

Across from our house, lived an old lady with Feng as her last name: we called her Grandma Feng. She was the most worry-free and open-minded person I ever knew. She was good-looking, with white skin and white hair. In the summer when she wore her white silk outfit, she looked like a true snow lady. This old lady had seen the world, perhaps because her son was the director of the Supervision Bureau and her daughter was head nurse at the People's Hospital. When she started a conversation on any topic with you, you would be surprised with how much she knew. Often times, she sat beside the front door of her house, shucking soybeans, and she would shout from across the street at my grandma, "What's for dinner today?" The two ladies would strike up a conversation just like that. Then, she would trudge over to our side of the street, a bamboo basket in her hands. Upon seeing me, she would say, "School over?" To my brother, she would say, "Did you get scolded by the teacher today?" Everybody loved her, and all who knew her also respected her. However, her unconventional past was well known to everyone in the area. When she was still very young, her husband had abandoned her and their two small children, and fled to Taiwan. How was she supposed to survive? Well, she started to find herself men friends. After no one knows how many men friends, she managed to raise the children to adulthood. They in turn built successful careers and established their own families. There were matchmakers always trying to hook her up with some man. She invariably refused, saying as long as her man was alive, she would wait for him to come back. Behind her back, people cajoled, "Wait? Is that called 'waiting'?" She was in fact happier than when her man had been with her. But no matter what people said, the fact was there: she had raised two small children with her own hands, not by enduring hardship and eating bitterness, but rather, she had completed that mission with a lot of small happiness.

We could not for the life of us tell how Big Lao Zheng's woman was different from Grandma Feng. Yet, somehow, we all forgave Grandma Feng, but not Big Lao Zheng's woman. It was not long before my mother was ready to show the Zheng family out the door. That night, mother made Big Lao Zheng tell the truth. He did, and what he said was not much different from what we already knew, but he added, "She is a good woman."

"I know," said my mother, "and you are a good person, too. This is not about good people or bad people. We are a respectable family. It's a matter of face. If we can help you two in any other way, we will. It's just.... Please don't make it more difficult for me."

Then, my mother added, "You're a businessman. You ought to know. Don't wait till you are completely ripped off by some outsiders." Big Lao Zheng managed a smile, and after awhile, he rubbed his hands and said, "I understand."

He left with his woman. My mother made the other Zheng

brothers leave also, just to be out of sight out of mind. After that, we never saw them again, nor did we hear anything about them.

That was fifteen years ago. How are Big Lao Zheng and his woman doing now? Did they separate soon after they left our house? Did they go back to their respective homes? In the first few years after they left, whenever it was summertime, *chengliang*, or wintertime, cuddling under the thick warm quilt, we would think of them. How peaceful and pure those times had been, like the imaginary bamboo forest in Putian, glowing quietly under the moonlight.... Now it all seemed so far away. Or perhaps it had never existed?

These years now, our small town is continuing to move forward with the times. A lot of things have happened. One day, my father thought of the Zheng brothers and said jokingly, "How can one ever explain this? These women start out selling smiles, and then they sell their bodies, but in the end they get emotionally involved too. Is that a specialty of a small town? I suppose ancient traditions don't die." My mother had her own opinion, "Not necessarily. If a woman needed to sell her body, then, sell the body. Why did she sell her emotions as well? That's worse than a prostitute."

Hmm, who could really tell about such affairs? All we could do was secretly gossip about them.

(Translated by Zhang Xiaorong)

The Kitchen

Xu Kun

Xu Kun. Born in Shenyang, Liaoning Province, in March 1965, Xu Kun holds a doctorate in literature from the Chinese Academy of Social Sciences and the title of "First-ranked Litterateur." As a professional writer of the Beijing Writers' Association, she is also currently a member of the Beijing Youth Federation, and on the National Committee of the Chinese Writers' Association.

Since 1993, she has published fiction and prose totaling over 3 million Chinese characters, including her representative novellas *Colloquialism*, *Pioneer*, *Hot Dog*, *Shenyang*, and *Young People Gather Together*; the short stories, "Kitchen," "Encountering Love," "Bird Droppings," "Damned Football" and "A Foreigner in China"; and the novels *Twenty-two Spring Nights*, *Love for Two and Half Weeks*, and *Wild Grass Roots*; as well as the drama scripts *Silver Fox* (adapted from Wang Meng's novel) and *Men and Women in Love* (staged by Beijing People's Art Theater in 2006). Some of Xu Kun's works have been translated into English, German, French and Japanese; or received prizes for outstanding fiction, including from the periodicals *Chinese Writers*, *People's Literature*, and *Selected Stories*. She has won the 2nd Lu Xun Literary Prize, the 1st Feng Mu Literary Prize, the 9th Zhuang Zhongwen Literary Prize, and the 1st Women's Literary Achievement Award, as well as many times taking *Fiction Monthly*'s readers' choice Baihua Prize.

The Kitchen

A kitchen is a place which is a woman's launch pad and safe harbor.

Glistening gracefully in the kitchen sits the china, from whose fine grooves, winding arcs and pure white forms gleams an exquisite light set off against the dark dusk. The brick wall and floor, flat and edgeless, with the aid of certain subtle associations, reflect the moist lights deeply back into the eyes. As always, the lips are duly dyed rosy, even to purple, by a slender bottle of red wine and sweet cordial made from blackcurrant, even making the breath incoherent. The transparent blue flame of the stove leaps up and down under the light, as the aroma of a teeming stew wafts about the steel stove supporting the pot. "Ss-la!" the intermittent puffs rise into the air and then dissipate, filling the entire house with a white fog. Fried asparagus and watercress display a rich pale green, while purple rice porridge and corn soup take their turn filling the room with their black and yellow.

Every of the components in the kitchen, with their lovely colors, aromas and tastes, whispers about the long life of this woman who has no idea why a kitchen is born female.

Never has she even thought about it. She resembles women of the past like her mother, entering the kitchen without even thinking about.

A summer dusk. After a sudden and violent storm, all the irritating heat and uproar has been blown away by the winds. The earth gradually falls still. In this city, the flaming setting sun burns directly above the overpass. Lazy red sunbeams radiate down into the kitchen, where is poised a busy woman named Zhizi. The sun decorates the outline of her beautiful body with gold, making her look quite dazzling from afar. The woman is quick and content with her kitchen appurtenances. She shoots a glance out the west window at intervals between movements. The setting sun turns round until it is overlooking the woman, while passing languidly by the branches of a lush magnolia tree near the window, as if there existed a tacit understanding between them.

Zhizi's eyes, therefore, also melt into a pool of red radiance, a humid and soft red radiance.

The kitchen does not belong to her. It belongs to a man. Zhizi is using her deeply ingrained kitchen lexicon to express her affection for him.

A fish is carefully cut numerous times, with sliced garlic, shredded green onions and ginger sprinkled on it. All these are put in a pot for steaming. Cabbage and lotus root are washed, piled in a plate with mayonnaise, superbly arranged, awaiting to be mixed together. Steam is rising slowly up through the gap between the stainless steel cover and the pot. Zhizi stops, takes a leisurely breath and casts a stealthy glance at the front room. Looking through the wide and transparent reinforced glass door of the kitchen, she watches the man, Songze, sinking himself cozily into the sofa, a large part of his face covered by a newspaper. His body, his hands and his feet are all long and big. From the short sleeves of his T-shirt bulge out his strong-muscled lower arms. His legs, wrapped in jeans, lie lazily sidewise. The jeans are tight, setting off the plump and powerful inner sides of his thighs. Suddenly Zhizi flushes crimson for some unknown reason, and a wave of uncontrollable joy sweeps over her. She swiftly withdraws her damp glance and hurriedly turns round, gazing at the setting sun through the window.

The large wheel of the setting sun retains only a semicircle now, held in the mouths of treetops and buildings of steel and concrete. These mouths are swallowing down and kissing the half wheel zealously. Again, Zhizi's face catches fire at the instant and another tide of blind happiness begins to rise in her.

"I love this man. Yes, I do."

Zhizi says to herself perplexed. At this moment, her heart feels full of bashfulness.

Zhizi is a so-called super woman who is already in her forties. Love does not easily come to a person of her age. Zhizi has a heart once sensitive and now forged by time, hard enough to remain indifferent to anything. Time has flown. Zhizi has gone through tough battles and turned from being a weak, tame, dependent and lachrymose girl into a well-known rising star in business circles. But after having her social identity and status fixed, unexpectedly, she wants to move from the tough business environment back into the hothouse and return to her family whom she once so resolutely abandoned.

No reason. She just wants to get back into the kitchen, and be home again.

Every lonely hard moment at night, the successful woman could not help missing her home, her remote kitchen and the warm orange light there.

Unlike during social occasions, she never gets tired in her home kitchen, never becomes so hypocritical, and never gets a terrible appetite. There are no traps here, no reluctant laughter, no cheating, no invisible yet unavoidable sexual harassment or the like; let alone the noisy karaoke invading your ears and destroying your appetite, which ultimately leads to terrible hearing and vision problems. Her kitchen would be quiet and warm. Every dusk it would see clouds of steam floating out of big stainless steel pots, and a while later the whole dear family soon gathering around the table to satisfy their eager appetites.

What if she could have a meal with her family! Only such a meal could be called real relaxation and rest. But how could she have understood this when still young and ambitious? Then divorced and away from home, she just got to feeling fed up with everything! Yes! She had become fed up with not only the tedium of life after marriage, but even the stereotyped kitchen and everything in there. She even came to bear a deep hatred towards trivial kitchen stuff. It was the repetitive tedious kitchen affairs day in day out that had killed her gift and eroded her genius, leaving her with no room to display her skills cultivated by a famous university. So, she had to leave. Yes, whatever was said, she had to leave, so that she would not stay in the kitchen all her life. She had to leave whatever the price would be. She had to dash to the new life in her imagination.

Sure enough, she had really left, climbing over the high wall of marriage, ignoring her child and abandoning her husband, without any hesitation.

But now she has come back, so voluntarily and willingly, yet so impetuous and resolute, throwing herself directly into a man's kitchen.

This is truly unthinkable.

If she had not fled, would she want to be back today?

She has never thought about this.

At this very moment, she simply wants to be back in the kitchen shared by her and another person. She experienced a marriage and a man she loved or did not, thus understanding the total difference between a single person and a married one. One single person does not make a home, and a kitchen belonging to only one person is not a kitchen. To fall in love with someone, make a family and share a kitchen with him is her current wish. She is willing to idle about in her own kitchen over and over and again every day, fiddling with every thing there without any serious intent, and touching every little decoration to make it tinkle. She also wishes to indefinitely prolong her cooking time, go to the food market to find vegetables in season, and carefully wash and pick every leaf and stalk. She will prepare each meal under the instructions of cookery books and never tire of balancing the proper nutrients. When she is doing all of the above, she attains a certain mood peaceful as water, no longer regarding it as a waste of her time or life. Even if her nice fingers get inflamed fingertips and rough joints some days, she would never complain about a thing. She just hopes she could kill time with a mild and hollow heart and ignore all the competitiveness outside. She would like to see two diners — her husband and child, of course — busy swallowing up her delicious food, too busy to have any time to praise and just burying their heads in the dishes until they get greasy and fatty mouths, growing stout and fleshy.

"Stout and fleshy?" Zhizi just cannot help tittering at the phrase.

Really, she is tired of all the bother of having to tighten her nerves to deal with people outside courteously but without sincerity. She has no idea why she always dislikes people. There are all kinds of people in the vanity fair: mean, dirty, petty, scheming and practical, enough to make her dizzy. Dealing with people all day has been crumbling her nerves. She wants to retreat into a deserted place such as a kitchen that can serve as a refuge.

A kitchen has never been so genial to her as it is now, and she has never been as affectionate toward a kitchen as she feels today.

Steam rises slowly out of the stainless steel pot on the stove, followed by Zhizi's fancy; and the sun is setting slowly in her fancy to beneath the treetops, and finally to the end of her fantasy. The long-limbed man has finished his newspaper, rises up to stretch and slowly moves to the kitchen, asking if Zhizi needs help. The woman is beyond excitement when she hears such a warm greeting from the man. "No, no," she says. It is the man Songze's birthday so she would like to complete the whole process on her own and feed the man with her own cooking.

Why does she offer to cook for the man? What will come next after cooking? She just does not want to think about any reason, which is cruel torture for her. She wants a vacant area in her heart. Let it be, she thinks to herself. Zhizi just hopes it would be what she wants it to be. Right now and here, she is really flattering rather than indulging the man, which seldom happens to her, a businesswoman star like her who is not short of male pursuers trying all means to please her. She has always turned her nose up at her pursuers and kept highly alert to every possible trap. Yet she automatically delivers herself to the man's door now. How can she explain this to herself?

Why should she mind? Whatever will come will come. Why must she waste energy explaining what has already happened?

The tall man, Songze, with his long hair hanging down, holds his hands in the air and orbits Zhizi twice, though he knows he cannot help in any way. Apparently Zhizi has with some sophistication planned out this meal. She knows maybe that this single man would lack many things in his kitchen, and thus the provider of meats and vegetables had to be herself. She has even brought all the seasonings such as oil and vinegar, as well as a soft white cotton turtleneck apron. Besides the apron, she wears a thin belt at her waist and has scattered little forget-me-not flowers all around her. The soft white apron is tight enough to highlight her slim waist to the perfect degree. Zhizi could have used a cotton hat for her hair to match the apron and protect itself from smoke, but she ultimately decided to throw the hat away, to pull her hair up and pin it loosely with a fish-shaped clip. In this way, Songze's vision is now filled with her black and shiny hair.

Gazing at the sylph makes Songze's heart beat wildly, and unsurprisingly, like all other artists, he is forever tempted by all the beauty he sees. They were close friends from a long time ago, and what led to this intimate relationship was after one of his art shows was successful due to Zhizi's financial assistance. Then their relationship evolved from amiable cooperation into intimate involvement, as the rough trajectory. However intimate they have become now, he still would not dared have considered asking her to come celebrate his birthday, let alone asking her to cook personally. What she is now doing surprises him, and it is too much for him.

It is the most wonderful thing to have a beautiful woman come to his home for his birthday. As a result, the man, while feeling himself highly honored, at the same time also feels it to be a great encumbrance, for there is nothing so inspiring for them to stay home for dinner the whole evening. An artist always tries to be creative. While Zhizi is cooking, several girls call him to go out partying with them, and he has to gently turn down each of them. Compared to a conventional birthday meal at home, hugging and pinching in a karaoke compartment is doubtlessly much more in line with an artist's creativity. In the long run, however, given the choice between going out with his young female devotees or setting good relations with his lady patron, the latter is obviously more handy for his future. Men tend to be more utilitarian. He ultimately decides to resolutely stay home to get emotionally closer to his patron.

Having made this decision, the man begins to concentrate on Zhizi, the cook in the kitchen, and gradually senses a different elegance from the woman's busy and orderly movements. Her movements are skillful yet tranquil, like a blossoming gardenia flower in the soya aroma of the kitchen. A woman's wonderful scent mixing with frying vegetable fragrance drives the man's imagination quite wild. Not knowing where to start, one of his legs stands as his gravitational center, with the other leaning against it, and his entire body leans against the doorframe. While waiting for a good chance, he frequently glances at Zhizi with passion.

Noticing the man staring, Zhizi becomes a little nervous. Her face, like a flower in full bloom before the spring breeze has arrived, grows flushed, and she finds it a little hard to breathe. She pricks her ears to listen carefully to the man's labored breathing, while she tries to order herself to calm down, to conceal her wild heartbeat and to make her movements natural. Isn't such a gaze from the man what she has been waiting for? Now she has got it! And is there any need to be nervous? No. Thinking these thoughts, her chopping gradually turns into half performance.

The kitchen is not big enough to have two people simultaneously turning around in it. Any movement would absolutely lead to body contact, and that is why they are standing still despite verbal interaction at intervals, but a tension rises out of both of them. This is mainly because the host has not yet divined the exact intentions of his patron. Though very adept at love affairs, he would never dare now to do anything unwise, for he does not know what she wants him to do or how far she wants him to go. He never forgets she is his investor. As a result, he just leaves matters to flow on their own and flirts with her aimlessly with momentary courtesy. After all, this man-and-woman occasion requires both an artificial and real love atmosphere.

The woman has no idea where to start either. She waits eagerly for some atmosphere that allows for a gradual and natural process. In fact, she is hoping for Songze to confess his love first, but if this really were to happen, perhaps she would then dislike him or refuse him. However, seeing him standing so still, she can not help feeling both eager and disappointed at the same time. She has chosen him and cultivated him because she saw a sort of wilderness and agility in his painting style. Yet her one-way love for him later grew out of when, during their association, she found he had already absorbed and digested this wildness and agility, able to apply it skillfully and agreeably, which is typical of an artist in her thinking. She used to think that all the people around her were much too civilized, but he was different, with his primitive wildness ever present in his paintings and his genius that could approach divinity. All this is what she desires deep in her heart.

Sure enough, with the financial backing of this lady boss, Songze made a sensation and became famous far and wide. She judged him by his excellent paintings, and thus fell in love with her commodity — this artist.

The prolonged tension begins to exhaust their bodies. Zhizi is already soaked with perspiration under Songze's gaze. If no further action is taken and the tension just goes on, Zhizi feels as if her thin waist will be snapped. She casts constant glances at the man, and from her burning face and body leaning towards him in soft, gentle, yet radiant and palpable encouragement, her eagerness and hesitation is evident. The man is the same, hesitating and irresolute in the camber of the soft body leaning towards him. His body sways slightly, in the end doing nothing.

The silence lasts for another while. Then Zhizi's fingers begin to swim in the sink and the noise of stirring water tells of some vexation. Too much tension and hesitation finally destroys Songze's desire to flirt. "I'll go set the table," he says, and then hurriedly gets himself out of the kitchen.

Only at this instant does Zhizi find herself time to relax. She raises her forehead and mops up the sweat on it quietly, while Songze is setting the table, making the tableware clink. It is a coffee table that serves as the dining table. Of course, nothing is regularly arranged in an artist's living room. Several soft cushions with embroidered flowers are scattered around the Persian carpet, and the bed is much lower than a normal one, in fact it is a mattress on the ground. The buffalo-leather sofa, nestling in a curve in the corner is surprisingly broad and comfortable, as if it may be the place where all daily activity takes place.

Songze puts the creamy birthday cake Zhizi has bought in the center of the table. In the light, dense caramel oozes out from the chocolate icing, looking very delicious. Songze stares at the cream, and thinks hard but comes up with nothing. Up to now, there still exists another mood flowing through his body that is not completely aroused, with the polite social intercourse that typically exists between him and Zhizi still persisting. "Another mood flowing" hints at the sudden physical igniting and wildness along with savagery that often occurs when he meets those girls crazy about art and willing to devote themselves to him, and which allows no end until each round comes to its end. Curiously, he never fails every time he deploys this wildness and savagery.

However, he lacks this feeling now. Why? Why on earth would this be? Songze begins to feel worried about his health. He does not know that everything becomes tedious once the ideas of identity and utility mesh, even physical impulsion hardly arises. Songze sits and opens a bottle of wine, at the same time glancing nonchalantly at the kitchen. Zhizi, cut off from Songze by the glass kitchen door, seems to know that her figure can guide the man's eyes, so she tries to coordinate her every unhurried movement with his tastes. Her beautiful figure, against the background of light and shadow, is subtly tacit with the outline of the kitchen. "What a good match I am with this kitchen. I make it come alive!" her silhouette seems say.

Songze's eyes are filled with a confused emptiness.

The sun has already disappeared from the horizon. The twilight glow takes back her last bit of beauty and fades away into darkness. Night falls and instantly blurs everything. The things that had been in the kitchen a moment ago have already been shifted onto the table, fragrant and lovely looking. Songze has been waiting nervously for a long time, and now he is worn out and needs something to eat. Though hungry, he becomes anxious and upset at such a big table covered with assorted food, wondering where to start the meal. He looks up at Zhizi, who is now sitting opposite him with newly applied makeup and staring at him affectionately. Zhizi had not forgotten to fix her makeup in the powder room after completing her kitchen chores. She carefully put on eye shadow to make her eyes appear fuller of love; she also colored her lips lightly with lipstick. Should her cheeks be blushed into an orange red? She finally decided not to. When the kissing gets to its critical stage, too much powder will turn her face into a mess due to the friction between the two people. After doing her face, Zhizi pulled a silk evening dress out of her handbag and took off the green and white-collared outfit she was wearing when she had first entered his house. The outfit was loose, unyielding, stiff and clumsy, keeping people far away; while silk has a softer texture and is much simpler and lighter. All these are what she has specially prepared for this night of love. Though requiring a little nitty-gritty planning, it does not baffle her at all, as a woman with her heart filled with sweet affection.

After returning from the powder room, Zhizi is ready in her ethereal long black silk dress, revealing the best parts — her long neck and smooth arms — out of her neckline and cuffs, with their skin giving off an ivory-like sheen. The rest of her parts are wrapped in silk, showing off their primal mystery, tempting the artist to explore them bit by bit with his slender fingers.

Though Songze is no longer in the mood, he is still a little shocked by Zhizi's attire. As an artist, he is good at appreciating and tasting beauty. He immediately shows his astonishment over her beauty. With an exaggerated expression, he puts one hand over a glass, while the other holds a bottle in the air. His eyes are set on Zhizi in admiration, and he seems to be saying to himself, "Oh my god! You are so beautiful!"

Zhizi is too shy to express her excitement, so she only implicitly says "Thank you," and then looks around to find a space to sit. Songze has cozily sunk himself into the sofa, occupying part of the table. At that moment Zhizi wants to sit on the sofa next to Songze, since that is… convenient, but she immediately gets all flushed and thinks of another thing: is that not a bit too aggressive? She shifts her gaze back onto Songze, and the man does not seem to be leaving her any space to sit. If he points out the place next to him and jokingly says, "It is unoccupied," she will take the chance to sit. He is, however, only pretending to be astonished by her beauty and doing nothing else, so she can only go around him to the opposite side of the table between them, and sit down gracefully with a desperate expression. After all, she is not willing to lose her identity so rashly, before anything seriously gets going.

The red wine in the goblets exudes graceful touches of romantic ambience. The dome lamps, wall lighting and floor lamps are extinguished by the host one by one, and only several red candles flicker in their stands. Speakers hiding in the corners of the ceiling are playing soft music, an exotic soft tune emanating from a distant saxophone. Zhizi softly and carefully cuts the cake into small pieces for Songze, and puts the piece decorated with a pink rose in his plate, leaving herself one with a cream green leaf. Compared with usual conventions — spoken wishes, drinking is more creative. They frequently clink their glasses. They not only drink to themselves but also toast each other again and again, as if they are trying to get deliberately drunk.

In fact, Zhizi is not getting drunk on purpose. She just wants to borrow some courage from the wine and muster enough nerve for herself to stick it out to the end. Songze, however, does not have so much in his mind for the time being. He is not failing to appreciate Zhizi's fine cooking, eating like a horse, only sparing his mouth to praise Zhizi's wonderful skill. The accolades fly into Zhizi's earlobes and cling to them, moist and like music. Zhizi has hardly touched her own chopsticks so far. On the one hand, cooks never want to eat what they have cooked, and on the other, Zhizi is paying no attention to food. With the help of the wine, Zhizi has acquired two intoxicated eyes totally naked, shooting fixedly across the table at Songze. The pair of eyes notices how the man moves his cheeks while chewing and how he blurts out fancy words to praise her.

The artist's long hair flies about frequently, and his powerful chin is shaved like bronze, like all other men's. All these things arouse Zhizi's tenderness, and set her face aflame until her eyes almost ignite in sparkles.

Right at this moment, hatred and love come together in Zhizi. She cannot help it, though her hatred already goes beyond anything, which draws more wine steadily into her mouth. She does not know how she comes across in Songze's eyes, but anyhow, he has made no move so far. At least, she thinks, he should have proposed a dance or something, which he is no doubt good at on such occasions. "What on earth else is he expecting me to do?" Zhizi thinks to herself, "I have done what I ought to, and I can go no further given the reserve and self-pride of my age." She believes that she cannot wait much longer, and if not satisfied, her hopes will not last.

So, Zhizi pours herself some more wine and drinks even more wildly, until her eyes and body are all wine-filled.

Songze continues with his accolades blindly, but when he stops praising his ears hear only the sound of his own words, not a peep from Zhizi. He reaches out to fill Zhizi's glass and takes this chance to glance at her face, only to find Zhizi trying to knit a net with her gaze. A desperate vision she exudes, soft and dense, wrapping him tightly and locking him in her love. Once bound, he would never be able to escape. Suddenly at this moment, Songze's heart trembles and his body shakes, accordingly spilling a great deal of wine out of the glass.

Zhizi picks up her glass with the wine spilling out, stands up unsteadily and says, "To tonight."

"Okay," Songze says, "to tonight."

Just as Songze brings his glass toward Zhizi, the latter clumsily reaches hers out close to his. But she misses her target, and the glass is forced directly towards the man. Songze blocks the glass reflexively with his empty hand, and the whole glass of wine spills all over his T-shirt and trousers.

"I'm so sorry," Zhizi blurts out in a panic. "Never mind," after saying this, Songze turns around to find something to wipe it up with. "Leave it to me," Zhizi says as she stops him and gets to her feet, stumbling into the kitchen where she finds a cleaning rag and tissues to dry the man's wet parts. When she comes out from the kitchen directly to him, leaning against the sofa, half squatting, to swab at his trousers, he cannot find time for polite rejection. He scrunches into the sofa with some difficulty and accepts her service, and she is now so near to him that her hair is brushing over his chin. Their bodies are almost clinging together tightly, and she can even smell the scent and wine on his body. A sudden hesitation then enters her half-sodden brain: should she take this chance to throw herself into his arms?

Even as she hesitates, her chance to naturally offer herself is already gone. If she did that any moment later, everything would be unnatural and distorted, and the transitional movements would become incoherent or inaccurate.

Love requires not brain but instinct. A brain is not necessary for love, she thinks, and with this idea in mind she feels extremely depressed, enough to bring tears to her eyes.

It is just as well that, at this time, two warm hands reach out and seize her passionately. "It would be unseemly if I did not do this," Songze thinks, and that is why he does her the favor of holding her waist and leaning her against him. Zhizi hears the man's powerful heartbeat. She puts her head against his chest with her eyes closed and drops of aggrieved tears ooze down on her cheeks, which she has no time to brush aside. Now her body has become so awfully soft she cannot even move at all. However, she did not feel her body soften until the man hugged her in his arms. Her armor of reserve collapses right away. She thinks, "I love this man, yes, and it is enough if I could stay with the man I love. It's alright."

The man feels his impulses aroused by the soft body in his arms. Wine and instinct are working, for they have blended together in his body and begun to foment. He lifts the face against his chest and puts his lips close. Her skin is as smooth as silk, so his lips can hardly stay still on her neck and face. Suddenly his tongue tastes salt. He opens his eyes slightly and looks from vaguely afar, only to find the woman is weeping, with tears running down the two sides of the bridge of her nose. He is touched by something he cannot name and holds up his lips to that face again. His lips slide down bit by bit from the eyes where they first drink up those teardrops, then to her lips where they complete a very tangible kiss. At first she is a little reserved and, though dizzy, closes her lips into a thin thread, leaving no chance of entry. Seeing this, the man employs his most advanced skills. While kissing her, he puts one hand around her back and caresses her there without stop until she is about to melt into a pool of water in his hands. The man knows that the right time has come, so he carries her slowly onto the sofa, where he sticks out his thorny tongue and presses it to the woman's lips. Sure enough, the woman's hot red lips open instantly like a clamshell. Without hesitation, the woman greedily sucks his tongue into her mouth in an instant.

Immediately the man is sucked in and cannot get out. It is not until then that he knows what her inhalation is really like. It is a strong and rude fervor rather than something warm or soft, powerful enough to swallow his life, as if keen to cling to him till death. The man, unable to bear it, hurriedly shifts his body slightly and tries to take most parts of his tongue out, with only the tip of his tongue traveling around in her mouth and touching and roaming everywhere, so that she cannot grasp a steadfast sense of inhalation.

While trying hard to engage the woman physically, the man is stunned and fearful: "Wow, this desperate woman is truly incredible. I can hardly deal with her." Songze has played this same game many times with numerous women, so he knows the differences between kisses, so even the subtlest differences can be sensed by his keen tongue. Women who are not serious do not kiss this way. They only kiss very softly and happily with a skip and a distraction, like the wind sweeping over water; their kisses simply a prelude to the games in bed. Amongst them, none would hang onto his tongue and seize him so tightly as if to prevent him from escaping; and none has been so serious, desperate and persistent as this one is now. Suddenly a startling idea comes into his brain: "Could it be possible that she is really serious and falling in love with me this time?" What she has done today is abnormal! All her deeds and kitchen syntax suggest to him that she would like to be the hostess of this kitchen, that she is perfect for this kitchen.

On realizing this, the man's burning body suddenly trembles and cools down within the shortest instant. The woman is serious this time, he realizes, and she has not come here today for fun but on serious business. Her purpose in being here is clear. What she wants is the final consequence, a concrete result, rather than something ambient, which he can tell from her kiss. Every word of her carefully encoded kitchen language gave evidence of her true feelings and ideas. He just was unable to decode it until this moment.

The man suddenly feels depressed, and this gloom goes around his body in a moment, and his body which had just become hard now softens. No fun at all, indeed. He is one who is quite capable of accepting false affection but not true love. He dislikes being weighed down. In this serviceable age, nobody likes to bind himself or offer to bear a burden. As an artist, he has always hated being shackled in any way. He wants to be free of any kind of weight, including family responsibilities, social obligations and so on and so forth. After selling his paintings, he never pays taxes until the taxman comes to him and leaves him with no other choice. Is he really going to accept her as his wife and support a family when his career is reaching its zenith? If that happens, how could he maintain his essential freedom and unruly style?

Who says that women are only emotional animals and have less rationality than men? They are as logical as men when they set their minds at a certain purpose. Yet the point here is that she has chosen the wrong guy, a man who wants no burden whatsoever and has no wish at all to be responsible to a woman. He is all right with games, but not with serious love. She wants him to be the one she can rely upon, but this is the kind of man he exactly does not want to be. Like any man who is the polar opposite of a woman, he hates any burden. When it comes to false love, he has practiced it on many a woman, and he feels it to be a safe and happy approach; and as for true love, he only has it for himself and his fame and gain, but not for anybody else. He is not afraid of games, but is very afraid of a serious relationship. False love in the face of false love is all right, for that is without burden or scruple, but true love faced with false love is irrational, let alone true love with true love.

He cannot, however, put an end to this game so abruptly with an icy rejection. Offending his useful sponsor in such a way would not be advisable; what is more, he is well known as a gentleman who cherishes beauty, so he should be well mannered to this lovely lady. Moreover, he can see no harm in playing a bit of a somewhat dangerous game with this beauty. It feels great and exciting to play such a game fraught with danger. Anyhow, he will hardly be assaulted or ultimately forced by her into the bridal chamber.

After the prolonged kiss, the woman feels exhausted and stills her tongue. When she opens her eyes, she finds the man staring at her with his mouth still holding her lips. The distance between their faces is so close that they, in a flash, look deformed in each other's eyes. The woman feels shy, so she hurriedly avoids his scrutiny and buries her head into his chest. The man caresses her back and hair as if he were tidying a puppy, and thus she takes the advantage of this moment to bury herself deeper into him with her clothes on, just like a real puppy. She closes her eyes and appreciates the dizzy feeling after the kiss, feeling that her mood, as well as her love, has finally touched down on the earth. To Zhizi, it has been so difficult to get this far. However, she does not know that such things have happened to Songze hardly just this once. As an artist, he has so many women devotees that they can hardly find themselves any space.

The woman Zhizi, however, is buried deep in her one-way love and is not in the mood to think about such things. Women confused by love are truly hard to handle. They are as fervent as fire or a rutting cat, and given any intimation, they will jump up at you and bite you crazily. The man calmly deals with what is happening, fights against her purpose with his skillful fingers and controls this game with interest. Once the woman's purpose is exposed, enthusiasm immediately fades away from the man's body, but his other interests will start at the same time. Now he has become part of the thing, but at the same time he is enjoying this performance of love as an audience, just like a director in charge of a whole opera accompanying an actress as a training partner. He has already taken her true love as something amusing, and he is also interested in appreciating the opera and training the actress. He is quite adept at entering his role, he thinks.

And Songze feels that he cannot help but be a little proud of himself.

The woman, so charming, is sinking in desperate passion. Her face is bursting into a flame that will burn her and the man into ashes. They are feeding wine to each other with their respective mouths. The woman nestles in the man's arms, as she cuts the apple down the middle and leaves her jagged teeth marks on each half. Then they nibble leaving marks bit by bit, until what comes next is their lips coming together kissing, and their bodies become one. Songze gently takes up all tricks from the woman, but never explores further on his own. He only squeezes her breasts through her clothing and then rubs her waist, trying to entice her, but then he stops and goes no further, determined not to explore what is inside the silk skirt with its high slits, as if he were indeed a real gentleman.

The woman just does not know what he means by this. Her customary signals get no reply, eroding her confidence. Maybe she is not charming enough? The woman thinks anxiously, sleepy and tired, that the moment he gives any signal or has any desire, she will devote her everything to him. She is so desirous of obtaining concrete experience in this love affair, some unforgettable souvenir of this love, which the man, however, is just not giving her, leaving her feeling tortured and pained. Anxiety makes her even more active and wilder, wrapping him more tightly with silk and not allowing him to relax at all. As a result, like an Indian dancer and flutist performing a snake trick, he attaches her lips to his, appreciates her body with his palms and watches every tiny change in her expression.

As they play with and stroke each other, several rounds have passed and it is already late into the night, which neither of them has noticed. When the woman rolls into the man's arms again and is absorbed in the perfect match of his masculine voice and rich expression, the man whispers to her, "Honey, look, it is two o'clock already. It's time I take you home!"

The woman is dumbfounded, taking her arms off his neck as her face turns towards him and her perplexed dewy eyes stare at him. "Go? Why? What does he mean? Is he driving me out of his house?"

The woman's thoughts do not gel at first for a while. Her sense of pride and self-confidence are badly hurt. "What's going on here? Is this it? What does his attitude suggest?"

Should she say no, anyhow? Could she offer to stay the night? If she did, just what would she become?

The man, however, simply ignores the woman's confusion. Allowing no explanation, he stands up, leaves the woman alone and goes to the closet for the jackets. His movements are resolute and firm, allowing no denial or negotiation, as if he is reminding her through his body language that he is not interested in accepting her. He has got enough from the woman and does not want to continue. He has behaved responsibly enough staying with her patiently for the whole night. In addition, he leaves her intact, not loving then abandoning her, and does nothing else more to her.

Given everything in her revelation, the woman's chest gives a heave due to her huge emotional loss and sense of pride. Her expression becomes violently distorted, and she cannot squeeze one word out. In no time after that, she suddenly smoothes the spasmodic muscles around her eyes, puts on the appearance of a smile, with her fingers sweeps her long hair over her forehead, trying to put on a bold face, and says generously and calmly, "Well then, let me clear the table for you." Her tone is almost a claim that she is an experienced lover and was already used to such typical things in the realm of love. While her tone suggests, it is as if she had come only to prepare him a meal and she not only gives a fine beginning but also a perfect ending to the whole thing.

Before the man can stop her, the woman begins to perform with great movements full of a certain uncontrollable exaggeration. She asks loudly where to put this stuff or that plate, quickly tidies up everything, and then fixes the makeup on her face that had gotten mussed up by the kissing. She comes out with a peaceful expression, in passing picks up the garbage bag on the kitchen floor, and says quietly to the man who is a little taken aback by this sight, "Let's go."

The leaves are rustling in the night wind, while the freezing dew reminds of inevitable approaching cold. Zhizi cannot help shivering because of the wind. The man comes over and hugs her shoulders appreciatively, but Zhizi says nothing. She ignores his flattery when her body is already beyond sense. They slide into the taxi, side by side on the back seat and the man wraps the woman into his arms. Zhizi, though replying with nothing, does not refuse him, still out of her senses, letting herself be embraced meaninglessly by him. She feels everything is just pointless at that moment.

The car is sliding quietly through the darkness of the night, in a light yet heavy way. The rear lights of cars in front leave traces of dark red. The night is dry, without the slightest signs of any moisture, she thinks. At the entrance to the building in a residential area, the woman climbs out of the car and the man follows her out, giving her an unnatural hug goodbye, then he lowers his head and climbs back into the taxi, which goes back along the way it came, following the other cars. The woman watches the red *Crown* fade in the darkness carrying him away. After all, he is not a bad guy — she tries to put a positive spin on it — and after all, he is not without any sense of responsibility, though his responsibility is only evident in that he accompanied her home for the short journey. His caring and warmth during the short journey will be enough for her to remember for the rest of her life.

A strong night wind blows through the door of the building and messes up her hair. Several strands of hair touch her face, covering her eyes. Her hands are trying to push her hair behind her head when they feel something wet on her face. She turns around, switches the corridor light on, intending to quickly run up the stairs. As she is taking the first step her leg touches a big bag. Looking down, she sees the bag of garbage that she has been holding onto tightly since she left the kitchen.

It is only then that tears, much like a violent flood, down her cheeks begin to fall.

(Translated by Zhang Ruiqing)

Sowing

Sun Huifen

Sun Huifen. Born in 1961 in Zhuanghe, Liaoning Province, Sun Huifen was earlier a farmer, a worker and a magazine editor, and is now a professional writer of the Liaoning Literature Academy, holding the national professional title of "First-ranked Litterateur." She is also a member of the National Committee of the Chinese Writers' Association and vice-chair of the Liaoning Writers' Association.

Her representative works include the short stories, "Rain Chattering before a Small Window," "Changing Tone," "Terrace," "The Steps," and "Dogskin Sleeve"; the novellas, *A Tale of Spring*, *Farmer-Workers*, *Two Women of Xiema Village*, and *Swallow Flying Southeast*; the prose piece, "The Creed of Streets and Lanes"; and the novels, *Xiema Village*, *The Story of Shangtang*, and *Jikuan's Carriage*. She has won many literary awards, including the 3rd Feng Mu Literary Prize for New Writers, conferred by the Chinese Literature Foundation in 2002; and the 3rd Lu Xun Literary Prize for Novellas, by the Chinese Writers' Association in 2005, for *Two Women of Xiema Village*. Sun Huifen is now living in Dalian, Liaoning Province.

Sowing

As soon as Dafeng stepped onto the sandy wasteland, she recognized the woman to the west. The moment she recognized the woman, almost like a hawk spotting a chick, she had a sudden premonition that good times were coming her way again. It had been a long time since Dafeng had met this Thin Fox — Dafeng always bore in mind that the mother who gives birth to a little fox must be an old fox, a skinny fox. Dafeng had come early in the morning to the sandy wasteland to turn up the soil; actually, she had not been looking for someone to fight with, she just had not known that Thin Fox would also be there.

When autumn had come on, her son, a migrant worker in the city, had brought back a girlfriend. From then on, she had stopped trailing Thin Fox, stopping abusing her. She no longer screamed out her curses. It was not that she wanted to be a good mother-in-law — she had never wanted to be one; it was that she did not wish her future daughter-in-law to find out that her father-in-law had become besotted with a mere girl of twenty-six and followed her off — which would only cause her daughter-in-law to harbor doubts about her son. She had felt oppressed for too long. When her daughter-in-law chatted with her, asking her time and time again what Uncle was away doing, or when her son and his girl were twittering and intimately carrying on with their affectionate chatter, especially when it was in the dead of night, with the moon shining through the window and casting a bright light on the heated adobe *kang*, a bed mostly vacant — she always wished she could leap up and run to the door of Thin Fox's house, pointing in her direction and abusing her, "You old bitch! You've offended god! He will therefore punish you by putting stones in the bladder of your man. You just cannot wait to see your daughter do me great harm making me live like a widow."

Dafeng really did not know that any god would present her such a chance. Actually, she happened to simply come across the idea of opening up a patch of sandy wasteland. The other day, when she was asking a fortuneteller to presage an auspicious wedding date for her son, he had told her, "This child has a fate of soil, sandy soil, which is not nourishing enough to hold onto a woman. But if you plant a furrow of winter green onions on some sandy land, and if it germinates in February, and your son gets married in March, all this will be settled." Now since Thin Fox was famous for turning wasteland into fertile soil, she herself first felt too disgusted to open up and grow things in the sandy waste. She had been hesitating. Of course, another reason was that, since her man had run off, she had endured the tough work of this summer and autumn without even having the slightest strength, and long yearned to take a good rest once the grain was stored and straw heaped up. However, she soon made up her mind and left her house for this sandy wasteland, since she wanted the girl of her son to stay and did not wish her son to lead a desolate life just like hers — she had been lonely for almost half of her life. Unpredictably though, she had not been able to avoid her enemy.

Dafeng stared at Shoulan (Skinny Orchid), saying to herself, "You Thin Fox, you really know how to stick a pin wherever there's room — you've chosen the same sandy patch! Perhaps you'll never dream of sticking a pin on my territory again." Dafeng noticed the skinny woman turn her head. Dafeng was sure that she could not see clearly who it was, for if she had, she would have run away immediately.

"She clearly didn't see me. That's great. It sometimes happens that a mouse bumps into the same cat a second time and for no good reason," Dafeng thought complacently. She chose another patch of sandy waste and began to dig and turn up the soil. She staggered when she stamped her foot on the spade. She had gotten good at such tasks, especially those needing heavy manual labor. Her husband used to be away all year round, so all the laboring work fell on her shoulders, such as plowing, furrowing, driving the cart, and threshing the grain. The few thousand yuan he brought home every year had trained her to become an expert farmer. She could not help feeling a gnawing pain in her heart, as if someone had tightly seized it. Actually, her staggering reminded her of her husband, and the accompanying ache made her involuntarily blurt out curse words, "You old bitch, you old fox!" Nevertheless, she articulated her curses voicelessly, as if the words had been absorbed by the bright light of the sandy wasteland as soon as they came out of her lips. Besides, she discovered that her enemy could hardly hear her no matter how high she raised her voice.

Dafeng shifted her posture to step the spade with her left foot. Her left foot was always defter than the other one, just as her left hand was always more adroit than her right at holding the plow. Dafeng felt revitalized after the adjustment. In fact, she was already fifty-four years old, not young anymore, so to speak, and with every passing year not as strong as before. In her youth, she used to like to do her work right under people's noses, and whatever she did, she seemed to have inexhaustible strength in her so long as there were people around her or she was in a crowd, like a child who became exceedingly naughty and excited when guests arrived. Well, what she really loved was the atmosphere of the crowding around of people like the vapor surrounding a steamer on the fire. Her strength could be likened to a bun in the steamer, which expanded and swelled with hot steam. But over the past summer and autumn, she had lost her "steam." Although she exerted the utmost strength in working as usual, any strength was not brought out by voluntary steaming but unwillingly by force. She pretended to work hard because she did not want others to see her broken down by her husband's absence. This summer and autumn, she felt she had been breaking down somewhat. Before she came to the sandy wasteland, she had feared the impending chore of sowing even more than she feared the labor of carrying stones to the top of the mountain. However, on this sandy wasteland, which was far away from people, with the first stamp on the spade, she found she felt as strong as a horse, which she had never thought she was before. The encounter with that old Thin Fox blew her up like an inflated inner tube of a tire. With her back to the woman behind her, Dafeng faced the sun, which imprinted her shadow on the sandy wasteland and made her as bright as the sand.

It was one of the most brilliant of days since the autumn had set in, and on such a day Dafeng came across her enemy. Originally, her enemy had been Thin Fox's daughter, for it was this daughter who had enticed her husband like a foxy succubus. However, why had that old fox not subjected her daughter to moral codes? Why had she herself enticed men in her youth? The fact that she herself had enticed men could not but turn her into her enemy. Like mother, like daughter. Thinking about this, Dafeng found a vent for her anger — the term "old slut." She used to abuse others with words such as "bitch" or "fox," but never with "old slut." Well, on second thought, what was she if not a slut? When that one was young, she had liked to dress herself up and put on rouge, even when her husband was not home. Whatever the work was, sowing or harvesting, she always kept her distance from the others, that is, she would either be the very first or the very last to show up. She just went out of the way to attract men's attention. Whenever there were people around flirting with each other, she had pretended to be embarrassed — her face got red and her eyebrows knitted tight together as if she alone were decent. In fact, that was no decency at all, but merely a trick for attracting men. The man, nicknamed "Big Bull," had been only one example. He had become so infatuated with her that, when she was in front he followed her, and when she lagged behind he would wait to meet her. Dafeng thought, perhaps her own man had been lured by the daughter's same affectation of silence and aloofness. That day, when they had come to blows and her husband left her, Dafeng remembered him saying, "Yes, I do love her because she is young, beautiful and quiet, not like you. You are noisy all day and every day like a nest of sparrows stirred up by a kitchen stick…."

"Quiet, could quiet take away men's hearts?" Dafeng spoke to herself. Dafeng did not believe that a woman could lure a man by keeping quiet and not speaking. She thought, when a slut keeps silent, she is sure to make eyes at men and must talk a lot with her eyes and brows. Her thoughts became more active in the sunlight. Why, could a woman attract a man and steal his heart if she was not seductive or flowery? She could not figure it out before, but today she found she had gained some ground, for she fixed on the thought of women's eyes and brows. She was quite confident that it must be women's eyes and brows that played the key role with the quietness. Dafeng raised her head in delight and took a deep breath, her eyes glancing swiftly from the sky afar across to the wild fields as if attempting to entice. After her husband had been lured and left her, there was this steady pain in her heart all the time like a saw-tooth pricking into it. But, when she came to imagine how Thin Fox had abetted Little Fox into enticing men, she seemed to enter another state of affairs — a state of affairs that had nothing to do with her.

Shoulan did not turn around from beginning to end, for she knew well how far her object was from her. It was a patch about two hundred meters long, and even with the greatest speed, it would take them both a whole morning to run into each other, which was to say, they would not meet until midday at least. "That's a long time," she thought, "long enough for me to think up the most beautiful and most powerful speech." She decided to pull out what had been tucked into her mind the whole summer and autumn, arrange things properly in order, shooting the words out like bullets from a machinegun when the time was ripe. "You complain that my daughter has corrupted public morals, but wasn't your husband answerable first? You know, he is more than twenty years older than my girl is. Should he not know better than her about the consequences of abandoning a wife and a son? Did he not know that he is old enough to be my child's father rather than lover? Didn't he spoil my girl's future in doing so? You say my daughter ruined your family, but what I want to say to you: it was your husband who ruined my daughter, not vice versa. Well, on second thought, as his wife, could you be excused from responsibility for what happened? You lived with your husband for more than twenty years and didn't win his heart, so who is to blame? You were always careless, fooling around all day with men in the village and having fun with them.... Wherever there was a crowd, you were sure to turn up, while your own home was in an awful mess. You never care about improving your appearance, winter or summer, your clothes are always filthy and wrinkled; day or night, your hair is disheveled and every time you step out of the door, it is as if you had just come out of the henhouse. No wonder your man ran away with another woman. You deserved it!"

The thought gratified Shoulan in her heart. "Nothing would be more satisfying to me than when those words are spoken out," she thought. It would shatter Dafeng's heart mercilessly. However, while wallowing in this indulgence, she could not help but feel a shiver down her spine when she thought about herself. "Am I not a good woman? Of course, I am, but didn't my own man have unfaithful intentions? How many men care a damn about women? Once a man has unfaithful intentions, how is it possible for a woman, no matter how virtuous she is, to pull him back?"

Shoulan planned to take advantage of the long time to prepare all her mind's ammunition to bombard her enemy with. However, she had never thought that her weapons would end up hurting herself in the first place. When she thought about her own man, her mind was in sixes and sevens like petals in the autumn fluttering in every direction in the air. Shoulan stamped her foot on the spade and found her foot weak; her withered breasts, protruding no more, hung sad and loose in the bosom of her dress.

Shoulan could not help thinking of the years past. In those

years of countless scars and sufferings, she had paid homage to her man, who came home every two months, as she would have to a god. While, on the one hand, the man had made her have children and labor at home, on the other hand, he had lived with a widow in a fishing village. The widow had given birth to two children for him, but he suspected that the children were from another man. Therefore, although she appeared decent enough in public in the daytime, she was almost beaten to death by the man when night fell. No one knew what had been happening to her. She only knew it when the widow called at her door. Her husband had not told the widow that he had been married from beginning to end.

There was nothing in the way of sunlight in the sky, not even a trace of cloud. Glints, interwoven by the wind and the sunlight, glittered on the sand and made her eyelashes cool again. Shoulan was afraid of the wind and the sunlight because of her eyes. Her eyes had long since become tearful when they met with the wind and the sunlight. Shoulan thought, "I must never mention those things, even if they could prove to be heavy weapons easily blowing the enemy up into pieces, for they could knock down both the enemy and me, and most probably I would be the first victim. Then, what should I say? What can best hurt the enemy without doing any harm to me? Shall I curse too?"

Yes, curse! Shoulan bent over, arched one foot and stamped the spade deep into the ground. She thought it was time for her to learn to curse. She did not know how to curse even now, except to call a little child "Little Devil," or curse the chicken and ducks; that was all. She never called a man or a woman by name. She continued thinking, "Well, in for a penny, in for a pound, today I am going to raise hell and make a scene like you always do. I will swear at your ancestors and the private parts in their trousers. Dafeng, you've cursed my parents and ancestors as 'old foxes,' 'old bitches,' 'worn shoes' (whores) and 'disgusting hooligans,' who were all talked about behind their backs. You have almost used up all the bad language there is, and as good as dug out my parents and ancestors from their graves, stripped them down and.... Why shouldn't I learn from you? Why should I be so tamed as to allow her to cast slurs on me to her heart's content? What a shame, I am unworthy of my ancestors."

Shoulan had let out a deep breath, and spat on the palms of her hands. Then, she cleared her throat. The way she cleared her throat sounded like swear words on the tip of her tongue. At first, there seemed to be nothing in the throat. However, once she began clearing it, she realized that her throat had been a little husky and clogged, not as smooth and clear as she had thought, like a window-sill, which looks clean, but when you put your hand on it, your hand gets stained with dust. The seeing was a far cry from the believing. Shoulan turned up the soil spade after spade. At the same time, she was plowing up her memory for the most powerful and sharpest swear words. Repetition of Dafeng's words was out of the question. Her words must be new and revised and — hit the nail right on the head. Then, slowly and unconsciously, Shoulan drifted away from her original intention to curse. She thought repeatedly about Dafeng's shortcomings and drawbacks. Dafeng was a famous know-it-all. No gossip could escape her ears, and then, as soon as she heard something, she right away spread it around. Dafeng was a famous shrew too, who never forgave easily when people erred. When things went wrong due to her gossip, she was able to absolve herself from all blame by being shrewish. She was a "flea in the crotch," no more, no less — a shrew spirit. She has also proved herself to be a "comet" (symbolizing bad luck and ill fate). Shoulan bet that, once these words were spoken out, Dafeng was sure to become angry. Only by making Dafeng angry would Shoulan feel avenged.

However, as Shoulan repeated the words once again in her mind, she inadvertently got stuck. The wording of "a flea of the crotch" would naturally remind Dafeng of the affair between herself and Big Bull, which she was most reluctant to mention, though there had actually been nothing between them at all from the very beginning. Besides, it was all very well to call her a "comet," but was she herself not the same? Her husband had been unfaithful to her, and had kidney stones after he retired from work. She had planned that, as a lifelong "public servant," they could rely on his pension for a living. However, his salary was delayed year by year in payment. Dafeng's man was unworthy of her, but, at least, he did not add trouble for her….

At this moment, Shoulan learned that it was no easy thing to curse without using obscenities. The Scud missiles she saw in the Persian Gulf War on TV could make turns to strike the enemy, while her abusive language made turns and ultimately hit herself. She was feeling so upset and worried that she could not concentrate on the job at hand, and over and over she could not dig deep into the ground with the spade. She was upset because she found herself disheartened, because she found herself weak, because she found she was ill-fated. It was as clear as day that she had done nothing bad, she was worthy of her husband, her children and her neighbors, and she had never hurt anyone including Dafeng. The only one that she felt unworthy of was herself but nobody else, if there were anyone else. However, because of her daughter, Dafeng vented her grievances on her while she could not fight back in the same way. It was annoying to think that what she used to curse others over had finally rebounded on herself.

Shoulan untied her kerchief, her face streaming with sweat. She had no idea whether it was through weariness or worry. She threw the kerchief aside on another patch of unstirred sandy wasteland and picked up the spade in no time again. Shoulan thought, "I will never let my enemy see through me. I, Yu Shoulan, must never show any of my white feathers and never be disheartened today, even if there becomes a need to fight desperately and risk my life on these sands."

Dafeng advanced quickly while turning up the soil; not that she did her work at a faster speed, but she did the digging at a different breadth. For every four furrows Shoulan turned up at a time, Dafeng had to turn up just one. The fortuneteller had told her to grow only one furrow of winter green onions in the sandy wasteland, and said that when they sprouted the next year, her son's ill fate would change. At a ratio of four to one, Dafeng was bound to be three times faster than Shoulan. Now digging, now stopping, Dafeng turned up the soil, feeling the loosened soil rise and fall with regular rhythm under her feet. She straightened up to look into the distance, where she saw mountain ridges and wild fields at the foothills. It was more than fifty years since she had first seen them. They had not changed much over the last fifty years — in the spring suffused with green of a different hue each tier, and in the autumn tinted in yellows of different hues. After late autumn comes on, all the colors become one — yellowish brown, the color of loess. Like all country folk, she was born to belong to green and yellow. The color of the mountains and the fields filled her with great joy and confidence — life, though ever so bitter and tiresome, still held hope. She would like to use her quick tongue and loud voice to stir a single color into a riot, which would remind her of a scene of many colorful flags fluttering in the wind. She loved to work before a crowd or under people's noses — she knew it was all because she had much, very much to talk about. So long as she could talk, she felt her days incomparably bright, as if she lived to talk and only by talking did she feel alive and live an acceptable life. When she saw someone remaining silent, she would shout aloud at them, "Why don't just die and go to hell! Of what value is life when you do not talk?"

Dafeng had never dreamed that there would appear such a deep hole, a black stain, in her bright days. Only after her husband had left her for the other woman, then came this deep and black hole in her life, did she realize that her desire to behave before a crowd and join in the fun and talk endlessly… was all due to an intact family, a steady life and a husband. After her husband had left and her family was wrecked, she lost interest in joining in the crowd, except when she quarreled with others. From that time on, summer or autumn, the mountains and the fields lost their colors and all looked like one color — the color of a dead man, dull, cold, ashen. But Dafeng would rather not see them again. Looking at them was but a prelude, in Dafeng's eyes much like a tune pitched before a song started. Dafeng's mind was on the woman behind her. If, before she had come, her decision had been to open up the wasteland and grow onions to avert her son's personal misfortune, then, after she arrived and found the woman, her only purpose to open up the sandy land now was to set herself against the woman. She would fight bravely against Thin Fox. She would like to see her scared, to scare the shit out of her, to have her wet her pants at the sight of her.

After Dafeng had opened up a stretch of wasteland, a germ of worry began to grow in her. She worried that Thin Fox would run away the moment she recognized who she was. If she ran away, Dafeng would suffer a big loss, as if a big piece of meat had been robbed from the mouth by a dog — cursing her was of no help, relieving neither hunger nor thirst. The only purpose was to give vent to her anger and thus make her unhappy life happier, which was hundreds and thousands times more important than eating fat meat. Dafeng had caught sight of Thin Fox. Every few moments, Dafeng turned around and took a look at her. To her surprise, she found Shoulan right there all the time. Dafeng could not believe that Shoulan had not seen her all this time. But then, why had she not been scared off? Dafeng had wished two hundred percent that Thin Fox would remain there to make herself a target for her anger. However, when Dafeng found that Shoulan was indeed still right there, she found herself in a flurry.

"Pooh, pooh," Dafeng turned around and spat in both hands. Then, in one breath, she turned up a *zhang* (3.3 m) of wasteland. "Why is Thin Fox not afraid of me? Does she naively imagine that I am going to make up with her because some people have put in a good word for her? No way! That is sheer dreaming on her part. Perhaps, I could consider it and get on well together again, were it not for that scandal of yours in your youth. That evening, Big Bull had happened to bump into me when leaving your house. The next day, he had come to my house and helped me store wheat and corn.... If there were nothing weighing on his conscience, why was he afraid of me? Ever since that evening Big Bull had come out of your house, you were shy about looking at me. Every time we met, you hung your head and blushed and did not dare to look up into my eyes. Do you think I noticed nothing! I am not blind! Old slut!"

This time Dafeng cursed hard, swearing audibly. The voice came out from her mouth and lingered around her ears for a long time, almost as if the words had circled around the wasteland and then returned into her own ears. Dafeng listened to her own voice, and to be fair, that was the only sound that she could hear, for it was quiet in the wilds. The voice, lonely and chilly, struck one as not flying up but falling down, as if a lonely bird had cried out. At that moment, when Dafeng sensed her voice falling down like a solitary bird crying on the wasteland, a thought awoke inside her: to curse was in fact no fun at all if there was no one around, or if only the enemy you aimed your curse at was on hand, all alone. To curse was not to reason but to vent spleen, pure and simple, and thus one must not lack an audience. One was avenged only by cursing wherever there was a crowd of people, much like putting on a play, the cheers from the audience and even the pleasant expressions in their eyes greatly encouraging the actors and enhancing their enthusiasm. To Dafeng, the more she cursed the more proficient she had become; the more people there were, the more melodious, clearer and louder her voice.

Many a time, Dafeng had purposely run into her at her doorway. At first, there would just be the two of them, so she just casually kept walking along, speechless, with vigorous strides — she would never speak when there were just the two of them. Nevertheless, when she would come to the intersection of Qianchuan and Houchuan villages, where people from three villages went to market and converged, she would suddenly blurt it all out. When the crowd, on hearing her cursing, began to grow, she would feel quite at ease and comfortable. She especially loved to see the surprised expressions in people's eyes when they moved their eyes from her face to Thin Fox's face — when she disclosed the twenty-year-old scandal about Thin Fox and Big Bull. To tell the truth, the moment her anger — bottled up in her for so many years — was given vent to, it disappeared in a flash. To curse was indeed very much like putting on a play: actors performing on stage needed cheering from the audience. Of course, there was a slight difference between cursing and performing. The audience cheered on the actors to encourage them to make better performances, and then felt satisfaction over money paid; while, when cursing, people wanted applause from spectators because they wanted to knock the opponent down with the aid of their cheers and applause and in the end have others pay up — to make others show pity.

When she realized that, no matter how loud she raised her voice, no one would be coming to the wasteland to watch the farce, her mood for a big quarrel with Thin Fox deflated rapidly. Dafeng stopped her work and tucked up her sleeves casually, biting her lower lip with her upper teeth. Her eyebrows knitted tightly, as if she had lost the battle already. All of a sudden, everything seemed to turn the color of shit brown, the mountain ridges afar and the fields at the foothills.

The sun, like the two women opening up the wasteland, moved along without a break and made the brilliance and the roaming winds of the autumn gather over their heads, reflecting colorful light. The colors were faint. When examined carefully, they disappeared, but with eyes turned away, they seemed dazzling — on close observation, the brilliant colors combined with the silvery white gleam on the surface of the wasteland. Shoulan's eyes always seemed to be brimming with tears, but she could not close them all day without using them. Not only were her eyes wet, her forehead, her lower jaw, even her chest were wet as well. Shoulan was very weary, for turning up the soil was extremely strength-consuming labor. Shoulan weakened with every passing year. Her chronic stomachache made her unable to eat with a good appetite while her stomach felt bloated. As soon as she started any work, she became wet through with sweat. She never told others about her troubles, even her husband. She thought it would be useless to tell others about her troubles. In this world, whatever you did, you have only yourself to rely on. She used to have stomach trouble years ago. When her husband was away and had not sent any money home, she had to go to work in the fields to get work points* and then cook meals after work, therefore she was always late for dinner and often endured the torments of hunger. This summer, after her daughter had caused trouble and Dafeng abused her in the street, saying that twenty years ago she'd had an affair with Big Bull, when her husband heard the rumor about her affair, he had flown into an uncontrollable rage as soon as the words had been passed on to him. He began to punish her day and night in order to give vent to his bile like a madman: when night fell, he pulled and hauled at her breasts and made her scream with pain; during the day, when it was time for dinner, he glowered and stared at her with both disdain and rage, making her feel bloated in the stomach before any food could be put into her mouth. Sometimes, when she belched at the dinner table, her husband would bang his chopsticks heavily on the table and scold her, "Goddamn you, will you let me finish my meal?" Therefore, to hide her aches from view was a most important and sensitive thing for Shoulan. Thus, she became even thinner, her shoulder blades protruding, like loosening door leaves.

Sweat streamed down Shoulan's wrinkled cheeks and neck like strings of rolling pearls. It was autumn and the sweat did not brew into hot steam, but was blown cool by the drifting breeze. Wiping the sweat with the palm of her hand, Shoulan was fully aware that she was sweating not only because she was weary and weak, but also because she had not come up with any swear words she could use against Dafeng, since it was impossible to avoid an abusive encounter

---

*Based on quantity and quality of labor performed, then payment earned, in the rural people's communes.

with her. Shoulan approached closer and closer to her object. Although she didn't really turn around and figure out the distance, but by instinct, and sidelong glimpses from the corner of her eye with an occasional turn, she knew that she was very close to Dafeng. She did not know that Dafeng was opening up one furrow of the wasteland at a time, so she was a little amazed by her speed, thinking that the woman was as energetic in her work as in her abuse. Shoulan's mind went blank as she got closer to Dafeng. Although the force of her anger had welled up from the bottom of the heart this morning, when she saw Dafeng also there on the wasteland, she was at a loss of how to vent her anger, how to wash off the stigma cast on her by that woman, and how to get rid of grievances, like she did with black stones in the wasteland. Shoulan was nearly at her wits' end. Her shriveled breasts hung from her chest like two wailing birds, but she just could not come up with any ideas. Far from thinking of any ideas, she was growing all the more flurried. Now at her wits' end, she unconsciously straightened up her back and turned round.

Dafeng was actually quite close behind her, only two *zhang* (6.6 m) away. Shoulan caught sight of her broad figure moving up and down: when it straightened up, it resembled a solid kitchen board; when it bent over, it was like a mare. Dafeng was one of the few big women in the village. Behind her back she was called "a big shaft-horse." Shoulan often looked upon any large, live animals she came upon in daily life as Dafeng, stirring certain unease in her heart. Now, when Shoulan could clearly see her back, who could have thought she would feel not a bit afraid. Moreover, exactly because she was not afraid, Shoulan unexpectedly changed her mind. She thought, "Why must there be quarrels and fights? Why could I not have a talk with her about my grievances, calmly and even-temperedly? Why not explain the whole story to her? — That day when my daughter had run in and told me that she was in love with Song Si and would marry him, I was felled by the news and had fainted away. When I had come to and found my daughter all in tears in my arms, I gave her a slap without thinking. I said to her, 'You little devil, get away, go away by yourself and never return.' Who could have known that she would really run away with Song Si…? I felt just like you when I realized that she had taken away your man from you — felt like tearing her to pieces. Yes, like mother, like daughter: she cared too much about improving her appearance and was always busy combing her hair, washing her face, and applying powder all day long. Nevertheless, I had never harbored any other designs like she did. She had worked odd jobs for no more than two months and bought a pair of earrings for me, saying that I did not live a happy life and did not show myself off to my heart's content.… But I had not given a second thought before I threw them into the stove. If I were what you call me, a 'bad woman,' a 'whore,' why would I not have put them on right away.…" With these thoughts, Shoulan calmed down all at once. At peace in her own mind, all of a sudden, colorful images seemed to emerge in her blank mind like on a blank screen. Shoulan made up her mind to stay near Dafeng and not abuse her. She decided that, even if she started the abuse first, she would not answer back. She would wait until the other woman had finished abusing or become too tired to continue, then explain to her the whole story exactly as it had happened: that she was not the kind of woman Dafeng made her out to be, and did not have anything to do with other men. Indeed, Big Bull had been kind to her at that time. She could feel the oft-cast sidelong stares at her, whenever sowing seeds or harvesting crops, which made her heart throb nervously. However, because her husband was not at home, she had to take a man who gawked so, as a bad man who bore her no good intentions.

In fact, she had always set strict demands on herself to be a good woman, after her mother had died a long time ago. Her mother had died of liver cancer when she just got married at twenty-three. The last words her mother on her deathbed had said to her were, "Though your man is away and you are alone at home, you must hold on to your good character." That year, when her children were still young, Big Bull had helped her to heap crops in the storehouse until midnight. In the moonlight, he had stared at her and, in a trance, soon looked as if turned to wood. Well, for a moment, her desire had been aroused, like a warm current flowing and pounding in her blood vessels. However, in the end, as she did up the washing in the courtyard, and he was ready to follow her into the room, she had turned around suddenly and pushed him out. As god is my witness, I did push him out, without even knowing where all my strength came from. After pushing him out, I had leaned against the door crying unrestrainedly without knowing why. The whole night, my mind was on men, but as god is my witness, I am clean and innocent. I did not have anything to do with him. From then on, he never helped me do any more fieldwork. For many years, every time when she assumed a target in harvesting, she took this target of a big harvest as Big Bull — Big Bull did not help her do any more fieldwork because she had rejected him, which further convinced her that he was a bad man with bad intentions.

Thinking of these matters now, Shoulan heaved a sigh of relief and felt an untold relaxation and comfort brush past both her body and mind, which she had rarely felt all morning, or even this whole summer. She relaxed: on the one hand, at this crucial moment, she had finally come up with an idea of how to face Dafeng; on the other, an even more important point was Shoulan now saw clearly and keenly that, twenty years ago it had been none other than herself who had pushed that man out with force. What an upright and amazing woman she was! For some time, even when Dafeng had shouted abuse at her, she had been also fully aware that there was nothing at all between her and men. Nevertheless, because her mind was perturbed, she had still not dared look at Dafeng; because she had still attracted such men, she had been secretly hard on herself. Well, in fact, it was nothing special, wasn't it? Who could guarantee that one had no evil intentions all one's life? In addition, who could make his way into another man's mind and see if there were no wicked ideas there? You know, I hadn't been touched by a man for several months at that time; and you know, when I pushed Big Bull out, his broad chest was really warm to the touch! The most difficult thing for a good woman to do is to muster the power to rid evil ideas once they did appear. This is most important for a truly good woman!

Shoulan did not open up any more wasteland. She straightened up completely and stopped to take a rest. She stroked her sweat-soaked hair and looked into the clear, blue sky. Shoulan felt herself bright, tall and big. Never before had she felt herself to be more aboveboard and loftier than she did now — she felt herself to be a woman of gigantic stature.

Dafeng quickly drew back her gaze from the shit gray mountains. She was the kind of woman who was unwilling to resign herself to defeat. Being deserted by her husband had been her biggest defeat so far. She had gone through her biggest defeat of her life and could not afford to allow another one today. Dafeng drew back her gaze and began turning up the soil again, her big wrists exposed as she rolled up her sleeves. Dafeng's wrists were strong, as were her legs and arms. Her bone structure was extremely large. In fact, she was not muscular, though at first she had been fat. She had to work and worry about her own livelihood, but she had been carefree and content, fit and happy. When she was displeased, she created rows and rackets to vent her displeasure. After her husband had gone, she remained in low spirits, but however hard she tried to make a row or a racket, her low spirits could no longer be dispelled, especially after her son had come to see her with his wife. She felt a millstone around her neck all day long, and every morning when she opened up her eyes, she would see it there. As soon as she saw it, she would feel a convulsive pain in her heart. From that time on, she had grown even thinner. She still looked big, but her belly had long sunken in, a fact she kept to herself.

Dafeng spared no efforts in her digging and turning. For a moment, she felt that the woman behind her had stopped. Dafeng thought that Thin Fox must have been preparing herself all the way along for how to beg for mercy but feeling afraid as they approached nearer. Dafeng could not help feeling smug. When she felt smug, she could fling the sandy soil far. Dafeng thought, "Hmm, how could a woman like you not be afraid of being cursed? How could you not be afraid of being cursed by a decent and upright woman like me?" When this last thought entered her mind, she suddenly saw the light. This was truly unpredictable light, like the sun rising in the dark night. Well, would a decent woman like me need to curse you? Why did I curse you? I never had anything with any other man except my husband. All I need to do is to stand before you, looking daggers at you for some time, without doing anything else, and you would tremble with fear, and your pores would enlarge into deep holes.

Dafeng at last worked out the best idea of coping with the woman behind her: draw near her, stand in front of her, and just stare cold daggers at her. The idea excited Dafeng: not only because the woman behind her would never imagine that she would come up with such an idea, but because she herself was a decent woman who Thin Fox could never match. She had been cursing her for more than half the year, yet it had never dawned on her until now that she could drive her into a fissure in the ground without saying anything. Of course, this strategy would not have worked too well when there were crowds of people around; it was only applicable to an encounter on this sandy wasteland. The lines on Dafeng's broad lower jaw suddenly turned into deep curves. Her sticky gray hair, which she had not washed for a long time, made a slight vibration. Dafeng broadened her face into a grin. Her mouth had been closed the whole morning, tasting bitter — there was always a bitter taste in her mouth as if she often drank the juice of wormwood. She was laughing at the soil before her, which she had opened up.

After the laugh of satisfaction, Dafeng became filled with an undying idea: "I am a good woman! I am a decent woman!" Dafeng thought, "Though my own man had not worked in the co-op, he is quick-witted and deft. Carpentry or bricking, tilling or plastering, he is expert in almost all jobs. When the individualized economy came into fashion, he did not feel he could stay at home any longer. In recent years, he had risen from being a skillful worker up to becoming a supervisor. Though he was never home all year long, I had never purposely lured men. In those years, you Shoulan used to not get on well with others and attracted men's thievish-looking eyes around you. I hated you to the very marrow of my teeth. I pretended to take no notice of you when I went to or came off work. Moreover, from then on, I didn't have any dealings with you. Of course, later on you began to enjoy a good reputation after your man had come back home. I built a house on the West Hill, which was far from you, and moved there, so we did not see a lot of each other. I mean, if I enjoy a good reputation, I wouldn't entertain others with a bad reputation. From the time I was young, I had been open and aboveboard, distinguishing clearly between right and wrong — I would not even give in a little over a small wrong. It is a pity I had three sons, and no girls. If I had a girl, I would have been sure to have her learn from me and be a good woman. She would never have been like you."

The more she calculated, the more confident and bolder she became. Since summer had come on, she had felt so vexed like a dog that she had wanted to bite people wherever there was a chance. Today it was very different; she did no longer wanted to bite because she was not so vexed any more. She thought, "Yes, my husband ran away with another woman, but I was stainless, decent and aboveboard. As the saying goes, evil does not prevail over the righteous, and when a woman of my virtue stands in front of a wicked woman, would there be the need to speak?"

A breeze sprang up over the sandy wasteland. It must have swept across the back slopes of Moon Hill before coming here. The wind, with the piercing cold of early winter, made Dafeng cool down all over. "How nice the wind is! This is what autumn should be like!" Dafeng thought to herself. Dafeng shook her slightly hunchbacked shoulders and tugged at the wrinkled front of her coat to smooth it out, feeling relaxed and comfortable. Thin Fox was only one meter away. With every breath, you could hear her puffing and blowing from the strain with every dig.

Dafeng made several hard digs. When she felt that Thin Fox was just behind her and was about to brush past her back, she stopped and straightened up. Once her back was straightened up, it was of a gigantic stature like a huge stake. Dafeng was not going to dig up any more wasteland. From this point on, all that was left to be done was to wait for the moment when they came across each other. At that moment, she would show her opponent what the expression in a good woman's eyes should look like. Dafeng did not think over what she would do next after that moment. All her mind was on the very moment when Thin Fox would shiver, shudder and tremble before her very eyes, her fine hair standing upright. Dafeng stood still, her hunched-over shoulders attempting to lean backwards, like a fighting rooster. Her eyes swept over the mountains in the distance, which were no longer shit gray, but glittering, shining and brilliantly dazzling as if dotted with gold.

Shoulan was waiting for Dafeng to start shouting abuse, which, in Shoulan's eyes, would happen without question. All of Shoulan's relief came from the fact that the sandy wasteland was far from the village and the crowds of people. Shoulan calculated, "I will take the floor when you have had your fill and gotten tired of your abuse." Shoulan had even planned that the first words she would utter to Dafeng should be "my younger sister," when her turn came. She was fifty-six and Dafeng was fifty-four. In earlier years, "my younger sister" had been exactly how she used to address Dafeng. Shoulan believed that, if she could only call her "sister" in a mild voice, even the hardest heart of stone would thaw. So long as Dafeng calmed down, she would get a chance to explain all her grievances as they had taken place. When she heard Dafeng stop, Shoulan's heart tightened involuntarily. Although she was fully prepared to get a scolding, she still could not help feeling nervous at heart, as she in fact approached right near Dafeng. But she did not betray her anxiety. She had been bending over, turning up the soil. She planned to wait until Dafeng finished cursing, and then straighten up her back and talk to her.

However, it was because Shoulan had made such a decision that the whole incident was brought to its unexpected finale. Because Shoulan did not look up at all the whole time, Dafeng's strategy of "looking daggers" at her could not be executed as she desired, for the other had brushed past her backwards; she never expected this to come to naught in the end. But Dafeng's heart was not troubled very much by the incident. She waited patiently, her eyes following Shoulan and gazing at her figure rising and falling. Not believing that she would not look up all the time, her eyes followed her closely. She saw that her hair had turned gray. And her slender waist could be likened to that of a mantis, which could be held in two hands. The skin on her neck was limp and loose, wrinkled like a deflated balloon. Since her opponent wouldn't look up at all, she had plenty of time to observe her carefully. When Shoulan bent over, Dafeng even saw the white bags, her breasts, hanging from her chest — her breasts! Though her neck was dark, her chest was quite white. At that moment when Dafeng saw Shoulan's fair and clear chest and the pair of hanging bags, a signal suddenly flashed in her head: the breasts! It must have been this pair of breasts that Thin Fox had used to entice men twenty years ago. They surely must have! And twenty years later her daughter must be using a pair of breasts again to entice her husband, a pair of young breasts! Almost in an instant, Dafeng burned up with wrath. When she boiled over with rage, she forgot not only the plan she had worked out just a few minutes before, but also all the swear words. She hopped and skipped over to Shoulan, grabbed her by the collar and swung her to and fro like she would a chicken. Dafeng could not utter a word. Her mouth and her eyes together sparkled off a raging flame, burning on Shoulan's chest, or to put it another way, it was Shoulan's breasts that had lit a fire that was burning in her mouth and eyes, making her alight and aglow.

Shoulan was not at all prepared for being grabbed by Dafeng. When Dafeng had stood behind her without uttering a sound, Shoulan had conceived hundreds and thousands of possibilities, but had never expected she would raise a hand to strike. At the beginning, Shoulan could clearly see the fury on Dafeng's twisted face. But as she was pulled and pushed back and forth, and when, in all the shoving and pulling, the collar tightened on her neck, Shoulan's head began to swim. For a moment Shoulan felt a little top-heavy and the sandy wasteland stood on end before her. Shoulan did not fight back; to be fair, the spade was in her hand now and, if she had held it up and struck it at Dafeng's back, Dafeng would have been sure to loosen her grip right away. However, she did not hit out, not because she had been laboring all morning and used up most of her strength, but because she was in a flurry, and flurried, she had simply lost her ability to fight back. Soon she loosened her grip on the spade, and in order not to fall, she clutched tightly at Dafeng's arms.

Shoulan's instinct to grasp at Dafeng's arms was just to keep her balance and not fall. But Dafeng had misconstrued this as Shoulan hitting back, so she exerted all her strength and hurled Shoulan away. Because she had not only used too much strength but also pulled her hands into knots at Shoulan's bosom, her pure white breasts were now completely exposed to the light of day. If this had not happened, and if Dafeng had made her fall heavily face down instead, she might have let her go instead of continuing. After all, she had held her up like holding up a chicken. She had won, and that was enough. She didn't want anything else and had never thought of beating up Shoulan. However, what was exposed but her shining white breasts — two bag-like breasts that had been played with by men. All these associations made Dafeng completely lose her reason in a flash. She sprang on her like a tiger would on a wild boar, seizing her by the shoulders and then her cheeks with her forceful hands.

Since Shoulan's numbed nerves had been awakened at the sudden moment of her fall, and because she had unconsciously opened her eyes wider and saw the savage and ferocious features when Dafeng pounced on her, Shoulan instinctively stretched her hands out to reach for the spade by her head. Shoulan was wondering, "What is wrong with the woman? Is she going to choke me to death?" When Shoulan realized that the woman was indeed going to choke her to death, strength welled up in her suddenly and she thought of her husband, her home, her livestock, and her life, as she did when she was too tired to go on working. All at once, she became filled with strength. Her body trapped under Dafeng, her hands groped for the spade by her head. She managed to transfer her strength to her left hand, though her body could not move. Dafeng's broad forehead butted against her cheek, and her neck was being gripped so tight that she felt a pain in her throat and could hardly breathe. Shoulan at last touched the end of the spade. She slowly held it in her hands and stabbed at Dafeng's back. Because she was lying on her own back and could not exert much strength, she could not gather enough power to strike but only stab with it — stab at the other woman's ribs on the side of her chest. She could feel Dafeng, who was astride on her, shake with the blunt noise. However, Dafeng only gritted her teeth to endure with dogged will, and seized her with both hands, showing no sign of loosening her grip. Shoulan was fully aware of how hard she had stabbed at Dafeng's ribs with the spade, but far from loosening her grip, she had only tightened it with her eyes opened wide like a cobra's, glistening. Shoulan was in despair, because she had little strength to spare while Dafeng's grip tightened more and more.

"Am I really going to die in this woman's hands? How could I die in this woman's hands? I have actually done nothing evil." Suddenly, when she came to realize that, though she had done nothing evil, she was being wronged and bullied for no good reason, and might even be choked to death, Shoulan felt a voice crawl out her throat like a plant out of the wild fields, "No — I was with a man — I had an affair." The crawling out proved difficult as a young seedling breaking through the soil, because Dafeng was choking her neck so tightly. But, choking with sobs, it did come out and emerge, intermittent yet extraordinarily distinct. Shoulan did not know why she in fact had cried out such words, as they were simply gross deception. But, when she heard her own voice coming out of her mouth, spreading out in the narrow space between her and Dafeng, she felt the hands clutching at her neck loosen bit by bit. There seemed to appear some space between her lower jaw and her neck. Pain was being drawn out from her throat, bit by bit like a spade stuck into the ground was being drawn out little by little, from the throat to the lower jaw, from the cheekbone to the skin of her face, and further on to the shoulders. Shoulan saw Dafeng's glistening eyes, opened wide, blur in the wink of an instant, as if her words were a handful of sand thrown into her eyes, or bullets shot into her heart. Feeling she was losing every ounce of her strength as if her soul had left her body, Shoulan felt very ignorant of how things could come to this. She had been most unprepared for those words. Shoulan lay on the ground limp, a smell, unfamiliar but pure and fresh, of the soil surrounding her. She had lost all her ability to move.

Dafeng loosened her hands and slid down off Shoulan. Her hands had already hardened, the part of the hand between the thumb and index finger half opened like a broken clasp of a chain. When Dafeng had seen Shoulan's breasts and thrown herself on Shoulan, she had been completely out of her mind and senses. At that moment, she had not known who she herself was, who the other person was, and what on earth she wanted to do. At that moment, except for the movements, there had been not a single signal in her head, which was as blank as the screen of a TV set cut off from any electric supply. Yet when Shoulan shouted the words intermittently in her face, and then repeated over and again that she had gone after another man, Dafeng had a feeling of receiving an electric shock and her head began to react owing to that jolt. Dafeng had never heard a woman say in front of her that she had gone after a man. She had been greatly shocked. Dafeng thought, "Shoulan said she was with a man, what did she mean by that?" Though feeling shocked, Dafeng had also been bewildered and confused for a moment, for she really couldn't make out what was meant by "with a man." Then in the twinkling of an eye, it got through to her. It suddenly dawned on her that the woman under her meant to say that her body had been touched by a man who was not her husband, but by somebody else. Only by being touched by another man other than her own husband and having an affair with him, could she be considered as having been with a man. In fact, for so many days and years, she had firmly believed and gossiped that Shoulan had indeed had an affair with a man, but she would've never expected that, once the words came out from Shoulan, personally and doggedly, things would turn out to be like this — making her out and out to be so foolish and dumbfounded. She felt pain all over, as if having been nastily shocked by electricity. The strength that had been welling up and surging and rolling in her only a moment ago dispersed all at once. Dafeng had loosened her hands and slid off Shoulan.

Because she slid off down to the right of Shoulan, on a hilly slope, she slid about one meter away from Shoulan.

The sun was shining quietly on the sandy wasteland, on Moon Hill where the wasteland stood, and on the wild fields around Moon Hill — an authentic picture of the wild fields after the autumn harvest, simple and honest, vigorous but bleak. Signs of plowing and tilling were laid bare on the ridges and furrows of the fields. By the side of the ditches and trenches where wheels rolled over, withered grass and leaves remained close to the ground. After they had sowed and plowed and got in the harvest, people no longer gave much consideration to what the ridges in the cropland should look like, or what a road or path should look like, especially in recent years, when there were other means of making money outside the village, and men did not put their energy and effort onto the fields any more. A gust of north wind swept the two women's faces, like a soft hand. They both lay on their backs, lost in their staring into the clear blue sky. What with digging in the field the whole morning and what with the hand-to-hand combat, they were both completely exhausted. They had both been exerting their own strength from the time they had grown up and were able to earn their own living. Even now, when they were already old, things had not improved very much. The two women lay motionless as if the purpose for which they had toiled and labored all the morning in the field was simply to lie side by side like they were now, looking up into the blue sky, extending their legs straight. A flock of wild geese flew overhead, forming the shape of an "A" against the blue sky. Fluttering their wings leisurely and lightly, the birds returned to the south after the autumn every year. Flying over the two women, the geese gave out sad, shrill cries. At that moment, as they made the sad, shrill cries, a voice was heard rising up from the sandy wasteland —

"I went with a man too — ," as if an echo over the distance to the wild geese; the voice was sad yet shrill, hoarse and husky, bold and vigorous.

It was Dafeng. Her voice — sad yet shrill, hoarse and husky, bold and vigorous — first rolling and projecting across the sandy wasteland, then soaring all the way up into the sky, resounding there. Shoulan listened quietly. When she heard Dafeng's voice go up in the air resounding there, a string of warm teardrops, like a string of pearls falling from the sky abruptly, streamed down from her face and dropped onto the ground, sinking into a brown stain.

Unaware how much time had passed, one hour or two hours, one year or a hundred years, Shoulan picked up her feet, feeling as if all her limbs were all out of joint, with little strength left in her. She took up the spade, as she made steps toward the edge of the field. She was in no mood for work now and wanted to go home. She was tired too. She said to herself that she could not be too unfair to herself and things could not go on like this. But when she arrived at the edge of the field, the sight of the scallion seedlings and the manure pile reminded her of her sick husband and her school-age son and the crop of Chinese green onions, which could sell for several hundred yuan. She hesitated, standing still at the edge of the field like a withered seedling. After a long while, she picked up the hoe and began to till the ridge by the turned-up field.

Dafeng rose a bit after Shoulan. If it were not for her rumbling stomach, she would rather have lain it out and not gone home, since her husband had gone away with someone else. Yet she felt hopelessly hungry. She was big and thus it was easy to get hungry. Dafeng picked up her spade and walked to the eastern edge of the field, half pulling and half dragging the spade behind her. Her ribs were aching from the stabs by Thin Fox. A bone must be broken there, but she did not want to think of Thin Fox, not in the slightest. She thought, "Go home. I am hungry. After doing the cooking, I will come back and sow the seeds and till the ridge of the field." However, when she got to the edge of the field and saw how far from home was this sandy wasteland, she felt a little afraid, and planned in her mind, "Well, I might as well get the work finished, or I might have to make another trip here and back again." She was now too reluctant to come back to this sandy wasteland and turn up the soil repeatedly. Therefore, Dafeng picked up a hoe and began to till the ridge in the turned-up field. With the first hoe into the field, Dafeng felt a fit of pitch dark before her eyes, with her forehead then oozing beads of sweat.

Two women, one on each side, both prepared to sow.

This was the sowing of autumn.

This was the autumn sowing on the sandy wasteland.

(Translated by Zhou Gang)

Weeping Forsythia

Ge Shuiping

Ge Shuiping. She is a member of the Chinese Writers' Association and holds the professional title of "First-ranked Litterateur."

Ge Shuiping writes plays, poetry and prose; and published the poetry collections *The Mermaid and the Sea* and *Women are Water*, and the prose collection *Soul Travel*. She began writing fiction from 2003, and has since produced 23 novellas, most of which have been excerpted by famous national journals and annual anthologies, and garnered much attention in literary circles. Therefore, she is hailed by critics as "a dark horse," "a writer in the Chinese literary limelight," for "her important contribution to Chinese literary circles." She has published the fiction collections, *Mountain Calls*, *Keeping Watch*, *Moon Sinking into the Desert*, and *Coal Scandal*. Her novella *The Sound of a Whip* was selected for the 2004 "Top Contemporary Chinese Literature List" of *Beijing Literature*, and won the 2006 Excellent Fiction Prize for Selected Novella. Her *Weeping Forsythia, Local Climate*, *Black Snowball*, and *Coming Before the Wind* kept her on the Chinese Fiction Society's Top Fiction List for four consecutive years. Her *Mountain Calls* won the 2005 People's Literature Prize, a Selected Stories prize, and the 4th Lu Xun Literary Prize.

Weeping Forsythia

1

Xunhong crushed leaves from the henna blooming in the courtyard between her fingers, the scent of the juice strong.

She sat in the sunshine carefully applying the juice to her fingernails, after which she tightly wrapped each fingertip with a piece of plastic film. She wanted to color her nails red. A girl shouldn't have two plain hands — red nails would look gorgeous, like the motes of gold scattered by the sun, in tiny flecks that now filled Xunhong's heart.

The sunlight appeared high, then low; bright, then dark. Shortly, the sun fell behind the mountains to the west.

Streaks of ruddy clouds alternated with the shadows of night as darkness fell obscuring everything.

Xunhong was eighteen. She had quit school when she reached junior high, and from them on had helped out at home. Her younger brother had to go school and her dad's explanation was, "There's no shortage of people to till the land; but our family is short of people to go to school. It's enough for a girl to be able to do her figures, because sooner or later she is going to marry and move away — so come home and take care of the house."

Her mother sat on a stone slab mending gloves by the light of day. "You're going up into the mountains tomorrow, you'll need good gloves. I have to patch the fingers with fabric; cotton-yarn gloves don't stand wear and tear," she said. "Picking stuff on the mountain is tough work, you have to rely on the strength of the fabric."

After darkness fell, the crickets began chirping at the foot of the wall behind the house, interfering with the sound of her mother's voice. Her mother raised her head and looked at Xunhong sitting in the middle of the courtyard. Having painted her fingernails, Xunhong's hands hung like chicken claws. Her mother tied a knot in the thread after making the last stitch, lifted the glove to her mouth and bit off the thread. She stood up, walked over behind Xunhong and slapped her heavily on the back. "What, are you crazy? The rations for the mountain climb tomorrow aren't ready yet. Your Dad's been working up there picking stuff on the mountain and will be coming back soon. Go and knead the dough for the pancakes."

Xunhong thought that if she could only cover her fingernails all night, they would become red through and through, but there was no way to get a whole night's time. To knead the dough, she'd have to use her hands. Having no other choice, she removed the plastic from her fingernails. Her fingers and her nails were a pale yellow — the color had not yet set. The wind blew, neither fast nor slow. Xunhong heard someone calling from the rear path of the village that led to the mountain. She saw her dad with a plastic woven bag on his back at the head of a group of people approaching gradually. Every one of them looked excited and was swaggering.

The mountain stuff they were after this season was called "green buds," which changed into "yellow petals" after splitting in the dryness of winter. It was a medicinal herb known as "weeping forsythia."

Wang Erhai's tractor-truck went by and stopped at the threshing ground on the riverbank. He leapt down from the driver's seat and rummaged around in the rear, took out his scales, and sat on the side of the truck, his mouth open, watching a long train of heavily burdened harvesters descending the mountain behind the village. Though tired after a day's work, they weren't totally exhausted but holding out, waiting for the money in Wang Erhai's pockets. As they walked, they appeared pretty energetic.

Xunhong concealed her private feelings, her feelings for Wang Erhai. A crow called weightily, flying from the old tree of heaven in the courtyard. Xunhong washed her hands and began kneading the dough. To knead the dough, Xunhong carried the basin to the slab-stone where her mother had been sitting. Her mother had gone to the back of the house to feed the pigs. Kneading the dough, Xunhong watched the scene unfold in the threshing ground across from her; the chatting and joking between young couples amidst the hubbub of voices floated across to her. Xunhong thought how lucky she would be if she could become Wang Erhai's wife. Standing there with him on the truck purchasing "green buds" in the summer and "yellow petals" in the winter, he would handle the scales, and she would write the receipts and pay out money. Her mother yelled at her from behind, "Are you going to knead that lumpy dough until tomorrow morning?"

Xunhong carried the dough inside and placed it on the kneading board. Rolling out the dough, she added some oil, chopped onions, salt, and pounded pepper. The iron griddle was piping hot and when the pancakes were laid on, the aroma rose. Outside, she heard her father say to her mother: "I picked fifity *jin*;* at one yuan and a half per *jin* — that's ten cents more than yesterday, totaling seventy-five yuan."

Looking toward the room, her mother shouted, "Bring the first pancake to your Dad."

Carrying the cake out, Xunhong saw her father stooping over a bucket of water, drinking like an ox. After drinking half a bucket, he looked up and belched a couple of times. He grabbed the onion pancake out of the bowl and took a bite, half of it disappeared.

Her mother decided that they had to get up at the fifth watch to go up the mountain. If later, the entire mountain would be overrun with folks, and they wouldn't get a thing roaming about for a whole day. She and her mother took turns with her father going up the mountain; one day on and one day off. No one could stand going up every day. Daybreak came earlier in the summer. Her mother called for her to get out of bed, and had her put on leggings and high-top tennis shoes, because there were snakes on the mountain slopes. Snakes were usually quiet, but once they struck with their long sharp fangs, they would spit golden venom. Her father was bitten by a snake on the mountain last summer. "The snake was like a black rope slithering lightly past," said her father, "My ankle felt like it had been poked and it soon swelled up and went numb." The villagers cut an incision in his ankle about an inch long and then applied a cupping glass. Her dad screamed like a stuck pig for several days. The villagers all said, "Your Dad was greedy — he wanted that last lush bush and then he was bitten by the snake."

All villagers were greedy when they found something in the mountains they could sell for money!

At the mountain peak, there was a continuous stream of human shadows swaggeringly coming close. They were all mountain people.

---

*Half a kilogram

Even without seeing their faces, everyone knew who was who. Xunhong's mother wanted her to follow her to the opposite ridge. They walked fast and amid the rustling of grass found themselves below a bush. Her mother said, "Do you see it: a huge green clump and so thick, won't that coarsen your hands?"

They started stripping everything from the bush into their bags; mother and daughter worked on the clump until the sun turned a pale pink. A cloud floated over from the horizon, getting ever denser. Her mother said, "The sky doesn't look right; it's going to rain." Xunhong looked up at the sky. It was just a cloud; she didn't see any trace of rain. The sound of thunder rolled in from the distance, decreasing as it came. Then the wind whipped up, blowing through the bushes, helter-skelter like rain. "Break the branches off," said her mother. "Carry them over there under the cliff to get out of the rain. There is lightning coming over the mountain."

Xunhong placed the branches on the ground. Then the rain started falling. Xunhong said, "Mum, let's go."

"Rake mine over; I'm going to pull some more down," said her mother. "When the rain stops, people will probably show up here. The mountain is everyone's — it belongs to whoever finds it. It'll all be gone in a few days, then where will we get money for your little brother to go to school?"

Xunhong hoisted the bag onto her back, grabbed it with her teeth so that it would not slip down, snatched up the broken-off branches of green buds on the ground and ran for the foot of the cliff. There was already someone there seeking shelter from the rain. Through the falling rain, the person at the foot of the cliff shouted, "Xunhong's Mum, don't worry about that little bit! Hurry up, lightning is going to strike."

Xunhong put down the green buds and dropped the bag she held in her mouth. The bag slid off her back and fell under her backside and she sat down on it without taking any extra trouble. She saw her mother running toward her, and like her, she was grasping the bag in her teeth and holding the lush branches of green buds in her arms. The thunder cracked, but it wasn't as turbid or as sticky as that which had just come through the clouds; it was dry and ear-splitting as if a huge detonation cap had been dropped from the sky. Lightning flashed downward and Xunhong watched as her mother went limp like a little bird as her clothes burst into pieces. Her mother looked as if she was going to take flight, but in a moment, the grass had swallowed her up.

Screaming in fear, Xunhong stood up and shouted, "Mum!"

The person under the cliff prevented her from running out. The rain tapered off and the clouds and thunder rolled away. Suddenly the sky turned blue, a vast and startling blue. The clouds passed over the mountain and another mountain. The person under the cliff ran with Xunhong to her mother. She saw that her mother was as white as a sheet of paper, her clothes in tatters, green buds lay scattered all around, and her mother was slumped on the ground like a bird with two broken wings.

On the gradually ascending mountain ridge, under an increasingly oppressive blue sky, Xunhong screamed "Mum!" once more, rending the mute sky.

The sobbing rose in the valley like surging waves and drowned in the sky. The people on the facing mountain saw the accident and ran over, knowing that someone had been struck by lightning. Most of the people looking on were men; the women stood farther off, discussing what had just happened. Someone carried Xunhong's mother back on his back; Xunhong followed with the green buds on her back. They seemed to fly back. The evening before, her mother had climbed upstairs and asked her younger brother to light and offer three sticks of incense to the Bodhisattva. Her mother had mumbled, beseeching the Bodhisattva to let her brother, Xunjun, pass the high school entrance exam, and that the days might pass in peace. But on this day her mother had departed and her brother had gone to the county seat to sit for his exam. She wondered if her mother's death would influence the outcome of the exam. Two streams of bitter tears flowed down her face.

2

Shangpo Junior High was ten kilometers west of Xihuo Village. It was ten kilometers along the riverbank, where the river ran like a trickle of urine. Xunjun was walking. His mother had sewn the three hundred yuan — thirty ten-yuan notes in all — into his shorts the night before. His mother was afraid that if he pulled out all the money when he bought something, thieves would notice, so she told him to take out only one note at a time. The money bumped around in his crotch. He couldn't hold out for one kilometer without going to relieve himself because of the rubbing money. The first time he went, he had to go pretty badly. On a flat stone, he wrote out two characters with urine: "High School." The first character was written unclearly and all he succeeded in doing was to raise some steam off the stone. The steam rose, carrying the scent of urine to his nose, which made him sneeze. He shook off the last few drips of urine, zipped up his shorts, fastened his belt, and continued on his way. He was walking to school to meet his classmates and teacher. Together they would take the afternoon bus to the county seat and sit for the exam the following day. Thinking of the next day, Xunjun grew excited and a little nervous as well. He did not really want to continue school, not only because he was making no progress, but also because it was becoming less interesting. If he did not pass the exam into high school, he would have to pay to go; if he could not get into a good high school, the second-rate ones would demand tuition. Where would the money come from? The poorer his test score, the more the tuition. He felt that everyone in the family had to work day and night just to send him to school. The next time he had to take a leak, he could not produce enough urine to write anything — he could only manage a few dribbles. The sun scorched his head. When he arrived at school, he saw that almost everyone was there already. He saw his quilt folded in a square along with his poplar-wood trunk. He had thought about carrying it all home the previous day, but then figured that if he did not pass the exam, he would have to come back and study again, so he left it all there when he went home.

Huang Guoqing, the Chinese language teacher who was leading the group to the county seat, called him outside saying there was something they had to discuss. He accompanied Teacher Huang outside the school to a shady poplar wood, where they sat down. "Whatever happens, it is your duty to sit for the exam," said Teacher Huang. "Don't think about anything else. For you, the future is the university. Going to university is the only way out of here for village children. Natural disasters may be unavoidable, but you still have to rely on your own efforts."

Xunjun was a little confused as to why Teacher Huang was speaking to him in this way. Normally Teacher Huang never paid much attention to him — he only concerned himself with the few best students. Never had he sat down and talked with him since he had begun junior high school. Staring at his teacher, he did not know what to say in reply. Teacher Huang rubbed his head a couple of times, stood up and said, "Go have lunch."

Xunjun watched as the teacher walked slowly back to the school. While eating, he discovered that everyone was looking at him. He felt a little frightened. Grabbing a classmate, he asked, "Why is everyone looking at me. Is my face dirty?"

"No," replied his classmate.

"Is there something wrong?" asked Xunjun.

"You really don't know?" asked his classmate.

"I don't know," said Xunjun.

"Your mum was struck by lightning," replied his classmate.

Xunjun shook his fist in the face of the other student.

The two started fighting. Teacher Huang ran over, separated them, and asked what was going on. Pointing at the other student, Teacher Huang said, "This is the entrance exam. If it weren't for that, I'd throw you out!"

"His mum was struck by lightning," replied his classmate. "It happened this morning. My uncle said so on the phone."

His uncle lived in Xihuo Village. Xunjun figured what he was saying must be true.

Xunjun threw his bowl at the other boy's back and, without a word, he turned and set off for Xihuo at a run. Behind him Teacher Huang shouted, "Stop! If you don't take the exam, you'll dishonor your dead mother!"

Xunjun kept on running without looking back. The money chafed, but he had not the slightest urge to go to the bathroom. All he could think about as he ran was the curse common among villagers: "If you want to make trouble, may you be struck by lightning."

His mum had been struck by lightning.

When Xunjun got back to Xihuo Village, he saw a number of people standing around the threshing ground. He ran to the ground, where he saw his sister Xunhong dressed in white mourning garb. When his sister saw him, she shouted, "Didn't you go to the county seat to take the exam? What are you doing back?"

Xunjun shouted, "Where's Mum?"

Xunhong did not utter a word; she turned and looked at a grass shed on the threshing ground. According to the village rules, villagers who died violently and suddenly outside the village could not be brought back in. They had to stop at the threshing ground just outside the village. Their mother had not been placed in a coffin — there had been no time to buy wood; she was lying on the grass, covered with a colored quilt. She could hardly be seen; she looked like another blade of grass. But Xunjun could not weep. Suddenly he no longer had the desire to see his mother and even felt that there had been no point in running all the way back from school. He plopped down on the ground and, tilting his head, looked at the mountain opposite. Thin clouds hovered over the peak, spread their wings and leisurely drifted away.

Xunhong walked over and grabbed him, trying to force him to stand up. "Are you crazy?" she yelled. "You didn't take the exam. Why did you come back just to look at the sky? You've dashed Mum's hopes. Why did you come back? Get out of here! If we didn't have to send you to school, she never would have had to work on the slopes gathering mountain stuff; if we didn't have to send you to school, I wouldn't have had to quit school so early. Get back to school. If you don't get going soon, you'll miss the last bus."

Xunjun did not move. His bottom stayed stubbornly glued to the ground and would not be moved regardless of how Xunhong tugged. Xunhong grabbed his hair and tugged. He was forced to stand up on account of the pain. He grabbed Xunhong's hand and pushed her away. His father ran over and hit him on the head and said, "What are you doing here? What is there for you to do here?"

Xunjun stiffened his neck and said, "There's Mum!"

His father replied, "If you don't get moving, you'll miss the exam. If you really have any feelings for your Mum, just go take the test and add some luster to her poor dead face!"

"I'm not going to take the exam!" said Xunjun.

"What do you mean, not take it?" asked his father. "If you don't, it'll be the same as your Dad dying too. Get going right now. If you miss the bus, we'll even rent a car to get you to the exam on time."

Still Xunjun did not budge. He plopped his butt down again. This time his tears started. The sunlight shining on the tears on his face suddenly traced two streams of light. The tears broke the stream and fell, pit-pat, pit-pat. Those watching turned their heads away, away from the light. Heaven also did not open its eyes. One member of a good family had been struck by lightning. Heaven crushes the weak!

After burying their mother, the whole family sat down. They had several matters to discuss. Their father was not a man to run a household, and said very little. As always people got up early to go into the mountains. The mountains close by had all been picked clean. Going to the distant mountains meant going to the mountains in the neighboring county. People started going in groups because they were afraid that they might end up fighting with people from the other county. After all, it was their mountain and taking things worth money would make them see red.

"We don't have anyone with a good education in the family," said their father. "We won't say another word about you missing the exam. You can see that your Mum is no longer here. There's no future if you don't study; with no future, all you can do is come back to Xihuo and farm. Look at Wang Hua's family at the head of the village. One of them passed the exam and got into university. What an honor! Everyone can see how the parents walk around with their heads held high. Out of fifty or sixty kids here in Xihuo Village, only their son has succeeded. One spends their whole life for the next generation. So what's it going to be — do you want to farm or study? You decide; your Mum isn't here to scold you anymore. Your sister's in charge of the house now."

Xunhong looked at her father, then she looked at Xunjun. Her father looked thinner than on that day when he had come back from the mountains, and the hair at his temples was now white. On that day he flew along with long strides, and his face was red in the sunlight. When he handed the money to their mum, she licked her finger and counted each bill. She would then bend over and put the money in the insole of her shoe. Without her mother around, her father had changed. When he spoke every sentence, he would cast a look toward that dark place where her mum used to feed the pigs, her slop scoop clanging against the trough. Xunhong suddenly felt she had grown up quickly. Looking at Xunjun she said, "You have to go to school. You won't be able to get by in the world unless you go to school."

Looking at her, Xunhong's dad said, "Check the vats of rice flour and grain, and go grind anything we are short of. We cannot fall apart because of the death of your Mum; we have to live on. When you're out of money, come and ask me for more. You have to take over all the jobs your Mum did. Xunjun, all you have to do is study. There is no future without studying. Your luck will determine your prospects."

"I'll go up the mountain tomorrow — one day's work is one day's wages," said Xunhong.

"I'll go too," added Xunjun, "I want to see how Heaven struck my Mum with lightning."

"Lightning pities no one," commented Xunhong.

"Someone has to stay and look after the house," interjected their father.

"Xunjun can stay," said Xunhong. "I'll go up the mountain with Dad."

"I'll go with Dad," said Xunjun.

Looking at Xunjun, their father said, "In that case, why don't you go with the others and make bricks for a month?"

It took a long while before their father pulled himself together, and walked over to that dark place to pick up the bucket to mix swill for the pigs. With the gourd ladle, he scooped up some bran into which he mixed boiled vegetable leaves. He banged on the bucket a couple of times and called Xunhong to come and feed the pigs. He said, "It'd be worth it to go make bricks for a month — I've heard one can make a thousand yuan."

Xunhong carried the bucket to the courtyard. She saw Wang Erhai purchasing green buds on the threshing ground outside. She watched for a long time as one person stretched her neck to examine the scales high above. Wang Erhai would bend down so she could get a better look. Xunhong thought that, given his age what he was lacking was someone to hold the scale. Her mother had lain on the ground for several days. During that time Wang Erhai had done his purchasing by the road outside the village without entering it. After her mum died, he even gave them ten yuan as a funeral contribution. He had not been seen for several days since then. Seeing him now she felt a twinge in her heart, an inexplicable twinge. As she fed the pigs, she thought of her mum and of how she was like a bird taken away by the sky. Coming out from behind the house after feeding the pigs, she found that Wang Erhai had already left. She suddenly felt somewhat lost. She looked at the henna growing in the courtyard, and heard those who had sold their green buds walking by their gate saying, "The road into the mountains is getting longer by the day. People are all over the mountain like wild bees — wherever you go you hear people talking and whispering. We'll rest tomorrow."

"Rest."

Xunhong went inside where it had turned dark. She washed her hands and carried a bowl upstairs to ladle out some flour. Her father commented on how tiring it had been dealing with all the business for her mum. He wanted to eat some millet porridge and fried pancakes. Xunhong checked the vats on the second floor — they had millet, rice, beans, and sorghum. Her mother had arranged things so that everything happened without a hitch. The house was filled with food. Her mother had been a good woman. Xunhong could not help but think about how her mum had met her death. Xunhong suddenly felt afraid and had the feeling that her mother's spirit was still walking the house. She still could not believe how her mum had been struck by lightning on what had been mostly a sunny day. After ladling out the flour, she quickly went downstairs, not daring to cast a backward glance. Downstairs, her father yelled at her, "You don't do anything as efficiently as your mother!"

Xunhong told her brother to add some water to the pot on the ground to make porridge; she herself worked the flour to make the fried pancakes.

Her father sighed, "All things are there. The only thing missing is your Mum!"

Their father stood up and made Xunjun move away from the fire. He bent down with a pipe of tobacco and inhaled. The fire made his face even darker and redder. His pipe glowed and faded. They should have turned on the lights, but their father did not want to waste money and waited until it was completely dark outside before turning on the lights. Their mum used to not let anyone turn on the lights, so everyone stood out in the courtyard and ate by the light of the moon. Only just before going to bed would they turn the lights on briefly. The first pancake was ready and Xunhong gave it to her father. He said, "Jun, come and eat, my son."

Xunhong felt that her father's tone of voice was just like that of her mother when she was alive. She wanted to cry. Tears fell from her eyes onto the griddle, giving off a hiss. No one knew that it was Xunhong's tears that hissed and raised steam upon hitting the griddle.

Xunhong carried a bowl of porridge and a pancake to the doorstep, where she sat and ate by the light of the moon. She had the constant feeling of someone coming and going, so she had to shift her legs to one side. If she had done such a thing when her mum was alive, her mum would have slapped her on the back of the head and scolded her, "Young ladies don't sit that way." Xunhong took a bite of her cake and looked at her father. As the smoke rose from his pipe, he said, "Your mother really is gone."

Everything became quiet. The sound of Xunhong slurping her porridge grew quieter too. The darkness under the eaves pressed down, pressed down on the henna, pressed down on the edge of the courtyard. The chirping of crickets was heard rising and falling.

3

Her mum's passing away was a shock striking Xunhong. In a fleeting moment Xunhong had joined the ranks of the mature village women. Each day was full: cooking in the morning, washing the dishes, and after the meal making pigswill with the dishwater, and feeding the pigs. Her dad worked the land. Major autumn crops were not ready for harvesting yet. So he took the short spell to harvest the small scattered plots sown with various grain crops. Cowpea was spread out on the east side of the courtyard, while red millet was piled on the west side. Working between them, Junhong used the handles of hoes and other farming tools to divide them apart. After feeding the pigs, she began to pound the beans. When her father returned from harvesting in the fields, he saw beans scattering all over the courtyard, and said, "You've never had pork? You've never seen a pig walk? Pounding beans, you scatter them all over. Think about how your Mum used to pound them."

Xunhong could not firmly grasp the mallet, as a result of which she developed blisters fairly quickly. She put on gloves to do the pounding. Her father said to her, "No village girl wears gloves to pound beans."

Looking at the scattered beans, Xunhong felt like crying. Turning away in hopes of wiping the tears from her eyes, she saw Xunjun returning home empty-handed from the mountain. "Nothing on the mountain?" she asked.

"Struck out," he replied. "I'm going to make bricks. I've already made arrangements with someone."

"You're not going to study?" asked Xunhong, pounding beans.

"What's the point?" Xunjun replied. "I won't pass the senior high school entrance exam. What's the point of doing the exam only to get into a normal school? I'm afraid I won't even be able to get into a normal school. After graduation, I'd still have to rely on connections to find work. With no work, I'd still have to do odd jobs. It is fate that I was born in a rural village?"

"Plenty of people are born in rural villages, you're not the only one," Xunhong reminded him. "Dad will worry if you don't go to school."

Xunjun didn't say a word. He took the mallet from Xunhong and sat on the ground to pound the beans. Xunhong stood up and looked at the threshing ground by the riverside. The ground was filled with the recently harvested grain. The grain of each household was separated by boards. Xunhong thought how Wang Erhai's truck would not be able to enter the ground. When her mum was alive, she would never let Xunhong sell the green buds, out of fear she'd be cheated by being unable to accurately read the scale. Xunhong thought that the mountain really had been picked clean.

The next day Xunjun left with others to go make bricks. When he left he only told his dad that he was going out to make a month's wages, despite the fact that he had thought about it quite a bit and had not wanted to say anything at all. His dad, also on his way out, calmly reminded Xunjun that he would have to go back to school in a month's time. Xunjun bit his lip and nodded. He left school carrying his bedroll on the bus. All the way during the journey, Xunjun figured that if he started making money away from home, he would never come back. The village was no good. There was no point in coming back. It was too boring. He wouldn't amount to anything by going to school — his ideals were out of touch with reality. He was a man. The family had to make money to send him to school; if it had not been for that, his mum would not even have been struck by lightning on the mountain. His mind was fixed on the future; he set aside everything to do with his family so as not to think about them.

It was nearly harvest time for major autumn crops and school had started already, but no sign of Xunjun's return. His father was so anxious that everything upset him; he just kept pacing back and forth, in and out of the house. His father took the previously cut red millet and milled it. He wanted Xunhong to go into town with some of the others, taking the money from the new crop, and look for her brother at the brick kilns outside of town and ask him why he had not returned to his studies.

When Xunjun saw Xunhong, his heart thumped and he blushed. Standing by the stacks of finished bricks, he took down a few for his sister to sit on.

"Why don't you want to come home and study?" asked Xunhong.

Without a word, Xunjun set some bricks down for himself to sit on. He took out a pack of cigarettes and pulled out one, lit it and took a puff. Seeing the cigarette held between his fingers, Xunhong gave it a slap, knocking it to the ground. "How old are you?" she asked. "Hooked on cigarettes? Where did you get the nerve to start smoking?"

Xunjun realized he had made a mistake. Accustomed as he was to smoking with the other laborers, he had done the same with his sister. He bent over, picked up the cigarette and put it in his pocket. Actually he felt somewhat relieved. Since it was like this, he wanted to speak openly. After all, it wasn't his dad in front of him now. "To tell you the truth, I don't want to study," said Xunjun.

Xunhong stood up, letting the cloth bag for carrying millet fall from under her elbow. It fluttered to the ground like a kite. She kicked it, and then stamped her foot. She felt like crying, but simply scratched the ground with the sole of her shoe. Sitting down, she retrieved the bag and wadded it up in her hands. Pointing a finger at her brother, she asked, "Why is it you don't want to study?"

"My head's not cut out for it, I forget everything right away," replied Xunjun. "I'm not really ambitious. Why didn't they let you study? It's easier to make bricks than to study. I might as well make some money now to support the family rather than wait."

"Was that your idea all along or did you just think of it?" asked Xunhong.

"I just thought of it," replied Xunjun.

"Dad says our family's not short of moneymakers or farmers, but we don't have any book learners," said Xunhong.

Xunhong reached over and pulled the cigarette out from his pocket. Looking at it, she said, "Dad smokes only the fifty-cent cigarettes, but you smoke ones that cost one yuan and fifty."

"None of our ancestors ever served as an official in the city or even as a worker," said Xunhong peevishly as she started to cry. "We're all counting on you; and this is great — halfway along the road you turn around before you've even achieved something."

"It's not that I don't want to study," replied Xunjun. "I thought about finishing high school and taking the college exams, since I detest technical schools, but I'm just not smart enough. I know that if I continue, it would mean throwing good money after bad. If I don't pass the high school entrance exam, it would cost more to pay high school tuition than to pay for college."

Xunhong knitted her brows and wiped her tears away. Her tears and the sweat on her forehead ran down from her temples. The sweat wasn't clear but dirty. Xunjun figured that his older sister had probably been covered with the dust raised by the trucks passing along the highway as she came to sell millet. Xunjun took the wages he had just been paid from his pocket and handed them to Xunhong, who looked away and hit the wad of bills to the ground. "You can make money. If you went to school, you'd make more than by doing this," she said.

Xunjun stooped down and picked up the money. When he stood up, he loosened his belt and removed the safety pin that held his pocket shut. He shoved the money in and replaced the pin. As he cinched up his belt, he felt the need to pee. He stepped behind a row of bricks to relieve himself.

Xunhong heard the sound of peeing. She leaned against the row of bricks and looked off into the distance, where water mixed with mud was dropping from a high-pressure outlet. Someone began placing the mud in the brick molds. If Xunjun did not go to school, he would end up doing that sort of work for the rest of his life.

Looking at her brother, cinching up his belt as he came out from behind the bricks, Xunhong said, "Dad said when he was young, he didn't want to study. After he grew up he wanted to study, but by then it was too late. People with no education always lag behind. If Mum were still alive, everything would be okay. The saying goes, like begets like, and that a child with clever and intelligent parents will do better than a child of dull and stupid ones. We villagers are the same, generation after generation. If you have mind to, just come home and study!"

Xunjun saw someone making bricks in the distance look in his direction and felt a little angry. "No, I'm not going to study," he said. "I'm not going home. You go home. You'll get married soon, so don't bother me!"

"You, if you've got a backbone, then don't come home," said Xunhong, standing up. "Even if a little boy who doesn't want to study is able to get to the city, all he will do is to carry mud and bricks."

Xunjun thought that, even if his mum were alive, he still would not have gone to school. The whole family was struggling to send him to school. If it had not been for that, his mum would not have been struck by lightning. All the villagers hoped their children would have a good future. But how many really did? More than half the village kids were not going to school — they had run off to the city to work as laborers on public projects or to get into some other sideline. Even the ones who did study never got anything for it in the end, but always came back to the village and picked up the hoe again.

Xunjun was about smoke a cigarette, when he looked at Xunhong and caught her threatening glare. He had no reason to look at her any further, and told her to catch the bus in the city, otherwise she would miss it. "See those people looking this way. They must wonder who you are!"

Xunhong looked at the sky and pursed her mouth. She felt like crying. She stood up and hurried off without so much as a backward glance, but did say, "You'll be sorry one day."

The harvest of major autumn crops began in earnest. Without their mother around, it was as if their father was missing an arm, in the house and outside. He did not seem to know where to store the grain. In the past, their mum would clean the upstairs and then, depending on what sort of grain, tell their dad where to carry it to and direct him where to store it. Rain was not a problem for the corn so it was stored in the courtyard in long woven grain bins. After the ears were braided, they would be hung from poles under the eaves. When Xunhong hung the ears of corn, many fell because they had not been tied properly. Her dad would slap her on the head. She wondered why her dad and her mum had both seemed to consider her an outsider. Her dad told her to pull up the henna growing in the courtyard because he wanted to put the corn there. Xunhong was not really pleased to uproot the boxy henna plants. They would bloom again in late autumn and Xunhong still wanted to dye her fingernails red. Seeing her lack of enthusiasm, her dad walked over and pulled everything up in a matter of seconds, discarding it by the edge of the courtyard. Without saying a word, Xunhong rushed inside and cut her nails way back. She could not say whom she was angry with; she just felt a girl needed time to herself. She was slowly becoming like her mother.

After autumn had passed, a matchmaker arrived to announce that Wang Erhai of Xiapo Village wanted to marry Xunhong. Hearing the news, her heart was all aflutter. She did like Wang Erhai. Her father, however, turned the matchmaker down, saying that Xunhong's mum had just died and her brother was still young. Even if he was not going to school, a new house would still have to be built and the other families had begun to apply for deeds to build new houses for their young sons. Her brother Xunjun would be old enough to marry in two or three years, and a new house would have to be built even if his mum was not around. Without the new house, there would be no way to find a wife for him. His older sister would have to take on his mum's responsibilities. After all, a girl, good or bad, could always be married off sooner or later.

Xunhong saw the matchmaker out of the village. "What your father said is right," said the matchmaker. "Village girls usually marry at eighteen or nineteen. If you were to marry now, that would leave only your Dad. Tell me what a household run only by a man who'd have to work in the fields and in the kitchen would be like. Tell me, if it isn't done right, then there'll be two unmarried men. Just wait until the house is built, then consider your own marriage. You're still young and you won't miss your chance. A girl never worries about finding a husband, right?"

Xunhong felt that these words were directed at her. She was too embarrassed to say anything, so she held her tongue for a while. Seeing that the matchmaker was leaving, she ran a few steps and tugged at him, saying, "Uncle, could you ask Wang Erhai if he'll wait for me for a few years? Even just a year."

"We'll see," said the matchmaker, pausing. "The family has only one son and they're short of hands and furthermore, they do a purchasing business — there's a pressing need for more help."

Xunhong did not know what else to say. The matchmaker turned his back to the wind and lit a cigarette. Looking at Xunhong, he said, "Go on home. It's windy."

On her way home, Xunhong thought about Wang Erhai, about how good he was in every way, and even though he was not tall, he was just right. If a man was too tall, you would have to spend more money on cloth to make clothes. Her heart called out to Wang Erhai, Wang Erhai. She felt she wanted to write him a letter. Before she could even get a sheet of paper on arriving home, her dad told her to store the grain in the courtyard and move out the old grain stored in the wooden bin upstairs, grind it and then sell it as new grain when a buyer came along. After storing and grinding the grain, she had to make supper. They had to go on living in a normal fashion, even if her mum was no longer around. When her mum was alive, they never used to eat later than other people. Her dad used to take his dinner close to the neighbor's courtyard. Those eating always got together to exchange the latest news from all sources. For second helpings, her mother would come to fetch his bowl and bring it back again filled with rice. Only after it got dark did her dad come home tapping his bowl, humming a tune. Her mother would hear his footsteps as he approached the door, and only then would she turn on the light — the bulbs always lot wattage. By that time, under the moonlight, her mother had cleaned up everything on the kitchen range. Xunhong now learned her mum's way of washing dishes and feeding the pigs by moonlight. After an exhausting day's work, Xunhong did not have the energy to think about Wang Erhai. She closed her eyes and was soon sound asleep.

Xunhong woke up around midnight, thinking of her mother and not daring to get up. She closed her eyes and listened to the sound of the darkness surrounding the village. She did not know what was making the noise. The vast darkness oppressed her; she dared not make a sound or go to the bathroom. Even her breathing became dark. It seemed as if daybreak would never come. Xunhong buried her head under the quilt. She seemed to sense her mother's shadow moving vaguely around her and felt as if she was going to suffocate. She drifted off to sleep and dreamed of looking everywhere for a toilet. While it was still dark, she heard her dad get up, throw on his clothes and sit by the stove, smoking a pipe. He didn't like cigarettes and found only a pipe would satisfy his craving. As he smoked, he coughed. He seemed to have some phlegm caught in his throat; it seemed to move up and down when he coughed, sounding very unpleasant to the ears. When she thought the phlegm was on the point of coming up, it stayed in his throat. She thought her father wanted to cough it up, but there it stayed without moving. After getting up, Xunhong went to the bathroom. The corn piled up in the courtyard seemed to have been split apart by the dawn. The half of the corn in the light bulged out of the woven bins; in the dark half was a hoe, looking much like a person standing there. At the same time she could see the village road disappearing into the darkness. Xunhong thought that it would be great if a person could just follow that road and leave the village behind. Then she heard her father shout from inside, "Let the pigs out. You should be making breakfast. There's a mountain of things waiting to be done — the field stubble hasn't been dug under yet. After breakfast, go and pick the kidney beans — they can be sold for cash."

At the edge of the courtyard, Xunhong took a deep breath. It was nearly dawn and the air was filled with dust and mist, coloring it a reddish yellow. The air seemed dense, enough to fill you up. She watched as her father shouldered his hoe and set off for the fields, as men and beasts started to stir another day. Her father always had his hopes. Even if her brother didn't go to school, he still had plans to build a house for him. If her mother were alive, he would consult with her; now that she was gone, her father kept everything to himself and mulled things over. Her father was a man with ideas, but when would he think of her?

4

Xunhong worked all through the autumn at home and in the fields. The work was never done. She kept, under the stairways, a pair of pumps she wanted to wear and show off, but never found the opportunity. She scrubbed the pots, washed the dishes, and fed the pigs; exposed to the autumn wind, her rough hands began to crack and her fingernails became short and thick. Handling the coal for the stove made her fingers black and she no longer looked at them. Coloring such fingernails would just look ugly. She felt her hands beginning to resemble ever more her mother's hands. When her father saw her several times looking at her hands absentmindedly, he said, "In winter, I'll go up the mountain and collect the yellow petals of forsythia. You can take down the corn; when the price is good, sell it. Next spring we have to get the title deed — if we don't build it everyone will laugh."

Two bins of corn sat in the courtyard out of the sun. Xunhong's hands would be raw all winter by removing the grains of corn from the ears. Yet a person had to live day by day. She tried to think of how energetic her mum was she was alive, but could in no way get motivated. She was born into this family, but it wasn't permanent — she couldn't imagine where she would be living in the future and where her home would be.

At the beginning of winter, people started patching their gloves again. The weeping forsythia that had formed seeds in the fall turned into yellow petals, and dry, they were worth more than those in the summer. It had been a while since she had last seen Wang Erhai. Toward evening, she saw exhaust rising from his tractor-truck, which was parked by the threshing ground. Xunhong was a bit excited. While waiting for everyone to come back from the mountain, she wrote a letter to Wang Erhai. She wondered where to begin and after a couple of false starts, she finally wrote:

Wang Erhai,

Autumn has given way to winter. Do you still remember in autumn Uncle Laicheng from Xiapo Village came as a matchmaker for you. But you know because my Mum died we are short of hands at home so my Dad turned him down. Actually, I'm willing. If you can wait till next year after my Dad builds a house for my brother, then I can marry you. Wait for me and I'll be yours sooner or later.

Having written to this point, she wondered how best to end the letter. While she was thinking, she decided to take another look outside and see what he was doing. If he was thirsty, he knew to come to her for water. What else was there to think of? Thinking that she hadn't put on her pumps, she went to get them from under the stairway. She tried to put them on only to discover that the ground moisture had disfigured her shoes and left them spotted with mold. There was no way she could wear them; momentarily disheartened, she stood in the doorway gazing at the threshing ground by the river. As she looked, she grew alarmed: there was a girl sitting and talking with Wang Erhai on the side of the truck, waiting for the people to come down the mountain and sell their goods. She saw how affectionately they spoke to one another, and, at a particularly happy juncture, the girl raised her hand and slapped him playfully on the head. Wang Erhai pulled his head back and laughing, tumbled from the truck. Xunhong stepped outside and walked to the edge of the courtyard, and the letter she had been writing became wet with perspiration from the palm of her hand. She crumpled the limp paper into a ball. She could clearly make out that the girl was Bi Xiaohong from Bi Fugui's family, living in the village across the lower rapids of river. She never expected to see Bi Xiaohong, daring as she was, sitting with Wang Eihai. Then she heard the aunt from next door come out to the courtyard to pour out dirty water, as she asked her, "Hong, what are you looking at?"

Embarrassed, Xunhong laughed and clenched the paper tightly in her fist, and said, "I'm looking to see if my Dad's returned or not. Those who went to pick yellow petals are all back. The guy who buys yellow petals is already here."

"Look at Wang Erhai," said the aunt from next door, "He's a good young lad from a nice family. In the early days of the autumn the matchmaker Laicheng wanted to make a match of you two, but your Dad wanted to keep you till you're a little older before allowing you to marry. Then Laicheng went and matched the second daughter of the Bi family in Xiapo Village to Wang Erhai. To judge by appearances, she is not as pretty as you. But fate is on her side.

Look at that little tease. Goodness, what a spectacle. What a girl, we never know what wind blows by which door. Take a look! It looks like her seat is on fire. She can't sit still for a minute."

The aunt next door took another look and twisted her mouth to spit. She turned to walk away, and straightened her shoulders as if to say to Xunhong, "Who cares about her? She is too crazy for Xihuo Village."

Xunhong felt that her sweaty palms had been blown dry by the wind and her back felt cold. She twisted the letter in her fist, but felt unsatisfied, so she walked behind the house and threw it into the pigpen. Thinking they were being fed, the pigs rushed over to the trough, but saw they had been deceived when she turned and left. Harvested ears of corn were piled in the courtyard. She sat down on a bench, and from under the bench she set up the post, pointing up. She took an ear of corn and reamed it from the base, and with a twist of her hands the kernels fell onto the flagstones. It would take her two months to do the two piles, after which her hands would be covered with blisters and calluses. Her dad wanted her to shell the corn, grind it, and sell it. They planted corn to sell it and make money. Her dad said they could make five thousand on corn for the year. Only by farming the whole year would they not lose money.

The days were pretty much the same as always, but Xunhong now felt something was missing. It had been that sound that often filled the emptiness — the sound of Wang Erhai's truck when started at dusk. Off in the distance, she could see Bi Xiaohong was standing on the truck bed, holding the scales as if she were his wife already. Xunhong felt that she should have been standing there; the one standing there now was like her, but not her. Seeing others smile, she could not smile. She felt sad. Night fell early in winter so her dad could not see the sadness on her face. She hated Bi Xiaohong, and sometimes when they ran into each other she would pretend not to see her and walk away. If they really ran into each other, she would smile first and smile until it hurt, just so as not to let others know how she really felt, but that smile came through such suffering.

With days of freezing weather, brick making was put on hold. In the county seat, Xunjun ran into Wang Erhai, who was in his truck after making a delivery to the Chinese medicine factory. Wang Erhai was heading back to the village and told Xunjun to climb aboard. There were several cases of beer in the truck, which Wang had picked up for a consignment store in his village. They ran into a number of villagers along the way who had been out selling or buying grain. The villagers would all say, "Hey, Erhai, let me rest my feet. Give me a ride."

"Climb on," Wang Erhai would say in his dog-skin cap.

He would not stop the truck for fear of a traffic cop coming along — he hadn't paid his road-maintenance tax. The walkers would have to quickly grab the side of the truck and climb up, while the people in the truck would help pull them on. By the time they had left the county seat, there were more than a dozen people in the truck. The truck swayed and the men and women were bumped around. One would shout that someone was stepping on his foot and to step a little more lightly. The other would shout that if they didn't stand close together, the cold wind would get in. Everyone in the truck laughed. Someone saw a motorcyclist with a passenger on the back from Shangpo Village, gaining on them from behind. He followed the truck wanting to pass but couldn't, and as a result had to eat a lot of dust.

Someone shouted, "He's carrying a woman on the back — it's his intended. They're getting married just before the Spring Festival.

He took his fiancée to the county seat to buy clothes. Now they're covered with dust — don't let them pass! We'll watch the fun and games all the way. We want to make him happy, completely happy. Let's have some fun with them before they marry."

Originally, Xunjun had been sitting in the middle of the group. Hearing this, he pushed his way to the edge and stuck his head over the side for a look. The man was wearing a large yellowish overcoat and dark glasses and a hat with earmuffs. The cold wind had turned his face the color of pig liver. The woman sitting on the back had her arms around his waist, her head to one side. The billowing dust from the road had turned her pale blue overcoat a brownish color. Anyone who wanted to avoid the dust would have pulled their head back, but she kept looking ahead. Discolored by the dust, her red scarf looked pretty ratty. They all wanted to see the girl's face, but the red scarf covered her face and a thin layer of frost formed around her nose. No one could tell what she looked like.

Someone said they had seen the girl and that her figure wasn't bad but her teeth weren't so neat.

Someone else added that, when getting engaged, she demanded that the boy's family take her to the city and have porcelain teeth made so that she'd have a mouthful of lovely white teeth.

Pursing her lips to keep the cold air from entering her mouth, one woman said, "Goodness, what sort of society are we living in!"

The man accelerated, trying to pass the truck. The people in the truck all shouted, "Don't let him pass; block him. He likes to show off his fiancée, he has to give us cigarettes; if he doesn't, don't let him pass!"

Everyone on the truck grew excited and struggled to get a look behind. Wang Erhai also grew a bit excited, as the clear snot kept running out of his nose and he had to frequently blow it away, while focusing on driving on the twisting mountain road. The people in the truck all said, "How can it snow on such a sunny day?"

"It's Wang Erhai's snot," replied one of the passengers.

Everyone started laughing. One of them shouted to the motorcycle that, if he didn't like the dust, he had to toss them two packs of cigarettes. The motorcyclist turned his head to speak to the woman behind him. She couldn't hear what he was saying so she leaned forward and seemed to climb on his back. Someone on the truck shouted, "You two kiss each other, that'll be okay too."

The woman settled herself again on the seat and took something from her bag. The motorcyclist accelerated again. Ahead the slope got steeper, and the truck was no match for the motorcycle. All that could be heard was its "putt-putt," and soon the motorcycle was passing. As the motorcycle picked up speed, two packs of cigarettes were tossed into the truck.

As the truck reached the top, they saw that the motorcycle was already halfway down the slope. The men, who were still a bit excited, lit their cigarettes and looked ahead in the distance. Xunjun wanted a cigarette, too. One of the people laughed and asked, "Anyone learn anything by going out in the world? Do you know what getting married means doing?" Xunjun's face flushed immediately. The women on the truck slapped the guy who had asked the question and said, "You're all immature. Getting married is to give birth to the likes of you!"

Everyone on the truck laughed. One guy lit a cigarette and placed it in Wang Erhai's lips. The motorcycle had stopped for some reason up ahead. Once again the people began shouting, "Hurry up, catch up with him, and make him give us two more packs of cigarettes." They were going downhill now, so Wang Erhai cut the engine and let the truck coast to save gas. As the truck was coasting, it hit a wet spot in the shadows that had turned to ice and, since no precautions had been taken, it began to skid. The women on the truck let out a collective scream. Out of control, the truck slid into a ditch.

Wang Erhai was injured in the accident and knocked unconscious; Xunjun was also injured — both his legs crushed. Everyone else suffered only minor injuries, such as cuts and abrasions.

Xunhong had never seen his father cry. The moment his dad saw Xunjun, he didn't choke out a sob, but rather screamed, "Son, just let your Dad take your place!"

The mountain echoed his father's scream, startling the cadres from the township government. As he knelt, embracing his son, his tears flowed like a river, wetting his clothes.

Their father was truly grieved. He cried and protested, "Disasters don't come singly. Who'd have expected a disaster of such magnitude? First your Mum died, to whom was there to complain? People say every wrong has its cause; every debt has its debtor, struck by lightning leaving some thunder, but nothing you can touch or see. Who can you reason with? Poor in life, suffering in death! Old Man in Heaven, open your eyes. You hurt me once and now you send a second misfortune. Who did my son offend? A whole truckload of people rolls into a ditch and you take both his feet; you have no pity and had to take them both. You didn't even leave him even one foot. I f--- your ancestors for eight generations and another eight generations! Huo Cuiping, up there in Heaven, you can't even protect our only son. No wonder Heaven struck you with lightning. Let Heaven strike your dead soul with lightning again!"

People were very pained hearing this. Xunhong listened, as her father started by crying about the accident and ending by cursing her mother, and could not help crying as well. When Wang Erhai's parents came to join the crying, Xunhong's wailing only grew louder. Finally, a car from the township arrived and set off for the hospital. Xunhong saw that Wang Erhai's face was as white as a sheet. Her brother's face was also very pale. She began to fear that the two of them would depart like her mother. Her heart began to thump, and she felt that life was pointless. Death came suddenly and that was the end. A thought of Bi Xiaohong flashed in her mind for just a moment and vanished. She asked her brother to pinch her hand. He began to moan and dug his nails into her flesh. She gritted her teeth. She would have willingly given her hand to relieve his pain.

In the hospital, her father trembled as he took out the four thousand yuan made by selling corn to pay for treatment. As her brother's condition stabilized, her father felt that he was in a hole. Why should he be paying out his own money? His good son hadn't gone in the ditch on his own — it was the person driving the truck. Wang Erhai should pay. Wang Erhai had passed out and so far not regained consciousness. When her father saw Wang Erhai's father, he said, "When your son comes to, we have reason to talk."

Wang Erhai's father had been a driver before he opened a garage. He was stout, dark, and coarse of speech. Looking at Xunhong's father he said, "We have to talk, if there is a reason."

Being angry did not mean there was no reason. Xunhong's father walked over feeling something was wrong. What he had said was clear to him. Now he grew worried at the possibility that Wang Erhai might not regain consciousness. He said, "My son didn't drive himself into the ditch, did he?"

Wang Erhai's father was on his way back to the hospital room when he heard the spiteful words. He turned with hands on his hips and said, "If my son hadn't given a ride to so many people, the car wouldn't have lost control and gone into the ditch."

Hearing this, Xunhong's father saw they each had their way of looking at the situation. He pointed at Wang Erhai's father and said, "My son lost his feet. He didn't lose them for nothing. If he lost one I wouldn't ask for a pair in return."

Not wanting to appear weak, Wang Erhai's father pointed his finger and said, "No wonder your wife was struck by lightning — you have bad intentions."

Xunhong's father was furious. He was never happy when someone exposed his shortcomings. He could curse his wife in such circumstances, but no one else could speak to him like that — it was tantamount to slapping him in the face. Those were fighting words. He threw the first punch, but Wang Erhai's father was ready and parried the blow; before the second had been thrown, they were tussling together. The people tending the patients dropped what they were doing to watch. The doctors and the nurses all came to gawk, after hearing people fighting in the hallway. Xunhong rushed out and the first person she saw wasn't the people fighting but Bi Xiaohong among the crowd. She stood on tiptoe to take a look and then turned and went back to the hospital ward. Xunhong thought that Bi Xiaohong was a kindhearted person. She had come to watch over Wang Erhai.

The hospital security guards pulled the two fighters on the ground apart. Xunhong pressed forward and could see that the whitewash from the walls was smeared on her father's face and on Wang Erhai's dad as well. Blue veins stood out on both men's necks as both returned to their separate sickrooms as ordered by the person in charge of the hospital, although somewhat unwillingly. They both said, "Just wait, you bastard."

Xunhong didn't know what to do to comfort her father. All she said was, "Dad."

Her father's temper found a new outlet. When he saw Xunhong, he said, "Instead of scratching the bastard a couple of times for your Dad, all you can do is stand there and say, 'Dad'."

Xunhong said nothing. She didn't know how she could go scratch anyone. She was just a girl who still lived at home. How could she go fight with someone? She poured out some water, moistened a washcloth and handed it to her father. Her father looked at his hands covered with white dust. He suddenly raised a hand and struck himself in the face. His action stunned everyone in the room. Speaking to the people in the sickroom, he said, "Could I be called a human being when someone hit me in the face?"

The people in the sickroom tried to comfort him by saying, "Every family has unexpected misfortune. As long as you live, there's always something. Life would be pretty boring without its troubles. Anyway, you still have a good daughter."

Her father threw a glance at Xunhong. At first he wanted to say that a girl wasn't the ridgepole of a family. Thinking better of it, he said nothing. He also felt saying such a thing lacked class.

Xunjun was on the mend. One foot was a stump, while the other was missing its toes; and he had to walk using two crutches. Looking at his two feet, Xunjun wept, depressed. Watching him weep, Xunhong felt pain at first. Then when she saw how her brother cried all the time, she couldn't help saying, "We wanted you to go to school, but you wouldn't go. Now look at how you've ended up."

Xunjun took the cup from the table at the head of the bed and hurled it at Xunhong's head. Xunhong bent down and picked it up and, looking at Xunjun, said, "If that settles things, then throw it again. Don't look at me as if I'm not a member of this family. This family has to count on me now and will rely on me in the future!"

Xunjun looked out the window without saying a word. His father also looked out the window. Their dad said, "It's the end of the year. Your auntie has been watching the house, but she has to go home for Spring Festival. We'll have to leave the hospital. Regardless of how much trouble it is, we still have to celebrate the Spring Festival."

They had grown familiar with the staff and patients at the hospital. The person in the next ward wanted to hire Xunhong as a housekeeper. He first asked if she was willing. She replied, "I can't make that decision. Ask my father."

When he asked Xunhong's father, he thought about it for a long time. Xunjun wasn't on his feet yet and they were short of hands at home, so they could not let her go. He shook his head and said, "Sorry but she can't go, there's no one at home."

That man said, "I'll pay high wages and I can also get Xunjun a disability card, which will allow him to get money from the state."

Uncertain, Xunhong's father asked him what he did for a living.

"I'm a civil servant working for the county government," the man replied.

"Why are you in the hospital?" asked Xunjun's father.

"To tell you the truth, as soon as one becomes well off, one gets sick," the man replied. "I've got a fatty liver, high blood pressure, diabetes, all diseases of the rich and prosperous. I get transfusions twice a year."

"That's expensive," remarked Xunhong's father.

"I have medical insurance," he replied.

Xunhong's father also did not know what a civil servant or medical insurance was. He figured that since he was in the county government, he surely had power, so he asked if a driver had to pay for his passenger's injuries if he drove into a ditch.

"That depends on the circumstances," the man said. "In most cases, the driver would have to compensate for injuries, but it depends on whether or not the party is able to compensate."

Xunhong's father immediately handed the man a cigarette. As he took out some matches, the man said, "Smoking is not allowed in hospital rooms."

"Put it behind your ear and smoke it when you go out," said Xunhong's dad.

The man refused with thanks, saying, "Tell me about your son's case."

"The guy who was driving the truck is still alive and is here in the hospital," said Xunhong's father. "I hear he is going to be sent to a hospital in the city after Spring Festival. He was injured pretty badly too and doesn't recognize anyone. He just stares wide-eyed at the ceiling."

"Then it's hard to say," he replied. "Getting anything by law will be difficult. For example, if the other party was driving without a license or was carrying passengers illegally in a cargo truck, even if the court awarded damages, the sentence would be difficult to enforce because he's in a sort of coma. People win lots of empty decisions in court. It's hard for a farmer to sue in court, and abiding by the court is hard too! If no one has any money, how are they supposed to compensate?"

"So you mean, I should be a mute victim?" asked Xunhong's father. "You mean, I should go broke paying for my son's hospital expenses?"

Patting Xunhong's father on the shoulder, he replied, "It's a big country and people are poor."

Suddenly Xunhong's father's eyes brightened. "Leader, will you help me if I let my daughter be your housekeeper? Help me get my own back."

"My name is Du," said the man. "It's hard to say if I can be of much help, but I'll certainly do what I can for you — not as an exchange, but because I think Xunhong is a diligent, good-tempered girl. If you let her come, then later if there is anything to be done we'll know each other and I'll be able to help. Let's be realistic here."

So it was settled for Xunhong. She would go home first and after the Spring Festival, she would work as housekeeper in Du's family. Actually, she would just be keeping an old woman company, because all of that woman's children were working and they needed someone to look after her and make sure she was fed, and inform her children if she got sick. Xunhong visited the woman's house with her father. The house was in the city, not out in the county seat. It was only half an hour away by bus. After she figured out the place and met the old woman, it was settled she would start work after the lunar New Year.

Before leaving, Xunhong stole off to visit Wang Erhai. His dad was already back in the village, and his mum was looking after him at the hospital. Wang Erhai was lying in bed looking up. A bottle of intravenous fluid was hanging there. Looking at her son, who was staring straight ahead, eyes wide open, his mother kept wiping away her tears. "Auntie, how are things?" called out Xunhong.

"That's the way he is — he's alive but doesn't know anything," replied Wang Erhai's mother.

"Has Bi Xiaohong been here?" asked Xunhong.

"She was here once, looked around, and hasn't been back since," said Wang Erhai's mum. "The wedding was set for this month and everything was prepared when the accident happened. With my son this way, unable to open his mouth, everything is off I'm afraid."

"He'll get well one day and everything will be fine," said Xunhong.

"If only everything could be okay," said Wang Erhai's mother. "Everything is bad now. The Old Man in Heaven just lets you work hard and struggle along from birth to death, in prosperity or poverty. Is there any reason for any of it? He's my only son. After the accident, everything in the house has changed. Nothing has any meaning and I'm not in the mood for anything. He's my only son."

Seeing her cry, Xunhong felt a pang and said, "Just take care of him and he'll recover in good time."

"Do I have any other choice?" she said. "The sky won't turn dark before evening no matter how anxious one is."

After Xunhong left, she thought of how Wang Erhai used to honk at folks he knew when he drove through the village. The sound of his horn was so spirited, so unlike her dad who, when he met someone, acted like an awkward villager. She thought about how she had wanted to marry him. If things had turned out, she would have spent her whole life with him, and that would have been a disaster. She felt fortunate that things hadn't proceeded. She started feeling sorry for Bi Xiaohong. Thinking that she would soon be moving to the city to work as a housekeeper, she felt happy. She wasn't responsible for Wang Erhai, but for her brother. Wang Erhai was Bi Xiaohong's responsibility.

5

After the lunar New Year, Mr. Du called on the eighth day of the first lunar month, and said that a car would come to pick her up. A box-like sedan did arrive the very next day. Xunhong had packed two bags of things to take with her, but they told her that anything she needed was available in the city and that there was no need to take anything. They even brought a wheelchair for Xunjun. Xunjun tried it out by sitting in it and turning the wheels with his hands, but he couldn't get the hang of it enough to control the direction. After going a short distance, his face was red and his hair was dripping with sweat. His dad laughed, mouth open, spraying stale saliva. Mr. Du found that the simple and unaffected villagers were easily moved by anything. He saw they were so happy to see a wheelchair, yet had no idea how painful it was to spend one's life in one. They didn't think too far ahead and were easily moved by a little good fortune. Mr. Du was moved too. He thrust out his beer belly and started laughing. Xunhong was busy looking for bags, big and small, in which to put new millet, corn, soybeans, and string them together. Just before everything was ready, a car from town suddenly appeared in the village. The car was not as good as Mr. Du's and was heading directly for Xunhong's home. The villagers felt it unusual — never in their lives had they seen a town cadre come to Xunhong's home, one having not so much as glanced before at her house when passing by. The sudden appearance of the cadres indicated that the visitor at Xunhong's home was a very important figure. The people who got out of the car looked at Mr. Du, who was laughing, his belly thrust forward. It was the town head and his deputy. They bowed right away, walking over with their hands outstretched. But Mr. Du didn't reciprocate by bowing or offering his hand, nor did he shake their hands, but instead only lifted his hand a bit to express his courtesy. He was not enthusiastic about shaking hands with them, and murmured, "Aaah," nodding his head to end the welcome greetings of the newcomers.

The town head and his deputy wanted to say something but did not seem quite to know what. The town head finally found his tongue and said, "Director Du, we are here to see Xunjun who left the hospital. You should have told us you were coming. Just give us a word and we will see to anything for you — you really don't have to trouble yourself by coming all the way to Xihuo."

Mr. Du laughed as he watched Xunjun turn, telling him to apply one hand when making a turn, while leaving the other loose. A firm grasp on the wheel would make turning easier. Without looking at the town head and his assistant, Mr. Du looked at Xunjun's wheels and said, "How did you know I was here? News travels fast."

"Yes, we heard you were here, but a little late," said the town head. "Why did you not stop by in town? We were in our office, doing our duty, even on the first lunar month of the new year. Even during holidays we have to hold fast to our post."

Mr. Du said, "I came here on personal business; it has nothing to do with work. It is Spring Festival and I don't want to put anybody else to trouble."

"You shouldn't overlook us when passing through," said the town head. "We don't consider it trouble. Return with us to town to show a little respect for our feelings. We'd be flattered if you came to see us."

Mr. Du did not reply. He only looked at Xunhong and said, "Ready? Bid farewell to your brother and father. We should be going now."

Hearing this, she suddenly felt loathe to leave home. In the past, as soon as she looked down the village road, she would wonder when she would ever be able to walk out of there. Now she was confused and uneasy at the prospect of actually leaving home. After she left, how would her dad and her brother get along? One was old and the other was young, both had to do everything in the home and outside. Xunhong went upstairs where she bowed to her mother's memorial tablet. Lifting her head, she saw her mum's photograph in which she was young and smiling. Xunhong remembered her mum as always nagging; she never once saw her smile so splendidly. Hearing the talking and laughter of the people outside who had come to see the wheelchair, she wondered what she could contribute to this home; she thought of her mum's presence when she was living; she was no longer scared, even though her mum was no longer alive, since as long as her shadow was there, her dad would have strength in his heart. Her dad often said, "Your Mum gave me a son and a daughter, and left before she could enjoy a life of ease and comfort. If your Mum were still alive, this home would look different." What kind of look? Xunhong thought again of Wang Erhai. If her Mum were still alive, she would probably be Wang Erhai's wife now.

She went downstairs to get in the car. Mr. Du opened the door for her to sit in the front seat, usually reserved for the leader. The villagers immediately felt that the girl would not be back nearly as quickly as she left — she had connections in high places. From her seat, she looked at her dad and brother outside the window. Her dad knocked on the window trying to say something to her, but she couldn't hear anything. Inside the car, Xunhong shouted, "Don't forget to prepare food for the pigs. When Mum was alive, the pigs ate one basket; now that they have grown, they eat two baskets."

The car drove away and did not stop in town. Mr. Du told the driver, "Give a honk to show our greetings. These people are such a bother!" Xunhong watched the town head and his deputy standing by the roadside wave and smile. In a flash the car passed the smiling people outside.

Xunhong was taken to the city and moved into the old woman's home. Before leaving, Mr. Du called Xunhong to the balcony outside the kitchen and told her, "My mother is not very demanding, but cleanliness is an issue. You must wash your hands constantly, and if she tells you to wash your hands, do as you are told. Otherwise she is easy to handle." Xunhong repeated to herself, "Wash my hands. I must pay attention to cleanliness." She nodded in assent. After getting her settled, Mr. Du went back to the county by car. Xunhong then understood that Mr. Du was the director of organizational department of the CPC county committee, in charge of checking up on and promoting cadres in the county. There being no cadres in her family, she didn't see Mr. Du as a leader; however, she felt that his walk was different from that of other people, as were his gestures and speech. It was hard to explain, but they were dynamic and had style. Xunhong felt that things would be easy and comfortable for her working in Director Du's family — even the town head dared not look down on her. Then she looked at it from a different angle — she was just a housekeeper, that's all. If she had been someone else's housekeeper, someone who did not supervise cadres, she would still be a nobody, still a girl from Xihuo Village. It was her job to keep the house tidy and clean, help the old woman change and wash her clothes, buy groceries and cook. The shopping money was on the tea table in the living room. The old woman did not socialize with Xunhong, but only told her what had to be done. When she needed her she would call her. When Xunhong finished any task, the old woman would repeatedly remind her to wash her hands. Xunhong did not know that it was an illness, an obsessive-compulsive disorder known as mysophobia. Sometimes, the old woman would stare at her for a long time and then tell her to wash her hands. After Xunhong returned from washing her hands, the old woman would take a piece of candy from her pocket and give it to her. Some of her movements were very strange — on account of age, her hands and head shook constantly. Xunhong called her "*Nainai*" and she was unhappy for most of the day, and said, "Am I old? Why do you call me Grandma?"

Xunhong did not know how to address her, not wanting to follow the village rule of calling her "*Shen*" for paternal aunt. She thought and thought, and finally decided to copy a TV show and call her "*Ayi*" or Auntie. The old woman was not entirely satisfied but nodded her head as a sign of approval.

Xunhong was allowed to have ample free time in the afternoon. She took walks all over the neighborhood, and memorized the street names in the vicinity. She saw many villagers coming into the city to set up small businesses, and became familiar with some of them. She listened to them talk about the woman cobbler across the street. She was from Wenzhou, and suffered a great deal because she had lost one leg in a traffic accident. Each day she came to repair shoes in her wheelchair. Every day, rain or shine, she was there on time and she was very nice to everyone. She had a family of four. Her husband was confined to bed with an illness all year around, so the whole family depended on her. She had sent her two daughters to college, both graduating and getting jobs in Beijing. They wanted her and their father to move there, but she said she did not want to go, because there was nothing for her to do in Beijing and she could not stay idle. If she repaired shoes on the capital's streets, her daughters would lose face; if she did not repair shoes, she would get sick just sitting around doing nothing. Anyhow, she did not know how to enjoy a life of ease and comfort anymore than she could remain idle. Looking at her, Xunhong thought of her brother Xunjun, who, though he had lost his feet, could repair shoes, too. She wanted to ask Mr. Du about getting a disability license so that her brother could sit on the street just as honorably and repair shoes. If a woman could support her family, there was no reason her brother could not support himself.

When her dad called her the first time, she told him of her idea. Her dad said it was a good idea, but the problem was where Xunjun could find a place to stay since he needed to be looked after. Xunhong worked as a housekeeper in someone else's house and couldn't have her brother staying there. Xunhong started looking around the streets again. Some time later she got to know a waiter at the restaurant across the street. The waiter was from outside the city and stayed in the restaurant at night as a security guard. When she knew him well enough, she mentioned her brother's situation to him, and he promised to help her. Some time later, he told Xunhong, "I have a way, but it's up to you to accept it or not."

"As long as there is a place to stay I won't say no," she said. She urged him to tell her about it.

"There are several blind people in our place who make a living as street performers," said the waiter. "They rent a place together. If your brother has no objections, he could join them and later, after he has earned some money, he could share the rent with them, so as to ease their burden." After he finished, he was afraid he might have offended Xunhong, so he added, "At first I thought he could stay with me in the restaurant without paying anything. But my boss asked how he could he guard the restaurant without any feet. It was just too much trouble to offer him a job. Then I thought of this way that I just told you about."

Xunhong thought it was a good idea. Why should she be unhappy about it? She was only afraid that she did not express her appreciation quickly enough, as she nodded in assent. Xunhong called home to tell her dad to send Xunjun to her. Xunjun, who hated to stay in the village, was interested in going to the city. He could not do anything during the busy spring sowing period and, besides, he hated being called a "cripple" by his fellow villagers. He didn't have any objections to repairing shoes. His dad waited till the green shoots of grain were growing everywhere after the hoeing and sowing before choosing a nice summer day to take him to the city. Xunhong, embarrassed about having her dad and brother come to her place, as well as afraid of seeing the reaction on Ayi's face, asked her dad to first come to the restaurant for lunch, after which she took them to the house where the blind people were living. The place was a dirty mess, flies buzzing all over the house that summer day. After Xunhong tidied the place up a bit, she asked Xunjun if it was alright. Xunjun said okay. Two blind people were out performing, playing *erhu* (two-string fiddle) on the street. Sometimes they played a short jubilant piece of music at the doorway of a restaurant or a shop and got some auspicious money. The two of them could earn forty or fifty yuan a day. Being blind, they hired a local woman who worked at odd jobs and cooked for them. Xunjun had to contribute his share after he moved in.

One has to spend a certain amount of money before starting to earn a living. Everything is hard at the beginning, and a person with no feet has to be even more practical. Xunhong and her dad went to see the woman who repaired shoes across the street and talked to her about Xunjun's situation, saying he wanted to learn her skills. The Auntie who repaired shoes listened to their story and agreed right away, since Xunjun, like her, had lost his feet. She said, "I guarantee he will finish his apprenticeship in a week, and also I'll buy an old machine for your brother. He'll make money the first year even though he's new to the job."

After seeing off her dad she returned to Ayi, who was angry. She then acknowledged that her dad had come to visit her, but knowing Ayi was so keen on cleanliness, they did not come to the house. Ayi then asked her to wash her hands with more soap than usual and to change her clothes as well. She felt that country folk were unhygienic and that many diseases in the city had come from the countryside. Xunhong thought Ayi was very sick, but kept washing herself even after the odor of soap stuck to her body. Ayi also demanded that the vegetables bought back from the market had to be soaked in soda water; otherwise, she had been told, the farm chemicals in the vegetables would poison a person if they ate them. The first change in Xunhong was that she had washed her hands until they looked like fresh kidney beans under the sunshine, so white and soft. Yet Xunhong did not like living her days in this way. This was not her home anyway, and she didn't know how many years she might have to wait for Mr. Du to find her a different job. When she went to visit her brother in the afternoon, she saw someone selling nail polish by the door of a shop, and bought one bottle of red. She also let the manicurist next door manicure her nails. All together she spent more than ten yuan, which pained her at first, but later, looking at her nails, she felt it was worth the price.

Walking to the shoe-repair place, she saw her brother sitting on a small bench, as if in a trance. It was summer and he had taken off his one shoe. His legs rested on the ground, and his two protruding limbs of uneven length looked quite pitiful. Passersby would drop one or two coins by his legs, at which her brother would suddenly turn hostile. Feeling belittled he would withdraw his legs to hide his handicap. Xunhong took two buns from her pocket and gave one to her brother and the other to the woman cobbler. She did not want it so she gave it to her brother. "We had buns for lunch so I took two before coming to see you," said Xunhong.

"Your brother is very diligent in his studies," replied the shoe-repair auntie.

Xunhong touched her brother's head, asking how his night was with the blind musicians and if he got along well with them.

Xunjun laughed. He had not laughed for a long time. Eating the buns he said, "When the blind musicians came home they counted their money — they count by touching, and were very accurate. But one of them wanted to practice the new tune they said they had heard on the street. They wanted to practice so that they could play today and catch up with the trends. Then they start practicing. They were quite pitiful. They touched my legs, and asked to me to go with them tomorrow."

"Don't go," said Xunhong. "You've come to learn a skill — kneeling to beg is shameful."

"I know," said Xunjun, lowering his head.

"You didn't go to school," said the shoe-repair Auntie to Xunhong. "If you did you could have passed the university entrance exam."

Xunhong said no more, she could not blame herself — she had to blame her Mum and Dad who thought a son was more important than a daughter, who never treated the daughter as a backbone of the family, but as an outsider.

When Xunhong returned to the house, Ayi noticed her red fingernails at once and flared up. She stood up and demanded that

Xunhong wash it off. But Xunhong couldn't. Ayi said, "The red must be washed away, or you'll clear out of here tonight!" Xunhong opened the balcony door, and out there she scraped her nails with a knife. After scraping and scrubbing, Xunhong looked at her nails, dull and pale again.

Ayi did not allow Xunhong to go out for two days. She asked her to think about her wrongdoing, saying she was a farm girl not a city social butterfly, who had to polish her nails red. She was a rural villager who had come to work as a housekeeper!

Xunhong could not understand who the hell would divide people born in the same society into villagers and city people!

Two days later, Xunhong was anxious to find her brother. The shoe-repair Auntie said, "Your brother hasn't been here for two days." Xunhong went to the place where her brother was staying, but found the place locked. Xunhong could not figure out where her brother could have gone. So she walked along the street onto a wider street. Wondering where she should go next, she caught sight of Wang Erhai's dad across the street, and called out, "Uncle —"

Wang Erhai's father, not expecting someone in the city to call him "Uncle," kept walking. Xunhong ran to catch up with him, calling him "Uncle" from behind.

Wang Erhai's father now realized someone was calling him, and stopped and looked at Xunhong somewhat confused. He could not place her, but was positive she came from the same river.

"Uncle, how is Erhai?" asked Xunhong.

Wang Erhai's father said, "Basically the same. He's still in the hospital, as he has been from the beginning. He's pretty much the same and doesn't know anything. The only good thing is that he can stand up to walk."

"That means he will recover soon," said Xunhong.

"Whose daughter are you?" asked Wang Erhai's father.

Xunhong did not dare to say she was the daughter of Huo Cuiping, lest he be unhappy, so she changed the topic by asking him, "Has he married yet?"

"Marry whom?" asked Wang Erhai's father. "His life is finished. What girl would ever marry him? Though he would recover sooner by marrying. Are you Erhai's classmate?"

"Yes," said Xunhong, "we were classmates."

Wang Erhai's father then continued on his way. Xunhong suddenly thought of asking him in which hospital Wang Erhai was staying. She shouted after him, "Uncle, tell me which hospital he is in."

Wang Erhai's father pointed ahead and said, "That one. Ward 305, Second Section, Internal Medicine. You're so lucky to be alive."

Xunhong did not find her brother, but did find out about Wang Erhai. She heard from her dad that Bi Xiaohong had married some other guy.

Xunhong thought that Bi Xiaohong had forsaken her conscience.

6

When Xunhong found her brother the next day, he was sitting on the ground rolling up his pant legs to show off his two disabled legs, a shabby old tea canister sitting in front of him, in which there was some money that had been dropped in by pedestrians. Facing him, Xunhong could not help but cry. She never imagined her brother would degrade himself by becoming a beggar. If he could not support himself, he still had her to help him. Why did he have to beg on the street? Xunhong walked over, bent down and said, "Lift your head. Look at what you have become. If you had gone to school, at least you would have had a sense of shame and would not ruin yourself like this!"

Xunjun lifted his head and looked at her. He had not lifted his head once since coming out that morning. He just kept his head lowered, thinking nothing. Once in a while he looked in his tea canister to see how many coins he had received and if they added up to a big bill. What ambition he once had completely disappeared the moment he lost his feet. He had never liked to use his brains, preferring to exert himself physically. Using all his strength, when making bricks he had tamped the mud with his feet. He did not like to study because he really did not want to study; he did not know how he could become a useful human being by studying. Did he lose his Mum and his feet because he refused to study? Xunjun looked up at Xunhong and said to her, "I don't know who you are. Get out of here!"

Pointing to her nose, Xunhong said, "You don't know who I am? But do you know Huo Cuiping and Li Ping'an? You should acknowledge they are your Mum and Dad, right?"

"You're disrupting my business," growled Xunjun.

Xunhong picked up the tea canister and tried to help Xunjun get to his feet to come with her. He refused to budge. Xunhong said, "Even if I have to carry you on my back all the way to Xihuo, I'll do it. Even Dad would not let you lose your human dignity like this!"

"I was fine before. Do you think I intend to be like this?" shouted Xunjun. "If you're so great, why don't you give me back my feet? Give me back my feet! If I lose face, it's my own face; if I am disappointed, it's my disappointment. Why don't you just treat me as a stranger?!"

"Even if I had no legs, I would still have hands and a brain," said Xunhong. "Why won't you live like the Auntie who repairs shoes?"

"I like to live this way; I like to lose face this way," said Xunjun. "At least I'm not losing face in Xihuo!"

Two blind persons behind them heard the squabble and stood up, walked over and said, "Girl, if we were born like you, do you think we'd lead this kind of life? We have the face given to us by our mothers, and who wants our unworthy face?"

Xunhong sat herself on the grass by the roadside and cried. She cried for herself, for her brother, and even for Wang Erhai. She thought of her home, her mother struck by lightning, whose death had deprived her home of half of its warmth. Raising a son to obtain a higher education had been her dad's hope, but his son did not like to study and preferred to make bricks. When her brother gave up on school, her dad shifted his hopes to building a new house, which was now put off because of her brother's legs. Every time the family had saved some money to do something, there was an accident. The family ended up with nothing at all, but she still thought of it as her family. Her family was humble and had no choices. She had just been pushed along by life. She could not choose her own life or fate. Even if Wang Erhai regained his health, could he compensate her brother? And her brother had failed to meet her expectations, but how could he meet them?

Xunhong stopped crying, but did not look at her brother either. The blind musicians sat on small stools playing their *erhu*. The music lingered on the street. A passerby dropped a coin into her brother's tea canister, clinking when it hit the edge, piercing Xunhong's heart. If you did not pay attention you would not hear the sound, but she heard it. Suddenly she felt she had grown up; suddenly she realized that a girl who polished her nails lacked good taste. She wanted to survive with style, and not be someone's housekeeper; she did not know how she could survive with style, but she knew she was no longer the Xunhong she had been before. She wanted to face life bravely, meaning to face herself. She then realized that it was life that had made her dad and mum so realistically practical. Even with life's pressures, her dad never gave up hope. Hope was like a kernel of corn that did not sprout, but when it did not sprout her dad would think of sowing other seeds that were more adapted to the season and the land.

Xunhong walked over to Xunjun and told him, "Go home and think long and deep, and then you'll understand."

Passing the hospital, she saw the sign "Peace Hospital" on the roof and thought she would go visit Wang Erhai the next day. He was, after all, one of the victims of the car accident, which would not have happened if he had not shown sympathy toward the villagers. Besides, she had once placed her hopes on him. Her dad told her, "Since no one showed up to purchase green buds, now besides working in the fields during the summer, people have started playing mahjong."

Looking at the city outside her window, Xunhong was lost deep in thought. Her dad had telephoned her before nightfall to tell her that, because she worked for Director Du, the village had allocated a land deed to her family to build a five-bedroom house. Thinking of her brother, Xunhong wondered what good the deed was if his future was in question.

"I'll find a son-in-law who will live with our family," said her dad. "We have to have a plan. The whole family is depending on you."

Her dad's new hope always appeared in good time. She did not sleep until dawn, and then she dreamed. In the dream, a cornfield that her dad had just harvested was covered with stubble. The villagers were passing the cornfield on their way to the threshing ground to sell green buds. Many people tripped over the uneven ground. She wanted to cross, but she could not, no matter what she did. It was not the stubble that prevented her, but rather her own emotions. Every step seemed to conceal a trap, and each trap looked like the roots of the stubble, which slowly turned into mouths snapping at her feet, and her feet now resembled her brother's. She grew pale with fear and, exhausted by life dragging her down into hopelessness, she screamed. She screamed: "This is not the life I want to live!" The sound of her own screams awakened her. Opening the curtains she saw the colorful clouds above the city, and sat and watched as they turned white. The sky grew light and she got up to cook and clean the house. It was the start of another day.

That afternoon, Xunhong located Ward 305, in the Second Section of Internal Medicine.

Arriving at the ward, she peeked inside through a small square window in the door. There were several beds, and Wang Erhai was sitting up in the bed by the window. She pushed open the door and walked in, but did not see his parents. He sat by himself looking out the window. Outside, white clouds hung in the blue sky, but there were no distant mountains visible in the city, just building after building. She stood behind him for a while, not wanting to call him to turn around and look at her. She did not know what to say if he asked her what she was doing there. However, she watched as he slowly turned his head — his eyes were lusterless. Giving her a glance, he lowered his head, not knowing who she was.

"Don't you recognize me?" asked Xunhong.

He did not reply.

"The buildings outside are very high," said Xunhong.

He did not reply.

Xunhong realized that he did not know anything and did not remember anything.

A wicked idea flashed in Xunhong's mind. "Do you know Bi Xiaohong?"

He then said one word, "Mountain."

A clever man had become an idiot, thought Xunhong. He no longer knew he had once purchased green buds with Bi Xiaohong. Her brother knew how to beg, but he did not know anything. "What do you want to eat?" she asked.

"Candy," was his reply.

"I'll buy candy when I come see you tomorrow," she said.

Xunhong did not have anything more to say. Watching him for a while she thought of her brother on the street, and decided to leave. He did not look at her. Xunhong then thought of evenings in Xihuo Village and how he used to drive his truck down the village road and turn down the hill to the threshing ground by the river. He had looked so handsome maneuvering the truck the way he did. At that moment Xunhong had taken a great fancy to him. Xunhong turned to take a second look at him, and discovered he was paler and fatter than before. She felt a pang in her heart, and she knew she still fancied him. As she turned to leave, she bumped right into Wang Erhai's dad.

Wang Erhai's dad recognized her right away and said, "You are Erhai's classmate. Whose daughter are you?"

Xunhong did not want to tell him that she was the daughter of Li Ping'an, whom he had fought with in the county hospital. The two families had become enemies on account of the accident and the lost futures of the two victims.

"You don't know my Dad," said Xunhong, lowering her head.

"That's impossible," replied Wang Erhai's dad, "I know everyone along the river. I just don't know you youngsters."

Xunhong, trying to avoid his pressing to find out who she was, finally said, "Uncle, you'd be angry if I told you who my father is."

"Angry?" said Wang Erhai's dad. "Knowing who your father is would make me angry?"

"Huo Cuiping in Xihuo," said Xunhong, biting her lip. "Li Ping'an is my father."

Wang Erhai's dad touched her head with his hand and said, "Good girl, you are more sensible than your Dad. Uncle knows you. Last year we tried to propose a marriage between you and our son, but your Dad wouldn't let you go. Still, it's better that way, otherwise, you'd be suffering now. What are you doing in the city? Into whose family did you marry?"

"I work as a housekeeper," said Xunhong. "I haven't got married yet. Now my Dad is looking for a son-in-law to come live in our home. My brother has no feet."

"Let me see you out," said Wang Erhai's dad.

They went downstairs. Wang Erhai's dad walked a long way to see her off. Xunhong now knew that, because Wang Erhai was hospitalized, his whole family, meaning his mum and dad, was focused on him. Originally his dad had worked as a truck driver, but because of his son's hospitalization he had quit working with others and ended up spending all his savings of about a hundred thousand yuan on his son's medical expenses. Now the dad stayed with his son in the hospital, and carried goods for others to the city. The mum stayed in the village to till the fields, otherwise they could not survive. Farmers survived on land. But the money spent on Wang Erhai was worth it — at first he could not talk but now he could, so there was progress.

Wang Erhai's dad asked about Xunjun's condition. Knowing

that he had lost his feet, he could not help but sigh and say, "We are all poor people. Who can we blame other than fate? One can be poor with lofty ideas, but poverty also breeds fear. My son was kindhearted enough to pick up your brother free of charge to save him some traveling expenses. If he had known what was going to happen, he would not have picked up anyone. Too many people in the truck made it lose its center of gravity and roll over. Poor people can get no redress from the law. I wanted to sue, and asked those who know the law. They told me I was lucky not to *be* sued, that I was actually lucky my son had become a vegetable. If he hadn't been injured when the truck rolled over, he'd have to go to jail. So it's good that he has become a vegetable!"

Wang Erhai's dad seemed on the verge of tears, and his voice quavered as he spoke.

"Uncle, I'll help you look after him for a while in the afternoon, so you can go do your work," offered Xunhong. "I believe he'll recover one day."

Wang Erhai's dad stared at her and said, "Which month or year might he recover? What virtue did I accumulate in my previous life to meet such a good girl like you?"

Xunhong did not see her brother when she passed the square. She knew he was trying to avoid her. A normal person's feet got tired walking such a long way, not to mention a disabled person's. It must be hard for him. Xunhong saw a billboard on the road that read: "You only have one life!" Seeing it made her shiver. She felt that, even a normal person had a hard time surviving in this one life, and there were so many others worse off than she was!

7

Xunhong kept Wang Erhai company whenever she had nothing else to do in the afternoon. They did not talk much, but she embraced him with her warm and ardent eyes. First he looked out the window for a while, and then turned his head to look at Xunhong. Closing his eyes he said, "I see you have turned a golden color."

His brain was slowly coming back to life.

Outside the sun shone splendidly all summer and autumn long. Xunhong knitted thick socks by the bright sunlight at the window. Winter would soon be here, and all the mosquitoes and flies would die in the cold. Her brother needed thick socks, but the wool socks she was knitting were straight tubes with no feet. "Where are the feet?" asked Wang Erhai.

Xunhong told him that her brother had lost his feet in the accident, and asked if he could remember or not? "That time, you fell down the mountain, after which you did not recognize anyone, my brother lost his feet." Wang Erhai could not remember a thing, but Xunhong kept reminding him. "You must have hit your head on the metal of the truck, hit it very hard. You were driving the truck to the mountain to purchase green buds, but in winter they are not called green buds, they are called yellow petals."

"Weeping forsythia, with yellow flowers, right?" said Wang Erhai.

Xunhong was so excited to hear him say this that she put down her knitting, and stood up to show him that there were yellow petals in his medicine. She took the medicine out and put it in his palm. Wang Erhai looked and looked at it, as if hit by something, but still he couldn't think of what it was. But there was a certain perplexity.

The doctor seeing Xunhong come every afternoon to keep him company, said, "What is your relationship to him? The patient needs someone to stimulate him. His parents are very anxious, but no one talks to him the way you do."

Xunhong did not know what to say about herself. Wang Erhai, seeing the wife of the patient in the next bed attending to her husband, told the doctor, "She is my wife."

The doctor said nothing, but when he saw Wang Erhai's dad, he told him discreetly, "Actually, your son does not have to stay in the hospital. The medicine he is taking is to control his condition. What he needs even more is spiritual therapy. Your son has a girlfriend he will marry, right? Your future daughter-in-law is very good; she can stimulate your son's memory. It won't hurt him to get married, and perhaps marriage will stimulate his central nervous system and speed his recovery."

Wang Erhai's dad was silent. He could not believe that anyone would marry his son. If he mentioned it to the girl, it would, without a doubt, be like boxing his own ears — even if the girl was willing, her father would not allow it. Li Ping'an was itching to cut off his feet for his son. Still, Wang Erhai's dad decided to leave the hospital and take his son to recuperate at home as he could no longer afford the hospital. To have his son take a wife was beyond his expectations, especially a girl as good as Xunhong.

The sun shining through the window warmed both of them. "You look great when you sit in the truck," said Xunhong to Wang Erhai. "When you go home ask your Dad to buy you another truck."

"If I buy a new truck, will you marry me?" asked Wang Erhai.

Xunhong turned her eyes and said playfully, "If you buy a truck, I'll marry you."

"If you don't marry me, what will you be?" said Wang Erhai.

Xunhong thought and thought, then said, "Weeping forsythia."

Wang Erhai picked some yellow petals from the bag of medicine and said, "If you don't marry me, every day I'll soak some medicine and eat you."

Wang Erhai's dad, standing next to them, dare not believe what he had just heard. Turning around and looking elsewhere, he said, "Girl, did I hear right?"

"Yes," she replied, "Uncle, I can bamboozle other people, but not him. His illness was caused by a truck accident. If you buy him another truck, he can drive — he does have hands and legs. Let him drive since he does know how. Learning again will stimulate his nerves. He can do it, and I can also learn. I can help him."

"I don't dare to believe what you're saying," said Wang Erhai's dad. "Girl, if you marry him, you will ruin your name, give yourself a bad name. A good girl marries a useless man, or a woman marries a vulgar husband — it's like sticking a lovely flower in a dunghill. If he can recover, that's good. I can still work to make more money. If he doesn't recover, I wouldn't be able to raise my head to look at your Dad. I would truly be indebted to him."

"Uncle, wait for me until next spring. I give you my word, but I have a favor to ask of you," said Xunhong.

"I'll promise you anything," said Wang Erhai's dad.

Somewhat embarrassed, Xunhong lowered her head and said, "I don't want any betrothal gifts. This is hard to say — what I want Uncle to do is help my Dad build a house, I have a brother and I have to give my father face."

"I'll do it, I must do it," said Wang Erhai's dad.

When Wang Erhai was leaving the hospital, Xunhong was not to be seen. Wang Erhai missed Xunhong so much that he demanded that his dad buy a truck. "Look at you like this, suffering on account of a truck and you still want one," his dad said.

"Don't forget! Xunhong wants one!" said Wang Erhai.

His dad then thought of the groundless promise he had made to the girl in the hospital and became angry at himself for his own stupidity. He made a special trip to Xihuo to see Xunhong's dad, without bringing up the marriage proposal. He said, "I haven't been here earlier to see you because I have been busy taking care of my son since the accident that also involved your son. We fought in the hospital, and that's a shame. It was my fault. Please accept my apologies. I've thought it over and sought the advice of someone who knows the law and found out it's my son's fault, though it could have been worse. My son is out of the hospital, and has more or less recovered. Though I am considered a well-to-do man by people along the river, this trouble has cost me almost all I have, though it could be worse. Tell me, how much do you want from me? We can talk in private. If you like, let's have a middle man mediate."

Hearing that money might be coming his way, Xunhong's dad thought that when a clay idol opens its mouth to give money, there must be some trick in which he'd certainly have to pay without mercy! But how merciless could a rural villager be, when their way of looking at things was usually narrow and shallow and never involved causing trouble for others. He calculated for a moment and said, "You think it over, it's a matter of a whole life, at least a house."

Wang Erhai's dad slapped his leg and said, "It's a deal. Let's find a witness. I'll ask Laicheng to deliver the money."

Xunhong's dad felt there was something wrong. Laicheng was a matchmaker, why have a matchmaker deliver the money? Yet he could not figure it out. After taking forty thousand yuan from Laicheng, Xunhong's dad started looking for sand and cement for building the new house. The villagers thought the matter strange, but he explained it to them by saying that Wang Erhai's dad was afraid his son would be put away.

Xunhong took the socks she had knitted for her brother to his place. Her brother accepted them after taking a look. Xunhong attempted to pare the hard skin on her brother's feet with a pair of scissors, but her brother wouldn't let her, saying he could do it by himself and that she should leave. "You never listen," Xunhong said.

Xunjun was silent, but his face was flushed as if he was up to something behind her back. He insisted that she leave. Xunhong pretended to go, but stopped at the doorway. Leaning against the window, she peeked inside and saw the two blind musicians, who were sitting on the edge of the bed, start to practice a new song. In the light, their eyes turned furtively. Their faces were wrinkled and their backs stooped. They played and when they reached a high point of expressing their emotions, white spots that sun had never touched appeared on their brows. After playing one song, they played the opening bars of another. One of them then asked Xunjun to sing. He knitted his brows, raised his nose, squared his shoulders, and started to sing. Xunhong then knew the three of them had become partners and were working together. The awkward expression on her face disappeared immediately; her brother knew how to live, she thought, and only a person who knew how to live knew how to adapt to life. Xunhong knew nothing about literature and art, but hearing the way they sang she recalled the songs she had learned in junior high. They looked so alive!

Xunhong walked back and thought of how clean Ayi was — too clean — clean enough to put other people off. The house was so spotless that nary a fly was to be seen there. Cleanliness was the old woman's hope in life. She had felt saddened and chilled because her brother had to beg for a living, but she never knew her brother could sing. Now he had hope, the hope of making others happy, and the happiness of others was also one's own happiness. Xunhong also thought of Wang Erhai and felt that, as long as a person had a small piece of ground on which to stand, it was enough, to warm other people, and at the same time provide warmth to oneself.

The following day, Xunhong went looking for her brother on the streets. She saw her crippled brother leading the two blind musicians, who were holding onto his shoulders. They stopped in front of a small shop and formed a triangle. There was no suffering in her brother's singing voice; in fact, he sang with great exuberance. The song he sang was happy enough to make people sway with the rhythm. Xunhong trembled with excitement. Her brother's song was like a flying bird, able to thaw the cruelest parts of life. Xunhong felt her brother had grown up.

When winter came, Xunhong left the director mother's home, but not of her own accord. After her son had met with trouble in the county and been placed under extra-legal custody, with such things hard to talk about and city people having their own problems, the old woman's mood worsened and she had dismissed Xunhong.

When Xunhong returned to Xihuo, it seemed as if nothing had changed. Her dad took her to see the land allocated for building and said, "When spring comes, we start building."

Xunhong had nothing to do throughout the winter, so she asked her father to take her to pick yellow petals on the mountain. "There's no one to purchase them anymore. The price is good, but no one is purchasing," said her dad.

"Someone will buy," said Xunhong with certainty.

Xunhong and her dad went to the mountain and picked yellow petals, which they stored in one of the grain bins for corn. Because the grain bin was woven with twigs of chaste trees, there were a lot of gaps. Xunhong asked her dad to wrap the bin with a piece of tattered matting. Father and daughter picked all of the yellow petals on the mountain around Xihuo. The villagers laughed at them for being so busy for nothing. Her dad looked at her somewhat confused, but she just smiled. If this had happened before, her dad would have scolded her, but not this time. Since Xunhong had returned, he never wanted to scold her because he had to depend on her. Sometimes he felt he had been unfair to her.

One day Xunhong told her dad that she planned to go into town to buy some things for the house. She was gone almost the whole day until the late afternoon, when the Xihuo villagers were busy playing mahjong. Suddenly the sound of a truck was heard on the village road. No one expected it to be someone coming to purchase yellow petals. Cigarette in hand, Xunhong's dad watched the villagers playing mahjong and said, "I'll see what the truck has come for. I'll see if the price of corn has gone up or not." He then saw his daughter sitting in the truck — driven by Wang Erhai. When his daughter saw any acquaintances, the truck would stop and Xunhong would offer them a cigarette from Wang Erhai. Xunhong's dad ran forward to meet them, but never expected the truck to head for his own courtyard. "Dad, we've come to buy yellow petals," said Xunhong when she saw him.

"Is there a scale? Shall I go borrow one?" her dad asked.

"Why? This is more or less in the family," said Xunhong.

Her dad did not respond, nor did he have time to, busy as he was calling for help to load the goods.

After loading the goods, her dad looked at Wang Erhai and said, "You've recovered, but my son hasn't."

"I'll be your son from now on," replied Wang Erhai.

Xunhong gave her dad a meaningful look. Failing to understand, her dad said, "I'm looking for a son-in-law to live with me. You're still your dad's son."

"Dad, I've got to go with Wang Erhai to deliver goods to the city tomorrow. I've got to accompany our goods so we won't be cheated."

Xunhong's dad let her go.

The moment the villagers of Xihuo saw someone there to purchase yellow petals, they left their mahjong games on the tables and went to the mountain to pick them. They picked everything nearby and then went farther. There were no snakes on the mountain in the winter to bite people, and no lightning in the sky to strike people. They were not afraid of the cold on the mountain, because they sweated all day long. In addition to Wang Erhai, who drove the truck to purchase their goods, there was also Xunhong.

"How will a girl who's not afraid of following a man around find a husband? Won't she become a laughingstock?" asked her dad.

Xunhong replied, "You've already accepted the betrothal gifts, so why worry if other people laugh?"

Her father then understood what the forty thousand yuan was for. It was to make a match for his daughter. He wanted to take the money and straighten things out with Wang Erhai's dad. The money was in the credit cooperative, but the staff working there said, "It's not liquid. Moreover, our business is done for the year and we have no cash available. You'll have to wait until after Spring Festival."

At that moment, her dad realized he had been duped, but there was nothing he could do about it. They had not said it was a betrothal gift, so his daughter still needed his permission to marry! But he still needed a truck to carry the building materials in the spring. He would go to court about the money after the materials had been delivered!

After the Spring Festival, when there was nothing to do, Xunhong's dad looked at the sky every day, waiting for the spring thunder to roar, so that he could start construction. Before the thunder roared, Xunhong waited for a good day to talk with her dad. "Dad, I no longer have Mum, and I don't know who I should talk to. Why don't you let your daughter get married? Your daughter is also expecting."

"Whose child is it?" her dad at once reflexively asked.

"The one who purchases yellow petals of forsythia," replied Xunhong.

Her dad raised his hand to slap her, but then he thought of that ancient saying:

A grown son cannot be managed; a grown daughter cannot be kept at home.

(Translated by John Balcom)

Perfect Journeys

Jiang Yun

Jiang Yun. Born in March 1954 in Taiyuan, Shanxi Province, of Henan origin, Jiang Yun graduated from the Chinese Department of Taiyuan Teachers College in 1981.

Since 1979, she has published fiction, prose and informal essays totaling almost 3 million Chinese characters. Her representative works are the novels, *Secret Blooming*, *Prisoners of Oak Trees*, *Beauty Dies Young*, *Shining on Your Branch*, and *My Hometown*; the short story collections, *Perfect Journeys*, *Escape from the Spot*, *Lost Games*; and the prose and informal essay collections, *Meeting Rodin in Spring* and *A Long Encounter*. She won *Shanghai Literature*'s Excellent Writing Prize, *Chinese Writers*' Dahongying Literary Prize and the 4th Lu Xun Literary Prize for her novella *Beloved Tree*, as well as other literary awards. Some of her works have been published overseas in English and French. Holding the professional title "First-ranked Litterateur," she is now a member of the Chinese Writers' Association and on the executive of the Shanxi Writers' Association, and vice-chair of the Taiyuan Federation of Literary and Art Circles.

Perfect Journeys

1. Hometown Flowing in His Veins

Liu Gang was born to his parents in a remote province in the northeast. His father was from a small town called Dongjing in Heilongjiang Province. A forested region, the town was located in Changbai Mountains, and Liu Gang's grandpa had worked as a logger all his life. Liu Gang's mother was from the beautiful city known as Mudanjiang.

Liu Gang's parents worked for a roving construction unit. It was a large group in some sort of bureau under the leadership of a ministry in Beijing. Soon after Liu Gang was born, his parents' unit was transferred from northeast to north China, and they settled in a city located on a plateau. His mother left Liu Gang with his grandpa and grandma in their hometown in the northeast.

Liu Gang was less than half a year old when his mother left him behind. Grandpa bought a goat to feed him, so he was fostered by fresh milk into a gentle and fair little boy. His skin always radiated a faint sweetness of mutton and green grass. This honest-to-goodness smell would follow him all his life. It had been stamped into his life by the herbivorous animals. Certainly, he also had other kinds of scent on him. For example, those of pinewood, fur, the hen house and the pigsty, rotting leaves and the luxuriant air of the summer woods. And these, of course, are no more than the normal smells you would find on any ordinary child from a forested area in northeastern China.

Dongjing was a peaceful small town, the days there as long as a slow, deep river flowing calmly on the periphery of the world. The sky there was eternal and lonely, filled with a boundless solitude and purity. Children growing up under that kind of sky often possess a temperament of aloofness and a misconception of the world.

On the vast winter snowfields, a snow sledge glided through the silver whiteness from afar, while the tinkling of the bell on the horse's neck was the only sound in a silent world. The sledge arrived and left, carrying away the little boy named Liu Gang. A total stranger took Liu Gang onto the sledge and wrapped him tightly in his fur coat. His breath felt as sharp and as chilling as shards of glass in the frigid freeze of thirty degrees below. The sledge carried them to the county seat, where they got onto a long-distance bus to Mudanjiang. It was the beginning of a long journey — a journey of no return.

Later in his life, that small hometown of his, where he was born, would appear in his dreams only. Sometimes he felt the place dear to his heart very far away, but other times he sensed it was close by his side. His hometown seemed to hide in his warm body like he was a tiny baby. The feeling was nice but also strange. However, whether too far away off the horizon or too close inside his body, he was never able to hold it in his hands as it had been separated from him forever.

The city he was taken into was the provincial capital of S Province.

2. A Ruthless Freezing City

In the beginning, he believed it was the largest city and the liveliest place in the world. Though it certainly was not.

He was used to nothing here, not its noisiness, crowdedness, filth or its aridity. Spring was the most uncomfortable season, when its ceaseless dry yellow winds sip up the last drop of moisture in your body until you feel like an air-dried mummy. His lips cracked and his gums bled throughout the spring. Failing to find any sense of thaw or mildness, all the newborn and green life burst off with a rather miserable though courageous fight through the endless sandstorms. Green became a color of tragic solemnity within a stirring frigidity. His feet stepped on the hard, ice-cold streets, failing to feel any arrival of the spring. He tried to remember how the spring would sneak into his body from under his feet back home, just like a seedling breaking through the soil and climbing up through his veins. Feeling he was being transformed into a tree, he raised his arms imagining the tender buds shooting slowly from his fingertips, to grow into green leaves. How marvelously warm and sweet the melting land had been then! Muddy all around, and the sound of dripping, cheerful human voices along with the fresh, resounding bird songs everywhere. Even your pulse quickened up in the spring back then. He suddenly felt passionately nostalgic about that kind of spring season. But as for here, you could be choked by the arid yellow winds and dusky skies, while the ugly, hard lineation of buildings had no birds coming to build their nests on them. Where was spring at all?

The weather was getting warmer though, and he took off the unwieldy padded jacket. The jacket was already very dirty, its front greasy and black with a layer of sheen. His mother nagged him, saying it was more a coat of armor than a padded jacket! She kept complaining angrily when she took it apart and washed it on a sunny Sunday. Ma would make him put on a sweater, a hand-me-down from his elder sister. The old red sweater was tight on him, exposing much of his arms. Ma sniffed at his hair like a hound, urging him to, "Go, go… go and give yourself a good wash! Just look at you. What kind of nasty smell is that?"

Those words hung on Ma's lips all the time: "Look at you, what smell is that?" But that smell could not be washed off. It was buried beneath his skin, deep inside his body, flowing along his blue, soft veins like a creek. That was his dear hometown air, the herbivorous animal's sweetness. Every spring it awoke and turned green. However, it inexplicably irritated his mother and stirred her restlessness, like a strong smell of estrangement. Failing to sense any kinship with this peculiar-smelling child, she just did not know how to deal with this strange invader in her household, other than to keep driving him toward the bathhouse.

The bathhouse was owned by his parents' work unit, and it was open to all the staff's families on certain weekdays. Naked people would bump into one another fighting over the few shower nozzles. All these nude bodies huddling together in the warm steam presented such ugly, terrifying scenes. Twisted and distorted in the water vapor, those bodies accomplished all manner of embarrassing and shameless writhing in the white mist, scrubbing and rubbing all their unsightly parts with vegetable sponges or pads. Liu Gang had no other way out but to try and hide his own body inside the waters of the white ceramic bathing pool. But even the bathing pool failed to be a safe place. Treating it as a swimming pool, stark naked boys swam and splashed water onto one another. Liu Gang's elder and younger brothers were among the noisy boys. Taking the dirty bathhouse as their little paradise, they exaggerated their joy while isolating their brother, their own flesh and blood, set apart from them.

3. The Origin of a Fairytale

I have lived in T City from my childhood. A number of shocking events occurred in my city during my teens, all having something to do with death. To be more accurate, these were several perfect or imperfect suicides. A woman climbed a factory smokestack in the city center one morning with the intention to jump from there to end her life. However, she came to regret it after climbing all the way up that high smokestack, so many people in my city got to witness a sight of a despairing human being struggling at the boundary between life and death. She was shown panoramically to the world atop this commanding height of the city, with nobody knowing what was detaining her up there. The traffic in downtown T City was jammed for several hours that day and people crowded on the roads around it. Then the firefighters arrived. Those heroes clambered up voicelessly like green tendril vines and rescued her eventually. The big net they held up was like a trap for life, and she was finally compelled to fall into the elastic net. Whenever I recall that scene, I still feel a sense of grief.

Then there was the man who was once my elementary school teacher, who taught us fine arts. It was he who gave me the highest score I ever earned in fine arts. My impression was that he was from Tianjin, with a distinctive hexagonal face and very high cheekbones. He was very hot-tempered, too. Once during a sketching class, students were asked to draw a picture of darning clothes or something like that, and one of my boy classmates made a terrible mess of it. So he brandished the student's work and shouted at him, "This is patching clothes? This is — wiping your backside!" The whole class burst into laughter, but it also made us feel that he had lost all self-respect. He quit teaching our class soon after, and no one knew where he went. However, it was this young Tianjin man with a hexagonal face and high cheekbones who later did something quite earthshaking — by touching a high-voltage cable in our city center.

The cause was unrequited love, after my fine arts teacher was jilted by his fiancée. He had to make great efforts to get a girlfriend at all, due to his shady background — from a sort of capitalist or small business owner's family. Yet even that girlfriend he had finally acquired ended up wishing to leave him. Therefore, the following scene occurred one early morning as my teacher climbed up a high-voltage pole in front of his fiancée, at a famous thoroughfare downtown. My teacher climbed up clumsily while his steel-hearted girlfriend was standing below, watching. Crawling up bit by bit, he stopped half way, held onto the pole, and gazed down. Perhaps he was hoping to hear some plea from her. However, the woman chose to say nothing except to flash a taunting smile from her mouth. There were all these pedestrians observing the fun, as if witnessing an ordinary young couple's fight. Some bench jockeys even shouted at him, "Hey buddy, keep going! Those who have not made it up the Great Wall are not true men!" Exhaling a great sigh, my teacher awkwardly continued to climb bit by bit up the pole. Since the sun was rising behind him, his last moment appeared extremely magnificent. He extended an arm, thin and long-looking like that of a gibbon. He touched the glistening high-voltage cable, and all of a sudden he was hanging like a fallen kite in the early morning sunlight.

People spread the story around. I felt very sad on learning the name of the dead man. I imagined my teacher climbing clumsily, with difficulty, toward his life's end, in that glare of the onlookers. He finished the tragedy of his life in the form of a farcical drama. But, though I was still young at the time, I believe I understood his loneliness and heartbroken sorrow.

There was yet another event, also a suicide, which happened quietly in a hospital dormitory. One day, a woman and a boy killed themselves in her dorm room. The reason was unclear, but they died peacefully. They were found hanging side by side, hand in hand, from a heating pipe. I have never learned why they died, and their death remained a secret throughout my teen and youthful years. I kept picturing their long, pure white and ice-cold corpses, feeling it to be a most mystical, thorough death. As I came to learn about it gradually afterward, it showed me a sort of beauty in death. Years later, I mentioned the incident at a reunion of old schoolmates. After I briefly described the episode, everyone present appeared at a loss. Nobody seemed to remember such a determined and poignant death occurring in our city. I asked, "But do you remember that woman who tried to jump off a high smokestack?" "Of course!" echoed everyone. "Then how about that teacher who killed himself by touching a high-voltage cable?" "Sure!" they answered unanimously again, because our city is not that a big place. Now it was my turn to feel at a loss. Not sure whose memory had gone wrong, I looked at them with confusion. I told myself, maybe it had never happened at all. The almost beautiful and dreamy nature of the incident makes it sound like a fairytale however you try to view it. Okay, let me complete the fairytale then, as it was perhaps the last fairytale of the twentieth century. Or we might call it, the last ode to the silver lining of all the clouds that gathered during the twentieth century.

4. Many Stories Occur at Railway Stations

One summer night in 1972, a woman named Chen Yizhu walks out of the T City railway station. The express train from Beijing was over six hours late. With the eleven-hour journey extended to nearly eighteen hours, the train finally made into T City, a pitch-dark and speechless city around midnight. Except for a number of dim streetlights on the square in front of the railway station, all the streetlights in the city have been blown out by the bullets of violent revolutionary fights or children's stones. This is a city bereft of her soothing nightlights. Standing in the vast and boundless darkness, the few streetlights on the railway station square look pathetically lonely and helpless.

The woman has no one to pick her up at her destination, so she has to walk into the waiting room of the railway station and wait there patiently until dawn, when the city awakes. The first bus in the morning does not arrive with a big yawn for another four hours, and that is if it is punctual. Luckily, the waiting room is not too crowded, since T City is not the type of busy hub like Zhengzhou, Shijiazhuang or others, perching on key nodes along a major railway or highway. Connecting T City with the outside world are just two minor lines known as the South and North Tongpu Railways. If not for the trains being unpunctual most of the time during this tumultuous period, there would be even less people in the waiting room of the T City station. However, despite all that, Chen Yizhu still easily finds an empty bench and now she has a sort of sleeping berth to lie down on finally. She feels greatly encouraged. After sitting on a hard seat in the train for eighteen hours, her legs are stiff and her feet swollen and numb. She lies down almost joyfully on the bench and feels at once relaxed. The wonderful feeling of relief and limb-stretching room swells in her and ripples through her body like warm waves, spreading and splashing out with a sort of secret sweetness. Chen Yizhu is an easy woman to please. Such self-contented women are not difficult to recognize. They are as fresh as plateau snow and as bright as sunshine among the dusky masses. Even the dust of life fails to tarnish them.

Right now she has arranged herself comfortably and put her head on her travel bag. She feels as if the narrow, hard wooden bench has become a broad and soft bed under her. It even makes her feel she is sleeping on an island, say, one of those beautiful, secluded islands in the South Pacific blessed with abundant sunlight and the plumpest tropical flowers and women. The grimy polluted air and the dirty waiting hall scattered with garbage seem to submerge in bright seawater. The woman feels as if she is resting happily under a starry sky, until she is transformed into a tranquil plant. So much so, that a lost child spots her rays, absorbing it all as soon as he roams into the waiting room. The day is dawning as Chen Yizhu opens her eyes. She stretches her curled legs tingling with numbness, but finds that she has just kicked into a human body. Then she discovers the child sitting at her feet. It is an eleven or twelve-year-old boy child, or one may say a lad.

She sits up.

"Did I snore?" she asks the child cheerfully.

"No," the boy answers.

There are many empty benches around but that child has chosen to huddle himself at her feet. It seems a little bit strange. Of course, these empty benches will soon be occupied by dirty buttocks, and the waiting hall will become noisy and crowded again.

Chen Yizhu raises her wrist to check her watch. It is a quarter past five and the first shift of buses should soon come from the parking lot. Just in time for her to wake up, she thinks. She pulls open her travel bag at once and takes out her comb. Scarlet red, the comb is made from either plastic or buffalo horn. She combs her hair quickly and the freshness rushes back to her face.

The boy keeps looking at her all this time.

"Where are you going?" she asks him casually.

"Dongjing Town," the boy answers.

"Where?" She is surprised she has never heard of the place and asks, "Dongjing? Do you mean Tokyo in Japan?"

The boy shakes his head, "In the northeast."

"Who's going with you?" she checks around her.

"No one," the boy replies quietly.

"Are you going alone?"

"Alone."

"Alone!"

She sees it now. This child is a street gamin in need of help. Yet how come this gamin's clothes are neat and his face pretty clean too, showing no sign of vagabondage. Chen Yizhu stops smiling. She looks at the boy carefully for a while with her clear eyes. What a bright child! She screams inwardly. There is a strange sort of bright air about this child but it is hidden by something right now. The lights in the waiting hall silently turn off at that very instant. The filthy air falls onto the child at once like a dust storm in the light of dawn. This is definitely not the right place for him to stay, she tells herself. She extends her hand to the boy.

"Let's go," she says, "Come with me."

Without asking where to, the boy gives her his hand trustingly after just a brief hesitation. His hand feels cold and smooth like a small fish just taken from a river. That feeling is fresh to her, as she cannot remember when she last held a child's hand. She is a … woman who hasn't given birth yet. She turns to look at the child and he smiles shyly at her suddenly. It is a moment of a bud blooming for the first time and the bright resonant quality in him radiates at once like a rooster crowing loudly at daybreak. She suddenly feels the throbbing of her heart. Fair and frail things never fail to make her heart ache and lament. She is so right, except she has no idea she has just taken the first steps into a tale of despair.

Chen Yizhu is a doctor, an oculist and a resident clinician in a hospital at T City. She is at the lowest grade of doctors, as there is a doctor in charge, an assistant director doctor and the director doctor above her, according to the icy and strict ranks. Hospitals are places with a strict hierarchy. In this respect, its stiff system of rank basically resembles the military.

Unquestionably, the hierarchy of the hospitals was destroyed thoroughly in the year 1972. It was a time when the director and the assistant director doctors perhaps had to wash toilets with brushes and decontaminate the hospital washrooms. A nurse, however, might have had to stand under shadowless lamps to perform surgery, such as burying thread into a polio patient, anesthetized with acupuncture. It was one of those many newly emergent phenomena in those years.

Anyhow, Chen Yizhu did not seem to see much change in her life. At least she is still doing her clinical work as before. Neither has she joined any "revolutionary mass organizations." She is known as the type who is "happy-go-lucky" by nature. The title of "happy-go-lucky" has brought her real happiness. She loves what that title implies, the wide-robed and broad-sleeved elegance and the rare poetic appeal. Her hospital is located on the fringes of the city. Hence she could see crop fields and vegetable gardens not far from her hospital gate. Once the green curtain of the tall crops has gone up, humans are easily swallowed by the sweet green. For a long while afterwards, this becomes the landscape the boy named Liu Gang becomes used to seeing, the only kind and bright corner in a gloomy and cold city.

On that dawning summer morning the woman and the child are walking into this green landscape. All the filthy odors, like the foul overnight air in the waiting room of the railway station and the nauseating gasoline smell in the bus, all ebb away from their bodies like receding sea tides, and they now feel air in their lungs as pure as by an ocean beach. The woman points to the boy where the corn is, where the rapeseed is. This is millet and that is castor-oil and.... The boy is silent. He knows these things, all of them. The fields, the soil, the growing crops and the manure scent, they are so powerful and appealing to him, cleansing him and irrigating him until he feels his feet turn magical and a spring gushes out beneath each of his steps as he walks. The spring water keeps rushing into him from his feet until he is softened and relaxed. After all, he has been holding that stiff posture for too long already. He follows the woman tamely and quietly, going upstairs, entering her room.... The first thing the woman does upon entering her home is to open the window to let the farmland sweetness rush in like rays of sunlight. The sweetness pacifies the child, and he does obediently whatever the woman tells him. He obeys her command to wash his face and hands under the tap, opening his palms under cool rushing water and feeling the charmed freshness of the water for the first time in his life as if it were flowing from an unseen river in the heart of the earth. After that, he sits quietly at the window and watches the woman busy herself going in and out. The woman comes in with a breakfast of fried eggs and corn gruel. The golden yellow color and white steam of the food blurs the boy's eyes all of a sudden. Tears flow from his eyes.

The woman sets down the breakfast. Good, she thinks. She sits down before the boy with her arms folded, watching him cry without trying to comfort him. She sees how the tears tumble out his black eyes like grapes, black eyes shining like chrysanthemums. First, one after another, big and heavy beads of tears fall down. Then the beads string into lines, as the silent, long cry cleanses all the dust off from him, spiritually and physically. The woman feels the morning light up — and she so loves light and bright things.

"What's your name?" she smiles.

We certainly know what his name is. We have known it for a while. We are aware of other things too, such as his family background, his loneliness and his loathing of city life. But all those are unimportant now. What is significant at present is that he has met this woman just as Cinderella met her fairy godmother. This is the plot of a typical fairytale. Now the woman plays the role of the fairy, listening to a lost child's pouring out of his sorrow. He talks hurriedly as if he were running. He says he wanted to go home, to Dongjing Town to see his Grandpa, Grandma, Flower Strong (his dog's name) and Black Nose (the kid of his nanny goat). He had been away from them for two long years. He asks the woman, "Auntie, do you know Dongjing Town? And Laoye Range? My hometown is in a forest region and we have Korean pines, larches, scale pines as well as the beautiful silver birches, fallen leaf oaks, maples, purple basswood and poplar trees.... Ahh, all the trees! When autumn falls, the trees' leaves turn light yellow, golden yellow, bright yellow, yellowish red.... So enchanting! Ahh, we also have Siberian elms. After a rain in summer, Siberian mushrooms — we also call them yellow mushrooms — grow under those elms. The mushrooms are so delicious when cooked, or you can make dumplings with them! We also have those shrubberies, hill tiger hazel and meadow sweet brush. So many delicious things can be found there. A creek sings behind the log cabin but no one knows where the creek comes from or where it goes. It is a rather mysterious. The cabin is where the forester lives. He is also my Grandpa. He used to be a lumberjack but then he got rheumatism in his knees so he went to work as a forester.... Grandpa has a liquor gourd hanging from his belt all the time. The gourd contains medicine wine made with pilose antler, ginseng and other items. When Grandpa sips liquor from his gourd, his neck root turns red. His face turns red from drink, even when he was young. But no one can beat his knack for drinking liquor...." Then one day they told Liu Gang that his Grandpa had passed away! They said something had been growing in his stomach, but Liu Gang would not believe it. Grandpa had nothing wrong except his old rheumaticky legs. He could eat five to six pancakes plus three bowls of corn gruel. How could he die? Also, Liu Gang's dad never went home for the funeral, saying he couldn't leave his work because he was engaged in the "all-out campaign!" Liu Gang asked the woman, "Auntie, do you believe it? Do you believe my Grandpa could die?" His black chrysanthemum-like eyes gazed at the woman with his question.

"Of course not," answers Chen Yizhu firmly.

The child bursts into tears at once, "I don't either."

It is so nice to be able to pour out what had been secreted away in one's heart. The outpouring turns him into a river inundating the bleak, harsh present. Yes, life was so hard and cold here that he often failed to find his own footprints. Except when it snowed but even the snow was dirty here. "What's that smell on you?" They keep driving him to the bathhouse, that terrible, disgusting bathhouse as if driving… a dog. He asks, "Auntie, have you seen how northeasterners kill dogs? They drive a dog into such a small vat and then pour a pot of boiling water on the dog. The dog struggles and twists in the vat so its fur rubs off against the sides. The fur falls off quietly, floating or falling to the vat bottom…. The bathhouse scares me but they always nag me about why I would fear a bathhouse. They, they …," he bursts out sobbing.

Chen Yizhu grips the child's hands. Now they feel warm like an animal woken up from hibernation. She holds both his hands gently for a while. The sobbing lowers gradually except for the welling tears. There is something terrible in the boy's story, ending with a bloody odor. It secretly alarms her.

"Liu Gang," she tries to make her voice calm, "Let me tell you this. I don't like public bathhouses either. They are definitely terrible places."

The child lifts his face.

"Look, both of us are not that brave, are we?" she says.

"But," she smiles, "this is not an intractable issue. For example, look, you just need a big trough." She points at something under her bed and there is indeed a big trough there. Made of jujube planks and painted with tung oil, the large trough sits there quietly. "We will boil a barrel of hot water and the issue will be solved, right? It's very simple," she tells the boy gently.

Everything seems to be simple with this woman. Things become simpler and brighter just like the blue sky with its white clouds, the red flowers with their green leaves and juicy fruits. That is the magical charm of fairytales. This woman is just magic and open-minded, possessing the power to turn complex things into pure enchantment.... The lost boy is so lucky to meet such a woman, and discover the rosy side of the world and a savior in his most dark days. His life changes tremendously from this moment on. However, that twelve-year-old boy was still to understand that, in that now long past summer morning. He just looks at her trustingly and stops crying, thinking in his mind how remarkable she sounds. Just a big wooden trough! Although it sounds an insignificant answer, somehow it strangely gives him confidence.

"Agreed?" she asks.

He nods.

"Look, you don't have to leave home," she smiles. "Your home, oh-oh, I mean, where do you live in T City?"

The boy named Liu Gang turns vigilant again.

"I don't want to go back. I want go to Dongjing Town to see my Grandpa. I must know if he is really... dead. I have to find out," Liu Gang speaks and his tone is firm as if he is trying to bolster a great determination about to dissolve. In fact, he already hears the melting sounds in his body clearly like the sound of spring thaw.

"Grandpa is not dead," Chen Yizhu tells him firmly. "Let me tell you, Liu Gang. If you love a person, he will never die. It doesn't need to be verified."

"If you love a person, the person will never die." These words sound like music from the heavens.

Things become simple now. Liu Gang eats a hearty, comforting breakfast of fried eggs and corn gruel plus the soft and fragrant bread with dried fruits Chen Yizhu had just brought back from Beijing. He even consents tacitly to Chen Yizhu phoning his father.

The poor man, near crazy already because of the "all-out campaign" and his son's running away, must have said "thank you" a hundred times. His voice then crackles over the phone, "I'll tie him up with a rope as soon as that little bastard comes home! I'll tear him to pieces!" To that Chen Yizhu replies, "Then I won't take the time to send him home since I need a son myself." That northeastern guy jumps on the other end of the phone, "Comrade, comrade, I am just muddleheaded because of this. I won't lay a finger on him at all. Oh, what have I done to come into such a little heir who is going to kill me sooner or later?"

When the sun is high in the sky, they step back onto the road they had come from a while ago. The crops smell fishy, baked by the sun, and the road has already turned dusty under pedestrian feet. Liu Gang's hair is still wet and his body clean and fresh. The sweet smell on him of the jujube wood trough and the rose-scented soap help transform him into an attractive and fresh green sprig of vegetable washed clean by a torrential rain. How safe and wonderful that jujube wooden trough felt! What a great feeling to soak one's body in clear and fragrant water! It is so secure and wonderful to be able to bathe alone in the white steam like floating in a kind of fairyland! Grandma used to catch him and press him into a wooden trough too. The broad trough had been made by Grandpa with birch bark. Most grandpas in the forested region were able to make all sorts of daily necessities like wooden barrels, basins or cradles using birch bark. Grandma's rough hands used to rub the base of his neck, his armpits, small feet and soft genitalia. Those were the feelings of home. Recalling his Grandma's hands, white hair and wrinkles, while sitting in the warm water in Aunt Chen's home, Liu Gang felt he was floating through a dreamland. He has come home.

He lowered his body in the warm water.... In the kitchen across the corridor, that fairy who just used the simplest magic to get him home in a wooden trough was slowly eating her delayed breakfast — the leftover corn gruel, the "Liubiju" pickled radish and the fermented bean-curd invented by Wang Zhihe. Birds were singing outside the window, house sparrows, swallows, and occasionally one or two magpies with black feathers and white bellies. They were hopping around and looking for food on the large poplar and locust trees, fully delighting in the joy of life.

Now they are finally walking on the road that leads back to downtown T City. He is walking quietly and cleanly by the woman's side, and tiny beads of sweat start to seep out the tip of his nose. His footsteps becomes slower and slower until Chen Yizhu notices. This main country road has been baked dry in the sun, so their shoes soon got dusty. Their bodies are feeling heavy and there is no wind at all. The leaves of corn and sorghum crops by the roadside remain still, their roots steaming. Liu Gang lifts his face.

"Where will this road lead us if we continue walking on it?" he asks.

"The bus station to enter the city," Chen Yizhu replies.

"What happens after that?"

Chen Yizhu thought about it before she answers, "We get out of the city."

"And after that, then what?"

"Enter the city again."

"How many times do I have to go in and out of the city before I will be able to reach Dongjing Town?" Liu Gang asks finally.

"I don't know," answers Chen Yizhu apologetically. Disappointment clouds the boy's face at once. Deep disappointment fills the child's face like a layer of frost after his gloomy vagabond night.

"But we could look it up on the map. You mentioned it is in the northeast, isn't it?"

"Yes."

"Which part of the northeast?"

"It's somewhere by the Laoye Range."

This is another strange name that baffles her. She is clearly not good enough in her geography. Having never been to the three northeastern provinces, she is aware only of such well-known places as Shenyang, Changchun or Harbin, which everyone knows. Oh, she knows Mount Weihu and Jiapi Ravine as well. These are names resounding in the ears of all Chinese people at the time.* Also, there is Jinzhou, a city well-known for apples, which appears in Chairman Mao's work on the Liaoning-Shenyang Campaign. What else? Oh, she knows the Greater Hinggan Mountains and Changbai Mountains too. The flashing by of the two place names lights up her eyes. They are like two huge flowers blossoming on a remote tree, these two names sounding hauntingly beautiful.

"It doesn't matter. So long as it's in the northeast, we can just walk in that direction," laughs Chen Yizhu and her laughter sounds bright and naive. "We could first go to Beijing. Many trains leave from there for the northeast, to Shenyang, Changchun, Harbin and Mudanjiang."

"I know Mudanjiang!" Liu Gang cuts in excitedly, "My mother's from Mudanjiang!"

"Really?"

"I went to Mudanjiang once. My Grandpa took me to see a doctor there and we stayed at my maternal grandma's home. There's

---

*Because of the nationwide performance of the Peking Opera *Taking Mount Weihu by Strategy* as well as a film of the same title.

a big river," says Liu Gang. Those were all the things that he remembered of Mudanjiang. "Auntie, will you take me to Mudanjiang, to the northeast?" he lifts his face and breathes quickly, "Are we going there by train?"

They soon arrive at the bus stop. It is the terminal of the No. 13 bus, or you may call it the starting point too. The No. 13 bus comes from the city, waits here for a few minutes before it returns to the city again. The name of the stop is "Hospital for Disabled Soldiers." That is not the one Chen Yizhu works at, even as the Hospital for Disabled Soldiers appears before them, sitting quietly across the road in the green shade of the poplar trees. Liu Gang remembers the place now. His class went there once, a visit organized by their school to see the criminal way the disabled soldiers had been tortured. The bare wire bed standing in the center of the gloomy floor branded him as an instrument of torture. Those human internal organs soaked in formalin: hearts, livers and lungs that looked so lonely, eerie and ugly, after being separated from their human bodies. They were turned into another kind of life form, into some sort of sorrowful and bloody eyes. That memory made his hair stand on end. Now this place looms before him again suddenly. He grips Chen Yizhu's hand tightly.

"Auntie, are we going to take a train? Are we leaving here for the northeast?" he asks eagerly.

"There are many ways for us to go where we wish to go," Chen Yizhu answers after thinking about it for a moment.

"How?"

Chen Yizhu looks at him gently: "Such as, with our imagination."

"Imagination?"

"Right," Chen Yizhu gets excited. She swings his small hand and tells him, "It will take us far away. We are in T City now but we can always go to a far, faraway place."

"That's only in fairytales," Liu Gang replies with some sadness.

"No, that is a different kind of living," says Chen Yizhu. "Say, let's try to go to some place now. How about a nearby place for now? Have you been to the Jinci Temple?"

Liu Gang shakes his head.

"Okay, let's go to the Jinci Temple then," Chen Yizhu looks up and the sunshine shimmers on her attractive face. "Now, we have to walk across this busy road," she points to her right. The road joins the dirt path through the green curtain of crops in the form of a T-shape. "It may take us half an hour of walking. Can you handle it?" Liu Gang nods excitedly. "Good! We should get to the Jinci Temple Highway in half an hour then. We can wait for the No. 8 bus at the Nantun bus stop as that is the closest one from here. If the bus is punctual, we will reach Jinci Temple in half an hour. We will need forty-five cents for each bus ticket."

"But I don't have money," Liu Gang sighs hesitatingly.

"That doesn't matter. I have it. When an adult and a child travel together, the child shouldn't worry about money matters. Isn't that right?"

"No, it's wrong to spend others' money. Grandpa and Grandma said we should not take other's things for free."

"Okay. Since you are a child of principle, let's say I will lend you the money. In the future, when you can start working and earn money, you could give it back to me. Is this arrangement alright for now?"

Liu Gang thinks about it and gives it some more thought, before he nods and smiles.

After the money issue is settled, they continue their walk. Chen

Yizhu starts to describe the landscape by the highway, saying, "Liu Gang, our bus is now rolling through the paddy fields. The area around Jinci Temple is the only place that has rice fields and harvests in T City. Jinci rice is extremely delicious, much tastier than the non-glutinous rice produced in southern China. The story goes that after being steamed, each grain of real Jinci rice stands up, looking crystal clear and smelling unbelievably fragrant. It is said that only one piece of land yields such valuable rice now but it is a pity we don't know which piece it is. Rice fields are so incompatible with our city on this arid plateau! It looks like an alien species that brings us the fresh air, moisture and beauty of southern China. Liu Gang, do you know why there is rice paddy in this area? It is because of the spring water from the Jinci Temple."

The No. 13 bus arrives and they get on it. The bus is bound for T City, but their imagination is running in the opposite direction and they feel as if they were walking on a totally different highway between paddy fields and lotus ponds. The summer lotus flowers are so dazzling! Colorful ducks and white geese are swimming in the ponds. Now the bus is stopping in front of the front gate of Jinci Temple Park. It is very quiet here as it is not a Sunday. Most of the visitors getting off the bus today are from out of town. They are here on official errands, investigating cases or visiting relatives. There is no one from T City. "The local people don't get on a bus to visit Jinci Temple on weekdays. They have no such carefree mood. But here we are, Liu Gang!" Chen Yizhu smiles contentedly and her smile makes her flow like a lively river glistening under sunshine.

"Good, Liu Gang. Here we go."

"Don't be surprised, child. In this ditch flows the spring water of Jinci Temple. Isn't it crystal clear? The water weeds look so soft and charming; see how it's so subdued and wavy — that's its way of survival. You'll see the source of the spring soon. Many fables and legends are told about this spring and I'll tell you some of them in a minute. Look, here we are entering the Offering Hall. It was built in the Song Dynasty. No, it might have been built during the Jin Dynasty. Its architecture is very unique. You don't see walls around it and no beams either. Isn't that so? Look again. There isn't a beam at all, right. We don't understand how it works because we are not architects, but professionals know. It is a miracle in architecture. Let's pass through the Offering Hall and keep going on. Stop and take a look now. We'll walk on a stone bridge with the blue stone floor and white stone railing. It is by no means an ordinary stone bridge, as it is known as 'Flying Beams over Fish Pond.' You see, how the bridge built was in a cross shape. Good, let's walk on it to better appreciate it. The cross plates stretch across the ditch. At present there are only two such cross-shape bridges preserved in the world. One is probably in Rome and the other is this one — 'Flying Beams over Fish Pond'! Our ancestors said that a round one is a pool and a square one is a pond. A single beam is called a bridge and a crossed one is called beams. That is why it is known as 'Flying Beams over Fish Pond'.

"Now look down and check out the spring water below. Turn left after we cross the bridge and we will pass another gate with stone steps. That is the only path for us to walk to the spring source. Look, this pavilion has a tablet with three characters written on it meaning 'Anchorless Boat.' Sitting in the water, doesn't the pavilion look like a boat anchored by the waterside? See the mouth of the spring from the cliff. The spring water gushes out from the 'Ageless Spring.' Just listen to its dingdong sounds. Isn't the water cascading down like a small waterfall? We will have to shout to hear each other when standing close.

"Let's walk down the steps. Be careful. The steps are cool and slippery, and the water vapor will spray us. The cool vapor rushes onto your face. Look, we've arrived at the 'Wise Uncle Ditch' now. Squat down, Liu Gang, you can put your hands in the spring and see how the water pats your palms and your hands, backing up and flowing through your fingers. Here, look here now. Do you see this stone dam? Do you see these holes in the dam? Count them and you will find ten holes. The spring water is split into two currents by the holes. The water flowing through these three holes flows to the west, while the water going through those seven holes flows to the east. Do you know there is a legend about it? It is the legend about 'Wise Uncle Ditch.' Now let's sit down in the 'Anchorless Boat' and listen to my story about that Wise Uncle and his ditch…."

The bus continues to move through the suburban and urban districts in its inevitable course toward the city center; yet in the whistling wind, they allow their minds to flow in the opposite direction, into the depths of folklore and botanical gardens, the Divine Mother Hall, the Water Mother Hall and the Shuyu Temple…. Liu Gang is taken across their ancient laps feeling a sense of boundless joy and unbelievable excitement. However, they soon arrive at the dorm gate of that construction unit. A man and a woman are running toward them. Their flustered behavior cuts short the climax of a most lovely journey.

Liu Gang's father kept saying, "Thank you! Thank you!" Tall, handsome and heavily bearded, he is a typical northeastern man. Even wearing a work suit, he doesn't really look like a worker. But Liu Gang's mother was yet to say anything. She just fixed her eyes on her son's hand which, in such an obedient, tame and trusting way, and in such an attached way, was now being held tightly by a strange woman.... The sight hurt her. Her son never allowed her to hold his hand in such an intimate way. Her son was so afraid to have his body touched by his mother. Like a piece of mimosa or a soft, sensitive insect, he was always scared, shrinking into a ball on being touched.

The sun was still shining brightly but this exceptionally bright noon was burning a hole in a mother's heart. The pain shot from her eyes to the depths of her body like seeds falling into the dark and warm soil. Of course, she at long last tried her best to put on a polite smile and said, "We owe all this to you!"

Chen Yizhu pushed the boy toward them gently. "He wanted to be a little Xu Xiake*!" she said happily. Refusing politely the father's invitation for lunch, she caressed the boy's hair and remarked, "Xu Xiake, come to me when you wish to travel."

Liu Gang smiled and at once tears began tumbling down his face. One after another, the big drops of tears were actually bullets hurtling towards his mother. Only, he was not to know this at all.

5. A Journey of Freedom

Starting that afternoon, Chen Yizhu became obsessed with one thing: to collect an atlas. She scouted all the large and small Xinhua bookstores in the city and bought an atlas of China, an atlas of world, as well as atlases of Chinese transportation and roads, the various provinces and physical geography....

Reading an atlas turns out to be such a pleasure. When familiar or unfamiliar names pop up before your eyes all of a sudden, you

---

*Noted Ming-dynasty travel writer and geographer

hear a kind of music following each appearance. For example, just turn a page of an atlas casually, place names such as Nagqu, Comai and Trashize show up like magic summoned by a mysterious and resonant call. Pure white and remote, they look as if heaven-sent.

Also, they resemble juicy fruit hanging from a marvelous tree, silent and secretive, forever anticipating something about to happen. Different types of places such as Hengtang, Yajishan or Xueyanqiao carry colors with them as in the landscape paintings of the Song and Yuan dynasties. You may even hear the ancient stringed *qin* instrument playing of mountains and waterfalls. But many more places remind one of everyday life — say, Liyujiang or Yangjiao-tang, without mysterious hues but filled with regular daily joy. However, other places such as Sanshili Pu, Manchuanguan or Luoshuihe sound like relay stations along desolate and lonely ancient journeys.

Of course, the first thing she did was to look for that name — Dongjing. It turned out to be quite easy to locate the town, sitting on a railway line, in southeastern Heilongjiang Province. The map's legend shows it as a small town adjoined on different sides by Langang, Ning'an, Wenchun and Mudanjiang.

She stares at it, the town's name on the map, for a very long time. She knows that in Liu Gang's eyes, this is his Grandpa, who coexists with Changbai Mountains. Sighing softly, she realizes that this must be the most touching and charming part of mountains to Liu Gang....

Now the home where she has been living alone becomes Liu Gang's favorite, most loved place. Almost every Sunday, the boy takes the No. 13 bus to come here, despite the tiring trip. As soon as he enters the room, he announces, "Hi, I am not late for the train, am I?" The journeys became the most important issue in his life now, more than meals, sleep, or playing with his little friends — even more crucial than home life with his parents. The glory of travel illuminates all the other hours in his life, and T City is no longer unbearable. He endures six dismal weekdays in order to welcome the bright Sundays. Like the radiating sun rising from the sea, Sunday leaps out from behind the horizon to light up the gloomy and tedious time, until everything becomes gilded by the brilliant rays of the sun.

They are the two best traveling partners: sturdy, enduring and energetic. Their bodies and hearts are equally sensitive, while their capacity to appreciate nature resembles plants knowing the four seasons. They sit in her small room, of a size less than fifteen square meters, and begin their journeys. The starting moment is always sacred and filled with a ceremonial solemnity. They hold their breath and put their palms together, before Chen Yizhu announces, "Good, let's start off now, Xu Xiake." Hence they start off with imaginary knapsacks on their backs. As soon as they set out on their journeys, they at once feel relaxed, as an immense joy fills their bodies. Each of their travel routes are planned carefully by Chen Yizhu. In the next several months, they make grand and arduous journeys to the west: to Xi'an to see the ancient Qin and Han dynasty wonders such as the Terracotta Warriors, then on to Gansu Province, to Lanzhou and Tianshui, to the end of the Great Wall at Jiayu Pass, until they make it to immortal Dunhuang in the Gobi desert, to gaze upon the ancient Buddhist cave murals. They also make scenic trips to south China. They visit the classical gardens in Suzhou, row a boat on Hangzhou's West Lake, then eat a dish of vinegary fish at the Louwailou Restaurant while sipping famed Longjing (Dragon-well) tea. They also make the cultural tours to ponder the Red Cliffs, ascend Beigu Hill and climb the Yueyang Pavilion, soaking in powerful nostalgic sentiments all along the way. The grandness of southwest

China bears their footprints, too. They sail from Wuhan and trace out the marvelous Three Gorges along the Yangtze River, before arriving in Chongqing. From Chongqing they take a train to Chengdu, and from there leave for Guizhou Province, arriving in Guiyang. Then Chen Yizhu pauses for a while, and suggests that they turn west from Guiyang, pass Anshun and Liupanshui, until they reach the Weining Autonomous County of the Yi, Hui and Miao peoples.

Without explaining why they must take on such remote, inconvenient and non-touristy places such as Weining, Chen Yizhu only remarks, "Liu Gang, did you know of Caohai (Grass Sea) there? It is the largest and the most beautiful lake in Guizhou." When saying these words, Chen Yizhu's eyes look as stirring and loving as the real Grass Sea.

Perhaps the place holds a secret in her personal life. But since she says nothing about it, Liu Gang doesn't ask either. He never asks about other things, say, 'Why are you different from others, without a home or a child?' He finds nothing wrong or strange about it, even though others gossip behind her back. He just likes what Aunt Chen is. She is not the type of woman like his mother. Aunt Chen is... a herbivorous animal. It is easy for Liu Gang to distinguish the descendants of those genuine herbivorous animals among the masses. So, even if Aunt Chen holds onto her own secrets, these must be open and honest secrets, which have nothing to do with any human shadiness.

Liu Gang passionately loves such a life. He feels that he has turned into a bird that can fly and soar everywhere. He loves such a feeling of freedom. He even feels his body transform to become as flowing and smooth as a bird, as if nothing could obstruct him now. What a wonderful feeling, that he can fly and soar! As this flight became real in his eyes, the life around him somehow turns unreal. T

City is no longer his prison cage. He knows how wide the horizons his spirit could now take him to.

There is only… only one place Liu Gang and Aunt Chen have chosen not to visit for all this length of time. This is none other than the town of Dongjing. And because of this, they avoid the entire northeast, including three big provinces. Their silhouettes wander along its boundaries several times, but they always turn away as soon as they approach the area. They travel to Qinhuangdao and Shanhai Pass, the other end of the Great Wall at the sea, to Chifeng, Hohhot and the Inner Mongolian grasslands. They roam along to the borders of these three dear provinces in northeast China, but at the last minute they always walk away.

Now Liu Gang has become a boy who loves maps with a passion. He reads maps like other children read picture books. Those places thickly dotting the pages turn into flower buds in his "annotations," which break into bloom when they visit them. His imagination gives him immense joy along with challenges knowing no bounds. He begins to search for even stranger place names on the maps, for example, Irkutsk, Lake Baikal, New Siberia, Tyumen or Moscow. In this way he sees the rail routes linking them up like a string of buds, still sleeping there soundly, radiating a sort of mysterious, dark exotic scent. He smiles, knowing they are calling out to him to visit them. So when he sees Aunt Chen the next time, he asks her, "When shall we go and see these places?"

Chen Yizhu is somewhat surprised.

"Sure, Liu Gang. But we have to do a lot of preparations, since this won't be an ordinary journey at all." Then she says something that sounds a little too profound to say to a child, "Russia is a dream of mine."

"Can we go there?" he lifts his face.

"I believe we have a way to cross the border."

He smiles. Of course, they can go wherever they want to. They are birds after all! Now he knows that the vast land has another name — Russia — besides its well-known appellations of "Soviet Revisionists" or "Old Hairy." Eventually he learns that the place not only has revisionists such as Khrushchev and Brezhnev, but also poets whose poems make that strange land appear kindhearted, beautiful and inspiring. Aunt Chen recites those poems with loving, hope-filled tears glistening in her eyes. They will go to that beautiful Russia, something truly exhilarating for them. He asks Aunt Chen time and again whether they are ready to go there. "Soon, Liu Gang, we are almost there."

All the trips eventually end at their terminus of the No. 13 bus, back at that lovely little home. It is always nestled behind the crop fields and vegetable gardens loyally waiting for them under the green shade of poplar trees. For these two, exhausted and travel-worn, the small room embraces and comforts them. Whenever the moment is up, Aunt Chen says to him, "Liu Gang, I have to go and boil water." She stands up and walks to the kitchen. And twenty minutes later Liu Gang is burying himself in the steamy and safe trough. This water caresses his skin warmly, as he feels himself transformed into a wispy beautiful water plant. He believes with all his heart that everything here looks so appealing, everything his eyes can see.... In the kitchen across the hall, the woman, just calming down from the thrilling emotional journey, sits by the stove quietly. Listening to the clear and unclear splashing water sounds from her room, she believes that these are moments filled with tenderness and goodwill in her own life, too.

6. Who is Our Enemy?

Now it is Li Shu's turn to step onto the stage. Li Shu has been waiting in pain for such a long time already. This woman is not a bad woman really. It is a common feature for such good women to be honest and watch their own nests with vehemence. Li Shu is an accountant. Sitting in an office all year round maintains her originally fair and smooth skin, making it even fairer and smoother. She looks like a Korean woman, although she is not. She is a mother of four, so she has started to gain weight and lose her former shape. Her waist is no longer as slender as a girl's. Her bottom is also no longer as compact as a girl's. Now it hangs loosely and heavily on her behind, making her originally slender legs appear much shorter than before.

All the years have been deposited in the fat accumulated on her behind, which is kind of saddening. That a young woman, fresh from accountant school with two big black braids, could erode into such a sad form at the twinkling of an eye. Certainly that was what her husband Lao Liu thinks, yet Li Shu herself instead feels rather proud of her wide and plump shape. This is the commemoration of posterity bearing fruit and what a fecund acre of land she has been — able to lustily breed and nurture. "How about you? You the hen! Have you ever laid an egg?"

More and more frequently these days, Li Shu dishes out such challenges. Women like Li Shu, ever alert to the scent of different species, can pick out an alien from the crowds with just one look. Incredibly sharp-eyed, even if they are blind, they are able to sniff out somebody not their type with just their noses. To them that odor is a sort of sex-laden mixture of green grass in the sultry summer, musk in the spring, the lure of incense and seminal fluid, plus the greasy sweet smell of rotting, fermenting apples. Li Shu could sniff that ominous smell from afar during that dazzlingly bright noon. It shrouded her son and became omnipresent about him from that day on. It was the light in the daytime, the darkness at night, the swallowing sounds of mealtime and her son's even breathing in bed. Her child has fallen into the hands of such a witch, thinks Li Shu gallingly. Nobody can see the truth better than she does. Her child was actually lost to her from that dizzy, evil noontide.

Sometimes she could even see a layer of foggy mist over her son, separating him from the normal world. She cannot reach him because that misty stuff turns hard as soon as she tries to touch him. Her boy hides behind this shield of fog like a prince hiding inside the skin of a frog or a big bear. It is the legendary invisible coat. Her son has disappeared without a trace after he donned it.

Even the old method of bathing cannot help now, and any talk of baths has become real disaster. Whenever she would ask him to go to the bathhouse, he now retorted, "I'm not dirty. I've bathed already." "Where'd you bathe?" Li Shu asked even though she knew the answer already. "At Aunt Chen's place," answered Liu Gang. But these words were terrible and unbearable to Li Shu. They sounded like a curse echoing time and again in their home, until it condensed into a thick layer onto their floor like fallen leaves, soft yet sticky, under her feet. She felt as if the sticky layer was glued to her feet and almost burying her entire person alive. The boy would extend his hands. The hands are clean. Rolling up his sleeves, his arms are clean too. Checking behind his ears, she can find nothing dirty there. Sniffing at his hair, nothing wrong there either. Her son is clean, smooth and shiny pure from the inside out, without even a trace of dirt or dust. Above reproach, however, his body yet carries and conceals the evil influence of that woman. It writhes beneath his skin like innumerable small snakes.

Trying her best to control her anger, Li Shu said to her son, "You are dirty even though you've bathed. Since you go to a hospital all the time, you get germs all over you, so you are ten times, a hundred times dirtier than before!" Her son grew furious. Yes, it was a flaming fury. When Li Shu blamed the woman, either openly or insinuatingly, her son's reaction was always fierce anger. He would look at her angrily, but soon his rage turned into sadness. Of course, the one who had to give in finally was the son, eventually forced to go to the bathhouse. Nonetheless, what was terrible was that the evil influence grew stronger and stronger after each time he returned. So she came to understand that the bad influence could never be washed off. Water failed to dissolve or dilute it at all. Instead, it kept growing, gaining increasing vitality as if irrigated by bathwater. What is it then, if you say it is not witchcraft?

Li Shu said to her husband, "Lao Liu, forbid your son from roaming to such places that far away. It isn't safe for him." To that Lao Liu answered, "What's there to fear? He even dared to abscond all alone, so why shouldn't he drop by there now? Also, how can we control his legs?" Possessing a carefree personality, Lao Liu was very busy with the project he headed in the all-out campaign at work. How could he worry about so many things? Not willing to give in, however, Li Shu retorted, "What an awful place that hospital is! Don't you worry about getting infected by those germs?"

"Stop fussing. Are you a glass figurine or a Lin Daiyu*? Why so fragile? Let him go if he wants to. Isn't it better than running away? Doctor Chen is so nice, and she is good at enlightening people.

---

*Frail young female character from *A Dream of Red Mansions*.

Don't you see now the boy has become much more open and happier these days?"

Good heavens above! Men are so stupid! More open and happier — was her husband blind or simply harboring other motives? Li Shu sneered, "Oh yes, isn't she the great one? It seems it's not just your son who loves going there, huh?"

"What nonsense are you talking about? Why do you, old haystack, have such a warped mind?"

"Ah, now you find me warped. Then why did you choose me from the beginning?"

In the end Lao Liu sighed, "Li Shu, I've been working sixteen hours. Can't I sleep now?"

Okay, let men fall asleep, even in the grave! Li Shu sneered again, "But I can't allow myself to be bullied openly like this, can I? I won't let others steal my kicking and splashing boy away from under my nose!" She remembered the opera, *Mu Guiying Takes Charge*. Yes, it is Mu Guiying's turn on the stage now.

If it had taken place nowadays, the two women would have chosen to meet at a teahouse or a quiet small restaurant with a graceful atmosphere suitable for a discussion. Such scenes often take place in soap operas. But it was not possible at that time, there being no such bourgeois settings around then. So Li Shu chose a park as their meeting place.

The park hardly had any visitors in late autumn. Fallen leaves were everywhere in the park, grumbling desperately under Li Shu's resolute strides. The two women were sitting side by side on a green bench by the lake. The sight appeared slightly bizarre, as the lakeside benches are generally used by lovers to exchange honeyed whispers. These two, however, were essentially hostile to each other. Li Shu tried to put on an intimate smile:

"Doctor Chen, please don't blame me for minding another's business. I want to fix you a date."

"Big Sister...."

"Don't decline my offer with whatever excuses. Let me tell you this: Engineer Bai is a good man in a million. His wife died two years ago and he has been alone with the child...."

"Big Sister," Chen Yizhu interrupted, "I really don't want to discuss the topic."

"Why not?" Li Shu stared at her with exaggerated amazement. "It is a big issue affecting your entire life. You cannot be alone forever, right? Doctor Chen, it is not that I want to criticize you. You have reached adulthood for a while now and you just cannot be this picky. Aren't all men the same in certain aspects? Get married and give birth to a child of your own, so... so you don't have to eye others' children all the time."

Li Shu said it — the words long buried in her breast. Chen Yizhu understood now. She understood one thing in that windy and cold autumn, but it was too late to realize it. Speechless, she looked at the woman, the boy's mother, sitting by her side, without knowing what to say. She realized the nature of their meeting now. A trap set up as a feast. She smiled sadly.

"Big Sister," she said after a long pause, "You can rest assured that nobody will take away your child."

"Doctor Chen, please don't misunderstand...."

"I haven't misunderstood," she replied and stood up, "I must go now, Big Sister."

She walked for a very long time in the cold wind, alone from one end of the city to the other. Autumn wind blasted her face and her face became icy cold. She did not know when her tears started streaming down. It shocked her, as she had almost forgotten when she last cried before, when her tears had been as precious as gold. She thought to herself: "Isn't it ridiculous? She is afraid I want to rob her son!" However, she failed to laugh out loud. She stepped on the fallen leaves scattered everywhere in the city and listened to their grumbling under the crushing of her feet. She remembered a saying: "Human hearts can be darker than the night."

Later she phoned Lao Liu, asking him to tell Liu Gang not to come visit her again. She was scheduled to take a long journey away from home.

She did leave home early in the morning that following Sunday. She went to visit an old schoolmate in the city whom she had not seen for a long while. She stayed at her friend's place the whole day. They had a good time making dumplings and drinking green plum wine. On bidding goodbye to her old friend, she said, "What a happy day we've had today!" Then she walked onto the chilly streets. Listening to her own steps, she asked herself, "Am I really happy?"

She almost kicked someone lying in the dark corridor. A person curled up at the doorstep of her small home sleeping silently like a dog. She knew at once who it is. That familiar, dear breath took hold of her again. He had been waiting for her the whole day! She felt something explode in her that moment. Nevertheless, she tried to hold herself, hold on.... She eventually said, "Did I not tell you I had to take a long journey away from home?"

"I didn't believe it," he replied peacefully.

"I meant it."

"But you've come back now."

"What if I didn't come back?"

"I would wait for you," he answered peacefully but resolutely, "forever."

She sighed, and her tears burst out suddenly. She asked herself why she has become so weak, but she did not try to control herself, instead letting the tears flow freely. She watched him stand up slowly and lean his small body against the door. A rock-solid posture in a most firm way. She shook her head and said, "Oh, Liu Gang, Liu Gang, what shall I do about you?"

7. Rose Garden

It is easy to imagine how angry Li Shu was now. Her effort at obstruction had failed and her son kept running to that damned woman's home on Sundays. How smug that woman must be feeling now. She would just say, "Sure, sure, he's your son." True as it is, just look at whom he is attached to!

The eyes of the smug and taunting conqueror haunted Li Shu's life, spreading an evil odor like that of salted fish everywhere. Li Shu told herself, "Don't you celebrate this early. The one who laughs last laughs best, isn't that so, dirty thing!"

Her son was distancing himself from her farther and farther each day. She knew this. Even if he stayed home, you could not tell where his soul has wandered to. He had stopped being a normal child like before. Would you ever see a normal child gaze at a dog-eared atlas as he does all day long? What mystery or secret lies in all this? Normal boys usually get together, fight one another or run around wild. That is how a boy should behave. But look at him! He talked strangely and senselessly besides reading those atlases. Of course, he did not repeat those strange words except to his younger sister Hongxia. In the family, only Hongxia is able to pry open his mouth. Playing the role of a messenger, the six-year-old Hongxia with two pigtail brushes would shuttle between Li Shu and her second brother like a dashing swallow. Hongxia told her mother, "Ma, Second Brother was in Guilin." "Nonsense!" snapped Li Shu. Not bothered at all, Hongxia would then run away to play her hopscotch.

On another day, Hongxia ran to her mother and said, "Ma, Second Brother went to Urumqi." Li Shu put out a hand to feel the girl's forehead but found she was running no fever. What nonsense was she talking about! Li Shu sighed, "It's terrible for our family to have one child bewitched already. Please don't join in that kind of play again, okay?" "No, not okay," Hongxia replied, and then flung her short braids and hopped away to kick up her feather shuttlecock.

Finally, the day arrived when Hongxia ran to her mother and said, "Ma, Second Brother is going to — Russia." Li Shu was truly shocked this time. Frightened in a big way, she asked her daughter, "My little devil, are you insane?" Hongxia replied, "No, I'm not. Who is insane? Second Brother said Aunt Chen will take him to visit Russia, to see the troika!"

Li Shu heard her heart jumping fiercely. Good, oh good, she thought. Suddenly her heart beat gave off a happy note. It was starting a happy tap dance now, the same dance Khrushchev did when he was drunk, kicking and tapping the mirror-like Kremlin floor with his big leather boots. How merry! Great! Li Shu told herself and even turned pale in her excitement. "How great it is for me to find the secret of the atlas. I've been waiting so long. I've earned this moment after all this long wait!"

There was once a term: "Sun-facing Courtyard." The term has vanished today, but it was once a newly emerging fad in the 1970s.

Now when we walk into such a "sun-facing courtyard," we sniff the scent of that era immediately. The essence of the bygone era has been sealed in historical terms such as this one, like those old bottles of perfume preserved and unopened for years. It will be the place where this story ends. As in those fairytales, there often emerges a beautiful park or a rose garden in its denouement. So our rose garden appears now and we are stepping into such a "sun-facing courtyard."

The "sun-facing courtyard" was bright without any dark corners. The life of all the residents here was exposed thoroughly under the blinding sunlight. Their life had to be transparent, clean and crystal clear. It was a crime for anyone to hold back any secrets.

But then, a single woman, a woman who never got married yet by her thirties, would be in itself considered a big secret and a huge dubiety. How could the sunny courtyard residents tolerate such an anomaly amongst them? Many knife-sharp, upright and strict eyes have thus been observing her! However, she has concealed herself so well, remaining waterproof and even airproof! She walks in and out cheerfully with her face written over with frankness and pureness all day long. Nonetheless, a woman named Zhang Guixiang was reminding herself at this very moment: "You will reveal your tail so long as you are a fox."

Zhang Guixiang is the chair of this sun-facing courtyard. A housewife in her forties, she is also Chen Yizhu's neighbor. Living in the same tube-shaped dormitory building, their rooms are only a few doors apart. The authority has true talent in selecting someone like Zhang Guixiang to be the chair of the dormitory courtyard. She is so sharp-eyed and clever-minded that hers are a match for the keenest ears and the most eager nose of a hunting hound. Wait, did she not even predict it? Zhang Guixiang had become really excited ever since that boy started to walk into their dormitory building. Zhang Guixiang had thought: "Just wait, the fox's tail will be out soon!"

In fact, Zhang Guixiang at first had not paid much attention to the boy's visits. However, it gradually began to appear a little unusual. How come that boy came so frequently and regularly? When Sunday arrived, no matter rain, wind or snow, the boy would always appear in the dark corridor stacked with junk. He took up all the spare time of that single woman. As soon as the boy arrived, the two of them would shut themselves in her room for at least half a day. No one knew what they were doing there behind those shut doors. You could only hear their talk rising loud and falling low from time to time. It was the woman who talked most of the time. Where did a woman in her thirties find all those things to say to a boy? Zhang Guixiang did try to get in there to check. Actually she went into the woman's room many times, using excuses of collecting water and electricity fees, gathering sanitation charges, borrowing things, or simply dropping around without any excuse. Every time she went in there, nevertheless, she saw basically the same scene. The two of them either sitting side by side intimately on her bedside, or sitting face to face across the table engaged in some exciting discussion. Nothing seemed suspicious. No, not really. What looked suspicious was the sense of intimacy between them. The kind of … intimacy you would see only between flesh and blood. Oh, there was also that bathing. The boy took baths in that single woman's bedroom! Sure, that woman generally stayed in the kitchen while the boy bathed. But was it not, according to the saying, a guilty person who so conspicuously pretends innocence? Zhang Guixiang smiled smugly: what else could it be?

Even from a distance of several doors, Zhang Guixiang seemed to be able to discern the sounds of water splashing. The sounds must be meant to cover up something. Ah, accompanied by such sounds, the woman must be caressing the boy slowly, stroking every part most intimately. She was holding him to her bosom, letting him... suckle her breasts! Things grew clearer and clearer now. Her suspicions became validated by those scenes in her mind. "Ah, she must have an illegitimate child!" Zhang Guixiang thought victoriously.

She became excited, unbelievably excited because she had been able to decipher the secret. "Hey, you, ha!" she called out the woman's name, "The most cunning fox is caught by a good hunter sooner or later!" She was sure she had finally ripped off that woman's mask of purity and pride.

The next day, she stopped that woman in the corridor and remarked, "Doctor Chen, did you hear the news — someone found an artificial leather travel bag at the No. 13 bus stop? Guess what they found inside the travel bag when they opened it?" "What did they find?" asked Chen Yizhu innocently. "An illegitimate child!" replied Zhang Guixiang loudly.

"That's a sin," Chen Yizhu commented.

"Isn't that so?" Zhang Guixiang giggled.

But good heavens, who would ever imagine things would turn even more dramatic, obscene, and simply shameless! A woman named Li Shu appeared before Zhang Guixiang one winter evening. Li Shu had been able to first locate the revolutionary committee of the hospital, and then she made it to the sun-facing courtyard. The chair of the courtyard, Zhang Guixiang, received the woman at her home. She was still unable to imagine what shocking or exciting news the visitor was carrying with her. Putting on her business face at the beginning, Zhang Guixiang told the visitor, "Sit down, sit down. Sit on the *kang* as I'm not equipped with an office desk yet." So Li Shu sat down on the heated *kang* bed and opened her mouth, "That damned Chen Yizhu!" Tears spilled out and she started condemning Chen Yizhu, on and on in tears. While listening to the visitor's accusations, Zhang Guixiang found herself soaked in a cold sweat. No, it was the cold sweat of excitement. "Younger Sister," Zhang Guixiang patted the back of Li Shu's hand, "I even thought the boy was her illegitimate child! Who could've thought... who'd ever have imagined?" Li Shu looked at her, choking, "Eldest Sister, are you cursing me? That's my own blood, my child from a ten-month pregnancy. I vomited whatever I ate while carrying him until my face turned green and I spat out my own gall. I felt as if my organs were being shattered, bit by bit spewing out whenever I opened my mouth! It was so miserable. I had a difficult labor when giving birth to him, and the doctor had to make a lateral incision on me — sewed me up with twenty-four stitches!"

"Sure, sure, Younger Sister, all of us mothers have been through the same suffering. We mustn't let our own blood fall into the lap of an evil woman! Who could ever imagine she even has plans to kidnap another's child and run away? What is most unbearable is her scheming to go to the enemy and sell out our country! She wants to run to the Soviet revisionists to live a bourgeois, decadent life! She must dislike our country for not having such freedoms! But we masses have sharp eyes and we must forbid her to commit such a crime so easily. Younger Sister, you have not even witnessed what she has done to your son's body yet."

"Big Sister, what has that witch done to my son? Oh dear, what has she done to my son? Tell me please, Big Sister!"

"Younger Sister, I really cannot tell you, you know, it's just too wicked! Oh, bear with me and I'll slowly try to...."

These two women, Li Shu and Zhang Guixiang, two mothers, sat together and talked heart-to-heart with such mutual understanding, mutual sympathy, and a common hatred against their enemy. One's own child born after ten months' hard pregnancy to become what another has tried to plunder and… *violate.* Yes, it was violating. The word burst out and at once shot right into a mother's heart. Then Zhang Guixiang recalled the bathing, the ambiguous and private sounds of water splashing. All of it appeared different to her now. She imagined the two of them stroking and hugging each other wet in that giant trough. Her stroking the tender parts of the boy to watch it rise erect…. It was so evil-hearted, that she shuddered. She gripped the hands of the grieving mother, and described everything slowly yet vividly, while trying to give her support and strength. Both of them were the type of people who with certainty upheld justice and abhorred evil….

They blew and firmly sounded the bugle.

8. Midsummer Fervor

The condemnation rally was held in the open space where children used to play in front of the dormitory building. Here, boys would kick balls, while girls played games of rubber-band skipping or handkerchief dropping. Surrounded by trees, mostly poplar and locust, the space with its cool green shade was a paradise for children in the summer. But it was winter now, and the trees were bare with a neat hard look. And the air was rock hard frozen with cold currents too.

But the fervor of the masses, like the fervor of midsummer, was red hot. The women had enough sunlight and heat energy stored in their bodies. What a horrible crime it was! Even treason and fleeing to an enemy country seemed less awful in comparison. What provoked these women most of all was the obscenity that shameless woman had committed on a boy…. They had already learned everything from Zhang Guixiang. More than once they had heard from her the story in all its graphic details. Now they were gathered here with their righteous anger, anger exaggerated to hide their excitement and peeping desires. They were yelling noisily now, demanding she confess her crime. After a while their yells turned to focus on a single target. That huge, shameless yet exciting vision flashed before their eyes, and they began to shout: "Did you stroke him? Did you touch him? Say it! Did you make him touch your breasts? Did you...?"

Yelling hotly, they lost any sense of shame and became even more excited. What a magnificent feat of collective masturbation! However, the condemned woman only clenched her teeth and kept her silence. Gradually, bombarded by the mad yelling around her, she felt herself going under and turning blind to what was happening before her. At first she had raised her face to stare at the sky. The sky above her was far and wide, a thin and bright ash-blue. Those happy journeys they made under the same high and noble sky! But stained and made filthy in such a short time. The friendship and the tender affection between a lonely adult and a lonely child had been so quickly twisted and polluted. Contaminated beyond recognition, it was kicked down into a dark abyss.

The silence of the condemned woman, however, only further enraged the crowd. Their forbearance was tested too far by her refusal to cooperate. Unable to confirm the evil and lewd story through her confession, they thirsted for more lurid scenarios. It fanned their pent-up cravings, until they could no longer control their indignation. They finally acted it out. While shouting, "Revolution is not a dinner party," they threatened, "Do you think we can't prove it if you don't say anything?" "Don't do shameful things if you don't want others to know!" "Why not check her breasts? Check if they are still a virgin's!" "They must be rubbed tender by others," and "They're a bitch's tits already!" They scrambled over to tear at her clothing. They pitched in to tear off her padded jacket, pull down her sweater and rip open her bra. Before they realized it, a dazzling scene appeared, as two most beautiful, pure, timid and noble breasts were exposed to the world, like two falling doves or delicate flowers. They revealed the woman's snow white and noble secret in the biting December freeze. The unscrupulous crowd fell silent suddenly, as if dazzled by a powerful sunbeam. In that awkward silence, the extraordinary and dazzling beam, like the bright Milky Way, blazed out the boundary between the dusty mortal world and the heavenly kingdom.

But our boy, after breaking through his mother's obstructions, was rushing there at that very moment. That Sunday morning his mother would not allow him to leave home no matter what, but he still managed to slip away when she was not watching. He was running toward that place. He was almost there. He stepped off the No. 13 bus. He started striding through the winter fields. The fields looked spacious and deserted without any crops now. House sparrows were hopping about looking for food here and there, the field enfolded in a serene atmosphere of peaceful life. The boy did not know that this would be the last peaceful and serene moment of his own life. Now he had entered the front gate of the courtyard and could see the crowds. He suddenly felt restless. Astounded for a while at first, he walked toward the crowds. Those standing in the outer circles saw him and instantly fell quiet. They moved to give way to him. He walked on and on along this long path, until he started to sense the odor of blood. He realized he was walking into a surrounding circle of fierce flesh-eating beasts. Then, all of a sudden, he saw the woman with her naked chest — the darkest, ugliest and meanest moment, but at the same time the brightest, sweetest and noblest picture in the human world.

That night, the woman killed herself with sleeping pills. Being a doctor, she knew which type was the most effective. She poured those little white, demon-like pills down her throat with grape wine. Spinning and flying in her body, the pills gradually led her toward another world. Before she departed the human world, she took a warm bath by soaking herself in the big jujube trough for a long, long time. She had boiled the balmy water with dried jasmine, chrysanthemum and golden bell flowers as well as orange peel. The woman bade farewell to society surrounded by fragrance and purity. The woman told herself: "I will not take the filth of human beings to where I am going."

People found the letter when sorting through her remaining things. The letter was for Liu Gang. Lao Liu delivered the letter to his gravely ill son. While his son was reading the letter, Lao Liu dared not look at the boy's face. The letter had been written as follows:

"*My Little Friend:*

This time, I am going to make the journey alone. This time I am traveling to the place that is the farthest place a person is able to reach.

You will eventually have to go to Dongjing alone, to face by yourself your Grandpa's grave. That is the reason why we kept on hesitating and hesitating to go there. We both understand this bit, don't we? My dear little friend, if you love a person, he or she will never die. This is also what I want to tell you as my last words for you.

We have spent the happiest days and made the most joyful journeys together. Now my journey is over. I have used the final power left in me to retain the most precious thing in my eyes — the beauty of dignity. Therefore, I chose this way to travel to my destiny. However, you still have a long way to go in your journey. It requires courage and an openhearted spirit. You have both. You must hold onto them throughout your life. Child, remember my words: Continue your journey well and go forward. Every single place your body and spirit will journey to, will be sure to give your old friend boundless joy…."

9. Leaving T City Behind

Liu Gang disappeared once again. This time it happened after he recovered from his grave illness. Careful readers might have realized that I altered the ending of the fable, even if I prefer the story to have both endings hanging side by side together. But that is not the truth. The actual story is that Li Shu got up that morning and found Liu Gang's bed in the outer room empty at barely 6:30 in the early morning. The day was just dawning and snowing hard outside. Snowflakes were dancing across the sky. Li Shu panicked at once. Her son had vanished into the whirling snowstorm without a trace.

Liu Gang has not returned home ever since. T City has lost that boy forever. This boy had come, then left again. T City once had a chance, to turn herself gentler, purer, more romantic and more humane. But this opportunity was ultimately lost. T City did not recognize valuable treasures, so she lost her last chance. In the following years, she spun out with the speed of flight, resonating the steel-cold, dissonant noise of a modern expressway heading into the next century.

As for the vanished boy, no one ever learned what happened to him afterward. Someone said he was shot dead trying to cross the Sino-Soviet boundary illegally. Still, there are others who claim that ultimately the boy became a poet.

(Translated by Ji Hua & Gao Wenxing)

Ending Where I Started

Fang Fang

Fang Fang. Born Wang Fang in 1955 in Nanjing, Jiangsu Province, in 1957 Fang Fang moved with her parents to Wuhan, Hubei Province. After graduating from high school, she worked as a stevedore for four years. Through the entrance examination she joined the Chinese Department of Wuhan University in 1978, and after graduation became an editor for Hubei TV. She was transferred to the Hubei Writers' Association in 1989 as professional writer. In 2007 she became the editor-in-chief of *Contemporary Celebrities* and chair of the Hubei Writers' Association.

Fang Fang began writing poetry from 1975, and published her debut fiction *In the Big Van*, followed by collections such as *A Song for Age 18*, *The Other Riverbank*, *One Singer and Her Chorus*, and *Floating Clouds and Flowing Streams*. *Scenery*, published in 1987, won the 1987-88 China Novella Prize. Her subsequent works, including *Grandfather in Father's Eyes* were highly commended. She has published over 60 fiction and prose collections, including her latest story collection entitled *Spring Comes to Tanhualin*. A wide selection of her fiction has been published overseas in English, French, Japanese, Italian and Korean. Her representative works are the novel *Wunihu Chronicles*, the informal essay "Old Residences on Lushan Mountain," and her novellas *Scenery* and *Blossoming Peach Trees*.

Ending Where I Started

What might have been and what has been
Point to one end, which is always present.
Footfalls echo in the memory
Down the passage which we did not take
Towards the door we never opened
Into the rose-garden.

— from *Four Quartets*, T.S. Eliot

1

When Huang Suzi was born, her father was in the corridor of the hospital reading the poems of Su Shi, the great man of letters in China's Song Dynasty. The man already had two boys and two girls, so he did not care whether his wife gave birth to a baby or not, let alone its gender. It was autumn, a season always resembling an ambitious man who easily gets quite depressed and emotionally unsteady due to lack of appreciation from others. Now the man was in bad mood. Thus the gloomy sky also seemed to take on a forlorn face, with pockmarked clouds scattered everywhere.

The corridor lights of the hospital resembled its mortuary, giving out this dim light creating an ominous ambience. The glass of the windows was broken in places, so the windows resembled angry lions with wide-open mouths. The broken glass reflected the glistening cold light. Wind brushed through teeth-like broken glass and whistled into the corridor. Huang Suzi's father sunk himself in a shaky chair reading Su Shi. He kept tucking in his neck time and again, with the chair squeaking from these movements.

Her father leafed through the pages quietly with his fingers. White and long, his fingers would sometimes cramp suddenly. The book had turned yellowish from age, its characters vertically arranged. On its cover was Su Shi's angular-faced and long-bearded portrait. This historic personage did not look as tall and charming as what Huang Suzi imagined. He had once thought angrily, "Could such a person be Su Shi?" He figured the painter of the portrait must have neither seen Su Shi nor understood his work. Her father had made a red plastic cover for this book, but it was not because he hated this portrait.

The time was autumn, 1966, the early stage of the "cultural revolution" in China. Huang Suzi's father was under criticism, and her pregnant mother had become frightened by the Red Guards searching their house.

Su Shi said: "So skilled at calligraphy and so learned, I should therefore be able to easily gain a chance to serve the king. I know how to choose or discard things and expose or hide myself in the proper way, so nothing should bother me. As long as I am healthy, I will greet my end, traveling at leisure and drinking like mad." Reading this and thinking of the big-character posters criticizing him just pasted up on walls, he could not help saying, "Absolutely wonderful, so well written."

Right at this moment, a woman doctor ambled gracefully over and said, "You have a daughter, 1.65 kilograms." As she spoke she shot an ill-intentioned glance at the book he was reading.

Huang Suzi's father closed the book in a hurry and said, "It is excellent, this article by Chairman Mao."

"Which one?" she asked.

He was so nervous inside, he replied hastily, "*On Practice.* It's so good. I've got an idea. I will name my daughter Huang Shijian*. My family name is Huang."

The woman doctor smiled and said seriously, "That is a name with commemorative meaning. I was once a member of a Publicity Group for Chairman Mao's Works. But you don't look like an activist in studying Chairman Mao's works." After these words she left.

Huang Suzi's father was soaked in a cold sweat.

His original plan had been to name his child, whether it was a boy or girl, Huang Suzi** after the poet, but this talkative woman doctor had strangled this beautiful and meaningful name in the cradle, and because of this her father harbored a certain degree of dislike towards this newly born baby — Huang Suzi.

Huang Suzi got to know how things had come into being twelve years after her birth. It was at a criticism meeting, where her father recalled what had happened in that hospital. When recalling the episode at the hospital, her father was bathed in tears and claimed that he would now return the name "Huang Suzi" to her daughter. All the people present — her father's colleagues and Suzi's students from her middle school — cheered at this news.

Huang Suzi was also present. She was then a shy and sensitive student just starting junior high school. Many students kept looking at her and whispering to each other about her, some of them even

---

*Shijian means "practice."

**"Suzi" (pronounced "Sutse"), or Master Su, is a respectful name for Su Shi, a great man of letters in the Song Dynasty (960-1279).

tittering, which made her so nervous that she wanted to pee. A boy, nicknamed Rascal, opened his mouth wide and said, "Huang Shijian the 'wretch' is becoming Huang Su Biaozi." *As he was saying this, his spit flew onto Suzi's face, and all the people around began to laugh.

The sound of the laughter rose and fell in the sunshine. Long shadows of the elms near the fences were projected among these people, mottled and speckled. One branch reached as far as the platform of the meeting and swung in the wind. Its swinging turned the sunshine into blinding silver shards in its shadows. At that moment, all the faces of people seated on the platform blurred and seemed light, like those of actors on a stage. The headmaster, also with such a mask, cried out on the platform, "Quiet! Listen to Mr. Huang's criticism of the 'gang of four'!"

Huang Suzi sobbed at low volume. Everybody became quiet then, but few people heard her soft crying.

After this experience, the non-talkative Huang Suzi became even more incommunicative, but her father had no idea what had happened. The next day he went to the residence registration agency and changed Huang Suzi's name. Back home, he declared to his family, "From now on, there is no Huang Shijian in the world. There is only Huang Suzi."

Suzi's older sister curled her lips and said, "A *shuzi* (comb)? Or a hairclip?"

Suzi's oldest brother said, "Huang Shijian is actually a more memorable name."

But Suzi's oldest sister screamed, "Is there anything memorable about the 'cultural revolution'? Papa was criticized badly and Jianjian was born. Nothing worth remembering."

Suzi's younger brother said, "Her pet name used to be Jianjian.

---

*This is a Chinese play on words: *jian* also meaning "wretch"; *biaozi* meaning "whore."

Now what should we call her? Susu or Zizi?"

Huang Suzi's father thought a while, and said, "Both are rather twisted, right?"

"There are really few in the world as deranged as you," said her mother.

After that, Huang Suzi was still called Jianjian by her family.

In such a noisy family she grew up, but she had always been a shy and quiet girl. Her two elder brothers and two sisters never took any special care of her for being the youngest, and neither did her parents — it was as if she was an extra person to this family. Simply because of this, perhaps, she always looked lonely and unhappy, but she never complained to her mother unless she was bullied by her brothers and sisters. Her mother, a housewife who did not have a good relationship with her father, occasionally helped her, but more often she just blamed it on Suzi as always asking for trouble. This always left Suzi at a loss when she was bullied. For the few complaints she brought up, her two sisters thought she was an "insidious" type of person.

Suzi's father never cared about whether his children quarreled with each other. He seldom stayed with them, since he dedicated his time entirely to his school and took rather too much care of his students, for which he got a certificate for merit every year during and after the "cultural revolution." He was busy from dawn until dark in his office, and sometimes he did not come home until night, so Suzi's brothers and sisters had to take meals to him at school. Huang Suzi thought her father was not so much a teacher to his students, but a father to them. Yet she could not remember him helping her once in any way, or ever teaching her anything gently. But one incident was buried deep in her memory. During a family meal he had gotten irritated just because she had not used the common chopsticks for picking from the dishes and had made a little noise when chewing.

He immediately pulled a long face and had shouted at her, "Use the common chopsticks for food and no noise when chewing! You should learn civilized manners at a young age!" She was too frightened to take any more food during that meal.

As she grew older, Huang Suzi became even less interested in talking, neither was she good at activities or sports, and even seldom smiled. Thus she had few friends. She always did her own thing and was indifferent or numb to anything else. This made her brothers and sisters, who never liked her, like her even less, and they always chastised her at home, "Are you soft in the head or what?"

Actually, however, there was nothing wrong with her brain, for she easily passed the entrance exam for the best middle school in her city, while her brothers and sisters had to make much more effort to do this. Worst of all, the school would never have accepted her second elder sister were it not for her father's stature as a teacher there and the family's extra sum of money.

Huang Suzi's sister was two grades above her, so when Suzi entered high school, the other was about to graduate. Though related, the two never went to school together, and never talked with each other even when they met on the playground. All the teachers of the school knew Suzi's father, thus they knew the two girls. They all said the two sisters were a bit odd. Suzi's father always took his reputation highly, so he was not happy about hearing such appraisal. He blamed it on Huang Suzi but not on her sister, for he thought it was caused by Suzi's arrogance. Suzi exploded into a mild spate of hatred towards her father. "It has to do with both of us, so why I am to blame?" she thought. Blamed by her father, Huang Suzi became more indifferent to her sister. In fact, they had never done anything actually harmful to each other, but they just could not get along very well. Gradually the discussion about them among the teachers ceased.

In the second half of her second year at high school, one of Huang Suzi's boy classmates suddenly began to chase after her and his love letters flew at her one after another, all extremely ardent. At first Huang Suzi tore all his letters into shreds, ignored the boy and concealed this from everyone, but the boy did not stop. At a school party, the boy handed her a letter in front of three other boys. The ardor hidden in the letter made Suzi pretty uncomfortable, the main reason being one of its sentences: "If we could become lovers, we could stay together all day long, and I would kiss you from head to toe without stop, and roam my lips all over your body." Suzi felt rather queasy. She wrote down three words — "Shame on you!" — on the letter and put it up on the blackboard.

This incident shocked the class, and the boy was summoned to the office. Great anger twisted Suzi's father's face. He wanted to slap the boy in the face. "A jerk like you would never get a chance to kiss my daughter, even in your dreams!" he snarled. Huang Suzi's father was proud that he was a refined and courteous gentleman and respected by the younger teachers, but this time he forgot himself for Suzi. He was being coarse, which was laughed at by the younger teachers. Even Huang Suzi thought, "You don't have to be this way even for me!"

Sure enough, these words had serious after-effects. From then on, some boys of the school often quipped with each other, using the following words, "It'd be real tough getting a chance to kiss Huang Suzi!" That boy, Suzi's admirer, changed into a scalawag. Whenever he met Huang Suzi when no one was around, he would tease her, "What difficulties must I go through before I can kiss you?" Suzi had no words to respond with, except for "Shame on you" or "Rascal," and she dared not to tell her teacher or father about this.

All these incidents brought nameless changes to Huang Suzi's feelings towards her father. She felt she was living under her father's thrall. A hurried traveler never cares whether the stone under his feet has been kicked into the weeds or a drain, for it is none of his business; he has his destination, but the stone's fate is changed due to him. Suzi felt like she was a stone kicked by her father into a drain and left in darkness, never to be able to see the sun again. He would not have named her Huang Shijian if he had not been reading a book when she was born; if he had not named her Huang Shijian, and then if he had not revealed the origins of her name at that criticism meeting, if he had not taken her sister's side, or if he had not chastised that boy using those words, she would not be what she was now. She would not be incommunicative and unable to smile when she wanted to.

After this idea took in on her mind, Huang Suzi could hardly speak to her father when she saw him. Finally, she just did not bother to even greet him at all.

Huang Suzi's father ignored this at first, but as time went on he found that she did not respond at all to what he said; when she had to address him, "hey" was how she began. Suzi's father felt unhappy because he was a father after all. One day Suzi heard her parents conversing, "Your daughter is not worthy to be a Huang descendant. She is not even at all civilized, as if she had been brought up in a low family."

Huang Suzi's mother said, "What are you talking about? Have you lost your mind or something? Do you think you belong to such a civilized strata?"

On hearing this Suzi in her mind agreed with her, "Mother is right. You're insane. Do you really think you're superior to others?"

With the upcoming university entrance exams, Huang Suzi decide she really wanted to get into a Chinese literature department. She liked literature after once reading this one writer. In his article, the writer had said that he had been silent from the time he was young, and that he talked with his pen because he was interested in literature. Huang Suzi wanted to do the same thing, so she asked to become a humanities student when her class was divided up.

Huang Suzi's father had once also been a literature student, but he did not agree just because it was Suzi's choice; on the contrary, he doubted and suspected her. He went to the Teaching and Instruction Director of the school to request she be placed into a science class, without Suzi's approval. At dinnertime he told Suzi about this in an indifferent tone.

Suzi was shocked. "Why? Why didn't you tell me in advance? Who is going to university, you or me?" But she did not speak this out, though her mouth did open. The family was busy eating and no one noticed her mouth opening. They thought she was just opening her mouth to chew. "All right! Kick me anywhere you want! I'm just a stone to you, and I'm already in a drain so I care about nothing!" Suzi ate down a mouthful of rice as a way of swallowing her unspeakable anger.

Suzi's father took her silence to mean she approved of his actions, so he told her before the whole family at the table: "How could you study literature when you're not that talented? Your compositions often go way off topic; you can't even use the right punctuation or spell correctly. You shouldn't have been my daughter. My compositions were always the best in my class when I was a student, and for that I got many awards. That's why I had chosen literature. What have you got? Why are you presuming yourself to be so high?"

His tone was not that acrid when he made his speech, and he was even being a little absentminded, but these words were like sharp needles to Suzi pricking into her ears. She could almost feel blood rushing down from her ears to her shoulders and further down to her arms and then to her fingertips. As she used her fingers to pick up the chopsticks, blood flew into the bowls along the chopsticks, and the food was dyed red. She passed the food to her mouth and chewed hard, so hard that her chewing noises were heard.

Her father said, "I've told you many times. Could you not eat in a more graceful manner?"

Huang Suzi did very well in the university entrance exam and was accepted by a university specializing in computer studies. Computer science was a hot subject for many people who could not get in. Unlike them though, Huang Suzi did not like it but was easily admitted. But Suzi's father could not have been happier, so he treated himself to a small drink to celebrate, which was unusual. After some sips, he said, "Were it not for me, would you be what you are now?"

Suzi remained indifferent, with neither a smile nor anger showing on her face. She just hung her head down to eat, and the snow-white rice turned red in her eyes. "So what.... Today, am I any happier than yesterday?" she thought.

Suzi's father drank up his wine, and after setting his cup down on the table he sighed deeply, "At long last, I've cultivated up one more talent for our country."

2

Huang Suzi's moved into her school dormitory. There were eight students living in a room, allowing for no privacy. Even such personal habits as changing clothes or fiddling with your feet would be seen by the other seven. Suzi was not used to it but luckily she slept on an upper berth, so she could keep her mosquito net hanging all year round and leave its door eternally closed.

Therefore, she spent much time staying inside her mosquito net. When spoken to by the other seven girls, she would reply politely like her father, but she never laughed crazily along with them. Every time she heard a joke, she would think: "What's so funny? Is it that funny?"

These girl students were at a bright and happy age, spirited and delighted every day, thus they did not like Huang Suzi who was silent or even somber. By the third year, they even seldom spoke to Suzi, but this did not make her unhappy.

That same year, the boy students were stirring, and regularly launched their attacks on girl students, but not on Huang Suzi. Phrases of the love letters back in high school had set her heart aflame time and again. As a result, she had been looking forward to being pursued by the boys. By the boys, she meant two boys — Wu and Chen — in her class. Neither of them were excellent students, but they were both handsome — up to Suzi's taste. However, they both kept away from her.

Huang Suzi passed by the woods one day, seeing the back of the girl who slept in the bed under her. The girl was on her date with a boy. Curiosity made her slip around behind them to overhear their prattle.

Her roommate told the boy with a smile, "Why did you hit on me, and not Huang Suzi? She's much more beautiful."

The boy replied, "Who would go for her? Don't scare me. You know what my roommate Chivalrous Wu calls her?"

"What? Cool Beauty, or something like that?" The girl smiled.

"Oho — Cool Beauty is a nice name," the boy said, "Everybody likes a cool beauty, but she's not like that. She's called 'Corpse Beauty,' and once this got out the nickname spread among the boys. Chen Guoqiang says she looks just like a real corpse."

The girl immediately burst into laughter. Her shrill voice made leaves fall off the trees onto Suzi's head.

Huang Suzi was somewhat startled when a leaf touched the tip of her nose. Suddenly she calmed down and walked out of the woods away from them. Passing the pair, she even stared at them for a while, giving them her best "corpse" eyes. She used this deadly glare to shock them pale with her abrupt appearance.

Later that day, Huang Suzi wept inside her mosquito net, but only for a little while. She then thought it no big deal, since she had already known Wu's and Chen's opinion of her. She thought to herself, "I may be a beautiful corpse, but better than you guys. Whom do you think you are? Wu, the fat guy, though not that fat, should be called Wu the Pig; and Chen has freckles on his face, so it is does him right to call him Chen the Freckled."

After this incident, she stopped hoping for boys' charms, and her original little eagerness for love also vanished. She would imagine after she talked with anybody, "Do they think I'm a terrifying corpse?" Then she would forget about it after silently muttering some dirty words, from which she could get some comfort.

It seemed that Suzi had developed the habit of silent swearing before entering university, but she had never ever blurted out any dirty words, for she really hated talking and was used to hiding everything she wanted to talk about inside her heart. As time went on, her curses accumulated like grain piled up in a barn; all the grain fermenting since the barn only gained but did not lose anything. The swear words increased and fermented. She even elaborately gathered various new extremely dirty words like a professional collector, and she grew excited at all dirty words she heard and began to see them as pearls. When graduation was imminent, she felt her heart unable to hold them any longer, so she inputted them through a computer onto a floppy disc. No one knew the existence of this disc, and no one knew she had such a unique skill. Silence was her exterior expression, and her silent dirty words were her essence. She would feel happy after she told anyone off, and if nobody was beside her after that, she even burst into laughter, and that became the only times she felt any need to laugh.

After graduation she was assigned to a government office, which was a popular job. "Though seemingly silent, she must have done everything necessary for her job stealthily," her classmates thought, "God knows whom she bought off in what way. Her deviousness is so obvious."

As a matter of fact Suzi had done nothing. The fact was that the government recruiting staff requested Huang Suzi after seeing her picture and report card. She had done very well in all her subjects. The teacher in charge of assignment work had wanted to recommend other students, like his friends' or relatives' children, but he was rejected. The school could do nothing.

Suzi quickly got used to the ambience of the office after her arrival, for she found it was perfect for her. Exactly like her, people there all had two sides, but they spoke out both on different occasions, which she never did. They spoke differently before different persons, but Huang Suzi only spoke her silent language to herself. Knowing others were similar to her, she felt much better and became a more amiable person than at home and in university. "It turns out that people all have split personalities," she thought.

Her coworkers knew she was naturally quiet, and they did not feel that she was hard to get along with. Besides, she was highly responsible about her work and took all assigned tasks seriously, which brought her many accolades that she had never gotten before.

Huang Suzi's Division Chief Liu was not so old, and he was the one who had chosen Suzi from school. He often praised her in public, and told others how he had insisted on choosing her when her school had recommended others. Huang Suzi's work had proven that he had made the right choice. Though never speaking out, Suzi bore good feelings towards her chief and so she worked even harder.

Soon the chief offered to introduce his younger brother to Huang Suzi. Though it was unclear whether one of the reasons he had chosen Suzi was especially for his brother, Huang Suzi did not despise his offer for she really had to go out with someone.

She compliantly met her chief's brother, and both of them had good feelings towards each other. The chief was with them during their first date, sitting there and drinking tea, as his brother exchanged addresses and telephone numbers with Suzi. They then conducted their subsequent dates all by themselves. Suzi was a naturally terrible speaker, and the brother did not know what to say either, so they went to the same place drinking cup of tea after cup of tea, with their silences much longer than speaking intervals. Only as they were about to leave, did the brother's light banter finally come out. He told her one about his primary schoolmates who had graduated from Suzi's computer science department. Suzi asked for the guy's name, and he said it was Wu Dasong — nicknamed Chivalrous Wu. Suzi immediately changed her expression, for Chivalrous Wu was the guy who had given her the nickname "Beautiful Corpse." Thinking of the past, she could not help cursing that guy in her heart. She was so absorbed in her cursing that what the brother was saying went completely unheard. Only just after they had parted, did Huang Suzi remember on the bus that the brother had said they could have dinner with Wu on the next date, and she began to tell them off in her mind: "Me, f—ing go for dinner with you guys? Go to f—ing hell! I'll be a whore if I go." She kept cursing silently and missed her bus stop.

She, of course, did not go for that dinner. But her chief's brother did not in fact come looking for her again. Her chief sensed she was pretending nothing had happened but he said nothing, which only reminded her of what had happened at the dinner.

Sure enough, most of her coworkers within a couple of weeks soon learned she was nicknamed "Beautiful Corpse." A driver, also her coworker, one day teased her by addressing her "Beautiful Corpse," making everyone around her titter, and Huang Suzi just pretended that she did not hear them and gracefully walked past the tittering crowd. The wind was strong but did not blow Huang Suzi's silent fierce cursing into their ears.

From then on, her chief never praised her any more.

Only a few years had passed after Huang Suzi started working there, when dramatic changes took place in the society. Everybody started getting rich except for government office workers. Of course, government offices were good places, but people working there could hardly make ends meet, so they became resentful toward their offices. Their superiors knew that without their inferiors' votes they would fail in their evaluations, and if their inferiors lived a tough life they would not vote, which certainly would affect the superiors' promotions. As a result, the superiors proposed they set up an assets company. The highest superiors said, "We must make the best use of our power and give all the money the company makes to our workers as bonuses."

The decision spread around quickly and was highly praised

by all. But when the notice to hire the general manager of the new company came out, nobody responded, for everyone thought, "It'd be good if I could make lots of money as the manager of the company, but if I fail I would have to take all the responsibility. What's more, if I don't do a good job, my future would be ruined because this failure would be under the eyes of the superiors." This situation lasted for several days. It was strange, for in the old days people would try all out to become a deputy division chief, but now nobody wanted this job as a general manager. This made the superiors feel ashamed and plaintive, "It's beyond our imagination why our officials are so shortsighted." Finally they had to appoint a general manager, and it turned out that Huang Suzi's division chief was chosen.

Huang Suzi's chief thought about it over and over again. If he refused he would be going against his superiors, which was even worse than being an unsuccessful general manager. So he reluctantly accepted the appointment. The moment he accepted he looked so sad, as if he had just adopted a lunatic child. Yet he did not forget to ask for something. He asked for two assistants so that he would not be alone. The superiors immediately consented to his request.

Her chief got two assistants — one man and one woman. Huang Suzi became the woman assistant. She had originally liked being in a government office, but since her nickname had become well known among her coworkers, she had lost interest in working there. When her chief appointed her as his assistant, she thought it no loss to move to another position. Her chief received some money from the government as startup funds and they rented an office using this. That was how their business started.

As a matter of fact, due to their powerful backers they did not encounter much difficulty starting their venture, which took off far beyond their expectations. The general manager, that is, the former division chief, had hardly made clear what was going on when they began to profit — and it was a great deal of money. Soon after that, they moved into a fine office building, and a few days later they bought a car better than those of their superiors, and their salaries kept rising upwards without being noticed. Too many bonuses took them beyond excitement, until they thought there might be something wrong with the world. Each of them now sported fashion of famous designer labels. They went to luxury hotels, to get drunk and indulge themselves without limit, saying they were already the same as those foreigners in those movies. Suzi felt she was lucky, though still she said nothing.

Huang Suzi moved out of her parents' house. She breathed out an intense effusion of emotions, and relaxed the moment she went out of the door. Her company allocated her a flat, which she fixed up very nicely. One day her parents came to visit. Seeing the inner rooms of her new home, they complained, "Unbelievable. I've worked for the revolutionary cause all my life but I don't have such a place to live in. Huang Suzi has worked for just a short time but she is now as rich as a capitalist." After that, they never visited the flat again, seeming to be elaborately isolating themselves from such capitalists. Suzi did not care, and thought indifferently, "Don't you think I like you visiting here!"

The company handed in some of their profits to the government office to which they belonged, but as with other companies of similar type, it held back most of the money through all manner of excuses. The general manager was shrewd. He was a born businessman, though not a good division chief. Huang Suzi was his assistant, yet she was not in charge of public relations. Her work was to organize files for the general manager. With her processing, all the files were well organized and clear, saving a great deal of energy for the general manager, so he often said, "Huang Suzi, do you know why I chose you as my assistant? You're really excellent." Suzi was happy about this, for she thought he probably was telling the truth.

One Christmas, the company treated many guests, including their former coworkers. Many of them offered bribes to the general manager for a position in the company. The general manager felt big from gaining so much face, and drank too much in his excitement. He really was not much of a drinker and soon got drunk, and then he began to blurt out drunken nonsense.

Those old coworkers took this chance to horseplay. They jokingly asked, "Why did you choose Huang Suzi instead of us? Anyone of us is better than her."

The general manager replied, "You're so wrong. None of you can beat Huang Suzi." He continued with his hand on Suzi's shoulder, "Yet, Huang Suzi, you must thank my wife."

The coworkers all laughed, "Tell us why."

"According to my wife, if I needed a secretary, 'Beautiful Corpse' should my exclusive choice, because I would probably sleep with any secretary except her. I dare not sleep with a dead woman. My wife is right. I have worked with Huang Suzi for so long but I've never got any ideas about her."

The coworkers at once burst into wild laughter.

Hearing this, Huang Suzi almost blurted out her dirty words. She could feel the blood vessels on her forehead swelling and her neck expanding. In her fantasies, their laughter had already been overwhelmed by her bawling them out. If the laughter were rolling waves, her curses were powerful storms. She silently swore at them for quite a long while, and did not notice when their laughter stopped. Then they moved to other topics quite different from the previous one.

This occasion was to last the whole night. There was going to be a masquerade later in the evening, but Suzi was not interested, so she left after an excuse. She told the general manager she was leaving. Though he was drunk, his mind was still clear. He pulled her aside and said, "Ah Huang Suzi, if you could occasionally give a smile, beckon with your brows and speak in a sweet voice, you would not be a 'Beautiful Corpse' at all, and all the men would want you in their arms. Your skin's so white."

Huang Suzi felt her whole body go numb and was overcome by a nameless fear. Then in no time this feeling vanished. Without a word in reply to his words, she walked away.

On her way out, she abused him violently in her heart, "You bastard! I am a 'Beautiful Corpse,' so what?" Then she used much dirtier words which made her private parts uncomfortably wet.

3

It so happened on that same night, Huang Suzi ran into someone. Suzi walked onto the street wearing her woolen windbreaker over her green short skirt suit — this was a rule of her company. Her ethereal clothes flew in the wind, looking graceful and pretty. A car was driving towards her with its lights on, which hurt Suzi's eyes, so she moved out of the way.

The car passed by but then suddenly stopped and backed up. It braked beside Suzi. The door opened and a man came out, staring at her, as he said, "Huang Suzi?"

Huang Suzi was startled. She looked him over, amazed: it was the boy who had written the love letters to her at high school. At this time, she saw in front of her again, his lousy signature, "Xu

Hongbing," at the end of those letters.

Xu Hongbing was not young any more either, but seemingly better off. With the help of the light, she saw that his clothes were even of better brands than her general manager's. She could also tell that his perfume was French, very fine. Despite all this, Huang Suzi instinctively said, "What do you want?"

Xu smiled, "You haven't changed at all. You, me, we are both adults now. Do you think I'd still bully you like I did before? On seeing an old classmate, doesn't it bring up any good memories?"

Huang Suzi said nothing, and all the passionate words of those love letters appeared in her mind again. As a matter of fact, she had often thought of those love letters in her lonely days, so she was now in fact more familiar with them than before. She nodded with an apology, "Sorry."

Xu smiled again, "You finally started talking to me. It's Christmas Eve. Are you free? Why not find a place to chat?"

Suzi was hesitating. Xu waited beside the opened door for about half a minute. Finally she moved her legs and sat inside.

They went to a quiet teahouse and ordered green tea. Xu Hongbing poured Huang Suzi a small cup of tea. The cup was red, and as soon as the boiled water fell in, an effusion of fragrance wafted up. This fragrance gave Huang Suzi a bit of a sweet feeling she had never experienced, this feeling overwhelming all the dirty words she had collected.

Xu Hongbing took the lead in speaking. He recalled some funny things that had happened to the students of their class, which awoke Suzi's memories. Huang Suzi remained a listener mostly, and did not speak unless Xu asked about her life.

Xu Hongbing said, 'I've heard of your company. It's a good company, but I can't imagine you in it, you being so silent."

Suzi replied nothing, but she thought: "So only those talented in talking bullshit deserve to work in a company?"

Their chat did not end until after midnight, with Huang Suzi the first to bring up the idea of leaving. She had had a busy day and was tired now, but Xu Hongbing was still in high spirits. He insisted on driving Suzi home. After refusing at first, she then agreed.

They remained silent all the way until reaching Huang Suzi's place. Xu Hongbing held her hand when she was getting out of the car and said in a soft voice, "It's been a long time since I was so happy as tonight. Shall we meet again tomorrow night?"

Huang Suzi's body trembled. She did not know how to reply. She wanted to decline, but she was not able to say it directly out loud. Xu Hongbing let go of her hand and saw her out of the car. Then he said, "I'll pick you up after work tomorrow." Then he waved at Suzi, and drove away quickly before she could give any reaction.

Huang Suzi forgot how she got into her house and bathed and went to bed. Only after getting into bed did she recall every detail of their meeting again as they had just done. The whole process was like a swimming fish. She tasted those details bit by bit and then unconsciously took off her wet underwear. Naked in the warm and soft quilt, she felt she heard flowing water, rising gradually, until soon she was submerged. She was clear about what she wanted.

The next day was a clear bright day, and Huang Suzi was absentminded. Her general manager, with a seeming smile, asked, "Did I say anything improper? Or did I trigger any physical reaction?"

Suzi said nothing but she silently cursed, "What f—ing nonsense!" Then she employed more sentences, filthy enough to kill. Those sentences were so strong, it was as if they had erupted from a volcano and hit her chest fiercely, making her ache inside. In this way Suzi became much cooler over the rest of that day.

After work, soon as Huang Suzi got out of the office she saw Xu Hongbing with a bunch of roses in his hand. He walked over to Suzi like an elegant gentleman and handed the roses to her. Huang Suzi's general manager was standing behind her just then, and his mouth fell wide open from shock at this scene. A few steps away from her, he could not even move his feet. Suzi frowned as if in thought, but finally stepped into the *Benz*. Whenever Huang Suzi's general manager saw his own *Audi*, he always said, "I have to change my car for a *Benz* eventually."

But before his dream could come true, Huang Suzi had already slipped indifferently into a *Benz*.

They had dinner that evening and went out for a drive. Xu Hongbing drove his car as swift as wind and lightning. Huang Suzi was a cool person, but several times the incredibly high speed caused her to scream. She thought her sharp voice would even shatter the glass into bits.

Xu Hongbing said, "I love your screaming. It's so feminine."

Cold wind was whistling outside but inside it felt like spring, so Huang Suzi took off her wool coat.

Xu Hongbing said, "You should have done so when you got into the car."

Suzi said nothing. Xu continued, "Take off your scarf, too. Aren't you sweating?"

She really was, so she took off her scarf, too. It was not normal for Suzi to wear a low-necked sweater completely exposing her neck. Suzi's neck was white, with smooth fine skin.

Xu glanced absentmindedly at her and said, "It's the first time I noticed you have such white skin."

Suzi went red and turned her eyes to look outside the car window.

The car was going along a small narrow street. The road was

not wide and the lights were dim. Though it was cold, the street was not that deserted, with many passersby. Xu stopped the car for a while, and said in loaded way, "It's called Lute Garden here, a very fun place."

Huang Suzi asked, "What's the fun?"

Xu Hongbing replied, "You'll find out later."

That day Suzi had expected some tale to unravel between them, for she knew that on such man-and-woman occasions a man would try some trick such as kissing or caressing or something further, but in the end nothing happened, which was not what she expected. Several times Huang Suzi could feel those moments trying to come out, and then the soft atmosphere would be broken by some trivial matters.

At twelve midnight Xu Hongbing drove Huang Suzi back home. When she got out, Xu seized her hand once more, very tightly this time, seemingly very excited. He said, "We had a good time today. Can we often hang around together?"

Huang Suzi nodded this time without thinking. "Alright," she said.

It was Suzi's left hand that Xu had seized, so this hand was valuable to her that night. She tried to keep the feeling in it by avoiding washing it. When she recalled Xu's hand, she could not help kissing this hand, because she thought Xu must have left a slight salty taste on it. She grew restless, as she got wet again. She wanted to caress her wet parts with her left hand, but after trying just a few times she forced herself to stop, and scolded herself for such immoral ideas.

It was another sleepless night, which made her almost late for work the next day.

That day her general manager was preparing for an important social occasion, which was to present some grease to the important superiors, since New Year's Day was coming. Red envelopes of money and gifts were made ready, but in her haste Huang Suzi missed a gift for a relatively low-ranking superior. The superior said it was alright, though his face suggested he was unhappy. Of course he would be angry, for he was the only one missed. Money was not as important as face here. Thanks to this incident, the general manager chastised Huang Suzi.

"I know you're in love, and I know you are tired from serving your lover at night, but business is business. You're in my charge by day, and are his only at night. Both jobs are important. He is rich, of course, so you would not like to offend him, but you shouldn't have offended me, either."

She almost spat out, "You son of bitch!" into his face.

Huang Suzi's general manager had decided to set up a women's fashion company together with a man from Hong Kong. Though a division chief and then a general manager, he had once been a boy from a poor family picking coal slag on narrow streets. He did not recognize his worldly potential himself but others did. After becoming a general manager, he always told others that his family was wealthy and he had relatives abroad and his father was a leader, and were it not for political activities which had brought his family's downfall, he would have been a man of the town much earlier. His story was so vivid that, after every interview, the reporters would report it in the newspapers. As a result, many people who knew the general manager thought he had a powerful family.

But this time, after he told his story to the Hong Kong man, the latter smiled, "Yes. It's a high rank being the counter chief of a foodstuff store in a rural town."

This struck the general manager dumb. The Hong Kong person continued, "Before we work together, how could I not get clear your background?"

Luckily the Hong Kong person did not care about his family background. What he cared about was what the company would be like and whether it would be profitable. Money being everything, nothing is more important. Knowing this, the general manager became relaxed. The Hong Kong person also said that if the company earned both a good name and lots of money he would move the general manager's family to Hong Kong. This promise excited the general manager, for his dream was to go to Hong Kong and be on the tiles there, otherwise it was no use making so much money. After that, he did whatever the Hong Kong person told him to.

The Hong Kong person said their company needed a woman as a negotiator, because a woman dressed in clothes made by their company could make it easy to launch a business. The general manager recommended his sister-in-law, but after seeing her, the Hong Kong person said, "She is good-looking but not the right cast of mind. Fashion needs no beauty. They need women with style." While saying this, he glued his eyes on Huang Suzi for some seconds and asked, "Who is this young lady?"

"My assistant," said the general manager hurriedly.

The Hong Kong person said, "She's what our clothing needs. How is she doing in her work?"

"Terrific, but she is uncommunicative," replied the general manager.

The Hong Kong person said, "You can never judge clothing only by words. You make your judgment only after they are put on. I would say she is the right person."

When the general manager was talking with the Hong Kong person, Suzi was holding a pile of files, sitting to one side. There had not been a word or a smile from her. Her mind was filled with

Xu Hongbing's voice and face. They were going out so frequently now in the evenings that Huang Suzi felt the days when they did meet were as long as years. She wondered whether she was in love with him. She did not know whether Xu had any other girl or whether he was married. Maybe she hated to even know these things. Even if he had a girlfriend or was married, so what? She needed him, everything about him, caring about nothing else but him. Inside Suzi's heart was all this excitement, but on the outside she was cool like a Buddhist statue. She had never been to Hong Kong but she knew it was not such a big place. How could one or two businessmen from a small place draw her attention? Her mind was occupied by Xu Hongbing, so how could she be interested in whether her boss and the Hong Kong man would make money or not? Being uninterested, why would she bother listening to them? That was why she in fact heard nothing of the conversation between her general manager and the Hong Kong man.

However, she did become the general manager of Ligang Women's Clothing Company — the company opened by her general manager and the Hong Kong man. When her general manager told her the news, she was startled but did not get excited.

Her general manager said, "The Hong Kong boss selected you! You are quite the somebody. He was convinced though you said not a word to him."

From the beginning Huang Suzi had not want to be a manager. She only wanted to get married since she was being mentally tortured by Xu Hongbing. Thus what she heard only annoyed her. Her calm expression belied her fierce cursing inside.

Her general manager continued, "Look at you. Your dead looks attracted the Hong Kong man. It's strange. There must be something wrong with him for not choosing a lovely girl."

In this way Suzi became manager of the company. When led to her manager's office by her general manager, she was still not clear what was really happening, until three days later when it all became clear. Both in the government office and in the company she had done a good job, proving her ability and intelligence. In addition, she had already been in business with her boss for years and familiar with everything about business, so she was capable of running a company very well.

Huang Suzi's company's initial business was to make clothing to measure for women of the "upper-crust of society." The so-called upper-crust women were mostly wives of high-rank government officials. They wanted to get beautiful clothes at low prices, so Huang Suzi only charged them minimally, sometimes even selling at a loss. She knew that what she was doing would bring in lots of money in the future. Suzi's general manager and the Hong Kong businessman were satisfied with what she had achieved so far. Her general manager said, "After several years of working with me, she has become very shrewd in business."

Huang Suzi always wore a blank face and never said much to her clients. Every day she changed into a new Ligang suit in a new style, sitting imperturbably in her office dealing with documents. Her silent disposition and graceful behavior gave people the impression: it is the Ligang clothes she is wearing that shape what she is. All the customers, elegant or not, wanted to become elegant, and after seeing Huang Suzi many asked for the clothing she was wearing. Gradually she became famous among these people. All of them said, "Hong Kong clothes are of course different from those ordinary outfits." Able to foresee such assessments, she did not get very excited. "It's no big deal," she thought to herself.

4

Xu Hongbing and Huang Suzi's dating had no slack season. At first they met every one or two days, and then they saw each other every day. After every date, Xu Hongbing would appear unwilling to part. He had also worked out many good ideas for Huang Suzi's company. One designer for her company had come back from Japan after graduation and been recommended by him; and this designer had already designed several popular suits. As a result, Huang Suzi felt love while at the same time gratitude toward Xu Hongbing. She felt herself waiting for his arrival every minute.

The Spring Festival was soon over, and spring arrived amidst people's elatedness and happiness. One night they went out for dinner in a star hotel. A piano was playing soft music in one corner, its melody consoling every blundering heart like a warm hand.

Huang Suzi sipped her cola and listened to the romantic music. Suddenly she said, "I am full of regret."

"For what?" asked Xu Hongbing.

"That I never wrote you back that year," replied Huang Suzi.

Xu Hongbing smiled and looked out of the window. A moment later, he said with a pained voice, "Spring is enchanting but too short." Then he continued spooning up his soup, as one song was replaced by another, keeping his head lowered, never raising it.

Huang Suzi thought: "Should I not have reminded him of the past? The past is sometimes kind and sometimes painful, but most of the time it makes you full of melancholy. What is he implying by focusing on his soup?" She lowered her head toward the soup, too, while her thoughts wandered.

She did not understand that the past gave people much more than she thought. Sometimes one has feelings beyond words, and so it was with Xu Hongbing here and now.

That same night they went to the cinema. There were few people there, so all the audience was sitting in the private boxes, out of which came the sounds of kissing and women's occasional moans, mixed with the music and the actors' lines.

That day Huang Suzi sat side by side with Xu Hongbing. The sounds coming from behind them made Suzi restless. She turned to look at Xu, who was staring at her with bright eyes. Huang Suzi hoped some thing would take off between them, but Xu kept still. "Maybe he is scared by what I used to be." Thinking of this, though Xu Hongbing was sitting on her right, she put her right hand on his right thigh as he was sitting on her right side.

Suzi whispered, "I will no longer be what I was."

Xu Hongbing smiled and held her right hand.

The rest of the time he kept caressing her right hand until the movie was over, and during the whole process he only said, "Your hand is soft," bringing Huang Suzi nearly to the point of collapse.

When the movie was over and the lights were turned on, Huang Suzi's face was all flushed and hot. She could feel herself trembling. A woman over thirty, she had experienced a man's caresses for the first time. Though very excited, she was far from satisfied. When Xu Hongbing was about to see her out of his car, Suzi sat longer, eager to say something but finally saying nothing. She then opened the door.

It was not until then that Xu Hongbing took her hand again. He said, "It's not so very long since we met again. I wanted to do something to you but I dare not, though I think you and I both want it."

Huang Suzi turned her head around to look at him and said, "I'll not refuse whatever you do to me."

Xu Hongbing put on a surprised look and said, "Truly? If you are serious, I'll take you to a place this Saturday. Aren't you afraid?"

Huang Suzi said, "I'll dare to go anywhere you take me!"

Xu Hongbing smiled. "Alright," he said, "It's a deal, but you'd better wear plain clothes like an ordinary person."

Huang Suzi got home feeling very excited. Her head was filled with fantasies about Saturday. She felt their critical moment was on its way, and untold love was going to be expressed, and she knew how badly she wanted Xu Hongbing. She knew what they were going to do on Saturday. She had learned about those occasions from books and even from videos, though she had never experienced it herself, so it would be very precious. For a few days she kept thinking about what underwear to wear for the occasion. Finally she found, in one of those joint-venture supermarkets, the right underwear, which was made of silk with embroidered flowers. The three fresh flowers on the bra and panties fell exactly on the three most beautiful parts of a woman. Huang Suzi pulled out three hundred yuan and resolutely bought them.

Then on Friday afternoon, her general manager told her that the Hong Kong boss was coming the next day. He would meet the city leaders, and after that Huang Suzi had to be present in her most beautiful Ligang dress at a banquet being held by the company.

Huang Suzi trembled and asked, "May I ask for leave tomorrow?"

Her general manager was startled, and said, "Aren't you clear what is happening now? Given such an opportunity, other people would be extra excited, but you want to ask for leave?"

"I have to because I have something urgent," she replied.

Her general manager jealously said, "You are meeting that Adonis, right?"

Huang Suzi said, "Whatever the reason, I must request leave."

Her general manager put on an annoyed look, "Huang Suzi, you think you are a manager and have a supportive man behind you, so you are strong enough to deal with anything? Honestly, I can fire you whenever I want. I am telling you."

Huang Suzi said, "I don't care. I am simply asking for leave."

Huang Suzi told the whole thing to Xu Hongbing. Xu clapped and laughed. He said, "Good. You dare to fire the city leaders!" They then got into the car, and their laughter made the car fly like the wind along the road.

Xu Hongbing said, "I will show you a place."

"Where?" asked Huang Suzi.

Xu said, "You'll know when we get there."

Huang Suzi said, "I'd love to follow you to anywhere."

Xu squeezed out one pregnant word, "Truly?"

The car sped along for a long time with music playing inside it. Soft music like a dusky wind blew over the willows on the riverbanks, evoking fantasies. The fantasies were not gorgeous with wild waterfalls, but rather more overwhelmed by a stealthy and mysterious mood waiting over a mountain.

When Xu Hongbing said, "Here we are," Suzi opened her confused eyes to find it was just a small street, ugly and worldly. It seemed she had been here once before. The street was dimmed by the night but not deserted.

Xu Hongbing said, "There is an interesting place here, named Lute Garden." Then he parked his car under a tree far from the street. The car was almost entirely covered by the shadows of the tree.

Xu was not wearing fancy clothes that day, instead only in a plain casual outfit. Considering Xu Hongbing's advice, Huang Suzi was dressed casually, too. They went along the street arm in arm. Among the dark shadows along the street could be seen some laughing and smoking garishly dressed women.

Huang Suzi said, "They are…?"

"Hookers. This is a red-light district. Unlike other ones, it is a place popular with poor guys. A lot of migrant workers hang around here."

Huang was startled, "What are we here for?"

Xu Hongbing whispered into her ears, "It's exciting here! Many families have rooms to rent. Tonight we will rent one and then…." He suddenly stopped.

Huang Suzi had gone red with embarrassment. She whispered, "Actually… I live alone. Nobody would disturb us in my place."

"I know," he says, "but the atmosphere is different."

Huang Suzi approved of his idea at once. She found she was getting excited. Blood was rushing into her blood vessels and her body was starting to tremble. Something was happening between them.

Xu Hongbing seemed very familiar with this area. Soon they had rented a room. The landlady claimed her family name was Ma, so Xu called her "Sister Ma." The room was not big, of only a size of about eleven square meters. At the center of the room stood a big bed and a big mirror with its surface unclean and foggy and its four corners very old. There was no toilet but only a red-painted night-stool. It was very old too, and the wood could be seen through its bracket's peeling paint.

The light was very dim. After negotiation with Ma, he entered the room and threw himself over her without a word, startling Suzi, who was waiting for kisses and caresses. She could smell the stinking sheets as she was crushed down on the bed. She wanted to say something but did not know how to start.

Xu Hongbing very quickly pulled off her clothes and threw

them at the feet of the bed — the three roses Huang Suzi had specially prepared for him — without even looking at them. After only seconds, Suzi felt a pain as if she had been hurt by a bayonet. She tried to find some feeling but she could only feel Xu Hongbing's heavy body choking her. He had been treating her like a gentleman, but now he was a wild animal, whose savagery and wildness was causing Suzi great pain. It was the pain of being torn apart. She could not help screaming, and then she recalled that Xu Hongbing had said he liked her screaming.

Everything he did was totally beyond Suzi's expectations. Before Suzi could screamed again, he was already finished, and pulling on his pants. Suzi had hardly any chance to see his skin even, given his agility, but she was still exposed before him naked and she enjoyed his scanning and appreciation.

Huang Suzi stayed completely still. She was naked and a little cold, but she would rather lay herself on the bed in this position, because she hoped that her naked body would awaken Xu Hongbing's desire again. Xu, however, just stared at her silently for a while and then moved to the window, lighting a cigarette. The window was old and small, with a curtain weakly hanging over it. He parted the curtain slightly and looked out. Suzi also looked out, just to see a streetlight giving off a ghostly light. "Was it all about sex?" she wondered, but she felt it should be more than what she had experienced. Huang Suzi said, "Why not come lie next to me?"

He turned around with a chilling expression in the light. Then a weird smile crept up his face, and Huang Suzi trembled. Xu said, "Mr. Huang would never have expected that one day his daughter would be naked in bed longing for me to take her. Was I good just now?" He burst into hysterical laughter, until he was almost choking.

Huang Suzi immediately went ashen. She gawked at Xu, seeming to recollect something. After his laughter, Xu said, "You think I would fall in love with you? My son is old enough to go to kindergarten. Look at your corpse-like face, bitch, take off your fair maiden's mask! In those years back then, your humiliation ruined my education, because all the teachers and schoolmates thought I was a scoundrel. Thanks to you, I lived a tough life. You could never imagine it. Now, you are only a whore in my eyes, just like the other hookers that I slept with in here, though you were once a university student."

Huang Suzi calmed down in the face of Xu's narration and abuse. She soon recognized it as a trap set long, long before, that Xu had been wracking his brains to avenge his unrequited love letters.

She suddenly felt completely tearless though she wanted to cry, and then fury set her aflame. All those dirty words buried by love exploded all of a sudden in her heart.

She said in a cold voice, "You think I wasn't playing with *you*? You were humiliated by me in that f—ing school, but you think you're now free of that humiliation? Son of bitch! I've been expecting all your traps, and why do you call your retreat so quickly? Why not wait till you make me pregnant with a bastard!"

It was Xu Hongbing's turn to be startled, at the exact same time as Huang Suzi began to blurt out all her deep-rooted dirty words phrase by phrase, allowing no time for him to think. Her abuse came at Xu Hongbing's face like an uncontrolled flood and forced him back against the door, with his originally satisfied face now in a panic. Suzi did not care about this at all. She continued her loud abuse with perfect pronunciation word by word. Those words were too dirty to be digested, and at once the whole room became filled with her stinking and wicked dirty metaphors. She had worked so long on these words that they were extremely effective when finally coming out. Suzi had never given so long a speech or used so many words in all her life, let alone cursing so loudly.

Backing off to the door, all Xu's elegance seemed to have been snatched away by Suzi's abuse. He looked a little timid, with one of his hands groping to open the door. Suzi shouted, "You didn't give it a perfect end. No debts, please. I am not expensive. Fifty yuan is okay. I charge all those blackguards who sleep with me this price, so you are no exception. Put it under the foot of the bed."

Xu pulled out his wallet and drew a hundred-yuan note from inside it. He said in a low voice, "No fifty in change."

Huang Suzi laughed loudly, "Then you can do it one more time. If it's not the right time today, you may come another day and do it for free. I'll be always waiting for you here."

Xu dropped the money and quickly fled.

When the door slammed, Huang Suzi collapsed in the bed as if she had been hollowed out. Her curses had stopped but now her tears ran amok. Her wild crying made her throat ache. Her mouth bit into the dirty pillow as she was weeping. Salty tears slipped down her cheeks into her mouth, but what was that other flavor? She had never tasted it before. That peculiar flavor rushed from inside the pillow into her heart and idled along her blood vessels all around her, and then came out of her pinholes and filled the whole room. Suddenly she felt this taste to be something familiar, but she could not remember when and where she had experienced it.

The landlady Ma heard her and came to ask her what happened, then before Huang Suzi could say anything she told her in an experienced tone, "Crying is good for you, and it is typical for a first-timer. Everything will get better later. All men are the same, but most importantly, they give you money."

Before Ma could finish, Huang Suzi uncontrollably started her abuse again. She meant to curse Ma, but Ma thought she was still cursing that man, so she sneered, "Believe it or not, everyone curses silently those whom they hate. Verbal abuse means you do not hate them that much. Once a country girl kept cursing almost till she choked, and then she started banging the wall till she began to bleed. It was her first time. Guess what happened later? She always stayed in here all day long, and one year later she married a rich man and got a son, but she still came here uncontrollably twice a month, like a junkie."

Huang Suzi's swearing stopped abruptly. Actually, she had not clearly heard what Ma was saying. She just suddenly felt that every phrase she blurted out had melted into the weird atmosphere in this room and put her into a kind of intoxication. Suzi felt she was melting into it, and she involuntarily stretched her arms and thought, "I didn't lose anything. Why am I so sad? Though he meant to deceive me, I abused him out the door. I'm not a virgin any more. I got to know the essential way of 'communication' between men and women. No big deal." As she thought this she stretched, feeling her favorite phrases as if they were dancing and entwining her arms while she was thinking. Those phrases were smiling enchantingly on her skin, and Huang Suzi put on an unconscious look, which she had never had before. She thought, "Those phrases were fermenting in my heart, suppressed. Now they have broken through and seen the external world. How dynamic and free and beautiful they are!"

At this moment, Huang Suzi seemed to have discovered the interface that harmoniously connected her with the world.

Day broke into Huang Suzi's nameless delight. Her tears had dried without leaving a mark. She thought, "Good! I won't need to mind tears any longer for the rest of my life."

It was a Sunday and Suzi did not need to work. She lay quietly in the weird atmosphere of the room. The curtain gap had remained as it was after Xu Hongbing had drawn it apart, with sunshine sneaking in. It was a sunny day, a brightly lit day.

Ma pushed the door open again. Seeing Huang Suzi was still lying in bed she said angrily, "Hey, it's time you get out. Others are waiting. If you don't leave, you'll have to pay more."

Huang Suzi pointed to the hundred-yuan note at the foot of the bed left by Xu Hongbing, "Is that enough?"

Ma immediately put on a smiling face, "Yes, yes! You're so up-front! I told you you'd be okay with it. Right? I often say that only astute people come to my place for this."

Suzi did not bother to reply. Ma noticed this and left with the money, but several minutes later she was back and said mysteriously, "Do you want more business? It's a frequent client. He sells pork and makes lots of money, so he doesn't care about money. I seldom recommend him to any hooker, but I can tell that you two are perfect for each other. He is absolutely healthy. What do you say?"

Huang Suzi felt those dirty words scattered around the room begin to assemble. Those words transformed into a woodpile in front of her and, as long as she struck a match, they would spark a prairie fire and zap Ma into ashes.

But Suzi had no such match, physically or emotionally. She was slacking and said without even moving her eyelids, "Okay."

5

Huang Suzi returned home feeling her body all covered with pig grease. It was dusk. The beautiful sun was setting in the west. The sunset glow dyed itself red coquettishly with the last of the sun's light. It was a beautiful world at such a time.

After stepping into her house, the first thing Huang Suzi did was throwing herself into the bathtub. She washed herself again and again, until an entire bottle of *Lanyoucao* bath foam was used up. The white foam in the tub was piled very high, burying her, with only her hair visible floating over the foam like weeds. The fragrance was so strong that the bathroom was almost expanded by it.

The telephone rang when she was still in the bathtub. The phone rang again and again, so she had to get out of the tub. Though the house was empty, she was not used to being naked out in it. She wrapped herself in a bath towel, put on her slippers and went to answer the phone. By the time picked up the receiver, the caller had hung up.

That call had been made by Huang Suzi's general manager. The next day when she arrived at her office, she found her general manager there, too. He never came like this to Ligang on his own first, instead, his secretary would call Huang Suzi to go to see him if anything came up. Most managers, even if they were only shoemakers or greengrocers formerly, would always put on airs with others once becoming general managers, and Huang Suzi's general manager was no exception, and besides he had been a division chief in the government.

The general manager did not look happy, but Huang Suzi was still expressionless as always. "Don't you think you should know how to smile since you have a man now? Are you so expressionless when you are sleeping with him? For him, you even can leave your work uncared, so why can't you change your style for him? When the city leaders asked why the manager of Ligang was absent, guess what I replied? I said her father had just died and she was away at his funeral. I could hardly say you were sleeping with a man anyway."

Suzi kept silent, but in her heart she was cursing back. She could tell her silent words were wicked enough to kill, for she felt them tearing about inside her organs and making them ache, with her blood approaching her chest bit by bit from the navel.

"Since you didn't answer my call, I must inform you myself: You are no longer the manager of this company. Go back to the company, and be my assistant again," said the general manager.

Huang Suzi said, "Today?"

"Yes. You'll have your original desk. There are some container lists and meeting forms on it, and you're expected to finish them today, and to return all the Ligang sample clothes you've worn."

Then the general manager looked at Huang Suzi, seeming to be awaiting her reaction, but Suzi said nothing. She even did not change her expression. She walked to her desk and organized her things.

The general manager said, "Nothing to say?"

Huang Suzi replied indifferently, "If I had anything to say, I'd say I was planning to quit and go back to my original office."

The general manager was a little surprised and asked, "Are you saying this deliberately? Why?"

"It's quiet there." After saying this to the general manager's face, she turned and stalked off.

The general manager stood still and sighed, "You are really a dead corpse. My wife is the only one who treasures you in the world."

Back at her office, Huang Suzi began to deal day after day with all the tasks her boss assigned her, as she used to do. Xu Hongbing had vanished like a passing wind. Huang Suzi did not hint at it through her appearance, but her boss sensed it anyway. He could not help taking pleasure in her misfortune. He asked, "Where's the *Benz* guy?"

Suzi said, "He's driven to another woman."

Her general manager said, "I was thinking how a *Benz* man could possibly fall in love with you, but you were so deep in love I didn't want to upset you. It's better for a person like you to have a dream than to have nothing."

Suzi replied, "You are so right."

The general manager had not got a *Benz* yet, so when he was sure that Suzi had broken up with the *Benz* guy he was very happy, almost as if the woman belonged to him again, though he did not like her and she had never had any kind of an affair with him. He was nevertheless filled with a possessive desire, though this beauty as cold as a dead corpse was only working for him next door.

It turned out that the general manager's sister-in-law had taken over Huang Suzi's office. One day she planned a fashion show and generously invited Huang Suzi. Before her invitation, she was afraid that Huang Suzi may not be in the mood to go. But the general manager said, "If she can get into bad mood over such a trivial thing, she doesn't deserve to be called 'Corpse Beauty'."

Just as expected, Suzi accepted the invitation and went to the show in fancy dress. Seeing the models walking back and forth on the uncarpeted stage and hearing their small heels clicking on the stage, Huang felt as if someone was hammering her head, making her feel dizzy and see stars, so many as melting iron pouring out from the furnace. As a result, though she tried to appreciate the show, she did not see even the colors of any of the clothing.

Suddenly a voice came to her ears, along with a woman's hearty laughter. Huang Suzi recognized it as her general manager's wife's voice. The woman said, "Oh, why do all the models look like your 'Corpse Beauty'?"

The general manager said, "Totally different. The models are sexy, but Huang Suzi is just a plastic woman."

His wife giggled.

The stars in Suzi's eyes suddenly vanished. She composed herself and looked at the stage again, as the show was just ending. Her general manager's sister-in-law was walking onto the stage with a big smile, like a terrible star, thanking the audience in an artificial voice. Huang Suzi's heart was full of unspeakable disgust, as she cursed inside, and left her seat. Most of the audience was leaving, so her departure was not very noticeable.

In the street, Huang Suzi felt like a lonely leaf falling off a tree with nowhere to go. At an intersection, a peddler tried to promote his goods to her. He said, "Miss, you have a nice figure. You'll look more beautiful and younger in my clothes."

Huang Suzi stopped at his stall and looked at his stuff. The peddler said, "They're all good buys. Don't you like any of them?" Then he picked out a low-cut, close-fitting short dress made of polyester, with several plastic buttons on the chest and a dark green flower design against its black background. Huang Suzi suddenly remembered seeing someone wearing the same one somewhere, so she took it. The peddler said, "It's only fifty yuan. You won't find a cheaper one anywhere else."

Huang Suzi pulled out fifty yuan and threw it at the peddler. The peddler, seeing her cross the street and leave so quickly, looked at the money in his hand and cried out, "You'll know once you put it on that you'll be definitely be much sexier."

Huang Suzi could not wait to put it on. She hurriedly took a taxi and once back home she immediately tried the dress on, forgetting to drink anything or even wash her hands or go to the toilet.

The dress wrapped tightly round her breasts and buttocks. In the mirror was a big mass of light hanging above her head. She suddenly found in the mirror another woman standing opposite her in the light. She had a white neck and high breasts, and her waist and buttocks formed perfect curves which made her resemble a dark green vase. Her face was expressionless like quiet, dead virgin soil; her eyes were confused, as hollow and white as a fog-dominated morning. It was a game, a mysterious game splitting one into two.

Huang Suzi was taken by surprise. She had never been so surprised in all her life. She could not help raising her arms and letting down her always bound-up hair, so her hair hung all the way down to her shoulders. By coincidence, she suddenly noticed all the cosmetics set out before her mirror. She knew what to do then, and began to make up an altered ego, elaborately.

Made up with thick foundation, her face turned plaster-white. Then she began to work on eye-shadow and her eyebrows, with dark browns, and used an eyebrow clamp that she had never used before. Her lips were dyed so red she felt they were bleeding. At last she sprayed perfume all over her body and allowed her unbound hair to cover half her face. Now before the mirror appeared a woman who was a total stranger to Suzi. She was so noisily colored and wild, yet artificial and worldly. That cool and expressionless Huang Suzi all of a sudden had vanished.

In her mind Huang Suzi recognized something clearly now. "It's so easy to get rid of a person," she thought.

Then she walked out of her house.

6

When Huang Suzi told the cab driver she was going to Lute Garden, the driver smiled vaguely. Several minutes after the car had set off, the driver opened his mouth, "You're working late?"

Huang Suzi said, "It doesn't matter." Usually she never talked with anyone who wanted to chat with her, but that day she had a strong desire to talk.

The driver said, "Your job must be exhausting but earns quick money."

"What do you think I am?" asked Huang Suzi.

The driver smiled, "If I couldn't tell, do I deserve to be a man?"

Huang Suzi said, "Then you're probably wrong."

The driver curled his mouth with scorn, "Even if I was blind, I could tell what you are by your smell. I deal with your type a lot. Xiao Cui and Lily, who also work in Lute Garden, use my car during every anti-prostitution drive. They use it to take the johns to the wild outskirts. Besides, I really wonder why they make it in such small places."

Huang Suzi flushed red in the darkness. She said unnaturally, "Really?"

The driver replied, "Of course. We're friends now. In the future if you need a taxi for work, please let me know. I am a good keeper of secrets. Once a policeman questioned me to find out who used my car but I didn't let out a word. I'd never surrender my sources of cash."

Huang Suzi felt less alert. She said, "Okay. I'll let you know whenever I need someone."

The driver immediately handed her a homemade business card with only a beeper number on it. He said, "Feel free to call me anytime."

Huang Suzi asked, "Don't you have a name?"

The driver replied, "Call me Xiao Liu. And you? Who are you?"

She hesitated for a while. She thought she was no longer

Huang Suzi, so she was not going to use those three characters. She was another woman, hence she should have another name. But she had not named that new woman yet, so she only said, "I'll call you, so don't trouble yourself to know so much."

Soon they got to Lute Garden. The driver smiled when he took the money from Suzi, "Once a veteran, you won't be afraid of telling me your name. You look like you're new here."

Suzi was surprised by what he said. She stood by the side of the road and saw the taxi fade away.

Now Huang Suzi was in Lute Garden. The light above her head was a dim mass, under which her last memories of being in this place were blurred. She had really forgotten how she got to Ma's that day, so she went blindly with casual steps and did not even know what she really wanted to do. Laughter from the two sides of the road came to her ears occasionally and made her feel comforted, as hearing her local accent which she had been missing for a long time.

Finally she got to a dark place in the street. Leaning against the wall of a house she looked at the passersby. Some twenty meters away from her was a streetlight that was not working very well. It went dark one minute and then shone bright the next. This reminded her of something but she did not know what it was. She only felt that she was just like this streetlight.

A man noticed her. He smiled and walked over to her. Right at that moment a name broke into Huang Suzi's brain. She thought, "I might as well name myself 'Darling Yu'." From books she knew that Xiang Yu* had this poem: "*Though powerful enough to turn a mountain over, and courageous enough to conquer the world, the current*

---

*Xiang Yu was the "Gallant King" of the State of Chu (232-202 BC), and Wu Zhui was the name of his charge.

situation is unfavorable, with even my Wuzhui unwilling to dash forward. What could I do to this horse, and Darling Yu, what could I do to you?" Suzi did not have a man like Xiang Yu, and neither was she interested in his lady Yu, who was unknown until after her death, but she liked the sentence, "Darling Yu, what could I do to you?" She thought, if there was someone who did not know what to do to her, her life would be worthwhile. "Such a lifestyle is also the rational choice," she thought to herself.

The man was standing before her now. His strong sweaty odor forced Suzi to pull one step back. Without thinking about it, she could tell the man was a migrant worker. Xu Hongbing had said that many of them liked to visit Lute Garden for enjoyment. They were spending their hard-earned money in tiny pleasures. Suzi remembered saying to herself at that time, "You can detest such people, or you can sympathize with them."

The man got closer and asked, "Do you want to do it?"

Huang Suzi's heart was beating wildly, but she tried to calm herself down and put on a veteran's mien, "Of course. I must make a living," she replied.

"How much?"

"How about a hundred," she answered.

The man said, "Don't you think that's a little too high?"

Huang Suzi did not care about money, so she forced her price down, "Fifty okay?"

The man said, "You have any safe place to go?"

"Of course."

The man said, "Who'll pay for it?" Suzi answered, "It's not so dear. You can pay if you want, or I will pay."

"You're very straightforward. What about splitting the bill?"

"Done," Huang Suzi said.

There were lots of short-term rooms waiting to be rented in Lute Garden, so they easily found a very small and simple one. It was not as good as Ma's, but very remote and quiet.

During the searching process, the man kept his arms around Huang Suzi as if they were lovers. Suzi was not used to his sweaty smell, but after about ten minutes she felt not a thing. She kept herself clinging closely to the man with occasional amorous gestures. She was not a born coquettish woman, so everything she was doing had been learned from hookers in movies or TV. At that moment she was not at all nervous and had become a totally different person.

They struck their deal for a room very soon and did not even have time to talk much.

The man was a little nervous. Huang Suzi said, "Why be so nervous? Go slower and you'll feel much better."

"What if policemen come?"

Suzi replied, "No big deal. What we are doing is just a physical need." The man calmed down on hearing this. Asked about her name, Huang Suzi said her name was Darling Yu, though it was apparent the man knew nothing about Yu or Xiang Yu's poem. He smiled, "An interesting name you got." Then he said his name was Shuigen.

Suzi was not at all interested in his name, for she had no desire to maintain a long-term relationship with him. She asked, "Are you working on casual jobs in this city?"

"Yeah, I do. Nights are always tedious so I came out for a walk."

Then Huang Suzi lost her desire to talk, as did the man. Action could remove a feeling of boredom, so the two weary and lonely people stayed in the crude tiny room until midnight.

"Darling Yu" took the five pieces of dog-eared paper money

from the man and left. She walked straight to the street and took a taxi home, the paper money, soaked with that migrant worker's sweat, was all given to the taxi driver.

The first thing she did after getting home was to rush into the bathroom. Though she had to scrub hard to get rid of the sweat smell left by that man, she felt avenged in a way, with her body and heart very relaxed and happy. She was clear, of course, what she had done would be criticized as depravity. Yet, at that moment she felt it too hard to be a good person.

When she climbed out of the bathtub and put on her silk pajamas, she became herself again. Her laundry was thrown into the washing machine. She pulled the quilt over herself and felt that this new person, Darling Yu, was covered, too.

7

Life was noisily rushing towards its own destination. Nobody could possibly stop its momentum.

Huang Suzi already had no idea how many identities she had taken on. Going to Lute Garden had already become part of her life. She was Huang Suzi by day but Darling Yu by night. Huang Suzi was the graceful and silent, pretty office lady on the surface, but inside she was a dirty woman who constantly cursed others with filthy words; at night she would become Darling Yu, the "hooker," cheap and obscene on the surface but desperate inside. She felt she was not prostituting herself just for the sake of prostitution; instead, she was trying on another lifestyle and fulfilling some need in her life. She split herself further and further, and then thought: "What a complex creature a human is — three-dimensional and made of different material, yet only paying attention to one dimension in life and becoming its slave because of vanity of contentiousness, afraid of being three-dimensional and making every surface shine. That was why all people were so stiff and dull, shortsighted and clumsy. Making their lives attached to their bodies languish like pickled vegetables, all their shining and vibrant qualities going sour due to this pickling process." Huang Suzi had already been pickled, so she knew what it was like. So now she would try to complete her splitting process to make her life real and three-dimensional. Thinking of these things, she seemed to have understood something, as if a truth was guiding her, and thus she thought she was living more rationally than anyone else, and simultaneously she found all people giving off a disgusting substantive smell that made her very sick.

New Year's Day was coming and she got her bonus. She bought a milky *Citroen*, since she needed a car to go to Lute Garden. Before that, she used to go home for dinner and then set off after changing her clothes, but without a car she could be seen by acquaintances who might look at her in a peculiar way and spread exagerrated rumors about what they had seen. After deep thought, she decided she should buy a car.

She put all her stuff, including Darling Yu's clothes, cosmetics and condoms in a canvas backpack she prepared. She had become experienced now and was a lone wolf in Lute Garden. Unlike other hookers, who often came together for excessive fun and went downtown with clients for singing and dancing, she only hung around Lute Garden. She would resolutely decline all clients who wanted to take her out. Compared to other hookers, she was thought to be the lowest because she wanted sex only — uninterested in fun and without taste. Huang Suzi ignored all these things, since she was clear that she was totally different from any of them. All her competitors worked only for money, but she did not. Money was nothing to her.

After the clients had left their money and disappeared deep into the night, however, Huang Suzi would ask herself, "What do I do it for, if not for money?" She had no answer. She tried hard to think and finally found the word: test. "I do it as a test, whether a person can have another lifestyle, and whether one can develop several altered egos," she thought.

After work, Huang Suzi usually grabbed a quick snack and drove to the parking lot in the central square, where she changed into her hooker's clothes and fixed her makeup. Huang Suzi had beautiful, fancy clothes and wore light makeup on her face, while Darling Yu only wore cheap and raffish clothes and raddled lipstick. After everything was ready, she walked out of the car as Darling Yu in the place of Huang Suzi.

Once she ran into her boss's brother. She got really nervous, since they had almost become husband and wife, but he did not recognize her despite glancing at her. He thought she was an ordinary hooker like the others. This made Huang Suzi very confident after that. Walking in the streets of Lute Garden, she was truly Darling Yu, and even someone who found her somewhat familiar would never believe it could be Huang Suzi. That was why Suzi felt at ease.

Huang Suzi never had a steady locale. She used whichever room she could find. At first she rented a room for a period, but after using it several times she found no interest in it. Besides, she did not want to become too familiar with any landlord, so she returned the room within a month, with no steady haunt again. Moreover, she found things were more interesting without a steady room. Usually she would stand in the dark corners of the street and solicit clients with a soft voice. In actuality, being silent was enough, for as long as she stood there long enough passersby would know what she was. In warm seasons, when short-term rooms were not available, she would walk clients along the railway and they would hastily spend their time in deserted work-sheds. Once she even made it with one of her clients in the open air, while looking up at the dark sky and sparse stars, thinking, "I am nature itself today."

On such occasions, she often charged less and the clients were usually poorer and quite vulgar, but Huang Suzi did not care about the money, let alone who the clients were. She would say to herself, "It's the business of Darling Yu. It's okay so long as she doesn't care."

There was a period when an anti-prostitution drive was at its peak and policemen could be seen everywhere searching for johns and hookers. All the clandestine hookers hiding in Lute Garden were very nervous and moved to others places, and the landlords refused to rent their rooms, giving various excuses. Unlike them, Huang Suzi still stayed put as usual. She went to Lute Garden every day alone, as if Lute Garden had become part of her life like salt.

"What if I get arrested one day?" she sometimes thought, but her ultimate conclusion was always just to wait and see. If she did not go to Lute Garden, what would she do at home all alone? Stay with the five lights on in the house? Listen to her neighbors' clamor? Watch the variety shows on TV? Or read a book in the deadly silence of her home? That was no better than being in police custody. So ultimately she came to the decision that she would not be able to live without her salt.

One night when the anti-prostitution drive was about to end, Huang Suzi and her client were both arrested. They were in Ma's room, and as the door was broken through, the idea occurred to her, "I will end where I started."

This had campaign paid off, with the police destroying many such dens of ill-repute. All the hookers and their johns were taken to the police station in a car. In the courtyard of the police station, the men and women stood against respective walls. They were all guys without any conscience, but at that moment they all lowered their heads due to fear or shame. Huang Suzi was the only calm and relaxed one, who casually looked at the policemen busy in the courtyard.

A watching policeman finally could not take the look on Suzi's face. He walked over and yelled out to her, "What are you looking at? Shame on you!"

Suzi answered imperturbably, "Why? What's the shame? It's my way of life and I need it. What is the difference between it and dancing, drinking and drinking in a bar."

The policeman was a little startled by her answer, but he opened his mouth again immediately after that: "Shame on you! It is the first time I've seen a person as shameless as you!"

Huang Suzi replied, "Don't you think you are being a bit extreme?"

A policeman, probably a supervisor, happened to hear her words. He got angry and motioned with his head to another policeman, "Take her upstairs."

Huang Suzi minded nothing on the surface, but her heart was beating fast for she did not want to be physically tortured. She stepped upstairs under the policeman's gaze. She spotted a toilet halfway, so she said, "I need to pee. You got to be a bit humane."

The policeman hesitated a moment, but did not think it possible for the woman to escape under his tight watch. He said, "Five minutes only."

Suzi replied, "That's too long."

Once in the toilet she began to feel nervous. She did not want to pee and only wanted to fine a chance to escape. Looking out of the window she found she could climb down the pipe outside the window to a roof next to the police station. Without even thinking, she climbed out and made a desperate climb down the pipe. Just as the tips of her toes were about to touch down on the roof, she heard the guarding policeman yell, "Finished? Come out! Now!"

She got flustered and fell down onto the roof, and then slipped along the roof right up to the edge. It was a coincidence that there was a branch right at the eave connecting the tree with the roof, so she jumped and hung onto the branch with her arms, without a moment's hesitation. The branch was long enough to allow Huang Suzi to land safely. Suzi could not believe what had just happened to her. She was not injured at all, only brushed by the leaves over her cheeks.

She ran as fleeing for life until she was back inside her *Citroen.* She only relaxed until after she had changed her clothes. Her hands were trembling so wildly that she could hardly drive. She sat in the car for a long while and reviewed what had happened over and over again. "A person can never know how capable he or she is," she surmised.

This terrifying experience almost knocked her down. For about half a month, Huang Suzi dared not set foot in Lute Garden. It was a long period for her. The atmosphere kept tempting her like opium. She fell into a constant sense of anxiety, and suffered from a dry throat and terrible headaches at night. What was worse, she began to lose a lot of weight, becoming near anorexic. Life had become tedious to her. Sixteen days after that, she said to herself, "I prefer to get arrested and beaten to death than to be tortured to death by so tedious a life."

Huang Suzi felt immediately relaxed after this thought. She went out and bought her Lute Garden gear before the shops closed. Then her car sped directly to Lute Garden. When seeing those familiar things again in Lute Garden, she could not help weeping with excitement.

The golden autumn was quickly over and a cold wind

overshadowed the season. Then the world transformed into a white one.

Anti-prostitution drives could not always remain at their peak, so now those fugitive hookers had returned, and again their sluttish laughter from the dark street corners could be heard. The righteous could never understand why these hookers could not be completely removed.

Darling Yu, however, vanished suddenly that winter. Several regular clients, who considered her very cheap but adventurous, started asking about her whereabouts. They all had an impression still fresh in their mind of that scene in the police station. They eventually heard that Darling Yu had escaped from the toilet. Their conversation seemed to prove that Darling Yu meant something different to them now.

But Darling Yu appeared no more.

One Sunday morning, a young firewood collector discovered a woman's dead body in a work-shed abandoned in the suburbs by the platelayers. Her private parts were exposed, her head crushed with her brains and blood oozing out. The winter wind had dried her blood. Her death was frightening.

The policemen arrived upon hearing the case. Apparently it was a murder. By her dress, policemen easily judged she was must have been a hooker hanging around Lute Garden. They took her photo to Lute Garden for identification. All who were summoned said, "Oh, isn't that Darling Yu? No wonder she had disappeared recently. She's that hooker named Darling Yu."

Not until the policemen asked about her address and hometown did people in Lute Garden realize no one knew anything about her. All they knew was she only came to Lute Garden in the evening and left at midnight. They even told the policemen about her escape from the police station, but there was nothing more to tell. It seemed the case would go no further, after reaching this point.

At the same time, Huang Suzi's boss was in a fiery rage for a few days, for Huang Suzi had unexpectedly left without telling him. They had worked together for many years and he had treated her very well, and nothing had transpired recently that could make her angry enough to quit, he thought. His files had always been dealt with by Huang Suzi, and as soon as she was absent he fell into trouble. He called Suzi's family every day but no one answered. One day he drove to Huang Suzi's parents to see for himself, but her parents only said, "How could we see her? She has stayed away for about a whole year." She must had found a better job or gone south for further advancement, but not dared or was too embarrassed to thank him for all his goodness, Huang Suzi's general manager calculated. He thought his judgment reasonable, so he hired a new assistant.

Several months had passed and spring was soon over. One day an attendant at the central square parking lot reported to the police station that there was a white *Citroen* that had stayed in the parking lot for quite a long time and no one had come to pick it. The police were good at following up on license plates, so they easily discovered the name of the car owner — Huang Suzi.

The policemen went to Huang Suzi's house but the door was locked, so they visited her company. Not until then did Huang Suzi's general manager realize that something was wrong. Was it possible that no one in the world knew where Huang Suzi had gone? Was it possible that some accident had happened to her?

With the help of the policemen, he broke into Huang Suzi's flat. There was dust all over with no signs of life. Obviously it had been deserted for a long time. No clues could be found in that car to suggest that Huang Suzi had committed suicide or encountered any accident. Huang Suzi's boss scratched his head and at once an idea came up — he decided to look for her through the missing persons' column of the newspaper.

Huang Suzi was a pretty lady with a nice face and demeanor, so her picture was striking when published. Whoever read the newspaper would take a good look at her and sigh deeply. One day the policeman in charge of Darling Yu's case read the newspaper. At first he also sighed, but on comparing he realized that Darling Yu's features looked exactly the same as the newspaper one. He had already put Darling Yu's tough case aside, but this picture gave him hope again. The same afternoon he went to Huang Suzi's company with Darling Yu's picture.

Huang Suzi's general manager was speechless at the news that Huang Suzi might have been killed. After looking at the picture, he immediately said, "I'm absolutely certain that's Huang Suzi, though I've never seen her dressed like that."

The policeman told the general manager the victim was not Huang Suzi but Darling Yu, a hooker in Lute Garden who had prostituted herself in recent years. These words almost knocked the manager down, and at once he discounted the idea that the woman in the picture was Huang Suzi. "If that is true, it would be impossible for her to be Huang Suzi. It must be someone else that looks like her. Huang Suzi's nickname was 'Corpse Beauty,' you know?"

When her coworkers in the company checked the photograph, the conclusion was reached that the woman in the picture was indeed Huang Suzi. But how had she become Darling Yu of Lute Garden? This problem confused the coworkers so much they only wanted to deny the conclusion.

The police station had its own methods. Age, blood type and various other forms of evidence told them that the murdered Lute Garden hooker Darling Yu was indeed the beautiful office lady

Huang Suzi.

For days the company staff members were all in an excited and distressed mood. Though the police station had confirmed that Darling Yu was Huang Suzi, they would not believe that this everyday hooker in Lute Garden, Darling Yu, was indeed the "Corpse Beauty," Huang Suzi; and Huang Suzi's boss was the one who believed it the least. He kept saying "no way," and that one day he would encourage Suzi to bring up a lawsuit against the police station after she came back. He said, "They are defaming her, and we will not settle with them unless they pay about a million yuan."

Huang Suzi's family had the fiercest reaction. Her father had retired. He often took part in activities organized by the neighborhood, and mediated between quarrelling young couples. In the morning he went to the park for exercise, and at dusk some students with poor grades would ask him for help in their Chinese language studies. He never went dancing, for he thought it dull and silly and only for ordinary citizens. He thought he was in a high position and should contribute more to the nation, and he could only live up to his reputation by doing so.

With only one glance at the photograph brought by the policemen he recognized it as his own daughter. When he found out what she had done, he beat his breast in agony. He was very anguished, but not for Huang Suzi's life at all. He kept crying, "How will I be able to endure such loss of face! Why was there such a bitch in my family? How will I face other people!" There were some dirty words in his abuse. He used many filthy words on Suzi, some of them being Huang Suzi's favorites. The policemen's ears could not stand them. They thought, "With a father so filthy, how could she not be a hooker?"

It was a fatal blow for Huang Suzi's father. He was unwilling to go out any more after that, for he thought the reputation he had earned all his life had been now robbed by Huang Suzi. Without such a reputation, was there anything meaningful in his life? So he only stayed home awaiting death. Huang Suzi's mother was much cooler. She said, "Anyway, Jianjian never regarded us as her parents. Why get so angry? You might as well forget her." "Technically she may be right, but the reality is not what she thinks," he thought, "If I went out, some people would certainly laugh at me surreptitiously."

For a long time the family cursed Huang Suzi every day. Before that, her family did not know how to curse, but now they all became experts at abuse, with their abusive words becoming extraordinarily dirty.

Six months or so later, Huang Suzi's case was gradually forgotten by those busy crime-unit policemen because of a lack of more clues, along with many other important cases.

Early one stormy morning in winter, a timid-faced old man came to the police station and surrendered to the police, and said it was himself who had killed Darling Yu of Lute Garden.

The old man who appeared provoked the curiosity of the crime-unit policemen. They made careful inquiries.

It was quite a story, simple yet sophisticated.

The old man was a sixty-two-year-old rag picker. When he was young he had been put into jail for stealing, and his wife had left him due to that. From then on, he had been living on his own and making a living by collecting rubbish. Stolen manhole covers or stuff with copper got him some money, and that was why he had some savings later. Once having gotten clothes and food, a man seeks other stuff, like women. The old man was no exception. He had frequently gone to Lute Garden over these years, but he was poor and his money was hard-earned, so he only visited cheap hookers. Darling Yu was one of them. In the old man's opinion, Darling Yu was easygoing, and she was not that serious even when he was bargaining with her. The old man said, "She was a different kinda hooker. It seemed she didn't do it for the money."

One night when the old man was collecting rubbish around the parking lot of the central square, he suddenly saw Darling Yu driving a car into the parking lot. The car was going slowly, so he could see clearly inside, and what he saw was that Darling Yu was not dressed like Darling Yu but like a refined lady on television. She was so comely and elegant that he at first denied his own eyes. "There are so many persons who look similar in the world," he thought. When a minute later he saw Darling Yu walking out of the parking lot coquettishly in her usual dress, he was greatly taken by surprise. Only then did the old man sense something very unusual. Due to his curiosity or something else, he began to observe this Darling Yu from then on. After several months, he thus discovered that Darling Yu was not just Darling Yu but was at the same time one Huang Suzi working in a company. She made a lot of money and had a white car and lived in a comfortable home. She ate outside after work, and then parked her car in the parking lot of the central square. She changed her dress for the attire of a hooker, and then she took a taxi to Lute Garden to prostitute herself.

When everything became clear, the old man felt that this must be the most unbelievable thing in the world, and that there had to be something wrong with the woman. At the same time he was wild with joy. He figured that nobody else knew this secret, and Darling Yu must be wanting to keep it a secret forever. Therefore an idea came into his mind.

One evening he went to Lute Garden very early and saw Darling Yu in the corner at her usual spot. Darling Yu did not know why he was waiting for her. The old man told her that it was because she was cheaper than the other hookers. Darling Yu said nothing and they went to a work-shed that had been deserted by platelayers in the suburbs. The old man had picked this place in advance, for it was desolate and he could do and say anything he wanted to. Because they were familiar with each other already and Huang Suzi often did it in such places, she was not vigilant.

After they went into that work-shed and did it, the old man abruptly spoke out Huang Suzi's real name, which gave her quite a shock. Given her character, she kept calm and said, "How do you know this name?" The man replied, "I know more than that. I know your company and your home address. You have no man so you are eager for this thing, and that's why you go to Lute Garden every day."

Huang Suzi changed her expression and started to leave. The old man did not stop her, but he said that if she went away he would tell everyone about her. After a moment's hesitation, Suzi sat back down and asked, "What do you want? Tell me." The old man said, "You're rich, I know that, and you know I'm poor. What I want is for you to give me two hundred thousand yuan one time, and then allow me to visit your place for the night twice a month — only twice, not too much, right?"

Huang Suzi told him in a cool voice, "I don't have so much money and will not let you come to my place for the night." The old man said, "How about I reduce it to one hundred thousand and your place once a month, if that is too much for you. I've never lived a well-off life, something you can't know about. Even living comfortably in a rich person's room for one day, I'll not regret it my entire life." But Huang Suzi only said coldly, "Stop day dreaming! Five thousand for you, and you never see me again. If anyone finds out my real identity, I'll send someone to teach you a lesson."

But the old man would not compromise, either. He said, "I can't go down much more. You probably don't realize how extremely hard it is to keep such a big secret from other people. You could give me five thousand and I'd keep your secret for three days. After three days I'd let it out. Those guys who've slept with you will go looking for you at your company. If they find out you're rich, they'll pay you much more. Though, if you take them to your house every night, you'll make even more money, enough for the rest of your life. That's good. In that way, you will not only enjoy yourself but also make lots of money without any cost."

Before the old man was finished, Huang Suzi began to curse him. She went at it with high speed and her wording was caustic and wicked. At first the old man cursed back, but ultimately he failed miserably. Huang grew more and more excited as she continued. She had gone red, and now the man who had to stop abusing her found himself set afire by her abuse. To him, Huang Suzi's words were like fireballs that were burning his body, which was no longer dry wood. He uncontrollably rushed at Huang Suzi and tore off her pants again. By that time he was already flaccid again, so Huang Suzi began to blurt out much dirtier words. The man, though sexually impotent, had his hands which were still strong, so he squeezed her neck and tried to cover her mouth with his. Huang Suzi desperately resisted and having struggled free she began to curse again. The old man wanted to stop her abuse, so from nearby he picked up a brick once used as a seat and hit Huang Suzi on head. She went silent at once. Still afraid she would open her mouth again, he tried with all his might to choke her with his two hands for quite a long time, for about one hundred years was how he said it. He thought in this way she would definitely stop her abuse, but by then she was already dead. The man became so terrified that he fled.

However, his ears could not get rid of Huang Suzi's curses, as if she were forever in his ears. She cursed him out with the dirtiest words without stop, until his ears hurt. He wanted to drink, until he fell passed out and never woke up again, but even when drunk or in his dreams she did not stop. Her constant cursing made the old man feel that all talk was evil. To him Darling Yu was not human; instead, she was a devil coming from the most mordant, acrid and indecent place in the world. He could not help swearing back loudly, but this elicited censure from all the people around him. Some of them addressed him as if he was a mad man, while others even chased and beat him. Such a life was something he could not bear, until he even thought death was better. As a result, he woke up abruptly one snowy morning, and went directly to the police station, despite the heavy snow.

After his speech, the old man pleaded with them, his eyes shining with misery, "I sincerely hope you kind policemen will shoot me to death. Please. Darling Yu's cursing is making my ears ache and my head explode. I cannot stand it another minute!"

The crime-unit policemen did not know what to think or feel. After questioning him, they laughed about this story over and over again, and discussed it for a long time, thinking the world was really full of strange happenings and people. They did not care whether the old man should be forgiven, for doubtlessly he would have to pay a price for his murder. Before that winter was over, he was sent to an execution field to be shot along with several other criminals. Unlike them, the old man was full of joy and occasionally bursting into laughter. He even joked with the policemen from the crime unit. His last words were, "Darling Yu, you can no longer scold me." Then a bullet ended the life of the laughing man.

This legendary tale spread until it was finally reached Xu Hongbing. It was already another spring. For some unknown reason, he drove to Lute Garden and went into Ma's house again. Nothing had changed here. The bed was dirty, the night-stool still had its falling paint, and the mirror was too foggy to reflect any face. He stood at the window thinking hard as he did when he had come with Huang Suzi. The night sky was decorated with numerous stars, with occasional shooting stars falling into the dust. Xu Hongbing sighed deeply. He thought, "Am I the one who first killed Huang Suzi?" But then he rejected this idea. "If not me, then who did it first?" he wondered.

He came up with nothing over the whole night, only feeling a little pain in his heart. As he was leaving the next morning, Ma asked him curiously, "You specially came to this place for a whole night without a woman, why?" Xu said nothing. He smiled and left.

His company is still making a great deal of money.

But on a nameless day, the woman Huang Suzi was finally forgotten on this earth, after having been the subject of discussion for quite a long time. Time is never too sympathetic toward people. All things, however sophisticated or strange, however weighty or profound, are transformed to mere dust and dew by time, with only a soft sigh not even a few people might hear.

Ash on an old man's sleeve
Is all the ash the burnt roses leave.
Dust in the air suspended
Marks the place where a story ended.
— from *Four Quartets*, T.S. Eliot

(Translated by Zhang Ruiqing)

Forever Autumn

Pan Xiangli

Pan Xiangli. Born in Quanzhou, Fujian Province, Pan Xiangli moved to Shanghai in her youth and has been residing there since. She went to Japan for two years of further studies, and has been working as an editor for literary journals and newspapers.

Her fiction collections are *No Dreams*, *Ten Years After*, *Slight Warmth in a Gentle Touch*, *I Love Sakura Momoko*, and *Plain Soup of Greens*; and her prose collections include *A Simple Letter from Me*, *Age of Innocence*, *At the Age of Believing in Love*, and *Sometimes Partial Perfection*. Some of her works have been translated into Japanese, English, Russian and Korean. She won *Shanghai Literature*'s Excellent Writing Prize, the Independent Chinese Pen Center's literary prize, as well as many other awards. Her short stories "I Love Sakura Momoko," "Miracles Only Come by Sleigh," "Plain Soup of Greens," and "Forever Autumn" (translated here) put her on the Chinese Top Fiction List for four consecutive years from 2002 to 2005. She was also given the honorary title "New Cultural Star of Shanghai" and won the 1st Youth Literature Prize, the 10th Zhuang Zhongwen Literary Prize in 2006, and the 4th Lu Xun Literary Prize in 2007.

Forever Autumn

Autumn just does not age. All those pleasure-seeking young men who used to go hear her sing at the Blue Crown Club years ago now flaunt protuberant bellies, as if no need to worry that others see them as "new money" with swollen portfolios. Some of these young men have gone bald at the top of their heads, and as a last resort have let the surrounding fringe grow long enough for them to comb it up to try to cover that crowning bald spot. In a popular witticism, this is quipped the "style of local governments in support of the central government." The wives of this set of men were once movie stars or fashion models. Of these women, who was not considered the most beautiful in her time within her circle? Now, you look around, every single one of them, if not for some paid nip-and-tuck jobs, breast augmentation and/or botox treatments, on top of the weekly "beauty maintenance routine" at the salon — even if they have managed to keep up the craft of their trade, none has been able to sustain their youthful appearance. Except, Autumn.

"Xieqiu Niang," our Madam Autumn still looks the same every year. Every time real-estate mogul K. G. Wang visits the "Autumn Kitchen," he goes through the same routine of babble: "Autumn, how you never change! Always so beautiful, you just don't grow old. It's so unfair, it almost makes the rest of us want to give up living!" If there are other clients present, Autumn just gives a small smile and ignores him. If no one else is around, she would, in that legendary, slightly hoarse voice of hers, once described as "the moon behind a cloud," answer in her unhurried way, "Stop trying to kid me. How can I still look young? I've never been young...."

Most people don't remember whether Autumn has ever been young. They only remember that she has looked this way for many, many years now. When she was in her early twenties she already had this same appearance. All four seasons of the year, she would dress in her classic *qipao* (cheongsam), made of not silk nor silk brocade, but more in the original Manchurian style, in ordinary everyday cotton, often of the plainest color. At most, the cloth might have some sort of small checker or simple muted floral pattern. She wears a pair of hard-bottomed black cloth shoes with black laces. From the back she looks like a clean-cut girl-student from the 1920s or thirties. But you have to wait for her to turn around. Then, your eyes are simply struck by a kind of bright, stark handsome beauty with a peculiar gossamer quality, and you just would no longer be aware of what type of dress she was wearing. That classic style of *qipao* gown had long gone out of fashion by then, with hardly any women seen wearing it. But Autumn would — and wear it like it was part of her. Like she had never worn anything else. Years later it would, in fact, come back in style. Suddenly all you could see on the streets would be *qipao*, somewhat modified to accentuate raised bosoms, to expose more leg, for a sexier, more eye-catching look. Yet Autumn would be wearing the same classic *qipao* she had worn before, as if to remind people that the new ways of wearing it reflected a certain shallowness. In the depths of winter, Shanghai can be quite cold and damp. All Autumn would do is to add a long coat on top of her plain *qipao*. The color of the long coat is always black. Her hair is gathered into a bun with a long sandalwood hairpin. This wooden hairpin seems to have no particular color. But it carries a faint scent, detectable only when you are close to her. It is believed to be a family heirloom. Except for this hairpin, Autumn wears no accessories of any kind.

More than one woman has been heard to say, "A young woman dressed like that is just not proper. It makes one look old, and people would find it unpleasing." And, of course, many of the fashionable young men of the "beautiful people" circles could not just tolerate this. They brought her presents, the trendiest and finest fashions of the time. Autumn would accept them all with a small smile. But she never once wore any of them. She would simply continue to wear her classic *qipao* made of cotton. Gradually everybody just had to cool off from any further efforts to try to charm her.

One person had not given up so easily. Dave Dai was a Chinese man who had grown up overseas. Dai was tall and handsome, "like a jade tree standing in the wind," and from an established family. He was a proud man who always aimed high. He must have owed some unpaid debt to her in a previous life. Now that they had met in this life, it was like payback time for him. The first time he laid eyes on her, he immediately said, "I would never have thought it possible to still find in China a woman like her, like someone who has walked out of a classic Suzhou gardens of old." None could doubt his devotion to Autumn. His flowers filled her dressing room in the Blue Crown Club. Every night his shiny *Benz* was parked out front waiting for her. The other female performers in the Blue Crown would in the end put aside their jealousy, and try to persuade Autumn, "How can you turn down someone like Dai? Are you hoping to marry a god?" Autumn would just smile her small smile. Autumn had always been a person of few words. When Dai finally came to bid farewell, he looked completely spent. Anyone who looked into his eyes would see signs of aging. Everyone sighed. And Autumn? No watery eyes. Not even the shadow of a rain cloud.

More than a decade had since passed. The bright-colored ones had faded, the gorgeous-shaped lost form. Then, like a late-blooming begonia, Autumn seemed only to blossom even more. Not only was there no change in the way she dressed, there was no change to her face and complexion, no change to her figure. The only change is there is now even more of this presence you could only call grace and elegance — in her glances, and in her mannerisms and movements. The shape and form of this begonia, having gone through so many moons and cold morning dews, has not changed. Simply so, the very color is even more for the eye to behold. That would have been quite remarkable already. But there is more. This begonia seems to have been painted with a layer of burnished finish, so the torrents of time and the dusty fallout of gossip have not been able to leave any mark. She seems completely oblivious to the vicissitudes of the ways of this world, and the rise and fall of the fates of the people around her. Those run-of-the-mill society "beauties," who had all gossiped behind Autumn's back, suddenly came to realize: Autumn is the woman who has been the most cunning. She had planned this a good decade ago, by holding on to her best. She has waited until today to slaughter them in the battle with time. How they now regret having hurriedly forced their own beauty to bloom fully, without preserving for all the tomorrows. And now, for them it is too late.

There is really nothing surprising in how things turn out. Autumn came from a family of academics and scholars, in a house lined with books. Her father was a musician, who had studied music overseas and taught music at the university. Her mother was a ballerina, who taught high school after Autumn was born. They lived in Fukang (Joy) Lane. Autumn's parents were a perfect couple who were deeply in love. After dinner, the gentleman would light up a cigar, and his wife would play the piano. It was only much later that Autumn was to know that what her mother used to play were Chopin's *Nocturnes*. For little Autumn they had a nanny, who would also do all the cleaning, tidying and various chores in the house and out in the garden, until Autumn was five or six years old. In the kitchen, Autumn's mother would do the cooking herself, making quite genuine delicacies in Huaiyang-style cuisine. For this couple it was a marriage made in heaven, with this pearl of a child who they had named Autumn. No one was prepared for what would come. Through no special effort on any one's part, the happiest and most perfect family was destroyed, shattered into absolute pieces. Denounced, put on a stage by a mob, their house ransacked, waiting to be evicted, Autumn's father could not hold himself up any longer. He chose to jump from a high building, far away from the family home, so that his wife and child would not be faced with the terrible sight of his suicide. His wife, a single-minded woman who accepted no compromises in life, killed herself by swallowing an entire bottle of sleeping pills. At that time, little Autumn was six years old. A flower bud in formation, suddenly facing a world frozen by ice, with no bridges and no roads leading anywhere.

After singing at the Blue Crown Club for three or four years, she became better known for her temperament than for her singing.

Never mind the plain and simple way she would dress herself, with not a trace of makeup, but whoever heard of a performer in a club or tearoom who would not offer a dazzling smile nor socialize with anyone? Even with her long-time devoted fans, she would still just be the most taciturn of women. No one could get close to her. And it was actually for such solitary ways that she became a well-known figure. Still, of course, some men would try. Unfortunately, especially for the ones who really cared for her — be it the successful businessman with money to throw about, the record company executive with the power to break or make a singer, or even that clean-living scholar — they all walked away without any fruit to show for their pursuits. All that remained was the gossip. Some said Autumn has a lost love her heart cannot forget. Others whispered Autumn had been betrayed, and left with emotional scars. Or, more simply said, Autumn was one fated to be an old maid.

In the end the one who finally succeeded in winning Autumn over was a diplomat by profession. This diplomat was about to be posted to a European country, when he met Autumn at a friend's birthday party. The minute Autumn caught sight of him, a special feeling welled up inside her. She could not stop looking at him. She even went over to offer a toast to the people sitting at his table. The diplomat was about to light a cigar, and without thinking she reached out her own hand and lit it for him. When she looked up in his face, a mixture of joy and sorrow rushed to fill her crystal-clear eyes. The next day he came calling by himself. Three weeks later they were engaged. The wedding was an absolute sensation. The newspapers reported it, and the headlines declared: "Ten Thousand Roses Mark the Day, Our Most Talented Gentleman and Most Lovely Lady Are Wed." On her wedding day Autumn, in a snow-white wedding gown, stood like a white cloud beside her blacktuxedoed groom, a quiet sweetness on her lips. After the wedding, this white cloud followed her husband to Europe. People did not even have the chance to succumb to jealousy. They could only sigh with envy, "Oh my, oh my, the ambassador's wife! Never mind the glory and honor of being an ambassador's wife, just the experiences and the kudos that an ambassador's life entails!"

When the cup is full, it tends to overflow. When the moon is at its fullest, it will begin to wane. This is a general rule that life cannot escape. Suddenly one day, Autumn came back by herself, alone. She had divorced the diplomat. No one knew why. Everybody looked hard at her to try to find the answer. And she looked just the same. Her face still clear, serene. No traces or marks of any kind. By then she must have been well over thirty years old. But that face would not even offer up a wrinkle or two. The owner of Blue Crown came to visit her, unable to hide the delight on his face. He was hoping to re-engage her to sing for the Blue Crown. Even before he had a chance to say anything of the sort, Autumn merely said, "We haven't seen each other for a long time. You're not putting up with that life in that place any longer, I hope." He then felt too discouraged to even bring up the subject.

Then, out of the blue there appeared a new hotspot in Shanghai, with the name, "Autumn's Kitchen." Those who did not know about Autumn would keep asking about it, just not understanding. They would say, "Big deal. Just another restaurant." And those who tried to explain would say, "Yes, it is a restaurant, but it is not just 'any restaurant,' you know." And the other would say, "A restaurant is a restaurant. How much difference could it have? Why are you getting all hung up...." "Hung up? Who's hung up? That foolish woman who is your next-door neighbor, you know, the one whose face is as round and as big and as flat as a dinner plate, and whose girth is bigger than a wheel-barrel. She is a woman, all right. And so is Maggie Cheung. Are you telling me between such women there is 'not much difference'?"

"Autumn's Kitchen" is indeed not the same old thing. In size it is one of those ordinary medium-sized restaurants. Its menu is no different from the usual sort of enhanced Shanghai cuisine. Its service is down to earth, offering none of those gimmicks such as waitresses serving on their knees, or nude female parts used as serving trays. Not only that, its waiters are without exception all young men in their twenties in tailored white shirts, black satin vests, with bow ties. Strictly conservative. Nothing too unique. But still, anyone who has eaten there comes away feeling it is unique. They just cannot tell you how it is unique. Everybody is simply puzzled why the place just feels so different. Thus making it even more unique.

Garment manufacturer Du Shifei, known as Big Brother Du, had long declared himself Autumn's big brother, way back in those Blue Crown days, when he was still just a small-time shop-owner. It was not many days after the grand opening of the restaurant before he brought a large group of people for dinner. The minute he entered, he was kept wide-eyed. The restaurant was very bright and open. The décor was more than fine. The tables and chairs were made of walnut wood, ever so subtly in the Ming style. The tablecloth and chair upholstery were of a type of champagne hue, with elaborately embroidered begonia blossoms. The menu was inside a lambskin binder, brush-written in black ink on fine rice paper protected by clear plastic. Lit by imperial-style lanterns, the restaurant exuded an ambience of boundless festivity. When you picked up a piece of the fine-bone china, you would immediately feel its fineness and its lightness, and realize it was made of the most translucent of china. The design and pattern? One you had never seen before. And it felt warm to the hand. By the four walls stood carved window panels. On both sides of these panels were faux windows with scenery painted that almost looked like you could walk right into them. Then on the other side of these window panels were the real windows, which if you opened you would look upon a velvety green lawn, ending in three hundred-year-old camphor trees. You could hear birds singing if the wind was in the right direction.

"On a clear night you can enjoy the moonlight," Autumn said with a smile. Du Shifei suddenly felt awkward in his golfing outfit, and felt that the guests he had brought didn't make the cut either.

The next time he came it was for his mother's eightieth birthday. He was wearing an Armani suit, and an Yves St. Laurent tie. Mrs. Du was wearing a Chanel suit and three or four necklaces, making the occasion quite a grand one. Autumn was as always in her *qipao*, but this time in an apricot shade, poetically bordered with a greenish yellow, and Chinese knotted fasteners. Under the big red palace lanterns, this all added festivity to the happy occasion. Autumn even wore a jade bracelet. She welcomed the venerable elder Madam Du with a smile, "Lao Taitai (Your Venerable Lady), I wish you fortune as deep as the East Sea, and life as long as the South Mountains." As soon as she finished her greeting, the music came on. It was *Blossoms under the Full Moon* (a popular Cantonese pop song of the 1940s). Being Cantonese, the old lady was completely delighted, and exclaimed, "How delightful! This place is wonderful." For the entire evening, Autumn stood behind Madam Du, keeping her cup filled and serving her the food. All the while, the jade bracelet slid up and down her wrist. It was easy to see how Autumn's beauty lay in her simple fine looks. That night, all of Big Brother Du's guests were charmed, some by Autumn, some by the food, and others by the décor of the restaurant. The eighty-year-old lady kept holding onto Autumn's hand. She could not stop showing her fondness for Autumn, and kept repeating, "My darling girl, are you a fairy? You are so beautiful. And so talented. And look at you, the poise, the way you carry yourself! You are more beautiful than a movie star." And Autumn said, "Well, well, venerable lady, if you really mean what you say, will you then do me the honor of allowing me to host this birthday dinner for you?" Then she would not allow Du to pay for the dinner. Du just felt so indebted that the next day he sent a red envelop. From then on, Autumn's Kitchen became his own dining room. He came to eat there a great deal, with or without reason.

Besides all her old friends, the new ones came as the word spread. Autumn's Kitchen became a place where all the big names hung out. Often people would go over from one table to the other, to toast or to introduce themselves. Then someone would loudly proclaim, "So, you are the famous so and so! I am so honored to meet you...." Then the two tables would join together into one, and the conversation continue. For those who had brought their money and their talents to Shanghai to seek or establish their fame, this restaurant became the place to hobnob. And the food was secondary.

Once there was this man who needed a favor from Honorable Director Zhang regarding some document. This man had come to the restaurant every day now for the last two weeks. When Autumn could not stand it any longer, she called the Director's residence, and found out he was out of the country for at least another month. Only then did this poor man stop coming and suspend his efforts in trying to meet the director. He thanked Autumn profusely. A young waiter declared, "Big Sister of mine, why did you have to find out for him? Why didn't you just let him keep coming every day? He was a very good paying customer." Autumn said, laughing, "That's horrible! He didn't come here for the food. He was so restless and anxious, and always only looking for his Director Zhang. That doesn't do justice to my good food and wine."

Occasionally some movie stars or famous singers would come, wearing dark glasses, clouded in a shroud of mystery. The waiters, being used to this, would serve these people just like everybody else. Autumn's Kitchen even made it into some foreign country's "tourist guide." Map in hand, even these foreigners would come looking for "Qiu Niang Xiao Chu" (Autumn's Kitchen).

Inside the restaurant by one side there is a hallway. This hallway is paved with glass in the center of which are placed green stone slabs for walking. Under the glass flows running water, with a few fallen leaves, and a few small fish. These small fish are almost transparent and unnoticeable until just when they turn around at the end of the hallway, then the metallic shine from their small bodies suddenly catches the eye. At the end of the hallway is a room for tea. A few diners are fortunate enough to take their after-meal tea in this room. The décor in this room is completely different from the world outside it. Simplicity is carried to its utmost here. On blue bricks, you'll find by the window a mahogany wide tea table in the shape of a banana leaf, and two armchairs with a few soft cushions of black velvet. Right across the room is a long low table with a rattan top, beside it a small high-backed chair with a simple seat cushion. The handles of the chair were carved in the shape of dragon heads. Hanging next to it on the wall is a calligraphy showpiece. Anyone can see it is great calligraphy, with strokes like a dragon's trail in the air kicking up a storm of clouds. Nobody can really read what it says, being, of course, not the point. There is no other furniture or anything else in the room. The whole place gives this feeling of a very quiet, uncluttered space. Until, of course, you accidentally push open the window and the green grass suddenly jumps into your vision and brightens your view. A great place to have some quiet time, or to engage in some private conversation. Of course, it is not just any customer or guest who can come into this tearoom. This is something very "special" for whoever gets the chance to be invited inside.

Regular customers to Autumn's Kitchen also become familiar with another "special" treatment Autumn may bestow. One day, K.G. Wang had just finished the ceremony to mark his success to win a new subdivision project. He took his team to Autumn's Kitchen to celebrate. Nowadays individual men have no more battles to wage to conquer more land for any kingdom. There are only real estate developers who talk of winning bids for tracts of land to expand their own business and wealth. Winning the right to develop a subdivision is just like winning a battle to occupy a town. The warriors would have to return with a victory celebration. That day, among the exchanges of toasts, the loud laughter and chatter, Autumn was directing more than half a dozen young waiters, who were weaving through the crowd. Towards the end of the feast, Wang suddenly realized, "Where's Autumn? Where has she gone?" A waiter laughed and said, "Our Madam Autumn is doing the cooking herself." Wang was so caught by surprise that he paused, and then said, laughing loudly, "That is rare! And this has to be a good omen for me!"

At that moment, Autumn walked in gracefully, followed by a young waiter holding a large covered bowl painted with a blue wave pattern. She said, "I can see today is such a happy day for Mr. Wang, and I thought I might do my bit to add to the festive occasion." Then she lifted the lid, and said, with the hot steam rising from the bowl, "This is called 'The Soup of Boundless Prosperity'." K.G. Wang cheered, and took a sip. He could not tell what was in the soup. But it was a very tasty and soothing soup. He gave another cheer. At the end, when he was paying the bill, K.G. Wang asked,

"Wait. Has the 'Prosperity Soup' been added to the bill?" Autumn replied, "I only made that because I wanted to." K.G. Wang said, with widening eyes, "All the more reason for you to charge me. You should charge me double because you made it." Autumn said, "Well, then just pay whatever. There's no price for this soup. You can't put a price on good feelings." K.G. Wang broke out into loud laughter, and declared, "Well said. You can't buy good feelings with money." He left double the money to pay for the dinner. The next time he came, he said to her, "Autumn, you should add this soup to the menu and call it 'Good Feelings'."

So, on the menu of Autumn's Kitchen there came to be this added item simply called "Feel Good." You can order it. But it is not every day that you get it. It depends on how Autumn feels. And this item is not any set dish. It depends on the season, the customer, the weather. It could be sautéed mushrooms with chili, with a bowl of plain rice to go with it. In the season when peach blossoms bloom, it could be a steamed *Coilia ectenes* (a type of freshwater fish). For a deep winter night, it could be tiny dumplings with fresh shrimp filling, all made by Autumn's own hands. When the bowl is put in front of you, the aroma of the soup hits your nose. The little dumplings afloat in the soup are translucent. You almost see the pink shrimp inside. But the soup is a milky white. Your mouth starts to water before you even take your first bite. Whoever orders this "Feel Good" dish would be, no doubt, doing some guesswork as to what to expect. And yet you would not want to be correct. Better to be surprised, when Autumn finally presents her "Feel Good" dish. This special "dish" has no set price. After you have consumed it, if you decide you really do not like it, it is on the house. When you leave, they would still see you to the door and bow their goodbyes to you ever so politely. If you did like it, then you pay anything you think is the right price. Those who have had the honor to be served this "Feel Good" dish, of course, would never think of losing face on such an occasion. The big shots would actually try to find out what others have paid, and they would try to outdo one another. To begin with, how many Autumns do you find in Shanghai? If Autumn feels good about you, my goodness, it is your good fortune and should only bring you more luck. Moreover, if you pay a handsome amount, it actually makes you feel good about yourself.

Autumn says it so well: money can't buy "good feelings." Too often, it is so puzzling that, no matter how much money some of these men make, they just don't feel good about themselves. When they are in this combat zone of the rat race, they feel no different from criminals on the run for their lives. When they are alone and having a rest, they are still not at ease. They feel like they are riding on a tiger's back with no way to get down, yet they do not know either how to forge ahead or to make a retreat. Or they feel there are traps set for them left, right and center, with someone lurking in the dark waiting for them to fall into one. Today you may have wealth and fame. Tomorrow your mansion may suddenly collapse and fall down on top of you. Or the tree where you as the monkey-king rule may get uprooted and all the monkeys will scatter and desert you. The ways of the world can really drive a man to insanity. So one needs to go to Autumn's Kitchen, to look upon Autumn, who never changes anything, not her dress, not her small smile. And then one can all of a sudden achieve a momentary peace.

The toughest man can have his moments of insecurity, and make this foolish utterance: "Autumn, should the day come when I meet with a bad fate, and I came to you, would you receive me?"

Autumn would be pouring into the cup some boiled water left to cool for just a few seconds, and then toss in a pinch of tea, probably some "Biluochun" (a green tea produced in Jiangsu Province). "Ah, Director Zhang, you really do think of us as a bunch of coldhearted people, don't you? Whether a high-ranking official or not, you still need to eat. Who knows, maybe you will be promoted to an even higher rank."

Director Zhang would then feel so solidly grounded. He would take a sip of the fragrant and invigorating tea, and feel so comforted.

But providence is not what one can plan for or avoid. Only a few days later, this Director Zhang was fired from his post. Then he was thrown into prison. And then it was discovered his crime was more than petty. He was sentenced to death. Then it was changed into death sentence with reprieve. In any case, there was no need to worry about how Autumn would receive him at her Kitchen. For there was no longer any chance he would be able to show up at the restaurant.

Autumn then said to the young waiter, "Take that cup out. Yes, I mean the glass one used by Director Zhang." When the young waiter handed Autumn the cup, she had already turned to leave. Without turning back she would say, "Throw it out."

One day an elderly gentleman came. His hair was all gray. His skin was on the dark side, and he wore a Panama straw hat. He asked for the owner. When Autumn came over, he stood up, his beard obviously trembling, and he spoke, "My Missy Xie, you've grown up! Heaven has its ways, the Xies' child survived…." While Autumn was still pondering all this, he went on to say, "You look just like Madam Xie, just like her…." It turned out this elderly gentleman, Mr. Duan, was Mr. Xie's close friend, from when he had studied overseas in university. Mr. Duan had not returned to China right after his studies. Instead he married a Malaysian woman, and went to Malaysia to become the principal of a high school. There he lived the well-off life, filling his household with offspring. He had seen Autumn when she was a newborn baby. When he later learned of Mr. Xie's tragic end, he had always wanted to find Autumn and take her to Malaysia. After all these years of searching, he had finally found her. "Why did you change your name? Oh, the things I have done to try to locate you!" Autumn replied, "I am just eking out a most ordinary life. I would never think of doing any injustice to that good name given by my parents." Mr. Duan then took Autumn's hand, and the old man wept, "My dear girl, you don't know how your parents treasured you. If it weren't that life had turned out to be harder to endure than death, they would never have abandoned you. My poor girl, you were just a tiny little child then. How did you pull through? If I hadn't found you, I would have presumed you dead and buried somewhere. Then I would certainly not have been able to meet my own death in peace." Through this whole time, Autumn left her hand in the old man's, as if she was listening to just any other story. After the elderly gentleman had calmed down, she said slowly, "My Uncle Duan, since you are staying in Shanghai for another few days, would you do me the honor of allowing me to host a dinner for you?" He answered, "That will be good. I shall bring my children. I'll let them meet you tomorrow. Oh yes, they must come and meet you. Now, they will no longer think that all these years when I was talking about you, I was only talking in my old man mixed-up dream world."

The next day, dinner was served only to one table, to the Duan family. All other customers had been asked to come back the day after. There was not a single dish from the regular menu. Every dish was Autumn's own creation. After the last course, the elderly Mr. Duan said in a shaking voice, "Wonderful.... Wonderful. You are the Xies' daughter indeed. You give honor to your family name."

And Autumn replied, "My Uncle Duan, you are so overgenerous in your kind words to me. This is just my way of making a living." To which Mr. Duan replied, "Oh no, I am only being fair and honest. This dinner you have prepared, for those who don't know, is simply a most delicious dinner. Of course, it is indeed a delight for the eyes to behold, and it is nutritious and perfectly put together for a healthy meal. But, your Uncle Duan knows better. Your Uncle Duan is, well ... quite well read. I knew right away, you were replicating the old classic recipes from that book, *As Tao An Remembers in His Dream*, am I right?" Everyone was stunned upon hearing this. Autumn quickly replied, in a delighted clear voice, "My Uncle Duan, you are right."

Mr. Duan laughed wholeheartedly and said, "I began to wonder after the first couple of courses. And the more I ate, the more I was certain." He started reciting, "*River crabs at the fattest when the rice is ripest. Lift the shell, and see all the fat piled up; as jade and amber, it does not crumble. Succulence unmatched, not even by the eight treasured delights.*" Mr. Duan pointed with his chopsticks at the dishes on the table, and continued, "*Seek the fat wind-dried duck, the cream from the cow, the crab the color of amber; stew the vegetables in the duck's juice, until it is as a slab of white jade. For fruit, oranges from Xie, wind-dried chestnuts and water-chestnuts; as drink, 'Ice in a Jade Pot' wine. For vegetables, 'Soldier's Trench' bamboo shoots; the rice, white rice from Yuhang. Let me whet my pallet with 'Snow on Orchid' tea.*"

"These were the passages from my favorite book. Since I was never able to taste any of these things, I had memorized the passages. This is food from heaven's kitchen for the gods. Oh, what a shame, what a shame. Even Zhang Dai* experienced only longing

---

*Author of *As Tao An Remembers in His Dreams*, Zhang Dai was a Ming-dynasty poet and historian who "specialized" in the art of fine living. After the fall of the Ming, he refused to serve the Qing court and became a recluse.

and desire for such food. So, how could we have resisted!"

Autumn smiled, and replied, "Uncle Duan has such a good memory. But today the fruit was only good old Zhusha (Mercurial Red) oranges. And the rice is just rice from Meihe. The tea is Longjing (Dragon Well) from the Mei garden. There is no longer 'Snow on Orchid' tea to be found." Mr. Duan put his chopsticks down, excitement still making his eyes leap, and declared, "That's fine, that's fine. It's the spirit of the thing that counts. What need is there to get weighed down by details? My dear Autumn, your Uncle Duan is a connoisseur too, not like those who are just snobs or old men with old closed minds. I can tell, you must be very well versed in the fine classics. A most refined woman — beautiful on the outside and wise and intelligent on the inside. You hide yourself well, but you no doubt have.... Oh, a gentle lady in a fine kitchen.... You fare better than Wen Jun*.... This is indeed better than the legend...."

Autumn's background has now come out of hiding. When one knew not a thing about the background she had come from, one did not even know what to wonder. But once you knew, you would no doubt wonder: all that tragedy and damage, where has she hidden it? You look carefully at her, up and down, and she is clear of any clutter; translucent skin with not a blemish; eyes clear as a cool spring. She moves with such clean elegance and easy grace, at total ease. You can detect no cracks. This is puzzling enough. But even more puzzling is that small smile which is almost always present. It catches you ten yards away. But by the time you have made it closer, standing by her, you know you cannot get another inch closer.

---

* A very talented woman in the Han Dynasty who was content to live a secluded life with her equally talented husband, in what is now Sichuan Province.

There's no getting closer to her. Yet you just cannot tear yourself away. This is, when you think about it, what a true desirable beauty should be. Not like those run of the mill "society beauties," who are just acting like pretty babies.

This is the type of beauty that Autumn just is. And she doesn't seem to age. It stirs everyone's imagination: how can she not have a loved one? Surely she is not going to grow old all alone, is she? Nobody would believe that. But then you think about it, and you realize that she is in Autumn's Kitchen day in day out. The restaurant needs her every minute of the day. She is kept busy until ten o'clock at night when the door finally closes. And then there is all the tidying up and the tasks that need to be delegated to her staff. It is midnight before she goes home. It is quite clear there really is no time for a social life. But how is it possible that, even among the many regular customers, there is not one man whom she likes? Maybe not enough to bring forth thoughts of marriage — but not even for companionship, or some romantic involvement? How can she, such a bright and wise woman, not know that one needs to appreciate the flower when it is still in bloom on the branch? Not when it is too late, after it has already fallen.

Among the newer customers there is Han Dingchu, a handsome man in his early forties, with a Ph.D. in law from the University of Politics and Law, who had also studied in the United States. Han had come back to China for just over a year. Already he had opened his own law firm and made quite a name for himself. When a man is successful, he carries a natural aura that gives him his good poise. Han is the elderly Madam Du's nephew. Big Brother Du brought Han and said to Autumn, "My mother told me to introduce my young cousin to you, so when he needs to be fed he can come to you. We are also hoping that you'll show him a thing or two about Chinese wisdom and virtue — before he has totally lost his Chinese ways and becomes a foreigner." Autumn stood up, and laughingly said, "That's exaggerating things. Eating is not the most important thing in life. I have this tearoom at the back. It is clean and quiet. If Mr. Han thinks it to his liking, I certainly hope he will now and then give us the honor of his presence."

Han had already heard a great deal about Autumn. He knew that when she was overseas, the company she kept was nothing other than the upper crust. He would never think of showing less than the greatest appreciation for her warm welcome. He immediately put on the broadest smile and said, "I have heard them speak of Mademoiselle Xie. It's just that, I would not think of rudely presenting myself without being properly introduced. Now that my Big Brother cousin has kindly taken the trouble to introduce me, I hope to visit often." And Autumn said, "I have almost forgotten all the English I learned. Now we can do some talking."

When Han was leaving the restaurant, his palms were sweating. He said to Du, "No ordinary type of woman. This Mademoiselle Xie."

"My dear venerable Dr. Han, what do you think of your Big Brother cousin after all these years? Did you think I was just going to take you to check out a pretty-baby type of a woman?" said Du.

The very next day Han went to Autumn's Kitchen for dinner. Autumn selected the courses: iced marinated jellyfish, sautéed shrimp, with vintage ten-year-old Shaoxing wine. The main dinner was knotted bean-curd sheets with braised pork, young bamboo shoots in oil, and a soup of bean-curd with green watercress. It was really nothing more than the sort of everyday home-cooked, sticks-to-your-ribs kind of comfort food. Han was by himself, so he begged for Autumn's company. Autumn sat down with him for a drink or two. In the middle of his dinner, Han out of nowhere gave a deep sigh.

"What's the matter? It's not your kind of food?" asked Autumn.

"Oh, please. It just occurred to me, now this is food. All those years in America, well, I just don't know how I lived. I had been eating sand and grit!" They both laughed at that comment.

After some days, it was plain to Autumn that Han is an intelligent, serene and understanding man. He is very well-spoken. He knows how to pay compliments, always to the point but never too overt. His words are just very pleasing and comforting.

When Han was ready for his after-dinner tea, Autumn took him to the tearoom. He took one look and said, "This room makes me feel like I am such an uncultured, earthy, common kind of person!"

Autumn boiled the water and rinsed the cups, and made tea with the Tie Guanyin tea that had just come from the tea company. She gave Han her own personal blue-vine-design cup, the size of a duck egg, just big enough to snuggle in one's hand. She herself used a sky-blue cup, the size of a walnut, an imitation of china from the Yue Kilns.

And Han is, after all, a cultured man. He took a small sip. He paused, a little astonished. He took another sip, and swallowed slowly. Then he merely said, "This is fine tea...." Autumn did not say anything. He looked up and saw her smile. She stood there with her arms folded. Her face was slightly flushed with the earlier wine, her complexion almost translucent, giving her almost a quality of crystal. Han could not take his eyes from her, and added, "Just like Guanyin, the Goddess of Mercy."

After that day, seven out of ten days Han would present himself at Autumn's Kitchen. Sometimes it is in the afternoon, when he would have tea in the tearoom and return to his law office to work. Other times it is in the evening, and he would just come for dinner.

On days when he was freer with his time, he would come for tea and stay for dinner, and then stay for more tea; and he would end up spending his entire day there.

Without realizing how time has disappeared, half a year has gone by. Spring has become summer, and summer turned into autumn. One day when it came time to say goodbye at the door, Han says, "When I arrived here today it was still daylight. Now, it is totally dark, and the world outside is ruled by neon lights. It catches you by surprise." Autumn smiles. There is a gust of wind. She turns her head away from it. He comes over to put his jacket over her, and says, "Don't catch cold." Autumn lowers her head and smiles again. She can smell some sort of fragrance in the air. Before he is able to clear his thoughts, Autumn has, as light and swift as the wind, already retreated up the steps. But she turns, before going in, and says, "Be careful with your driving."

In the legal circles the news spread, that the famed lawyer Han Dingchu has fallen in love with the lady owner of Autumn's Kitchen. Some of these lawyers actually come to see for themselves, and then conclude that, yes, Han knows how to choose his women. And Autumn? Everybody is talking about her. How could she not be moved by a man like Han? Never mind the wealthy prestigious family he comes from. And never mind his big name in the law circles. You just cannot find anything wrong in him, not even in his looks. Moreover, he had already divorced his wife, when he was still in America. He is your perfect, most eligible bachelor. Also, the two seem to have endless topics to converse about. Judging by all that was taking place, she would no longer to need to work herself so hard. Soon she should be able to lead the comfortable life of a successful lawyer's wife.

K. G. Wang, because of the long-standing friendship between them, has no fear of taking the risk of displeasing Autumn. He asks her directly, "If you are going to get married and close down Autumn's Kitchen, what are we going to do?" Autumn replies, "Are you also taking all the gossip seriously? Why should I close down Autumn's Kitchen? I will keep it open for another ten thousand years." K.G. Wang roars with laughter. "You may wish to. But we shall see."

Mrs. Du also came to put in her bit to try to talk Autumn into it. "Our dear young sister, you know, in the end, we are women. Why should we work ourselves so hard if we have the opportunity to depend on our men to live the good life?"

Autumn smiles her small smile, and says, "Are men any good to depend on for a good life?"

Mrs. Du feels jarred. She thinks about Big Brother Du's carrying-on outside of the family home, and she catches herself releasing a long sigh. Self-pity takes over. "Then what can a woman depend on if not her man?"

"What to depend on? Well, in this world, nothing is dependable," says Autumn. Her eyes dim a little, no moonlight but only cloud in her beautiful voice. Still, the smile is there. Just that it is more like the sunlight that appears on a snow-covered landscape, completely devoid of warmth, making one actually feel colder.

Mrs. Du is all caught in her own thoughts. She completely forgets she is supposed to try to persuade Autumn about marriage.

Han had initially thrown his whole being into establishing his practice in Shanghai, and had not yet thought of buying a home. He was content renting an apartment close to his law office. But these days he seems to have a change of plan. He has been pestering

Big Brother Du to look for a house for him. Lately Du begins to complain the minute he sets foot in Autumn's Kitchen: "This is too much. He has been dragging me to look at building sites. I could trip on the uneven ground. I have to wear a hardhat too. And I am all covered in dust and dirt from all this." Autumn hands him a hot towel, and asks, "Have you found the right thing?"

"I believe we have finally come across the right one. Over a hundred and sixty square meters. This should be big enough. And it's in a good area. It's near.... Oops, what am I doing? I should let him talk to you himself!"

When Han is talking to Autumn about the house, he keeps his eyes on her. There is still the same clear, clean and serene face, not a hint of happiness yet neither any care of any kind. Only when he gets around to telling her about the interior design company he has hired, then she says casually, "That is the right thing to do. Time is too precious a commodity for you."

Han cannot help but wonder: is this supposed to be an understanding of, and sensitivity to, his needs — or is this a way to say that she wants no part of this? Just when he felt he was so close and about to seize the opportunity, she would then make him feel that he was still not close enough. Well, sometimes the wisest can only resort to the most straightforward, down-to-earth approach. He asks her to go with him to look at the new house. "There is still a lot to do. I am not good at this. It would be so good if you could take care of this for me. In any case.... Well, it is what you like that counts."

Most rumors are just that, rumors. But when it comes to gossip about people's love affairs, sometimes rumors turn out to be the real thing. Everybody is saying Han and Autumn are an item. Does this conversation not sound like Han is, in his subtle kind of way, proposing to Autumn?

On this day, as Autumn is seeing Han off, out of nowhere a beggar pops up in front of the doorway, and says, "Sir, can I read your face to tell your fortune?" Han says, laughing, "There is no need. I already know my fortune. But I can tell you your fortune. For sure you are not having a good time of it." After that, he climbs into his car and drives off. The beggar kept on mumbling to himself, "Within three days there will be blood. It's another one of those. Another one…." Then a gale of cold wind gusts up. It is suddenly so cold it could go right through the skin and chill the bones. Autumn has this feeling, as if the entire world had just shuddered. Winter has already arrived.

Out of a clear sky comes a loud clap of thunder, strong enough to jolt the heart out of one's chest. Han Dingchu has been killed. A hired hand at the new house, knowing Han was a very rich man, had been stalking him. It was just supposed to be an ordinary robbery. But Han would not submit. He fought with this man. The robber was actually no match for Han in a fistfight. He pulled out a sharp knife and stabbed Han once. The knife went into his heart.

At the day of the funeral, wreaths stretch from the large hall of the funeral home to the lobby. In front of a huge picture of Han are arranged gigantic floral sprays from Han's law office and the Lawyers' Association. Their elegiac couplet reads: "A piece of the sky has fallen," and "Heaven has taken our most brilliant."

Many people, wiping their eyes with handkerchiefs carefully ironed the night before, are looking for the legendary woman, Autumn. But she is nowhere to be found. Those softened by life whisper, "A woman… no matter how strong, how can she take this? She must have found her own hiding place to do her own crying."

On the front door of Autumn's Kitchen there is a notice: "We are closed for today to conduct inventory." Inside several young men are in the process of changing the decorations. Autumn is watching them take down the red imperial-style lanterns, and put up lamps made of a kind of tree bark, imported all the way from Russia. These lamps are made of a special type of bark, which is of a kind of beige color with tints of brown. It is hard to tell what kinds of birds are painted on the bark. But they are colorful birds, all in pairs. Suddenly, Autumn sees the young man, the dishwasher of Autumn's Kitchen, opening the doors to the cabinet that held the tea sets. She says to him, "Take out the cup on the top shelf."

The young man hesitates. "Yes… do you mean the one used by Mr. Han?"

"That's right."

The color disappears from the young man's face. He takes his time in reaching for the top shelf to get the tea cup with the blue-vine pattern. He asks, "Do you want to dispose of it?"

Autumn comes over and takes the cup in her hand. She looks at it for a while, like a collector looking at one of his collected articles. Then, suddenly, the sound of broken china. Fragments of brilliant white china are all over the floor.

"For something so easily breakable, having it broken actually makes one feel more at peace."

Everybody is stunned, frozen, like they were clay or wooden statues. Then Autumn turns around and speaks, "I am going to check out the river crabs. The customers who have ordered them for tomorrow are true gourmands."

(Translated by Yuvonne Yee)

The Surgery

Sheng Keyi. Born in 1973 in Yiyang, Hunan Province, Sheng Keyi started writing fiction from 2002, since publishing nearly 2 million Chinese characters in influential Chinese literary journals, including *Harvest* and *People's Literature*. Her works, featuring somber, deep reflection and her distinctive, sharp narrative style, have been included many times in the annual *Chinese Top Fiction List* anthology. Some of her writings have been translated into English, German, Japanese and Korean. Her representative works are five novels, including *Milk and Water* and *A Question of Morality*, and the short-story collection *Tender Yellow Willow*. She was awarded the Chinese-language Literature Media Prize for "Most Promising New Writer" in 2002. She is now working for the Guangdong Writers' Association.

The Surgery

The instant her body was covered with the surgical sheet, Tang Xiaonan began to shiver.

Her body is covered, leaving only her left breast rising above the surgical sheet, standing upright, lonely.

What she just saw becomes blurred and her ears prick up, sensing a scalpel suspended in the air. Now, with her rich imagination turning into self-intimidation, Tang Xiaonan's sensitive ears can witness the whole process of the surgery.

The surgeons had said that, with the local anesthesia, she would not feel any pain, but she could not believe it, or found no use believing it, for she is waiting for the sensation of tingling when they begin to cut — anxious, with her teeth clenched. The sound of metal apparatus colliding with one another could be heard, and Tang Xiaonan senses that the surgical tools are being spread out, with those clattering sounds as if they were being thumped on her chest.

She was right; it is a tray of glittering surgical instruments.

The surgeons are choosing the ones they wanted, with the sounds of clatter as the background music serving as accompaniment to their talking and laughing. They were talking about salaries and the benefits at this hospital — now something about patients like Tang Xiaonan, and the surgery she is undergoing, from which the hospital could make no profit at all. Thus, she came to understand that there is really nothing serious with her left breast and it is only a minor operation. As a result, her shivering eases and her tense nerves relax.

Li Han was the one who had discovered the problem in her left breast.

Seven days earlier, while Li Han was fondling Tang Xiaonan's right breast, he had felt a small lump, which he though suspicious. Anyway Xiaonan had been feeling strange herself, so they went down to the People's Hospital to do a checkup. The color Doppler report said it was "hyperplasia of the mammary glands," a normal physiological phenomenon. Tang Xiaonan had just heaved a sigh of relief, when the doctor stopped the transducer on her left breast. After searching repeatedly, she said rather indifferently, "There's no problem with the right breast, but there's something wrong with this left one — this unidentified swollen lump suggests a possibility of carcinogenesis."

Why, Cancer?! Tang Xiaonan nearly fainted, her heart breaking with the sad news. She was very healthy, never catching even a slight cold all the year round. How could she think of being afflicted with such a lingering and incurable disease? Besides, she and Li Han loved each other so much that she could just not stand this terrible blow, and was at once frightened into tears. Li Han was five years younger than Tang Xiaonan, and he, too, never having thought of such occurrences, was a little bit muddled. Li Han comforted Xiaonan in a manly way, saying, "The doctors are just lying; they want to cheat patients out of more money; let's go to the tumor hospital tomorrow and find my dad, and get a thorough checkup." Tang Xiaonan thought, "The doctors may want to make some money, but they wouldn't fool around about such a thing." She began to think of the issue of death. She had heard that patients with cancer lose all their hair, and at advanced stages, they become exceptionally ugly, and have to use morphine as a painkiller; and with these thoughts, she could not help but become filled with fear — thinking about people and things to say farewell to, suddenly finding so much to be sentimentally attached to. She was filled with grief.

Li Han's father was in his fifties, lean, with a pair of large-frame glasses and a serious expression. The skin on his face was dry and wrinkled. He, a surgeon-in-charge at the tumor hospital, was well known throughout the medical profession in Harbin.

"Xiaonan, my daddy is quite shrewd, so you've got to insist that you're twenty-four. Do not relent, or you will not see me again if he puts me under house arrest!" Li Han told Tang Xiaonan countless times before they went to the hospital.

There was not only a problem with the left breast, but one with age as well. Tang Xiaonan felt oppressed, but she had to do as Li Han said.

At that moment, Dr. Li was looking at patient X-rays.

"Dad, this is my classmate, Tang Xiaonan, who I told you about," Li Han introduced.

"Follow me," Dr. Li said, throwing her a quick glance to size her up, his face expressionless.

Tang Xiaonan had been in a depressed mood due to her malady. Furthermore, when she found that Li Han dared not disclose their relationship to his father, and even wanted to hide her age, she became even more filled with grief. Now she also found that the old codger was a man of penetrating insight, and it seemed that he did not want her to be his daughter-in-law at all. Under pressure from all these things, her heart felt heavier than ever.

However, at present, the issue of the left breast was the most important issue.

When she was getting the color Doppler done, Dr. Li was watching alongside and touched her breast. The color Doppler map was the same as the one that had been done in the People's Hospital, but the report from the doctor differed: "The sonogram of the left internal mammary reveals a benign fibro adenoma, with no possibility of deterioration. Resection could be done either immediately or after a period of observation." Dr. Li seemed to know something about Tang Xiaonan's misgivings, so he invited some other authorities of the hospital to each touch her left breast, and they had unanimously concluded that hers was benign and there was no big problem.

Now that she could rest assured she could survive, Xiaonan cried once again, just like some philosopher said, "Happiness is when the pain lifts." This time she was crying out of joy, as if she had nearly lost her life.

Then, as for the adenoma, should she get it cut it or not? Tang Xiaonan was not an assertive type. Although, the fibro adenoma in breasts is as dispensable as love in a marriage, much like jealousy in love, not mattering much, she still felt uncomfortable. After all, there were other things growing in the body. The doctors said there was no possibility of deterioration, but would they dare guarantee it? Many of those who have no love in their marriages still do not resign themselves to the fact — did they not then seek "love" outside marriage? Moreover, did sometimes jealousy in love not deteriorate into rather devastating results?

Some of the authorities thought there was no need for a resection, or at least, there would be no need for an operation for a long time still. Tang Xiaonan stole a glance at Li Han, who kept silent, a perplexed expression on his face. Li Han's father then said decisively, "Since it has to be cut sooner or later, it's better to do it sooner." His tone sounded like a relative of the patient, which startled Tang Xiaonan. She began to think him a man of excellent judgment.

The doctors are squeezing the left breast, groping for the tumor one centimeter in diameter.

Tang Xiaonan does not know when they administered the anesthetic.

At this moment, her left breast has lost its sensitivity, and it seems that it has nothing to do with her body. She feels they are touching her with something, or that her left breast was but a slice of frozen meat in the fridge, and her body just a saucer under it. She cannot tell how many fingers are searching her left breast. She is sure that Dr. Li's fingers must be participating in the search, for he feels about it with strenuous effort and complains that the tumor is hidden deep among the lumps of mammary hyperplasia and thus not easy to find, and it is especially harder when the muscles stiffen after the injection of anesthetic. He also says that, if they fail and only cut off a hyperplasia lump, she will have done the operation for nothing and would have to suffer a second operation. Xiaonan senses that it is the doctors' fingers that are talking, showing their irritability and professional indifference, just like butchers moving back and forth over the pork on a cutting board, incomparable with Li Han's affectionate fingers.

Xiaonan cannot help shivering, her hands clenched, and her palms sweaty.

Tang Xiaonan, now definitely knowing that she will not die, begins to worry that the scars after the operation will repel her. Besides, according to the present situation, it is not known yet how many scars will be left on her breast. If this operation does not work, it will be a mess. The breast that suffers one operation is already like the virgin who has lost her chastity, unprovoked and regrettable, and if it suffers still another one or two operations, it will be almost the same as being cruelly violated.

"Ah, yes, I got it," about four or five minutes later, a doctor exclaims in surprise.

"Oh, Ma…!" Tang Xiaonan shouts to herself, and then she hears the doctor pick up a scalpel from the tray. She feels her left breast is like a balloon about to be poked, burst by some children playing a prank. Since Xiaonan has never seen a scalpel before, she can only imagine it like a carving knife used to cut steak when having Western food. The only difference is that this knife is narrower at the tip, and the blade is so much sharper that one dare not look straight at it, making it like a mirror, refracting the incandescent light of the operating theater, the whole of which gives a quaking effect with every single turning of the scalpel. If this scalpel were used to cut steak, it would likely cut through the plate as well.

Tang Xiaonan feels nervous all of a sudden.

She hears the doctor acting without any hesitation.

Before the scalpel falls into the breast, she exerts herself to capture the pain when it cuts the breast open.

At that moment, there is a tension in the air.

Tang Xiaonan hears the knife poke the left breast, like the knife in a butcher's hand, after estimating the weight the buyer needs, gently cutting through. Because the knife is too sharp whereas the flesh delicate and smooth, it will split like mud without any effort from the hand. Therefore, the doctor uses his quick and exquisite technique, the blade seeming to slide across water.

The first cutting finished, the knife becomes glossier.

She hears blood gushing out, gurgling continuously.

The left breast is like an eye filled with tears.

Perhaps the blood flows down her back every two seconds; there is a piece of gauze-like stuff wiping her skin, stiff as ever, not so gentle as Li Han when he wipes away tears for her. She hears worms wriggling on her back, and the blood extending longer and longer like earthworms. Suddenly, a gust of cool and a refreshing feeling sweeps through her left breast, her chest like a wilderness, littered with rugged rocks.

She hears the left breast open.

The open left breast is like a house whose window has been left open, empty with a cold wind whizzing through. Her heart, which originally lay next door to the thick wall, is now saturated gradually with this cold breeze, and soon chilled to the bone. She imagines that the doctors have opened up her left breast like opening the cover to a cellar. Badly mutilated, she does not know what might be left in there.

She does not feel any pain, not the slightest bit, but she feels blasts of cold air move here and there.

The cold feels hard, rather like a spraying car making the street clean and humid all at once.

She tries to remember the sensitive warmth of her left breast in Li Han's palm, but now it is more like a mass of plastic.

Seeing that she can hardly do anything to cooperate but lie there quietly, Tang Xiaonan suddenly has a feeling of being occupied with nothing. It is like when, at a certain stage in love, one does not know how to carry on. The pain that had been deliberately expected did not come, and it seems it will not come at all actually. Just as at times, when she could not find a sense of feeling alive in this too bland life, she would become eager to throw a tantrum at Li Han.

If you cannot feel any pain through an operation, this is also a pity, much as when having sex, you cannot climax. Therefore, Tang Xiaonan feels disappointed, unexplainably so, since she is afraid of pain.

For the moment, she is really hoping that she can feel a little pain, to let herself know what the doctors are doing with her left breast.

In fact, she is not necessarily even afraid of pain. She can remain motionless even when someone pinches her on the arm until it bleeds. Because she can see it with her own eyes, the sense of pain would be weakened without the imaginary self-intimidation. Just as it is the monsters in the night that one is afraid of, but not the night itself, what Tang Xiaonan has is the fear of the unknown. She does not know when the monster (the scalpel) will come out, and with what momentum it would appear (if the extent of the pain is within her endurance), and what kind of raging results it will cause (the length of time during the pain). And her relationship with Li Han is like the night in which the monster appears, seeing no light and perhaps, sometime in the future, a merciless knife will cut him off from her side.

Anyone who forces love to collide with reality is either an idiot or a person who is mentally challenged. Tang Xiaonan is not stupid.

Tang Xiaonan is now quite certain she will not feel any pain, and gradually relaxes. Only at this time does she trust the doctors somewhat with the left breast, no longer carrying a psychological burden. However, in an instant, she feels guilty over the left breast, like not having taken good care of a child entrusted by others.

Since she got to know Li Han, Tang Xiaonan's left breast has been extremely sensitive. But she could not figure out the relationship between Li Han and her sensitive left breast. Neither can she tell, "What came first, the chicken or the egg?" She suspects the one-centimeter tumor is the troublemaker. In this way, she begins to worry there would be terrible scars left on her left breast and, if it became lifeless, who would pay attention to it any more? Which part of her body would replace the sensitive left breast in its function of adding fuel to the flames during her sex life?

"Love is as irreplaceable as the most sensitive body parts," Li Han once said, while grinning cheekily.

After Li Han moved in to live with Tang Xiaonan, he still went and stayed with his parents for two days every weekend. Financially, Li Han is not independent from his parents, so he has been living with his parents while studying English for the IELTS outside, where, he falsely claims, he is sharing an apartment with a classmate. One evening, the other day, Li Han argued with Tang Xiaonan until midnight over some trivial matter. Some comment of Li Han's had so irritated Xiaonan that she had even told him to get out. But then, by just after midnight, they both seemed to be on good terms again. In the morning, Li Han said goodbye as usual, then he disappeared for three consecutive days. Early in the morning three days later, Li Han knocked on Tang Xiaonan's door, held her tightly, and sobbed loudly. Tang Xiaonan, still drowsy and now frightened, did not know what had transpired. "I cannot live without you!" Li Han shouted, holding Xiaonan even closer, as if never wanting to let her go. Xiaonan was shocked, pressing her face close to his face, frozen by snow and wind, unable to utter a word.

This incident reveals two levels of information. The first is that Li Han had been ready to leave at any moment. Being with her, he just wanted to enliven his life. So, had he loved Xiaonan at all before this? When did he fall in love with her? Tang Xiaonan does not know. Moreover, she is afraid that even Li Han himself does not know. The second is that, after Li Han had made up his mind to part ways with Xiaonan, only after his departure did he find that he could not live without her. Therefore, this is evidence that Li Han was determined. What should he do since he could not leave — keep on enjoying the carnal pleasure until they become tired of one another — which people say, only by so doing could one have no regrets.

Li Han is quite good-looking, quite able to attract the attention of women on the street. In Tang Xiaonan's opinion, the expressions in the eyes of those girls or women show obviously that they are eager to get into bed with Li Han. Xiaonan is very aware of the fact that she is not a gorgeous woman, only another passing traveler in this city. All of which is destined to reveal the fact that her love with Li Han has no foundation and cannot be fully developed. Privately, as some song or other goes, "If he deserves your love, give him your love; if he deserves your hatred, give him your hatred; but you must reserve some for yourself." Therefore, Li Han's love became both a pleasant surprise and an unpleasant fear for her — she really cannot tell why Li Han is sentimentally attached to her; if love truly comes right at one's face, should she reserve some for herself at all?

Perhaps the one-centimeter flesh pellet has gone missing again, or doctors are equivocal by nature. Now, Tang Xiaonan hears the doctors rummaging around in her left breast, just like dustmen choosing and weighing alternatives on a rubbish heap, the fingers in rubber gloves stained with blood. The left breast is no longer a breast but a piece of streaky pork or some other such item on the butchers' cutting board, or the doctors are expert meat buyers — Xiaonan feels this from their fingers. She can only hear some muffled sounds, like someone flicking and pulling a rubber band, as if they were in the room next door. She knows that the doctors have put the scissors to use.

"If this does not work, we have to cut out a big section," the doctor on the left says. It sounds more like the strategy in Chiang Kai-shek's massacre of the Communists. Tang Xiaonan feels that the pinches of the doctors' fingers have become blows. The change touching a raw nerve, she dare not imagine what "a big section" might mean.

"I'm afraid it will affect breastfeeding," Li Han's father says on her right, and his words make her warm.

"Ah, we've got to look for it slowly. I don't know if the anesthetic was enough.... Hey, if you feel any pain, just yell," Tang Xiaonan hears the doctor on her left shout to her, wrinkling his brow.

"Heavens!" Tang Xiaonan clenches her teeth in despair, and regrets feeling disappointed earlier because she had not felt any pain.

Tang Xiaonan also recalls that one night when Li Han said in a low voice, "Once you feel sexual pleasure, just shout out. The more pleasure you feel, the more you should shout; the more you shout, the more pleasure you will get!" Now the doctor is asking her to shout. If she senses pain, she is asked to yell, and then they will use more anesthetics. Ah! She exerts all her strength to try to utter a sound. She forgets how she shouted out when she got pleasure on those nights. She wants to imagine the pain as pleasure, and then shout out, and then she will feel pleasure.

The pain will soon come from some unknown place. Tang

Xiaonan endures the situation anxiously, like expecting pleasure, expecting it to get to her human body from a distant place. The knife moves back and forth in the left breast, the cold deeper and deeper, more real. Xiaonan's right hand holds on to the edge of the surgical bed, and her hand feels the ice-cold iron bedstead, apprehensive.

"Li Han, Li Han, my Li Han!" she shouts to herself, as pained as if dying, beads of sweat bouncing out from her brow.

"Where are you from?" Dr. Li asks. His thigh happens to press upon Tang Xiaonan's right hand.

"Hunan," Tang Xiaonan answers, and she begins to feel a little more relaxed.

"Oh, why come here from so far south?" Dr. Li questions her closely.

Tang Xiaonan is about to say, "I'm a journalist and I work in Harbin doing interviews." However, all of a sudden, she remembers what Li Han told her, so she just says "yeah" in an equivocal way.

"Li Han tells me you've had a positive influence on his studies," Dr. Li seems to laugh.

At this, some pleasure emerges in her mind, and a faint smile even plays on her face, buried under the surgical sheet.

"You cannot extend the incision more!" Dr. Li reminds the doctor on the left. Tang Xiaonan becomes all keyed up over this, holding back her tears and pricking up her ears.

She hears that the left breast is a mess.

A breast, in perfectly good condition, suddenly deformed beyond recognition. Why is the right breast safe? Is that because the left breast had been too lewd previously and must now suffer such punishment? Tang Xiaonan and Li Han have been passionate about making love for three consecutive months. She had never tried making love so frequently, and has enjoyed it to her heart's content. Suddenly she thinks of the idea of karma in Buddhism.

"Li Han, come quick, Li Han," Tang Xiaonan shouts to herself, feeling dizzy, a few tears falling from her eyes. How could Li Han dare enter? He dare not even say that he has ever touched Xiaonan's breasts, and how it was his very touch that had exposed the problem with the left breast. He only told his father that Tang Xiaonan is one of his classmates, and asked Xiaonan to hide her age by four years. Tang Xiaonan knows Li Han's predicament — his father does not want him to look for a marriage partner at present, much less a woman of twenty-eight.

Tang Xiaonan secretly feels wronged by Li Han, but she suddenly think of the words Li Han said to her before the operation, "I'm here, don't be afraid." Thus, she understands his difficulties, puts up with him, and becomes a little stronger.

She hears that Li Han is smoking outside the hospital (it being forbidden to smoke inside), where the temperature is minus twenty Celsius; he's smoking red packets of *Blessings*. He is facing the window of the operating room, his nose red with cold.

He looks like a mature smoking adult.

At that moment, Tang Xiaonan thinks, he is her man.

Tang Xiaonan remembers Li Han constantly holding tightly onto her hand, when she was feeling scared at the People's Hospital, no matter when — walking, eating, and even sleeping at night. He never let it go.

"I'm here, don't be afraid!" It is the first time Tang Xiaonan has heard a man say such words to her.

Tang Xiaonan does not know if she had ever given a man the chance before to say this to her, or whether no man would like to say such words — or at least never men in their thirties, whereas maybe only men a little over twenty would have the courage. Xiaonan used to complain that Li Han was still green, but then seeing him behave as if he would sacrifice his life for her, she was deeply moved. Aware of her situation, Li Han said, "If you're dying, then die quickly; if you're going to die, I won't go abroad. I will stay here with you." This left her dumbfounded, yet she could not be sad about it either. Li Han intends to study abroad and his visa may be issued any time. As soon as they established their relationship, this result was ordained.

Tang Xiaonan was also aware that Li Han, no matter what he says, just wants to put her heart more at ease.

Now, under the surgical sheet, she wants to cry aloud. She feels that she should have paid more concentrated attention to what he was saying: there was one occasion, when she should not have lost her temper in front of him; another time, she should have given him a kiss. The more she thinks about it, the more regret she feels. She thinks she will certainly love him more carefully to make up for what he has done for her.

In the last few hot days one autumn, Tang Xiaonan had gone to Beijing.

Before this, she had declared on the phone to Jiang Bei where she stood — she cannot be his lover, and she does not want him to be hers. Tang Xiaonan had made up her mind to remain single, until she reached her twenty-eighth year of life when she discovered, being another's lover amounted to nothing. Besides, she had gotten to feeling more and more that men were good for nothing. They only wanted to have fresh experiences with sexual partners spread over every corner of their beloved motherland. Meeting again many years later, they would make routine love to their partners, as if reliving an old experience, with their sexual prowess being their gift.

After that, they would ask all manner of questions and feign concern for the partner. On other occasions, there were gifts aside from rings, necklaces, or even pure RMB yuan. But this sexual type of gift was also full of tender feeling, while separating itself from the vulgarity of money. In short, during this age when explosive sex was regarded as a gift, Tang Xiaonan suddenly felt she wanted a family, a fixed man and a quiet life.

With this clear goal, Tang Xiaonan began to preserve her chastity. From her side, unconsciously, sex became the opposite of marriage, and the two began to contradict each other. Men would not marry a woman who had casual sex with men — such was the simple fact. Therefore, if she wanted to marry somebody, she had to start with the issue of sex, meaning, abstinence. Having been snubbed by her, several men complained of her indifference to such an enthusiastic human body; and they all abused her when leaving, "You sexless bitch!"

One of her friends' sexual partners had introduced Jiang Bei to her. He was a married man without children, but an extremely serious hitch arose in his marriage. Jiang Bei had said himself that, as soon as she proposed a divorce, he would sign the paper immediately — he would definitely get a divorce, it being only a matter of time. It had been one year since Jiang Bei's wife had left Beijing for Shenzhen to start up a company, and they had not interfered in each other's life for a long time. In this case, Tang Xiaonan was sure that, following this crack, she could make his marriage disintegrate and build her own castle on the ruins of his marriage. Her friends also encouraged her to win him over.

When the feelings between Tang Xiaonan and Jiang Bei had arisen as they were talking on the phone, they discussed the marriage issue several times.

Jiang Bei said, "It is possible for me to get a divorce any time; as for us, since we've not even met each other, who to say what could happen?"

Thus, in those last few hot days in the fall, Tang Xiaonan finally made it to Beijing. It was her first meeting with Jiang Bei.

Tang Xiaonan had arrived in Beijing one week ahead of schedule. She was on a mission. Jiang Bei's wife had suffered a business setback, and feeling bereft, had been moaning tearfully to him several times on the phone, so Jiang Bei had to fly there to fulfill his obligations to console her. Xiaonan immediately pictured a scene where the couple would find their long-felt needs satisfied. At this, she became very angry. Jiang Bei had originally planned to stay in Shenzhen for one week, but as soon as he had arrived in Shenzhen, he received Tang Xiaonan's call, saying that she would reach Beijing the next day, and she would only wait for him for one night.

Sure enough, Jiang Bei had hurried back the next day. On meeting, they felt an immediate liking for one another; and if marriage was to be considered, there appeared to be no problems. Although Tang Xiaonan experienced some pleasures of conquest, she ultimately resisted his body (feeling sure he still carried his wife's body temperature, even though Jiang Bei repeatedly stressed they were a sexless couple); using this as an excuse, she gradually wove this into a resolute attitude.

They shared the same bed the whole night, serene and eventless, but both of Jiang Bei's eyes turned red with frustration. Tang Xiaonan wanted to hold on to her sexual desirability until their wedding day, wanting to keep something for herself in this way, lest Jiang Bei might get tired of her body before their marriage, and if so, she would just be screwed once again for nothing. Xiaonan knew that many marriages were spoiled by sex — after being fed full in advance, what enthusiasm would there be for marriage? Many sex lives begun after marriage also ran into difficulties — without understanding the body of the other, how would a couple know if their sex lives would thrive? For Tang Xiaonan, she was more afraid of the former, since what she wanted was not sex but marriage. One step at a time, for getting to marriage was the first stop, but after marriage would be another stop. Jiang Bei did his utmost to express his own ideas, and he said, "If we do not make love, without this deeper perception, how would I know you are mine? How can you use the oldest trick in the book, in this modern day and age?" Jiang Bei believed in physical feeling. Besieged in the fortress of age, he was already profoundly familiar with the value of sex. Thus, each holding onto their own opinions, the two of them had a run-in all night long, but their opinions did not synchronize one with the other, like gears that could not mesh.

When day broke, Tang Xiaonan came to firmly believe that Jiang Bei just wanted to make love to her, and that he, being a man who only needed a sexual partner, did not intend to marry her. Xiaonan felt that she had been taken in, so she vented all her resentment against men on Jiang Bei, relentlessly picking out and criticizing his faults. Chosen as representative of all men for no reason, Jiang Bei found it hard to vindicate himself. He had been hoping to enlighten her, and to try to get along genuinely with her and work things through gradually, but found in an instant that Tang Xiaonan had become so furious she only seemed to want to get even with men. Besides, he felt that they were very different from one another, with difficulty communicating. Thus, the two parted readily.

Such was the case, how Tang Xiaonan and the man with whom she had considered marriage had come to be so quickly over.

"Is this it? You give it a feel, touch it."

"Well, it feels like it."

"Ah, yes, that's it."

"Cut it longer, cut a little more."

"Well, that's enough; if it's too long, it will be harder to sew up."

The doctors' voices droned on in her ears.

The scissors moved a little bit, and Tang Xiaonan hears them. The sound resembles that of cutting a length of a rubber band, made by the tips of the scissors. Once, twice… she hears the emptied left breast shrivel up slowly. The doctors do not seem to want to leave her alone. They are still gnashing their teeth, like they were cutting up a piece of cloth, left and right, horizontal and vertical. The scissors become colder and colder, and harder and harder, as if stretching into her heart. Tang Xiaonan suddenly feels cold.

"Oww!" Tang Xiaonan lets out a yell. In fact, it is only a small pain from being given a needle. She yells out on purpose in an exaggerated way. It is not so much the pain as it is the horror. She hopes to attract the attention of the doctors — she feels pain already; no more pain for her, or she will not be able to stand it.

Eyes brimming with tears, she tries to hold them back, her desire for an impassioned wailing gone in a twinkling as well, leaving behind only a very gloomy frame of mind. In fact, even if she had sobbed out loud, she would not have known what she was crying for or why she deserved to cry so bitterly — she had known long before, the result of her relationship with Jiang Bei.

Tang Xiaonan sat on the train, as if attracted by the sights outside the window, a twilight sunset on one side of her face and a pale shadow of the light on the other. The sun, like an egg yolk, suspended at the end of the sky, would fall and vanish any moment. On the small square table in front of her, the white baby's breath flowers and a red plastic rose without any luster were buried together in a heavy vase.

Burial — this was what crossed Tang Xiaonan's mind — this was burial. Burial, was a state that had become fixed, that could not be easily changed over a very long period of time, as in permanent death — there was no doubt about it; such as an unpredictable marriage — saying that marriage was the tomb of love, it could also be summed up as a word, burial. Some burials were happy, and others were unhappy; some are happiness in disguise, while others are a mishap in disguise. Since she had never been buried, what kind of burial did hers belong to at all?

Hunger was irritating Tang Xiaonan a bit. The waiter was still by that young couple, holding a ballpoint pen in his hand, facing the blank menu form spread out before him, as if he were sketching. Every time the man chose a course, he would ask the girl if she liked it, then, after making a study of it, the two of them would make a positive or negative decision about the course. With a sweet look of being in accord with the man, the girl seemed to be showing off in an even more affected tender way, laughing contentedly. Hunger irritated Xiaonan a bit more. Maybe it was just due to hunger; otherwise, it had nothing to do with her, Tang Xiaonan, no matter how long they studied the menu and however much they made eyes at each other. Now Xiaonan really was hungry, whereas they, occupying for a long while, the only waiter taking orders in the dining car were wasting time, time in which Xiaonan could have filled her stomach. The young couple's attitude toward ordering seemed much like how they treated their love, seriously, with care, not in the least perfunctory. They perhaps were studying the menu more carefully than they did each other's bodies, far too unnatural.

Tang Xiaonan suddenly wanted very much to swear at someone, not at some specific anyone, but in any direction — at life, at history, at the figures of men and women. She wanted to shout abuse at love all over the streets.

"You are going to feel a little pain. Bear with it, the operation will be done soon." The doctors, knowing it would not be so painful under the circumstances, have not taken her yelling seriously.

"Do you need more anesthetic?" Dr. Li asks.

"There's no need. This girl does not feel pain, only the fear of pain." The doctor is right. Indeed, Tang Xiaonan shouted because she was scared by the pain. Now, the slight pain is disappearing rapidly. Xiaonan, unable to shout out, now clenches her teeth silently, tears falling, streaming down from the corners of her eyes. Xiaonan dares not move her left hand, and Dr. Li's thigh presses her right hand, which cannot be moved. She cannot hold back her tears, and regardless of what she is feeling, the tears, like a passing visitor, indifferently rush along their journey, by way of her cheeks. Tang Xiaonan cries as she prays to herself that the operation will be over soon.

"When is your son going abroad?" A certain doctor is chatting with Dr. Li.

"He is expecting his visa, two months at the latest," Dr. Li says.

"Miss, are you also planning to go abroad?" Dr. Li asks Tang Xiaonan, immediately after.

"No." Just after her answer, the surgical lights go out, only dark before her eyes.

When Tang Xiaonan had first stepped into compartment No. 17, she found herself falling into darkness, her eyes taking quite a while to adapt to the surroundings. The lights in the compartment went out so early, leaving only the small lamps in the wall near the floor giving off a dim light. Xiaonan could not figure out her sleeper, though she saw clearly enough that every berth was empty. This frightened her, as if walking into a scene in some horror movie. After shuffling forward about ten paces, Xiaonan could not help but turn around and beat a hasty retreat. She was puffing loudly as she rushed into the duty room of the train.

She said, "There's not a single person in the whole compartment. Who dares sleep in such darkness?"

With a smile, the attendant led Tang Xiaonan again into the compartment No. 17, and said, "This is 19, your lower berth. Isn't there a person on the opposite berth?"

"Are you a man or a woman?" Tang Xiaonan asked after the attendant had left, half believing, half in doubt, as she faced the spread-out quilt.

"I'm a man," the person on the berth said and sat up, the lamp casting its dim light completely on his face.

"Ah, thank goodness, I was so scared." Xiaonan put aside her huge backpack and sat on her own bunk.

"Yeah, I was thinking earlier, alone here, nobody would know it even if you were murdered," the man on the opposite bunk had obviously read many murder novels.

"That's odd, indeed! Why isn't there anybody else?" Tang Xiaonan said, realizing the importance of the person on the opposite bunk.

"This is the compartment for the train staff to rest in. It's the way they earn quick money." The man on the opposite berth held both of his knees in his arms, and Tang Xiaonan found his features were not bad.

Xiaonan's eyes gradually adapted to the dim light, which seemed to have gotten brighter.

The man opposite stood up, his tall frame casting a large shadow over her eyes. Tang Xiaonan raised her head, distracted all of a sudden — what an exceptional boy!

The boy came back from the bathroom, his face clearer now, and Xiaonan was distracted once again — never had she come across such a handsome boy!

Smiling at Tang Xiaonan, he said, "My name is Li Han."

Tang Xiaonan was growing rather restless and fanciful.

Chatting by the dim lamp, the two gradually became familiar with one another. They knew that both lived in Harbin, not far away from each other, and it was possible for them to meet again.

Perhaps because the light was too dubious or because, frustrated by her experience with Jiang Bei, her attitude had undergone a 180-degree turnaround, Tang Xiaonan began to feel a longing for something, in this compartment where there was only a solitary man and woman, amidst the clacking noise of the train.

At some point Li Han asked Tang Xiaonan, "Are you married?" "No," she said.

"Why aren't you married?" Li Han said.

Xiaonan thought for a while and said, "Marriage is only something that common custom has left us with."

At this, Li Han let out a cry at once, "Well, exactly!"

Then there came the baffling silence.

Tang Xiaonan had not said it intentionally. She regretted it somewhat. There were many layers of meaning to her words, but Xiaonan had not actually caught on to any one of them. Li Han then echoed her idea, which he had obviously misunderstood. Li Han said that he had been close with several girls, but had never gone to bed with them. He was afraid of them wanting to marry him. He did not have sex with them, so he would not have to take any responsibility, let alone getting married.

Late at night, the two went to their own beds. Tang Xiaonan could hear Li Han's breathing, now heavy, now light, now long, now short, or even not at all. She saw him lying there with his eyes open, his arm hanging down the bunk edge, fingers bending naturally, and palm up. He seemed to be expecting something to fall down.

Tang Xiaonan's body, gradually warmed up in the quilt, was still restless and ready to make trouble.

She felt she was a faucet. Tightened up earlier for Jiang Bei, she had been watertight. Now, she was leaking, tiny streams dripping at the bottom of her heart. The streams gathered in front of the dam, stopped, finding no vent, gradually forming a deep pool of water and countless whirlpools.

"You asleep?" Li Han asked, his body moving a bit, facing her on his side, arm still placed that way.

"Not yet," Tang Xiaonan's voice was so gentle that it surprised her.

"What are you thinking about?" Li Han did not seem to be putting on any bad guy act.

"Why aren't you sleeping?" Xiaonan was trying to sound him out.

Li Han did not speak, but his fingers moved.

Tang Xiaonan's fingers pressed and held his, and as if drawn by some powerful gravitational pull. Li Han, following her hand, rapidly fell into Xiaonan's quilt.

"Marriage is only something that common custom has left us with." Tang Xiaonan believed that feelings are sacred, but there was this distilled sentence, which, on the contrary, unexpectedly served as a lubricant for a relationship between a man and a woman.

Ants have started crawling and then biting her left breast; Tang Xiaonan feels it burn a bit.

Now that the muscles have become soft and she has slowly regained consciousness of the left breast, the hard and ice-cold metal apparatus makes her tremble, and she utters a heavy "ah," indicating she is suffering some pain.

"We've begun to sew it up. It will be over in a moment," the doctor says. The suture pulling inside the left breast, Xiaonan hears the sounds of her mother stitching soles for cloth shoes.

"Well, not bad, the incision is not too long." As Dr. Li is checking her wound, his thigh presses harder on Tang Xiaonan's hand.

"Will there be a scar?" Xiaonan asks very innocently.

"There will be some, but no big problem. It won't affect…." Tang Xiaonan does not know exactly what Dr. Li has meant by "problem" or "affect."

Tang Xiaonan's mind is a jumble.

After two months living together, Tang Xiaonan brought up the issue of marriage with Li Han.

"In fact, I want to get married." Pushing Li Han away, who has climbed onto her, Tang Xiaonan mouths such words for no reason.

"Why? Didn't you say that marriage is but a remnant of common custom? In addition, you asked me to remember we would be the closest couple forever." Li Han grinned cheekily. Left without an argument, Xiaonan had not expected that these words out of Li Han's mouth would turn into a sharp weapon, stabbing and hurting her hard.

"Yes, I said that marriage was only something that common custom has left us, because I believe only feelings are sacred. Yet I am a worldly person, so I also want worldly things." Tang Xiaonan could not help but put aside her package of pseudo-theory. She knew within her: from the perspective of love, marriage was indeed something that common custom had left us. Love is the resting place for love, not marriage. Therefore, love had nothing to do with marriage and Li Han's ideas were not incorrect. Nevertheless, she could not agree with what he had said in such a way. At such a stage, living together without marriage made her feel like a solitary ghost in the wilderness. Li Han was still young, so he could afford to lead a casual life. However, as a woman almost thirty years old herself, she could no longer waste her time and feelings.

"You want to get married with me out of love, or only because you're not so young anymore, so you've got to get married?" Li Han was not so confused either.

Tang Xiaonan could not come up with an answer for the moment. Undoubtedly, her body loved Li Han, her left breast loved Li Han, and her heart was willing to be together with Li Han, though there always seemed to be a barrier between them, a little something preventing one from going deep into the other. Apart from the fact that Li Han had no social experience (he was not to blame, having been a student until now) and that he had no ideas of his own when doing things, she could not think there was anything wrong with him, and he was better even than any one of her former men.

"Do you want to marry me or not, after all?" Tang Xiaonan did not answer his question, but asked him again more seriously. She knew that Li Han would go abroad and it would be impossible for him to marry her now. But her dear friends had advised her: "Get married while he is hot for you; get divorced while he is cold with you." Besides, everything would be "cold" when he left, and she did not know when she would again find love, which would be as vibrant as Li Han's.

"Of course I will, but now I have nothing. If I marry you, it would mean not being responsible to you," Li Han said.

"If you do not marry me, will that be responsible?" Tang Xiaonan argued.

"You know I am not independent, how can I be responsible for you? Love alone is not enough!"

"Then when are you going to marry me?"

"How can I tell exactly? If I then don't fulfill that, won't I be fooling you? You aren't young, would you fool around with a solemn pledge of love?"

"What do you mean exactly?"

"If I ask you to wait two years for me, who knows what things will be like in two years? What if I become a beggar abroad? What if I encounter sudden death? Even if we were to get married regardless of everything, could you face a possible divorce in a few years? Are you willing to make such a vulgar mistake?"

As for Li Han's objective reality and his remarks, Tang Xiaonan could only compromise; there was no room for rebuttal. She knew that a commitment would be empty. What she precisely wanted was just an explanation, one that Li Han was sincerely willing to marry her. She even wished that Li Han would strongly insist that she wait for him — wait until he comes back.

Tang Xiaonan lowered her head, not so much savoring slowly what Li Han had said, as trying to catch his deeper meaning. She was attempting to know his inner life through his words.

"You should not doubt my true love for you. I'll surely come and see you when I get back. No matter where you are, if your body still belongs to me, I will come find you. If you regard this as an oath, I will make a pledge."

Taken as a whole, this declaration from Li Han satisfied Tang

Xiaonan's potential emotional needs, and she made up her mind to wait for him, determined to be moved by this marathon love, involving her.

"Ow, it hurts!" The point of the needle is shuttling back and forth inside the left breast. Tang Xiaonan lets out a cry, without any exaggeration; on the contrary, she is exercising some restraint. Her voice seems to concentrate the pain, therefore it sounds more real and sonorous. The anesthetic has lost any effect. As if after experiencing the muddled stage of passionate love, she comes back suddenly to reality.

Tang Xiaonan had come upon the problem with her left breast when she was beginning her marathon with Li Han.

The problem with the left breast brought about new problems.

"No matter what happens, we should first settle the problem with the left breast. Everything will be all right when I'm independent." During the time when Tang Xiaonan had been waiting for Li Han's father to make an appointment with the doctor for the surgery, Li Han had gone home once, and upon coming back, he said these words to Xiaonan, who was completely without a clue. "What do you mean?" Xiaonan asked. "It's nothing to do with you. It's something about my family." Tang Xiaonan felt indistinctly that this was no ordinary matter — but in a battle of wits, Li Han would certainly lose this round to his father, that shrewd old man. Perhaps Li Han failed to hide what he had been trying his best to hide from his father, who had given him an ultimatum.

Li Han must have had a confrontation with his father.

Tang Xiaonan did not feel bad.

She liked everything to be transparent.

The surgical lights flash, bright and dazzling once again.

"Women, ordinarily, by your age have already fallen ill and had injections. You shouldn't be so afraid of pain," says Dr. Li.

Tang Xiaonan thinks of what Li Han had said — "My father is a shrewd old man." She is afraid Dr. Li has found out her real age, and blushes to the ears. Afterwards she inwardly blames Li Han for having made her so embarrassed.

"I rarely go for injections, I've been afraid of pain from when I was little," Tang Xiaonan disputes in a low voice.

"During any surgery, there always some pain. The anesthetic has some effect, but you cannot fully depend on it. When it no longer has effect, you will have the sensation of being brought back to reality. That feeling is real and more painful; nevertheless, you will feel all right soon."

Tang Xiaonan is stricken speechless. Dr. Li's words sound awkward — she feels he is talking about love, in particular the feelings between her and Li Han.

"Remember to tighten your bra. Don't worry, this type of minor surgery doesn't take much time to recover from." Dr. Li's thigh presses against her no more, and the surgical sheet no longer covers her.

Tang Xiaonan's right hand has gone numb. She cannot raise it for a long time. She remains still on the surgical bed for some time, her upper body naked.

There is only one person, Tang Xiaonan, remaining in the operating room. The left side of the surgical sheet is stained with blood. Tang Xiaonan puts on her bra slowly, and following Dr. Li's instructions, she does up the inner snaps, the lace of the bra fitting tightly across her back.

The left breast is but a heap of gauze.

"Li Han, where's Li Han? Why has he not dared to come in

yet?" Tang Xiaonan puts on her jacket, and glances out the window. For a moment she cannot remember what happened before the surgery.

"Take the thing in the cup to the fourth floor for a pathology diagnosis," Dr. Li comes in and tells Tang Xiaonan.

"Where's Li Han?" Tang Xiaonan's lips move, but no sound comes out.

"You have to get a pathology test — take the cup and follow me," Dr. Li adds.

Only now does Tang Xiaonan catch a glimpse of the table by the wall, on which a translucent plastic cup sits, with a little round ball steeped in it. She walks over, holds the cup close to her eyes, and sees it clearly. It is a fleshy ball: it looks very much like streaky pork, red with white in between.

She is aware that this was the problem with her left breast.

"Where's Li Han?" Tang Xiaonan asks herself, holding this cup with the "problem with her left breast." Then following behind Dr. Li, she passes on the "problem" to the doctor, to await the final analysis and conclusion.

(Translated by Zhou Gang)

Editor's Recommended Reading (in Chinese)

Growing Up with You (Ban Ni Zhangda) by Wang Jingyi

Woman on the Brink (Zuonü) by Zhang Kangkang

The Small Woman (Xiao Nüren) by Ye Mi

Sisters (Zimei) by Wei Wei

All the Evenings of the World (Shijie Shang Suoyou de Yewan) by Chi Zijian

图书在版编目（CIP）数据

永远有多远：英文 / 何向阳 主编
北京：外文出版社，2008年（21世纪中国当代文学书库）
ISBN 978-7-119-05436-0
I. 永 ... II. 何 ... III. ①中篇小说—作品集—中国—当代—英文
②短篇小说—作品集—中国—当代—英文 IV. I247.7
中国版本图书馆CIP数据核字（2008）第134636号

责任编辑：曾惠杰
英文审定：Kris Sri Bhaggiyadatta May Yee 李振国
装帧设计：视觉共振设计工作室
印刷监制：冯浩

永远有多远

主　编：何向阳

出版发行：
外文出版社（中国北京百万庄大街24号）
邮政编码：100037
网　址：http://www.flp.com.cn
电　话：008610-68320579（总编室）
008610-68995852（发行部）
008610-68327750（版权部）
制　版：
北京维诺传媒文化有限公司
印　刷：
北京外文印刷厂
开　本：787mm×1092mm 1/16 **印　张**：29
2008年第1版 第 1 次印刷
（英）
ISBN 978-7-119-05436-0
10800（平）
10-E-3897P